SEVEN WAYS *to* START *a* FIRE

Rachel Mahood

For Layla, Leo and Kitty

Saturday 10th August

Dalt

When do you panic? How long should you wait? When do reasonable explanations become unreasonable and when does an absence become a disappearance?

Nell had left for a run just before 7 a.m. A quick glance at his watch showed it was now 2.15 p.m. – over seven hours later.

Don't panic. Gut instinct, that's what he should trust – isn't that what they always say on those survival programs, where well-tuned guts frequently save enlightened folk from near-death situations? But Dalt's special gut-instinct-antennae seemed to be malfunctioning, the indicator wavering wildly between panic and chill out, man, she's got previous for this.

Which was true.

Nell had gone missing before. There was the time she'd followed a stream to find its source, the time she'd spent hours rebuilding a collapsed moorland wall, and the time she'd never even gone out at all, but had been in the attic, searching for something. She'd never said what. Then there were all the other occasions that she'd simply lost track of the time. But she'd never been gone *this* long.

So, should he panic *now*? There should be courses available for this sort of thing. Admittedly, the advice he was looking for was rather niche. *What to do if your wife doesn't come home*. He'd follow it with a course on, *How to be a better husband*, although *How to be an 'ok' husband* might be a good starting place. Don't run before you can walk and all that. These courses would surely be over-subscribed. Dalt would probably be on the waiting list, whilst finer men than he learnt to understand the inner-workings and complexities of their wives.

A friend of his father had come to dinner one evening when Dalt was a child. The adults chatted over drinks, discussing a husbandry course the friend was due to enrol on. Husbandry, what a glorious idea, thought nine-year-old Dalt. Even at this tender age, the girls in his class bewildered him, left him tongue-tied and blundering. His imagination led him down a tree-lined avenue to an imposing manor house, through the formidable front door, up a magnificent, sweeping staircase to a grand room where paintings of elegant women and fat, cherubic infants hung on the flock-papered walls, their gazes adoringly set upon handsome, self-assured fathers. A preposterously long table took centre stage and a distinguished, heavily moustached man stood at its head (was that a slightly smug expression Dalt had seen on his face, even then?).

'The core subject matter,' boomed the magnificently moustached man, 'will comprise of practical husbandry skills, including car maintenance, mortgage management, bin emptying and toilet seat protocol as well as more...' a long, calculated pause, heavy with the weight of one hundred held breaths, '...advanced learning. A handful of successful students...' Mr Moustache had continued (at this, a hard stare at the gathered audience) '...will be able to move on to what we call *Intuitive Husbandry*: compliments, reassurances, small white lies and so on and so forth.'

Dalt had always had quite the imagination. Yet, even then, even on his own imaginary husbandry course, Dalt knew he'd never be one of those 'successful students.' He'd never be one of those who was going to make the grade.

It was years later when Dalt realised husbandry related to agriculture. Someone's missed a trick there, he'd thought to himself. Maybe it was him.

What he wouldn't give to have Mr Moustache here now. He'd lay a heavy yet reassuring hand on Dalt's shoulder and tell Dalt whether, indeed, it was time to panic. He'd tell Dalt whether his wife had just popped out, forgetting to tell anybody ('Unusual,' he'd say, 'but not impossible'), or whether she had gone totally, truly, not-messing-around-this-time missing.

Huck, his son, had noted Nell's absence at breakfast together with the presence of their dog, Turnip.

Panic scale reading then: zero.

'She's probably gone for a longer run, got carried away. Too far for Turnip,' he'd told his son without a second thought. Turnip usually ran with Nell, unless it was too hot or the run too far. Dalt hadn't been concerned.

'Yes, she was wearing her backpack – I saw her out of my window,' Huck said, and the matter was dropped.

At the speed Nell ran, she would be close to completing her second marathon by now. She liked a long run, but this was a step (or sixty thousand) too far. Dalt felt a tightening in his chest. Was it guilt, or a feeling of neglect? A feeling that he had one job to do and he had done it badly.

After breakfast, Dalt had spent the morning working in his office, which hadn't been as productive as he'd hoped, due to Turnip whining insistently at his door. At around 1 p.m., his rumbling stomach had nudged him towards the kitchen, where he'd quickly prepared himself a cheese sandwich. Each to their own for lunch in this house. He'd taken it back to his desk, where the next hour had slipped by undisturbed.

Afternoon coffee was usually more sociable. At 2 p.m. like clockwork, Dalt turned on the heavy, industrial coffee machine that looked as if it would be more at home in the local café than in their kitchen. The chugging and gurgling of the machine as it warmed up and cleared its lines of old grounds never failed to act like the pied piper's music, luring his wife from the depths of wherever she may be.

But not today.

'Nell? Nell? Coffee's ready!'

Dalt scouted the house, Turnip at his heels, calling his wife's name. In their bedroom, her phone sat on the bedside table. He tapped the screen. Dead. She had a terrible habit of letting the battery run out. In fact, sometimes he swore she did it on purpose.

Panic scale reading: three. This was unusual. Nell loved her coffee but had never bothered to learn how to work the machine. She wouldn't miss coffee o'clock without a pretty good reason.

Dalt stood outside on the decking, scanning the garden. He was still brandishing the two coffee cups and mulling over Nell's absence when his teenage son and Amelia approached from the lower lawn.

'Have either of you seen Nell?' Dalt called.

'Have you seen Mudder?' Huck shouted at the exact same moment.

'Not since she left for her run this morning,' Dalt said.

'I did tell you at breakfast that she wasn't back.' Was it the sun making his son squint, or was Huck scowling at him?

Yes, a scowl, definitely a scowl, with a side-portion of blame and a sprinkling of implied negligence thrown in for good measure. Or was Dalt imagining it?

'Have you called her?' Huck asked.

'She didn't take her phone.'

'If she was here, Turnip would be with her,' Huck added, noticing the animal whining at Dalt's knee. 'Amelia hasn't seen her either,' he added.

Amelia didn't seem to mind being spoken for. Dalt thought she looked a little glazed; a shimmer of sweat glistened on her forehead. Not surprising – it was bloody hot. The lawn where they stood was fully exposed to the sun; a muggy, unpleasant heat that unleashed in him a desperate urge to seek the ice-cold waters of the river and plunge in fully clothed.

Amelia must have noticed him staring.

'I haven't seen her. I presumed she was back from her run and had taken herself off somewhere to write where she wouldn't be disturbed. I'm sure she's fine,' Amelia said.

A possibility, until Dalt nagged at it and, like a frayed edge, it began to unravel.

'Maybe, but it's odd. She would have showered and changed before starting to write, and I haven't heard anything.' The clunking and vibrating of the old pipes that carried hot water throughout Moordown House was a constant source of irritation for Dalt. The property was over two-hundred years old. The pipes, along with dodgy wiring and a leaking roof, were annoyances that Dalt kept a mental note of, but ultimately had resigned himself to.

Huck had made a good point about the dog, too. Turnip was Nell's. She'd found him wandering the moor when she was out running one day and brought him home. Nell was besotted with the hairy creature from the start. There had been phone calls – Dalt made them – to the local vet, to the police, to a dog rescue centre. He'd even put a *Dog Found* post on social media, but no one had claimed him and so Turnip stayed, always by Nell's side.

But not today.

A dull pain above his eyes. Where were his sunglasses? He rarely remembered to wear them. The glaring, early afternoon sun was making him squint. He rubbed the back of his hand across his eyes until dancing black dots appeared.

'I'll go and look for her. I'll run the route she normally does.' He felt momentarily relieved. He had a plan. Mr Moustache would be so proud.

Huck nodded. 'Want me to come?'

Dalt shook his head. 'No. Thanks. Stay here. Have a look around.' Why did the thought of running with his fifteen-year-old son make him feel nervous?

'Okay, we'll see if we can track her down,' Amelia said. 'I'm sure she's fine. Maybe she had a meeting or something and had to dash.'

Not impossible, thought Dalt, but Nell's car was in the drive and her keys were on the table – he'd checked whilst the milk frother heated up.

He finished his coffee (negative husbandry points) then began the search for his running shoes, eventually locating them buried at the bottom of the old shoe box, covered in dried mud. He stood for a moment on the decking, banging the soles together hard, a smog of mud and dust rising around him, the band of pain above his eyes tightening.

What had happened to the runs he and Nell used to go on together? He remembered them laughing, breathless and out of control as they hit the final downhill mile full pelt, a race to touch the bars of the unlocked, twisted-iron gates of home. It felt so long ago. It *was* so long ago. He hadn't run for months. A year maybe. And even then, not with Nell. He had no idea if the route he was going to run now was even the way she'd gone that morning, the way she ever went, anymore. But it was the route they used to run together. It was worth a try.

Leaving the house by the back door, Dalt cut across the lawn, past the willow tree and down to the river, which flowed parallel to the bottom of the garden. Upon meeting the wooded track, which followed the river in both directions, Dalt turned right, and ran alongside the gently flowing water for half a mile, calling and scanning for Nell as he went. A stile in a stone wall marked the boundary of their property. Once over, Dalt continued for three riverside miles, before taking another turn, and climbing steeply over wild, rugged moorland. In the distance, the chimneys of their house, Moordown, were visible if you knew where to look. No sign of his wife though. Finally, high up on the moors now, he followed the old granite tramway until one last turn led to a steep descent and (in the old days) a sprint finish to the front of the house.

Back in the day, he could cover the seven and a half miles in under fifty minutes. Back when he was fit and keen (and not integrating a search for his lost wife into his daily fitness regime).

Not today. Muddy, sweaty and beaten, Dalt leaned against the white, concrete pillar that housed the keypad to the new, heavy electric gates. He still wasn't used to them. Nell had insisted on their installation a few years ago, and he'd agreed. With her book sales skyrocketing, and her worries about obsessive, stalker fans, he'd seen her point. He missed the old gates though; ornate, Gothic affairs with twisted railings and arched tops, they'd embodied the wildness and the mystery of Moordown.

Dalt entered the code and the gates opened smoothly. He crossed the drive and took the stone steps to the porch two at a time. The front door was unlocked and, as he entered the wide hallway, cool air hit him, the whitewashed walls and granite floor of the old manor house providing much needed relief from the heat outside.

'Nell?' he called. 'Nell?'

No answer.

Heart and head both pounding now. Sweating from both the exertion of the run and the worry. Where the hell was she?

Even Mr Moustache would have had trouble with this one.

Panic scale reading: five, he concluded, six at a push. Nell could be erratic, someone who easily lost track of time.

But this much time? It was coming up to 4 p.m. And in this heat?

Panic scale reading: seven.

Unconsciously, he massaged the outline of his mobile phone in his shorts pocket and a conversation with an emergency operator played out in his head.

'So, just to clarify, your wife has been missing for nearly nine hours. It's the hottest day of the year so far, and there's a distinct possibility she's not carrying any water. She's most likely up on the moors, where the risk of an accident is high. And you're only calling us to tell us about it NOW? Have I got that right, Sir?'

Bad husband. Bad husbandry. But that's the problem with husbandry: the wives. They're all so unique, so individual, and so terribly unpredictable.

Panic scale reading: TEN.

Now. We panic now!

'Huck! Amelia!' he shouted.

Heavy footsteps on the granite floor, a door opened, and Huck appeared in the hallway just as Amelia approached from the kitchen.

'Did you find her?' asked Amelia, as Dalt kicked off his running shoes and headed past them, into the drawing room.

'No. Have you both searched the house and gardens?' Searched. Why that particular verb? Panicking.

'We've looked everywhere, and I've gone through the calendar, just in case Nell had an appointment or something,' Amelia reported. 'But we didn't find anything.'

'Maybe she tripped, and she's injured,' Huck said.

'Yes, maybe. You said she took her backpack. What else is gone?' Dalt asked. 'Water bottles? Food?'

'I've looked, but I can't tell,' Huck replied.

'I definitely think we should call the police.' Amelia's voice was higher than usual, her face flushed. 'Should we use 999 or is it that other number, the non-emergency one, that we need to ring? I can never remember. Not that I've ever needed to know. It's not like I'm always making calls about missing people.' Not just higher – quicker – hammering through Dalt's head like a woodpecker on speed.

Focus, he told himself sternly. Meandering thoughts will not get one's wife back, but googling '*how to report a missing person?*' might be a good place to start.

'101,' he instructed Amelia as the search engine quickly produced the goods. Amelia was poised, phone in hand, finger hitting the numbers on the screen as Dalt spoke, as if immense speed now would counteract the dream-like inertia that had characterised their response hours earlier.

'I'd like to report a missing person,' Amelia began. 'I mean, I wouldn't actually *like* to report her missing, God that sounds awful. I mean, someone's gone missing and I want to tell you.'

Amelia shot a panicked look at Dalt. This wasn't going well. He gestured for her to pass the phone, but fear seemed to have welded it to her hand (or his miming wasn't very good; he'd never been great at charades). One stride took him over to her, where he tapped the phone in what he hoped was an assertive manner. The spell was broken, and Amelia released the phone to him gratefully.

'Hello. This is Edward Dalton. I'm concerned about the where-abouts of my wife – Nell Davenport.'

What followed was a mild, out-of-body experience, in which the details and events of the day so far were carefully packaged up and passed like a neatly wrapped present from Dalt to the call operative. As if looking down from above, Dalt found himself marvelling at this calm, assertive man who could report his wife missing so coolly and articulately.

An intake of breath, the rhythmic sound of fingers running confidently across a computer keyboard, recording. Actualising.

'Don't panic, Sir,' (see – he knew it was too early to panic). 'Seventy-five percent of adults are usually found within twenty-four hours. We've got all the details we need for now, and we'll assign an officer to visit you as soon as possible.'

Dalt tapped the red phone symbol to end the call, the motion acting like the release of a seal and sucking him back into his body, a place he wasn't sure he wanted to be. He breathed out deeply and looked at his son. Huck was staring out at the garden, dwarfed by the floor to ceiling windows. Dalt had always thought they were too much, leaving the room and its occupants too exposed – vulnerable even. As he gazed at his son's strong back, an involuntary shiver passed through him.

Huck

H uck felt like crap. Last night, the house had been stifling; too hot to sleep. He had lain restlessly in bed, beneath the sheets at first, then beneath nothing at all, his unencumbered legs doing little to help. Frustrated, he'd got up and walked from room to room throughout the house, opening all the windows, creating cool breezes which soothed him temporarily but ceased the second he crossed the threshold into the next room. The enormity of the old place was brought home to him when, mission completed, he'd returned to his own bedroom feeling hotter and more uncomfortable than when he'd left it, the effect on his body of walking up two flights of stairs to get there. The irony was not lost on him.

He'd heard the electric fan whirring in Mudder's room on the first floor as he'd passed. It did little to disguise the muffled voices of his parents arguing. Business as usual, he'd thought, snaking his way past.

He must have fallen asleep eventually, as now it was morning. The cold touch of fresh air on his bare skin had woken him, the wide-open window another hangover from his (possibly too vigorous) house airing the night before. He pulled on a t-shirt and crossed the room to close it.

It was then he saw her; a flash of fluorescent yellow and black, like a wasp, he'd thought to himself, no, a bee – kinder, less stingy – jogging across the lawn and heading down to the river. In the seconds it took for him to lean out the window and catch hold of the lever, she had gone.

When Mudder hadn't returned for breakfast an hour and a half later, nobody had seemed that surprised. The morning was a good one – fresh, crisp and full of promise. Sunshine poured into the kitchen through the French doors at the far end of the room, which opened out onto the decking and the garden beyond. The mugginess of the night before had dispersed into a beautiful new day – who wouldn't want to be out in it?

At the kitchen table, Dalt read the paper with absolute focus, as if there would be a quiz on the headlines later in the day. Amelia picked at her toast like a bird whilst editing her writing from the day before, crossing out, substituting, engrossed. Huck ate his breakfast, spoon-to-bowl-to-mouth, spoon-to-bowl-to-mouth, a task on his to-do list, rather than an experience to be savoured. Although, in his defence, breakfast consisted of two Weetabix and some cold milk; it was hardly Michelin starred.

'Mudder's normally back by now,' Huck had said as he gathered up his breakfast things. 'And how come she didn't take Turnip?'

'She's probably gone for a longer run, got carried away. Too far for Turnip,' Dalt didn't even look up from his paper.

'*Carried away.*' The phrase lodged itself inside Huck's head, where it grew restless, flitted about and sprouted wings. Carried away. By whom and to where, Huck had wondered?

Dalt and Amelia hadn't dwelled on Mudder's absence for long.

'Amelia, would you like to take this opportunity to look over those sketches I was telling you about?' Dalt, always unnecessarily formal, Huck thought (cruelly?) as he loaded his bowl into the dishwasher.

'I'd love to. I'm struggling to visualise the characters I'm writing about. I'm hoping your work might help!' Amelia: bubbling, energetic, enthusiastic. Fawning?

He left them alone to their plans, his own day, empty, stretching out in front of him like a blank page.

School had broken up for summer just two weeks earlier, but Huck still felt tainted by its touch, the way that the smell of smoke lingered on clothing long after the flames of the bonfire had burnt out.

The last day of term, kids saying goodbye like it was going to be for forever, not just for six weeks. Patrick, Huck's only friend, had been taken out of school early, to endure an arduous (his word) family car journey to Scotland to visit his aging grandma. Left on his own at school, Huck had found himself inwardly pouring scorn on the dramatic farewell hugs, as if loved ones were going off to war rather than to all-inclusive holidays in Italy, arms thrown wide, to capture and claim, squeezing tight, holding on for long seconds like snakes with their prey. He'd looked away as a group of boys jostled and teased and signed each other's shirts in bright, colourful marker pens, then drew ridiculous moustaches on each other's faces. He'd turned up the volume on his iPod and looked at his watch, waited for the buses to arrive and for it all to be over.

And now it was, and the summer was his. Aside from a deal he'd struck with his father to do a little housework, he was free to do as he pleased. Mudder and Dalt weren't the kind of parents to plan activities. They were too caught up in their own work. So, what should he do today, with this day? Huck considered his options. He liked to walk. He could easily walk all day, headphones on, notebook in his bag, stopping when he had an idea to jot down, or if he felt like a rest. He'd read an article in the Sunday paper a while back: *The*

Daily Routines of Famous Writers. 'Walk,' they had said, and walk they apparently had: Wordsworth, Blake, Dickens and (somewhat randomly thrown in, he'd thought) Stephen King, walking for hours each day, being inspired, gathering ideas, formulating plot lines. Stephen King, he'd figured, probably walked around cemeteries and old lunatic asylums (can you say that these days? Lunatic?) Whilst Wordsworth must have idled through fields of golden flowers. Huck longed to follow in their footsteps, both literally and figuratively (well, maybe not actually into the lunatic asylum, maybe he'd just skirt around the edge a little).

Dare he even think it, to consider it? To be a writer, an actual, paid, doing-this-for-a-living writer, like his mother. That was his dream. A little predictable, he supposed, like those talent show wannabes on Saturday night TV, who gush that to sing, or to dance, is, 'All I've ever wanted to do since I was born, no – since I was in the womb – no – even before I was in the womb, since I was a bunch of cells.' (Is he being too cynical?) But in his case, it's true (not the womb bit – just the early desire).

Huck had a recurring daydream, one that flooded him with an internal warmth, in which he'd walk into a stranger's house and peruse the unfamiliar bookshelves whilst someone (a fatherly figure usually) poured him an amber drink (a whisky and soda, Hemingway's favourite). Huck would trace his finger along the spines of the books, until there, on the middle shelf, bound in soft, tan leather and embossed with his name (yes, yes, he knew that books weren't made like this anymore, but this was his fantasy, alright) was his book. Recognised, acclaimed, and distinguished, like Mudder's. Although Mudder didn't just have one book, on one shelf. Mudder was something else. Mudder's books took up whole shelves, perhaps even small bookcases. She'd once been described as '*possibly the most prolific author of her generation,*' and the old adage, quality not quantity, didn't apply to her either, as each book – every, single, one

– had an outstanding review in some esteemed journal or literary digest. And as if she wasn't productive enough, somehow Mudder also managed to produce a highly regarded, widely read, weekly short story in the town's paper, the *Stonebrook Gazette*, making her something of a local celebrity, albeit one who was read rather than seen in her hometown.

Green-eyed, covetous, emulous? No. Huck was proud, protective and defensive. Safeguarding, shielding, sheltering (too much?). Mudder was a 'mother like no other mother', if you will. As far back as he could remember, Huck had felt it was his job to look after her. To guide her, to steer her, to protect her and to help her survive everyday life.

Survive. Overly dramatic? Sensationalist? At the very least, un-usual? Perhaps. But not if you knew Mudder.

At the age of five, coinciding with his own entry into primary school, Huck had begun versing Mudder in the art of playground etiquette (Huck was already aware that there really was an art). Whom to greet and whom to simply 'nod' at, when to approach and when to hang back and how often and for how long. He could sense, even at such a young age, that these seemingly trivial school-gate in-teractions with other mothers made Mudder's quick-witted tongue impotent, and he could not bear, even then, to see his brilliant, clever Mudder reduced to a graceless, awkward husk, like a clumsy buffalo joining a herd of graceful antelope at a waterhole.

It hadn't been smooth sailing. Only weeks into his first term at school, Ms Jamison had beckoned Mudder over at the end of the day, when the other parents were gathered tightly together (was there a collective noun for a group of parents at a school gate? A sting? A storm?).

'About packed lunches...' Ms Jamison had begun, 'the other chil-dren aren't, how shall I put it, very *fond* of the food Huck brings in. I think it's only fair to tell you; he's been sitting on his own for over a week as the smell is quite overpowering, and frankly, Ms Davenport, I can see why the other children don't want to sit too close to him.'

The expression on Mudder's face had upset him far more than the embarrassment of sitting alone at lunch ever had. Huck had first seen panic, then anger, frustration and bewilderment, and then something that even at five years old he could begin to understand – resignation – a giving up of sorts. He hadn't cared all that much that the other kids didn't want to sit with him. He wasn't sure he wanted to sit with them either. He'd quite enjoyed watching them from his table across the room. He supposed, on the positive side, that he might quite like to sit with the red-haired girl with the fringe that went into her eyes. Her lunch smelt a little bit too, and no one talked to her much either.

He'd squeezed Mudder's hand, managed to catch her eye and silently tried to tell her, 'It's okay. I'm okay. You're doing fine.'

Back home, he'd sat up high on a kitchen stool, whilst Mudder questioned him like he was an anthropologist, recently returned from a visit to a remote, previously undiscovered tribe.

'Just cheese or ham – no sardines or even tuna? And no pickles or chutneys? This sounds terribly dull, but if you're sure...'

Gently, patiently, he guided her through the whole new world of a socially acceptable five-year old's school lunch.

'And no egg, Mudder. No way.'

Huck had tried to picture Mudder as a kid at school, eating her lunch. What did she used to have? He was pretty sure the weird, wonderful, 'smelly' foods Mudder gave him didn't exist when she was a child. Mudder understood so little of the reality of school life. He couldn't imagine her ever stepping foot inside one.

'So long ago, it's hard to remember really,' she'd said once, when he was older and had enquired about her experiences at secondary school. 'It was called Saint Catherine's. It was an all-girls school.

Horrible things.' He'd always wondered if she'd meant schools, or girls, but had never asked.

In the end, he had gone for a walk that morning. Not as far, or for as long as he'd intended (sorry Hemingway). He'd like to say he returned to jot down some ideas that he couldn't afford to forget, but the truth was he had a headache that refused to shift. The coolness of the early morning was gone, and the thick, oppressive heat of the last few days had returned, inescapable and exhausting. He hoped the weather would break soon. It was going to take an almighty storm to sort it out. After his walk, he'd gone to his room and made a start on one of the books from the recommended reading list his English teacher had handed out before the holidays.

Around 1.45 p.m. boredom took him to the kitchen. Late for lunch, he knew, but he didn't feel all that hungry. His legs felt kind of wobbly and weak and his balance was off. Sunstroke? He'd been out for hours the day before, lying on the lawn pretending to read but really doing nothing at all.

Since the holidays began, it was Huck's habit to make his lunch, usually just some fridge leftovers thrown together, and eat it in the garden. He'd try to track Mudder down and tempt her with some small offering, a piece of cheese and some crackers or fruit, to remind her to eat too.

Enjoying the blast of cool air from the fridge, Huck stood for a moment, bathed in the yellow light, looking but not seeing. Too slow sucker. The fridge started to beep, a sure sign that the door had been left open too long and he was 'titting about,' as Patrick would say. Huck shut the door, then opened it again, taking out some cheese and salad. He made up a small plate of food. Any other day and he might have felt annoyed as he surveyed the fridge's contents: jars of pickles and relishes, home-made humous, leftover cauliflower curry and vegetables, vegetables, vegetables. Their fridge was like an advert for the local farm shop, not a processed item in sight. On so many occasions he had wished his fridge were more like Patrick's, or the other kids at school, loaded full of yoghurts, cooked meats, sausage rolls, fruit juice cartons and ready-made salads. Fridges stocked by parents who weren't obsessed with being self-sufficient. Parents who weren't immersed in their own creativity ninety-five percent of each day and actually went to the supermarket rather than just their own allotment. Parents who were just that, parents.

Job done, Huck grabbed a fork from the cutlery drawer and made his way out the glass doors onto the decking at the rear of the house. Back into the glaring sunshine.

On the deck, six cushioned, aluminium chairs sat around a large, rectangular light-grey slatted table, a large, white, sun umbrella promising coolness and shade. The perfect place to eat lunch, and yet always empty at this time of day. Huck pulled out a chair and sat and ate alone, saving a small chunk of cheese for Mudder.

Full, he picked up his plate and headed towards the river. So hot. Maybe he should go for a swim later. It might make him feel better. The neat, recently mown lawn ended abruptly, giving way to tall, wild grass and meadow flowers.

'Mudder?' he called.

No reply.

'Mudder?'

A giggle erupted inches away from where he was standing.

'God, Amelia, you made me jump!'

Amelia was half-sitting, half-lying in the long grass, notebook and pen in hand, a bottle of water propped up on a stone by her side.

'Huck!' (Giggling. Were forty-year-old women supposed to giggle? Mudder certainly didn't, so why was this friend of hers so childish?) Amelia clearly found it funny that she'd taken him by surprise. 'Huck! How's it going? Another beautiful day! It's just so inspiring.'

So inspiring? So predictable more like. Huck thought that Amelia must sleep with a book of '*stock, pretentious phrases to be used by aspiring authors*' under her pillow. The word 'inspiring' appearing at least once in every conversation he'd ever had with her.

She raised her notebook slightly and smiled happily. 'I'm writing. I know it sounds corny, but it's like something has been unlocked, and the ideas are just flowing organically. I don't know if it's any good, but it's a start.'

'I'm pleased for you. They say starting is the hardest part.' Vague – who were *they*? But Huck genuinely meant his platitude. It must have been hard for Amelia, knocked and knocked again by the world of publishing, whilst Mudder made it look easy. Tough, he thought, to watch from the wings, wanting (desiring, craving, coveting) for something so much. He really was glad that Amelia was feeling inspired at last.

Amelia eyed his plate. 'Is it lunchtime already? The morning has just disappeared.'

Another interesting choice of word.

Enough of this small talk.

'I'm looking for Mudder.' His voice came out gruffer than he'd intended. The perils of his age.

'She's not down here, or if she is, I haven't seen her. Maybe try up at the house?'

In his pocket, Huck's fingers rhythmically caressed the smooth, hard body of his cigarette lighter, a habit he'd begun in his early teens in the school playground, the object highly forbidden there, but the power, satisfaction and reassurance gleaned from its touch worth any penalty put upon him. He didn't even smoke, apart from that one-time Patrick stole a couple of cigarettes from his older sister. It was for lighting fires mostly, campfires up on the moors with Dalt, and occasionally, fires just for the hell of it. Just to watch something burn.

'Huck? Did you hear me? She's not down here. I said try up at the house,' Amelia's insistent tone jerked him from his reverie.

There is a defining moment, one moment, when something changes irreversibly. One infinitesimal moment when a reaction happens, and the ash and the smoke that were the campfire logs cannot ever be the wood again. Later, Huck would pinpoint this – now – as when it all began; the moment they knew Mudder was gone.

Amelia

The Willow Tree

Velvet fronds like Neptune's fingers probing the eddy,
Magnificent and revered. The star of the show.
A hundred years of theatrical splendour,
Its living curtain the keeper of secrets and mysteries never to be revealed.

Not bad for a few hours' work, Amelia decided, pushing the end of the pencil against her teeth as she reread her writing. She was no gardening expert; the age of the tree had been a total stab in the dark. The poem was perhaps on the figurative side, but surely that was the nature of the beast. There really was something truly compelling about that willow tree. Her friend Surami (Amelia still thought of her as Sarah – it's terribly unnerving when a person changes their name in their forties, as much as people try to pretend it isn't) would probably say (in breathy tones) that Amelia was connecting with the tree's very essence and conceptualizing the experiences imprisoned in its very core. She'd definitely felt a connection.

Damn it, the pencil in her mouth slipped and jabbed her hard in the gum. She rubbed her mouth with her thumb. It was so hard to focus. Even in the shade down here by the river, it was ridiculously hot. She took a gulp from the water bottle next to her and pulled the large brim of her sunhat down over her eyes. She was particularly pleased with this hat. She'd seen one like it in the window of the charity shop in town, its pinkish straw bruised from being stuffed into picnic bags and rucksacks, and as luck would have it (she could hardly believe it herself) she'd found a brand new version, cleverly fashioned to replicate the battered, vintage look in the boutique next door, but without that distinctive lingering odour of carefully preserved sweat and mustiness resplendent of charity shops throughout the country.

She'd hardly realised her eyes had been closed, when she heard Huck crashing through the long grass towards her, calling for Nell. It amused her to think that he had no idea that she was there. She imagined catching hold of his leg as he passed, then swiftly dismissed the idea – he didn't seem the type to appreciate a surprise. He'd probably kick her in the face.

She was giggling to herself at the thought when he noticed her, propped up in the long grass.

'God, Amelia, you made me jump!'

She took in his flushed face and startled expression and let out another peal of laughter. Not funny, Amelia, she told herself, as Huck's body tensed and his eyes narrowed angrily. Was she the only one to find his behaviour aggressive? And what was on the plate he was holding? It looked like a small, sweaty bit of blue cheese. Teenagers – a whole world she didn't understand. But social etiquette and false niceties were things she was very aware of, and this was the son of her good friend and host. She must remember her manners.

'I'm writing.' Her voice sounded falsely high-pitched and a little bit manic, but Huck didn't appear to notice. 'I know it sounds corny, but it's like something has been unlocked, and ideas are just flowing organically. I don't know if it's any good, but it's a start.'

Surprisingly, Huck seemed interested. Maybe she'd read him wrong. In the short conversation that followed, he was even complimentary about her work (although she didn't show him the poem, that would be way too much) before his demeanour abruptly changed.

'I'm looking for Mudder.'

'She's not down here, or if she is, I haven't seen her. Maybe try up at the house?'

The boy was clearly out of sorts, breathing fast, rubbing something in his pocket. Oh, dear god, was he...? She knew teenagers were uncouth creatures, but surely he couldn't be? This was downright disgraceful behaviour.

'Huck? Did you hear me? She's not down here. Maybe try up at the house?' Amelia practically shouted the last few words and Huck's hand flew out of his pocket.

'I'll walk up with you,' Amelia said, forcing her voice to stay steady, keen to be out of this long grass and back with Nell and Dalt.

As they neared the house, Dalt appeared on the decking. Was he calling to them? Amelia could see his lips move, but if there were words, they were lost on the air. She glanced at Huck. He was still carrying a plate and that odd piece of cheese which, to put it frankly, stank, and was making her feel rather nauseous. As they got closer to Dalt, Amelia could see the worried expression on his face.

'Have either of you seen Nell?'

'Have you seen Mudder?' Huck said at the exact moment his father spoke.

'Not since she left for her run this morning,' Dalt said.

'I did tell you at breakfast that she wasn't back.' Huck was definitely exuding stroppy teenage vibes today.

'If she was here, Turnip would be with her. Amelia hasn't seen her either,' Amelia realised Dalt was staring at her, waiting for her to speak.

'I haven't seen her. I presumed she was back from her run and had taken herself off somewhere to write where she wouldn't be disturbed. I'm sure she's fine,' Amelia had added, after a pause, cringing at her own voice, which even to her sounded cheery and false. '*Daddy will be home soon,*' as the bombs begin to fall.

Suddenly assertive (Amelia had rarely (never?) seen him like this) Dalt issued instructions. Stay here. Look around.

Watching him go, Amelia peeled her blouse away from her clammy skin, and considered for the first time that something really might be wrong.

Monday 19th August

The Stonebrook Gazette

The Stonebrook Gazette yesterday published a blank column in honour of Nell Davenport, local author and the paper's feature writer, who went missing from her home on the morning of Saturday 10th August.

Despite a large-scale search of nearby moorland involving specialist agencies, efforts to locate Ms Davenport, 40, best-selling author of the Daniel Hargreaves detective series as well as wife and mother, have so far proved unsuccessful.

Amelia Early, a close family friend of Ms Davenport, told reporters, 'We don't know what's happened to her. We miss her desperately and just want her back.'

Davenport, who was last seen at 7 a.m. on the day she went missing, was known locally for her love of trail running, a pursuit which often took her well off the beaten track.

She is thought to be wearing black running leggings and a distinctive fluorescent yellow t-shirt.

Huck

Another mention of Mudder's t-shirt. All the papers had focused on it. He didn't even know how they'd got hold of the details. It made Huck think of that old gameshow, *Family Fortunes*.

The question again: what do you think is the most distressing aspect of the disappearance of Nell Davenport?

You're going for, 'The fact that she was wearing an inappropriate, comedy t-shirt.'

Our survey says, (cue high-pitched celebratory sound-effect). Not only is that our top answer, but you've won a spot prize of a holiday for two in the Maldives!

Over to the Kerridge family. You're going for 'the fact that she's been missing for over a week and has no warm clothing, food, money, or phone.'

Our survey says (low, two-syllable, loser sound-effect), it's not there. Not a popular answer I'm afraid.

Amelia, too, had focused a considerable amount of her energies on berating Mudder's 'choice' of disappearance outfit.

'Can you believe she was actually wearing a t-shirt that said, *YOUR PACE OR MINE?* on it in huge, black print? Seriously, why was she wearing that? Who gave it to her? Of all the clothes to go missing in, why that?'

As if one can control what one is wearing when one goes missing. As if Mudder should have dressed with more consideration that morning, searching her wardrobe for the perfect disappearance outfit. Huck pictured her in front of her mirror giving a little twirl.

'Should I wear the emerald-green, moisture-wicking technical top that matches my eyes but at the same time promises to absorb both sweat and blood, should I happen to be violently abducted, or should I wear the long-sleeved, fleece-lined, orange number, that offers both warmth and high-visibility, should I happen to trip over a cliff edge, break a limb and lie undiscovered for weeks on end?'

The irony of the whole thing being that Mudder was actually the kind of woman who would not have spent more than a fraction of a second considering her outfit anyway. Here was a woman who hadn't bought a new item of clothing during his entire lifetime. Here was a woman who wore other people's cast-offs, and clothes she had owned since her twenties without a second thought. Mudder cared not one iota about what she wore, or what she looked like. He doubted whether she even knew her running t-shirt that day had writing on it, let alone that it looked to some like she was inviting trouble, and that some people thought trouble had taken her up on the offer.

Huck sighed audibly, pushed the newspaper away and stood abruptly, his chair making a loud scraping noise on the tiled kitchen floor.

Nell Davenport has disappeared.

Mother is missing.

Mudder's gone.

A visceral pain; he almost felt grateful.

'Huck, sit back down,' his father said. 'You don't look so good.'

Dalt's no nonsense tone acted like a hypnotist's trigger. Dalt was a man of few words, which when they came tended to be in the form of commands: climb, swim, find, build, and now sit. As a child, out on the moor, Huck had learned young to heed these words if he wanted to stay safe.

He lowered himself into the chair his father had pulled out for him and scrunched his eyes together tightly. He took a few deep breaths before opening them again. The clenching feeling in his gut had passed and the room was no longer spinning.

'I know how you feel,' Dalt said. 'The article... it makes it real. But we can't lose hope. We have to stay strong, for Mudder.'

Cheesy, thought Huck, but maybe that's all that's left in times of crisis: people talking in clichés about hope and strength and sticking together. Funny really, we shouldn't 'lose' hope, but we lost Mudder. Is it easier to lose a feeling or a person, he wondered?

His brain kept doing this, running away with an idea, taking it further and further from the start until he almost lost sight of where the thought had begun. Maybe it was a coping mechanism. He must read up on it. Either that or he was losing the plot. He saw his father looking at him, concern etched on his face.

'I'm okay,' Huck managed. 'The article threw me, that's all. I'm fine.'

Dalt stood, and placed his hand (encouragingly, reassuringly?) on Huck's shoulder. For a large man, his father's touch was surprisingly gentle.

'Well, if you're sure you're ok, I'll be in my study if you need me.'

Huck watched as his father cleared away the breakfast things and left the kitchen.

Dalt. Dad. Edward Dalton. Father, illustrator, husband.

An old school friend of his father's had phoned the house many years ago, and toddler Huck had picked up the handset.

'Is Dalt there?' a voice had asked.

'Dalt. Dalt. Dalt. Dalt,' he'd repeated, and the nickname his father had been given at university had stuck. To Huck, his father would be Dalt for ever more.

Mudder's name had also been spawned by his own infant mouth, unable to form the word mother. It too had stayed. It suited her perfectly, a mother in her own way.

Nine days, 216 hours, twelve thousand, nine-hundred and sixty minutes, seven-hundred and seventy-seven thousand, six hundred seconds (he may have been emotionally fragile since her disappearance, but he was nailing 'missing mother maths') and still no sign of her.

Too much time to ponder, reflect, ruminate, to deliberate, muse and contemplate (ruminate is his favourite). He entered the hallway just as the clock struck nine and the memory of a Saturday just over six weeks earlier hit him, when the clock had chimed, and as if in harmony, the frenzied buzzing of the electric gates' intercom had notified them all of Amelia Early's arrival.

He'd heard of her before then. Mudder talked fondly (albeit rarely) of her student days, and marginally more frequently of her good friend and roommate, Amelia.

Unexpected. Unforeseen. Unanticipated. Unwanted?

He'd pressed the button, opened the gates. Minutes later, Amelia Early stood on the front doorstep, the low morning sun behind her sending out flares that he should have read as a warning.

'Hi', she'd exclaimed. (Anxiously? Nervously? Apprehensively?) 'You must be Huck. I'm Amelia, Amelia Early, a friend of your mother's. Is she in?'

He'd stood for a moment, blinded by the sun and the surprise, wished he'd had a camera, one of those instant ones that could capture the moment, the light, the colours and the shapes and contain them forever in a three-by-three-inch square.

'Nell!' The moment shattered, and the stranger had brushed past him into the house and thrown her arms exuberantly around Mudder, who'd stood rigid in the embrace, Turnip barking and jumping between them as if to say, 'Back off; she's mine.'

North and South. Opposite poles.

Mudder: angular, uncompromising, 'gauche' (he tries the word on his tongue, is pleased with it – he hasn't used it before, but he likes how it feels: stately, sophisticated, cold) versus Amelia: flowery, flowing, bohemian.

He remembers feeling like he should avert his eyes (he didn't). He can't remember the last time, if indeed there was ever a time, that he saw Mudder make Actual Physical Contact with someone.

Floored, sucker-punched (him or Mudder?) (Do you have to follow the rule of three? There's a definite pause, an absence if he doesn't). Who cares? He's going to rebel, make his own rules.

The crazy thing is, Mudder looked like she was enjoying it!

'Huck, it's Amelia!' Stating the obvious, but at least Mudder had eventually remembered he was there, and she'd even attempted an introduction, going well beyond her usual efforts when faced with social conventions.

'Hi,' he had managed. Mousy. Vanilla. Unremarkable.

'I've heard a lot about you,' he'd added (a poor attempt to pull it back).

'Such a long time...,' Amelia had enthused, whether to him or to Mudder, he hadn't been quite sure. 'Can you believe it? Sixteen years since we last met! I know we've been in touch along the way, but still, sixteen years! And look at you now – best-sellers in every country of the world! You did it! You made it!' To Mudder then, definitely to Mudder.

Huck had caught Mudder's eye straying to the open door behind him, where a bright red suitcase was waiting (unsolicited?) on the doorstep. Amelia had caught the glance too, and Huck recalled how she looked momentarily off-balance.

'Do you remember me mentioning Henry? Henry Cooper? Well, it's over. Mutual and all that. It's fine, I'm fine,' (this last bit said with a shake of the head, pre-empting Mudder's concern perhaps?)

A pause. The concern didn't come.

'Anyway, it all needs a bit of time and space to bed-in, so to speak – to settle down, or rather, we need a little time and space. I was going to Olivia's – remember my sister? Then I realised you live practically enroute, so I thought I'd call in, catch up and all that. I won't stay. You must be so busy with your writing, and your family too,' (a quick glance in Huck's direction). 'Anyway, I just wanted to see you, to say hello.'

Amelia's words dispersed into the hallway, like trapped air violently and suddenly expelled from a whoopee cushion, leaving the three of them standing self-consciously in the silence left behind. Amelia, too, looked deflated, as if she'd just that moment realised what a ridiculous idea this surprise visit had been.

They made for an irregular triangle.

Amplified sounds: the angry buzzing of a fly trapped behind a curtain, the ticking of the hall clock and the heavy release of his own held breath.

Snap, the shutter closes, the picture freezes.

Then Mudder had smiled.

'Come in, come in properly! Huck, can you fetch Amelia's case? Run it up to the guest room?'

Amelia had grabbed Mudder's hand and squeezed it (playfully?).

'It really is *so* good to see you.'

'Whatever you need,' Mudder had replied.

A fly landing on Huck's cheek brought him back to the present moment. He brushed it away with his fingers. How long would it take for flies to cover a body, lay their larvae, infest?

Stop it, damn twisted thoughts. Terrible, awful notions that pervaded his mind uninvited, like drug addicts squatting in a monastery (note to self: simile needs work – museum?).

The clock had finished chiming many minutes ago. The house was muggy. The fly was still circling. What was he still doing here, standing in the hallway daydreaming?

'Huck, are you okay? Has there been some news?'

Amelia, creeping up on people like a middle-aged, hippy ninja, dripping her sweet concern all over them like poisoned honey.

'No news,' he told her. 'Unless you count an article about Mudder's t-shirt as news?'

Amelia looked tired. Who wouldn't, after just over a week of worrying, waiting, missing, hypothesising, talking, guessing, wondering? He was tired, too. Tired of her more than anything, still here, intruding on their loss like one of those birds that steals nests. The hen cuckoo, he thinks. Dalt told him about it once, how it ejects the eggs from another bird's nest, only to lay its own there instead.

Well this wasn't her nest. It was time for her to bugger off and leave them to their... their what? Their worry? Their pain? Their fear? Their grief?

'You should rest,' he told her. 'Maybe no news is good news.' Now he was doing it, the cheesy clichés, but he could hardly say what he really wanted to and tell her to get lost and leave them alone. Clichés would have to do. For now.

Amelia

U p until Nell disappeared, staying at Moordown had been like attending a rather empowering writers' retreat, all thanks to Henry bloody Cooper. Not that she was about to thank him, the cowardly toad, dumping her out of the blue like that, just after she'd booked a holiday for the two of them to Rome. Amelia had torn up the tickets (a little dramatically in retrospect and lacking the intended impact; she had actually ripped up some scrap paper symbolising the tickets as she hadn't got around to printing the e-tickets yet) and packed in a frenzy. It was on the train, on the way to her sister Olivia's, when the name of a passing station jerked her memory and the proximity of her old friend Nell and the idea of a visit had occurred to her.

Although they had talked on the phone a couple of times a year, Amelia hadn't actually seen Nell for years. Or rather she hadn't seen the real-life Nell for years – she was frequently confronted by photographs of Nell on the flysheet of her latest crime thriller, or promotional cut-outs of Nell's fictional detectives in the local bookshop. It spawned a curious feeling in her: pride and admiration, for sure, but also the question, 'Why Nell? Why her?' Hadn't they both shared the salubrious role of most talented students at university? Hadn't they both been voted, *'Most likely to write an international best-seller before they were thirty,'* in their graduating mock awards ceremony?

Nell hadn't just proved successful at writing. The house, the husband, the son – she had it all. If Amelia had been a different kind of person, she may have found the whole scenario frankly unbearable. But she wasn't. And when she'd buzzed the intercom on the gates at Moordown just over six weeks earlier, and Nell had appeared, Amelia had felt their old connection instantly. No hard feelings.

She'd been right to get off that train when she did. Comforting days had followed. Remedial days that alleviated the hurt caused by Henry. Chicken soup days, Amelia liked to think of them as – although she hadn't actually eaten any chicken soup, just delicious, simple, homemade meals made with vegetables plucked fresh from Nell's vegetable garden. This house was restorative. She'd go as far as to say it had magical healing powers. The creative energies that flowed here were unbelievable. Her writer's block had boarded a plane and flown off into the sunset, taking any residual feelings for Henry Cooper with it. The words were literally flowing out of her. Down by the stream, she'd written a two-page poem she'd entitled, *The Betrayal of the Magpie*, that contained both the words eschew and pontificate in one sentence. And her friendship with Nell had been rekindled. She'd wondered if it would be weird, just turning up out of the blue like that after so long, but Nell had welcomed her in. Karmic timing. Nell seemed to need Amelia like Amelia needed Moordown.

But to put it mildly, things had gone rather down the pan since then.

It appeared that Nell really had disappeared.

On the Saturday of her disappearance, Nell had been missing for twelve hours by the time two police officers turned up at the door at

7 p.m. The mugginess of the night before had returned, and as the officers entered the hallway, the female officer removed her hat and wiped her forehead with her forearm, leaving a glistening, wet slug trail on her skin.

'What can I get you to drink?' Amelia had blurted, openly staring, then panicking that her expression of repulsion had been noted. She regretted her behaviour immediately. These were highly trained police officers gathering information, forming all-important first impressions. They'd been called here to investigate the disappearance of a mother, wife and famous author and instead of being 'Concerned and Worried Friend', Amelia was being 'The Hostess with The Mostess.' What was she playing at? She felt guilty for no reason, like when she walked past security guards in an airport, convinced they thought she might be some kind of middle-aged drug mule, smuggling Class A substances, ground into the beetroot pesto in her organic wild-pink salmon and grilled asparagus wrap.

But the damage was done, and the drinks orders were taken. Four minutes and two clinking glasses of ice-water later, Amelia returned from the kitchen, following the voices down the hallway into the drawing room.

A drawing room – how stately, she had thought, the day she first arrived at Moordown, when Nell suggested they take their coffee in there, without even the hint of recognition of the grandeur the term implied. And grand it was, or rather, had been. It was a room at odds with itself. Stylish modern furniture in shades of paint from one of those ridiculously expensive catalogues that Amelia loved to flick through, and floor to ceiling windows that monopolised the southern end of the room, a vast expanse of glass that bequeathed divine views of the manicured lawns (they must have a gardener – surely, they had to have a gardener?). Hedges and rose gardens were visible to the left side of the house, whilst straight ahead lay a lawn *Gardeners' World* would have been proud of, sloping away towards what? A river perhaps? In the distance, the top of a magnificent willow tree had caught her eye, its thick, vibrant branches like arms waving a welcome.

The other half of the drawing room sat in stark contrast: dark and old-fashioned, stuffed too full of furniture, like an overcrowded, under-loved antique store. A piano had been plonked in the centre of the room, various sofas and shabby hard-backed chairs scattered haphazardly around it. Let the good times roll, Amelia had thought, picturing an alcohol fuelled, drunken knees-up. Maybe in someone else's house, she realised now. Not here. Never here.

The room, at least, offered a choice of places to sit. Huck was seated next to his father, both in single, hard-backed chairs, the two police officers opposite them, squashed together into the centre of a brown sagging sofa. If they weren't already a couple, they might be after this house call. Amelia handed out the glasses of ice-cold water. The female officer, who had taken off both her hat and jacket and slung them over the back of the sofa, threw Amelia a look of gratitude. Amelia sat down quickly and gave her attention to the officers.

'You missed the introductions,' the male officer was blunt. Amelia supposed that there was little time for niceties in their profession, or maybe he was playing 'bad cop'. Was she stereotyping? Too much TV? Was good-cop-bad-cop even a thing?

'I'm Officer Pearson, and this is my colleague Officer Henley. We've come to gather some details.'

'I'm Amelia – Amelia Early. I'm a friend of Nell's. I've been staying here, visiting, for the last five weeks.' They'd need details, wouldn't they? Specifics. Amelia managed a strained smile, which neither officer returned. What were they thinking? Freeloader? Polyamorist? Did it show a lack of confidence, of character, to presume another's low opinion of oneself? She'd have to explore this in her next talking therapy session with Dr Sasha at The Sanctuary.

Amelia supposed that the officers had already been informed of her presence as house guest, as no further questions were asked of her. Officer Henley turned her attention directly to the matter at hand.

Flick. Flick. Flick. Pages of paper moving backwards and then forwards again, the officer tapping her pencil and scanning her notes whilst simultaneously trying to shuffle out of Officer Pearson's lap. Notepads? Surely the police department were more high-tech than this?

Apparently not.

'Ok, Mr Dalton, I know you gave the call operator a lot of details, but I'm afraid you're going to have to repeat a lot of the information again. It's important Officer Pearson and I know all the details first-hand. There's a standard MISPER form we'll go through with you. Sorry – missing person,' Officer Henley explained, looking apologetic for her lapse into police speak.

Dalt nodded his assent.

'Can you tell me your wife's full name?'

'Eleanor Margaret Davenport. But everyone who knows her calls her Nell. '

'Davenport? Not Dalton?' A question in a question.

'Davenport, not Dalton,' Dalt repeated. A statement not an answer.

Amelia averted her eyes, the awkwardness palpable.

A brief pause. 'And her date of birth?' Officer Henley glanced briefly up from her notes.

'16th May 1979. We shared a birthday,' Dalt said.

'Unusual. What are the chances of that, eh?' said Officer Pearson.

'One in three hundred and sixty-five.'

Officer Pearson looked taken aback.

'Ooookay. So, she's forty. I was born in 1979 too. A good year, a good vintage.' Officer Pearson looked like he was warming up, a slow start to a bad stand-up act. 'And can you describe Ms Davenport – height, eye colour, hair colour, build?'

'She's five-foot-nine, tall, willowy.' Dalt looked to Huck, who nodded affirmatively. 'Green eyes, red hair – mid-length, wavy. It would have been tied up; she always ties it up when she's running. She was wearing black running leggings and a bright yellow t-shirt that had something written on it.'

'Your pace or mine?' Amelia interjected, unable to hold back, hoping she'd kept the judgement out of her tone.

Huck gave her a funny look. Perhaps her disapproval had been evident or maybe it just seemed as if Amelia was propositioning an officer of the law.

'That's what the t-shirt said,' Amelia was quick to explain. 'I'd seen her in it a few times. I didn't see her this morning,' she added, worried that aspersions would be cast in her direction.

'Mudder gets her clothes second-hand. She isn't into fancy stuff. She'll wear anything. She must have picked the top up somewhere. She liked it because it was high-vis.' Huck's tone was sulky. Defensive. Amelia sensed he was annoyed with her.

Officer Henley nodded, and made a note. 'Footwear?'

'Trainers. White with blue stripes, Adidas I think. Pretty old and worn,' Dalt said.

Amelia had seen the trainers left abandoned on the decking on a number of occasions, presumably lying where Nell had flung them after her run. She wasn't the tidiest person, Amelia had noticed.

'And did she take anything with her? Have you noticed anything missing?' Officer Pearson asked.

'She took a running bag. She normally only takes it when she goes on longer runs. But we don't know what was in it. It's hard to tell what's missing.'

'Ok.' Officer Pearson made a note in his notebook. 'It would be very helpful to know if Nell took any clothes or supplies with her.'

'She didn't take her phone, or wallet. They're both here. The bag's pretty small,' Dalt offered. 'She wouldn't be able to fit much in.'

'She didn't take Turnip, either,' Huck gestured to the dog curled up at Dalt's feet. 'He usually goes running with her. But not if she's going out for a big one – maybe ten miles or more,' he explained, noticing Officer Pearson's raised eyebrow. 'Or if it's too hot.'

'Okay. Well, it makes sense that she wouldn't want to take him out in this heat,' Officer Henley was scanning the room, eyes lingering on the empty piano top. 'Have you got any recent photos of Ms Davenport? Something we could circulate?'

Amelia looked questioningly at Dalt, who looked at Huck, who looked at the floor.

'We're not a very *photographic* family.' Dalt put an odd emphasis on the word. 'Nell used to take all the photos, years ago, when Huck was small, but lately...' his voice trailed off. 'Lately, it's not been a priority, and I haven't taken any. The camera on my phone's been broken for months.'

Officer Pearson looked questioningly at Huck. 'What about you, son? Any on your phone? It's so easy these days, isn't it, with camera phones? My kids are always taking photos of me when I don't want them to, messing around. Got any of your mum?'

'I haven't got a phone.'

Two jaws dropped, Huck's reply blindsiding the officers. Forget the missing person, Amelia thought, amused – a teenager without a mobile phone – this was the biggest mystery they'd had to solve all year.

'No phone? Are you serious?' Officer Pearson looked admiringly at Dalt. 'How'd you manage that? My kids think they're entitled to call ChildLine if they haven't got the latest all-singing-all-dancing iPhone ninety-nine, or whatever it is these days.'

'I don't want one,' Huck said, saving his father the difficulty of an answer.

The Officers looked to Dalt for further explanation. It didn't come. If the police officers wanted details, they'd clearly come to the wrong family.

As another silence threatened, Amelia spoke up, surprising everyone.

'I've got some photos on my phone. Nell and I took the rowing boat out a few times. We messed around on the river. I took some pictures. They're probably not very good, but at least they're recent. Or you could use one of Nell's author photos at the back of her books. She's got a new book out so there'd be a good one in that.'

Amelia took in Huck and Dalt's matching expressions of surprise and could see the questions in their faces. Officer Henley noticed too and caught Officer Pearson's eye. This wasn't what Amelia had intended. She'd been trying to help.

'Can we take your phone before we leave, Ms Early? We'll download the photos and return it to you as soon as possible.'

'Of course,' Amelia sounded brighter than she felt. Take her phone? Would they read her messages and check her calls as well as her photos? Did they think she had something to do with this?

'Are there any vehicles missing?' Officer Henley asked, referring to the missing person form on her lap.

'No. All accounted for,' Dalt said.

'Ok, fine. We'll get that description circulated straight away. Officer Pearson, do you mind?'

'I'll get on it.' Officer Pearson struggled to get off the sagging sofa and put a hand down to steady himself.

'My leg.' Officer Henley did not look impressed.

'Sorry.' Flushed red from embarrassment or from the heat, it was hard to tell, Officer Pearson pulled his two-way radio from his belt and left the room hurriedly.

'Right – a few more details and we're done.' Officer Henley looked dishevelled, her brown fringe damp and clinging in strands to her forehead, her cheeks blotchy. 'Talk me through this morning again. When you each saw Nell, and where, and what time it was.'

Huck spoke suddenly, a catch in his voice at the start of his sentence. 'I saw her, from my bedroom window. She was too far away for me to see properly. She was going for her run. I could see she was wearing yellow and black. It was about five past seven.'

Officer Henley's pencil scribbled furiously. 'Thanks Huck. Which direction was she heading?'

'Straight down the lawn towards the river.'

More scribbling.

'I saw her at about five to seven.' Dalt's turn now. Amelia couldn't help but think of the old nursery rhyme, '*Who killed Cock Robin?*' Tasteless, but apt, with all this 'I' business. 'I said the sparrow, with my bow and arrow. I killed Cock Robin.' Or was it: 'I, said the son, with my smoking gun. I killed Nell Davenport.'

Amelia Early! Amelia mentally chastised herself for her abominable thought process. Missing – Nell was missing, not dead, and what reason did she have to throw Huck underneath the bus?

'Nell always gets up then. She was getting dressed. She woke me up, shutting a drawer. She apologised. I went back to sleep.'

'How did she seem to you, Mr Dalton?'

Dalt paused, considering the question. 'She seemed fine. The same as usual. I mean, we didn't talk, I was still half-asleep, but she seemed fine.'

'Was there anything bothering her yesterday, or over the last few days, or even weeks? Anything that you can think of that might have been troubling her?' Officer Henley cast her question out to all three of them. Getting down to the nitty gritty, Amelia thought. 'Speak now, or forever hold your peace.'

Dalt spoke first. 'Nothing I can think of. She was busy as usual. The latest book in the Daniel Hargreaves series was released a few months ago. She was still pretty wrapped up with that, liaising with her publisher and agent, doing PR, that kind of thing. Not Nell's bag really, but it had to be done.'

Officer Henley looked to Huck and Amelia, inviting them to speak.

'She seemed fine to me,' Amelia said. 'Like Dalt said, she was pretty busy in the daytime. I didn't see that much of her to be honest. She had her routine – run then work. But when I saw her in the evening, she seemed relaxed. Happy.'

'Huck?' Officer Henley asked.

'Fine. The same as usual. Busy.'

Description circulated, the hulk of Officer Pearson reappeared in the doorway and seconds later he'd resumed his position on the sofa. Questions were thrown open to the floor now. Assessing risk, Amelia figured. Had Nell had any financial pressures? Personal issues? Was she on any medication that they knew of? Had this ever happened before? Had she been involved in any disputes?

'No,' 'No,' 'No,' 'No,' and 'No.'

An anti-climax. Both officers leaned back at the same time, the delicate balance of the sofa disturbed again, this time Officer Pearson's meaty thigh slipped over Officer Henley's regulation navy trouser leg. Another red-faced, flustered apology.

'Okay, so I think we've got all we need for now.'

Amelia felt a churning in her stomach as Officer Henley read aloud the information she'd gathered, summarised the facts of the day, the details that would later become a timeline, the description of Nell that would become front page news.

'I do think we need to start to look into this immediately, especially considering Ms Davenport's public profile,' said Officer Henley. 'First, we'll check local hospitals, see if anyone has been admitted that fits Nell's description. We'll deploy some officers in the area in which you informed us that Ms Davenport may have been running this morning and we'll conduct some local enquiries in case anybody in the neighbourhood saw anything. Then we'll take it from there.'

A collective outtake of breath. Amelia felt relief wash over her, glad that the problem had been outsourced and a degree of pressure lifted. She'd never been good with stressful situations – she was a Pisces after all – highly sensitive, how could she be expected to be? She was going to need a cup of something soothing. Camomile tea perhaps, with just the smallest shot of gin, to settle her nerves and take the edge off the worry.

The Officers were standing now and heading for the doorway, the plan in place.

'The best thing for you all to do,' Officer Pearson told them, 'is to stay here at the house. Hopefully, Ms Davenport will return of her own accord. If she does, then notify us immediately. In the meantime, if you could all think very carefully about Ms Davenport's actions, and indeed your own interactions with Ms Davenport over the last few weeks, that would be most helpful indeed, just in case you think of something that might aid our enquiry.'

'Oh, one last thing,' Officer Pearson said, hand on the doorknob. 'Do you have your phone, Ms Early.'

Amelia put her phone into Officer Pearson's outstretched hand and told him her lock screen password. It felt so wrong, so intrusive, so out of her control.

Then they were gone.

Dalt closed the door behind them and turned to face Amelia, his forehead shiny with perspiration.

'What was all that about the rowing boat?'

'It was just a little fun, something spontaneous, to get inspired. I'd been reading an article about water and its effects on creativity…'

She'd stopped, aware of the look of incredulity Huck and Dalt exchanged.

'Where did you go?' Dalt asked, his expression one of mistrust before she'd even opened her mouth to answer.

'Not far. We stayed near the jetty. We were never out for long.' The hallway seemed to have narrowed and Amelia felt intensely aware of the heat of their bodies, the clamminess of her shirt and the smell of her own fear.

'You went more than once?' Huck said.

Amelia nodded. 'A few times. What's the big deal anyway? Did we do something wrong?'

Neither Dalt nor Huck answered. Dalt shook his head almost imperceptibly. Huck looked confused.

'I can't just stay here and wait, whilst Nell is out there somewhere,' Dalt said, the subject changed abruptly but clearly not forgotten.

Amelia nodded and tried to make the right soothing noises.

'Empathy, my dear...' her therapist was fond of saying. 'Empathy is key.'

Put yourself in Dalt's shoes. What must he be feeling? Pretty rubbish she imagined. Losing your wife was never the best start to the weekend.

'Amelia, you stay here, answer the phone if it rings. Wait for any news. And Huck, can you search the house again, and the outbuildings and garden too. We've probably just got time, before it gets dark.'

Huck had sullenly nodded his agreement, looking every inch the stroppy teenager.

'I'll have another good look around the house,' Amelia had told Dalt.

But their searches had been fruitless. Nothing found, not a trace.

And it had now been nine days since Nell disappeared, since the police officers first visited, and what little progress they'd all made in that time. The photos had been downloaded from Amelia's phone (and God knows what else! Amelia hadn't wanted to ask. No one had said). It had been returned, with its floral cover looking manhandled and grubby. Amelia felt much like her phone: violated, probed and examined. Dalt and Huck were treating her differently, she was certain. Whilst she had sensed that Huck had never been sure of her, now he was going out of his way to avoid her. Dalt, too, was different: wary, suspicious even. Not that she saw much of him – he was out searching the moor from first light, returning beaten each evening, the moor and his mind relentless adversaries to battle.

And yet here she was, on the inside like this, within these walls, witnessing first-hand the actions and emotions of two people in turmoil. She felt almost honoured, privileged – a most unusual situation. She'd begun to see it as her duty to jot down the events of each day that had passed, each interaction with the police officers, the searches, extending way beyond the house now, right down to the river and across the moor, involving dogs as well as people, members of the public as well as police officers, and even, on one occasion, divers in thick black neoprene suits, 'knights of the deep,' she had written, (perhaps somewhat romantically in retrospect), 'using torches instead of spears to bring their fair maiden home.' Far too whimsical, she decided on a re-read, but tricky to find the right tone. Calls had been made to local hospitals, and then not so local hospitals, enquiries made in town, then in surrounding towns, but nobody knew anything. Gone, without a trace. Was that title already taken? Probably, thought Amelia, it sounded familiar, but she jotted it down anyway, just in case.

Nell's disappearance was big – national news big. Public interest was huge. Reporters had been camped out at the end of the driveway since the news broke, just visible from the house, kept at bay by the gates. Reporters jostled for titbits thrown like breadcrumbs from the police officers stationed on twenty-four-hour watch.

Amelia had seen the headlines online:

INTERNATIONALLY ACCLAIMED, BEST-SELLING CRIME AUTHOR INVOLVED IN HER OWN NOVEL DISAPPEARANCE, (Amelia imagined that someone must have been very smug about that one) and *REAL-LIFE PAGE TURNER: THE PLOT THICKENS*. The story was news gold. Suddenly, everyone had read one of Nell's books. Everyone knew who Nell Davenport was. An amazing marketing ploy, book sales were probably going through the roof. What amazing PR for Nell's new book release, Amelia had caught herself thinking, before giving herself a virtual slap. The green-eyed monster was a hard one to slay; it lurked in the shadows, seemingly always waiting for a chance to rear its ugly head. A fair point though. Bloody good marketing.

With Dalt's permission, police officers had searched the house, taking away Nell's computer and phone. They'd searched the gardens too. Whilst his colleagues worked, one elderly officer had taken great joy in regaling Amelia with missing person statistics. Someone is reported missing every 90 seconds in the United Kingdom, he'd told her. 170,000 people are reported missing every year.

Was he trying to make her feel better or worse?

And why didn't he tell her how many of those people were found?

Dalt

That bloody blank column yesterday wasn't going to help things. Nice idea and all that, but ultimately sentimental tosh. Ironic really, if Nell were here she would have been mortified at the waste of good publishing space.

'A perfect opportunity for a junior reporter to submit a piece,' she would have said. Anyway, it was done now, and Dalt had feigned thanks when Frank, the *Stonebrook Gazette*'s editor and, more than that, his good friend, had called his mobile.

'Still no news, Frank,' Dalt felt guilty that he had nothing more to offer him.

'I'm sure she'll be home soon,' Frank said before they ended the call.

Sure? Dalt wanted to ask. Really, sure? He'd file Frank's certainty right up there with his mother's 'I hope', his stepfather's 'I bet' and all of the other aspirational expressions of desire for a positive outcome that he'd heard over the last week. People are just trying to stay optimistic, he reminded himself. People are just trying to help.

The stress of the last nine days was taking its toll. His body ached from tirelessly searching the moor. His legs were slashed and his hands torn from battling through dense, thorny gorse, forged to withstand strong winds and torrential rains, his exposed skin no match for their brutal resilience. Yet the physical pain did nothing to distract him from the mental one. Constant thoughts of Nell, out here alone, exposed and suffering, sent him wading through pools of thick, black sludge and sliding on his belly into stony crevices, searching desperately for a trace of his wife.

On the rare occasions he was in the house, he'd taken to not answering the landline, which seemed to ring continuously, unless the caller's name flashed on the display, and sometimes, even then, he'd choose to ignore it. Interesting, how many people felt the need to get in touch and pass on their thoughts and best wishes. Interesting that months could go by, years even, without hearing from aunts, cousins and old friends, and now the phone practically rang off the hook. He supposed that they all meant well. And, in fairness, it had been his and Nell's lifestyle that had kept them apart rather than the other way around. Writing, drawing, his and Nell's were quiet pursuits, perhaps even bordering on antisocial, as Diana, Dalt's mother, would have said. Had said, on more than one occasion. Water under the bridge, Dalt mused. She was one of the most prolific callers. She telephoned from New Zealand daily, each call, a tree planted to offset the emissions of guilt that she harboured for moving so far away after his father, Charles, died. He could often hear Laurence, his stepfather, in the background, his mother in the middle acting like a translator. 'Have there been any updates? Are they still searching the moor? Have they gone underground? Looked in any of those old pit holes?' (This last question he'd pretended not to hear.) Two more people that meant well, but ultimately couldn't help find his wife.

Dalt could smell his own stale breath rebounding from the phone handset. Coffee, coffee and more coffee. Dalt imagined if he was cut open it would spurt from his veins instead of blood.

Cut open. Dark thoughts he couldn't shift. Thoughts that made no sense – no sense at all.

Like the rowing boat.

Nell hated being on the water. More than hated. She was terrified of water. Hardly surprising when her younger brother, Toby, had drowned in the same river thirty years before. It was a shocker of a tale, and one which Nell had never spoken of to Dalt. Nell's father, Dennis, a pleasant man who Dalt felt he had never really got to know as well as he would have liked, had given him facts about the day Toby died that he could count on one hand. Toby had been eight when he'd toppled out of the rowing boat into the river, a heavy rucksack strapped firmly to his back. He'd gone out alone, to investigate the dragonfly larvae. *'A budding scientist,'* was how Dennis had described him. Nell had been ten at the time. *'A bookworm even then'.* So absorbed in her reading that she hadn't heard the splash as Toby entered the water.

'And it's true what they say. Drowning is a quiet affair,' Dennis had said, a faraway look in his eye.

Toby: a tear in a tapestry, the fabric mended neatly, without a fuss. Precise, short, quick darns. Was the damage repaired, or just hidden from view?

But Dalt couldn't work it out. He'd seen the photo Amelia had taken. Nell was laughing. He didn't understand it. In all the years that he had known Nell, she had never set foot on-board a boat.

After the police had left on the day Nell went missing, Huck had come to find Dalt in his bedroom.

'I asked Amelia if she knew Nell had a brother. She said no. I told her all about Toby and how he drowned. Amelia looked shocked: genuinely horrified. I really don't think she knew anything about it.' Huck told him.

'I just don't get it. It makes no sense at all. Why would Nell have kept it a secret? And why go out on a boat?' Dalt said.

Huck looked as puzzled as Dalt felt.

But the photographic evidence was there, Nell has done exactly that. They couldn't deny it. What was missing was any rational explanation.

Tuesday 20th August

Amelia

Amelia was still annoyed. Annoyed with Dalt and Huck. Annoyed with the boat. Annoyed with Nell for asking her to keep a secret.

Annoyed with herself for being such a sucker and blithely believing Nell's spiel.

Amelia had only been at Moordown for a few days when Nell had knocked lightly on her bedroom door.

'I want you to help me with something!' Nell had said excitedly. 'A little project.'

'Whatever you need,' Amelia had replied, a conspiratorial smile reflected on their faces.

Dalt busy working, Huck at school, Amelia followed Nell down to the river, where they turned left and walked until they came to a small, brick boathouse with faded, blue, wooden doors. Covered in green leaves and vines, it looked like it was hiding and had morphed over time into the trees and bushes around it.

Nell pulled on the padlock, scattering faded blue paint like snowflakes. Sliding it off, she caught the edge of one of the doors, and pulled it firmly over the tumble of weeds and grasses that had grown up in its way.

'I came here not long ago,' she told Amelia. 'It took me ages to clear the weeds enough to open the door. The padlock was so stiff, I had to use pliers to force it open.'

Amelia watched, fascinated, as her friend wedged the door open with a rock, and stepped into the gloom of the boathouse.

'Come in,' Nell encouraged. 'Your eyes will adjust in a few minutes.'

The two women stood, side by side, just inside the doorway. Amelia could make out the shape of a boat, concealed by a large tarpaulin. Nell leaned forward and pulled off the covering.

'It was my father's boat,' she told Amelia. 'He used to take it out fishing on the river. It's old, but I think it will still float. It looks to be in good condition. I brushed it down when I came before. I couldn't see too much wrong with it.'

Amelia stepped forward and rested her hand on its bow. She knew a little about boats, more recently from floating lazily about on rivers with Henry and bottles of champagne. But before that, before stupid Henry, there had been a time in her early twenties when she'd joined a sailing group and learnt how to sail.

This obviously wasn't a sailing boat. Two metres long at the most, the boat was simple in design. Sturdy, with a fibreglass hull, neat wooden seats in the middle and either end and a faded orange stripe of paint around its base, Amelia imagined that it used to look rather fine on the water.

'I want to give it to Huck,' Nell said. 'As a surprise, for his next birthday. But first I want to fix it up, get it out on the water, see if it still floats.'

'What a brilliant idea!' Amelia had exclaimed. 'Does he know about it?' Most teenagers would have taken it for a spin by now, Amelia thought.

'I don't know. I'm not sure I ever mentioned it,' Nell had replied.

Huck definitely wasn't a typical teenager.

'What's the plan?' Amelia asked. 'Should we try it out on the water?'

An awkward pause. Did there used to be so many awkward pauses, back in their student days? She couldn't quite see Nell's face in the gloomy light to gauge her expression.

'Yes. That seems like a good idea.'

'How the hell did your dad manage this on his own?' Amelia asked, five minutes later, as the two women stood either end of the boat, bent double with laughter, hands covered in years of thick dust tinged with orange paint, the boat only a metre from its starting position.

'He used to leave it moored on the river. There's a jetty not far from here. It only came to the boathouse for repairs and over winter. And then when he stopped fishing altogether.'

'He'd have struggled to do this on his own! Okay, after three. Let's try again,' Amelia instructed.

It took a few more rest breaks, but between them they finally got the boat down the rutted concrete path and into the water. The wooden jetty Nell had spoken of was still there and more surprisingly, still intact, stretching out a couple of metres into the river.

'Let's see if this thing is watertight,' Nell said, her voice trembling with what Amelia could only presume to be excitement.

Amelia reached into the boat to find the end of the thick mooring rope, impressed when the length unravelled, frayed but complete. Kicking off her sandals and wading up to her knees into the calm water, she tied the rope tightly to the wooden mooring on the jetty.

Nell was staring at her.

'Can you swim?' Nell was always so direct. Not one for small talk, Nell.

'Of course I can swim. I love to swim. Back in London I swam a couple of times a week. In fact, I'd been meaning to ask you what the river was like for wild swimming. It's something I want to get into. Kristna, my acupuncturist, swears by it. She says it's amazing for reducing stress and inflammation. I mean, I try to drink turmeric smoothies for that, so I've probably got it covered, but cold-water immersion sounds worth a try, too.' Looking at her friend's bemused face, Amelia realised a yes or no was probably all she'd been looking for.

'In fact, this spot looks ideal,' Amelia added.

A handful of large, flat rocks, perfect for changing on, littered the water's edge, as if nature had designed this pool with bathing in mind. She was no expert, but the water looked safe. The river, no more than eight metres wide, didn't appear to have any fast-moving currents; in fact, the water hardly looked like it was moving at all. Perfect for splashing about in.

'Do you swim here?' Amelia asked. 'Dalt and Huck love to swim don't they? I bet this is one of their favourite spots, so close to the house.'

'They swim, but not here. They prefer to go up onto the moor. Will you teach me?'

Nell dropped the question in so quickly that Amelia wondered if she'd heard her correctly.

'Teach you? You can't swim?'

Nell shook her head. 'But I want to learn. Another surprise. They'll never believe it.'

Amelia hadn't known that Nell was such a fan of surprises. But then she hadn't known that Nell couldn't swim either.

'Yes, sure, I'll give it a go. I'm not sure how good an instructor I'll be. But it'll be fun…' she said, warming to the idea. A challenge, a way to repay Nell's kindness for letting her stay.

'The boat's still afloat!' Nell exclaimed suddenly. All this talk of swimming had distracted Amelia from their original mission. The boat looked different now – the water had washed the dust and dirt off its sides. It looked happy, if a boat could look happy; like it had been given a new lease of life.

'I'm not sure I trust it entirely. Definitely not in deeper water, but here maybe. In this pool,' Nell had mused.

'Why don't we change into swimsuits, so we're prepared if we fall in? Then we can have a swimming lesson and a boat testing session all in one go?' Amelia suggested.

'I don't have a swimsuit,' Nell said.

'You can borrow one of mine. It might be a bit big, but it'll do the job.' Amelia had brought a selection of swimwear with her in her suitcase. Something for every occasion: pool party, boating afternoon. None of them screamed 'river swimming', though, but they'd do.

They'd left the boat where it was. Nell seemed certain that neither Huck nor Dalt ever ventured down this way. They'd headed up to the house to change when the sky turned dark and large drops of rain started to fall.

'Tomorrow?' Nell asked Amelia.

'Definitely,' Amelia replied.

It had felt good, then, this secret of theirs, exciting and bonding. Not devious and dishonest, like it felt afterwards, with the eyes of Huck and Dalt upon her, examining her, judging her.

They had returned the following day. The boat was miraculously still afloat. They'd tested it, still tethered to the jetty, first with Amelia's weight and then their weight combined.

When Nell took her first, tentative step aboard, her pale skin and trembling hands belied the depth of the fear that until now she'd kept hidden. She'd stood, hunched, inside the gently swaying boat, one hand gripping the side, the other holding tight to Amelia's arm, her fingernails digging painfully into the soft flesh.

'Sit down. Sit,' Amelia had hissed, fear suddenly contagious.

It had been odd, that first outing. Whilst she was physically there, perched on the wooden seat at the back of the boat, Nell seemed absent in spirit, far away in thought. Amelia had taken it steady, rowed the little boat through the calm water, looking for any leaks or problems, chattering as she did so. (She didn't find any. Despite its age and neglect, the old boat manoeuvred easily and efficiently through the water, staying dry inside throughout).

Arriving back at the jetty, Amelia had helped Nell out of the boat. It wasn't until Nell's bare feet and ankles were submerged in the cold water of the river that she seemed to occupy her body again, an expression of bewilderment on her face.

'Are you okay?' Amelia had asked. Nell nodded.

'Sorry. I'm fine. Just feeling a little lightheaded. Let's not swim today.'

As the days passed, they fell into a routine. Nell would run, then work, then mid-afternoon, after coffee, they would meet at the jetty. First Nell only waded into the icy water, let it lap about her thighs, but gradually she grew braver and more accustomed to the cold. Amelia, taking her role as swim instructor and lifeguard seriously, had ordered arm bands and a large rubber ring to be delivered to the house. Nell hadn't seemed to care that she was trussed up like an infant. In fact, the more inflatables she was surrounded by, the more comfortable she seemed. She made progress quickly, and within a week, Nell was treading water further out, where she could still put her feet down if she needed to but could try a few swimming strokes too.

Two weeks in, and the rubber ring snagged on a branch and deflated. Nell ripped off the armbands, threw them into a bush, and declared it time to move on.

Amelia felt like a proud (but nervous) mother duck as she watched her protégé wade out to where the water got deep and launch herself in. Her heart nearly stopped when, for a second, nothing happened, just Nell, lying face down, inert in the water.

'Swim!' Amelia screamed. 'Swim!' and Nell jerked to life, furiously kicking her legs and wind-milling her arms, sending sprays of water into the air. It wasn't pretty, but it was effective. Nell had swum back to the jetty in moments. Swum!

'You did it!' Amelia shrieked excitedly, as Nell's pale hand reached up to firmly grip the wooden post nearest to her. 'You did it!'

Nell hadn't looked as thrilled as Amelia had hoped. Rubbing at her eyes, she'd looked upset.

'Thanks. Thanks for teaching me, Amelia. I really appreciate it. Everyone should know how to swim – so important...' She'd trailed off, before wading back to the shallows.

They hadn't gone again after that day. Nell had obviously ticked 'learn to swim,' off the list. And she never mentioned the boat again. It was all a bit strange in retrospect.

Their secret, but now it felt muddied, like the river after heavy rain.

What was Nell doing on the boat, they'd asked?

At the time, Amelia hadn't understood their distress.

But when Huck told her about Toby, Amelia had felt physically sick. Nell's brother, dead. Drowned. Toppled from that very boat. In that very spot. No wonder Nell had looked shaken the first day they'd taken it out. No wonder Dalt and Huck had looked confused when they heard that Nell had been out in it.

Like a puppeteer's plaything, Amelia felt used, violated, made to perform. Why hadn't Nell told her about Toby and about her fear of water? Had Nell really intended to give Huck the boat and surprise them all with her newfound ability to swim? Knowing the history of the boat, it seemed doubtful – perverse even.

And yet, Amelia hadn't told Huck the truth either: that Nell intended to give Huck the boat, and as a surprise she was learning to swim. Why did she feel like she had to protect Nell, when Nell hadn't been truthful with her? And what was she protecting Nell from?

It had felt so good to be Nell's confidante. No one else in Amelia's life needed her. But Nell had. Nell did.

No. Amelia wasn't going to share their secrets. And keeping them wasn't going to harm anyone, was it?

Dalt

It had been bothering him all week. He just didn't buy it – the crap about the boat and artistic inspiration. Nell must have had a reason for getting on that boat. Amelia had to be hiding something.

Nell – boat – boat – Toby. Toby: the name Dalt kept returning too. The linking piece? He was at the heart of this somehow, Dalt felt sure.

He'd woken at dawn as usual, but instead of pulling on his hiking boots and searching for answers out on the moor, he was determined to find some right here at Moordown.

Come out, come out, wherever you are, Dalt thought to himself, as he moved through the old house pulling out drawers and rummaging through their contents. There must be some information about Nell's brother in here somewhere.

On the wall of the drawing room, next to a framed, pinned butterfly, its vibrant colours long gone, he found a photo of the two of them, Nell and Toby. Dalt took it down and turned it over. The faded, handwritten date on the back of the frame gave away their ages: Nell nine and her brother seven, the picture taken a year before he died.

The nine-year-old Nell in the photo reminded him of a sunflower: a long, lanky stem encased in green corduroy trousers, a bright yellow t-shirt and a mass of curly orange hair. Even her face was sunny, a broad smile, freckles prolific and vivid against her pale skin.

And like a sunflower, her head tilted up to look at her brother. He stood beside her, on a small stepladder, a mossy wall behind them, a specimen pot in his hand. A smaller version of her, the main difference to be found in their expressions: hers joyful, his, focused and serious. A budding scientist, Dalt remembered.

They weren't touching, but a tenderness emanated from the Nell in the photo that Dalt had only ever seen on a few occasions in their life together. Dalt rubbed his thumb gently across the glass, clearing the dust away from his wife's face. His throat felt dry, his eyes suddenly painful.

Toby's death must have been hard. Must have ripped them all apart. No wonder Nell behaved oddly in the years that followed. Wouldn't anyone who'd lost a sibling in such a traumatic manner?

Dalt sighed and reached to hang the photo back on the wall, but as he did so, the back of the frame came loose. A piece of folded paper dropped out onto the carpet. He unfolded it.

Toby's birth certificate.

Toby Dennis Davenport. Born, Stonebrook Hospital, 13th March 1981

Folding the paper to put it back, a pencil scribbling on the back caught his eye.

Died: 10th August 1989.

The tenth of August.
The date Nell went missing.

Wednesday 21st August

Amelia

A melia thought of the atmosphere in the house as 'Eau de missing person,' cloying and oppressive, it was definitely an acquired taste in the perfume world. She needed to get out. The town of Stonebrook was only a couple of miles away. They could do with some groceries. They still needed to eat and drink (especially drink). Amelia had observed her own alcohol intake increase significantly but was enjoying the sensation of dislocation that accompanied the lunchtime glass of gin, as if the hand that poured it wasn't hers.

The days were passing in a blur. They were sleepwalkers, the three of them, blundering bleary-eyed through the hours that suddenly were so many in number. Police visits, questions, phone calls, reporters at the gates and that awful, unrelenting, gnawing sensation eating away at her the entire time. The weather hadn't broken, either. Inescapable heat. Oh, for this to be over – Nell missing, the heat, the whole bloody thing.

She definitely had to get away from Moordown. Was it egotistical that she had spent over an hour this morning considering what to wear? It had felt wrong, trying on outfits up in her room. What was she hoping to achieve? Bereft, sleep-deprived friend with the beginnings of a drinking problem was a challenging look to polish. But she was going to be photographed, that was for sure. There must be at least ten reporters at the gates. She could hear them calling out questions whenever the police officers came. They always got the same answer: 'No developments. We'll let you know if and when there are.' She needed to be ready.

Would the reporters even know who she was? How would she be referred to in the newspaper? Family friend? Fellow author? (Who was she kidding?) Amelia sat down on her bed with a thump, frown lines bunching on her forehead. Hadn't her mother taught her to never waste an opportunity? And this might just be that. What to wear then? She had forced herself back up and had decided, in the end, on a long, green dress, loose enough to be flattering but light enough to be cool. In emotional turmoil or not, she didn't want to appear in the national press with big, ugly sweat patches under her armpits.

She'd told Dalt and Huck late last night, when Dalt had returned from yet another day on the moor, that she was going into town and together they had made a list of things they urgently needed (how helpful she was being). When Huck had asked her for a very specific 'cave-aged' vintage cheese from the delicatessen at the top of the high street, 'but only if they've got the walnut and date crackers and the damson jam in stock too. Middle shelf to the left,' she'd been a little taken aback. Was he making a fool of her? It felt like it.

She was ready. She felt rather like she was taking her first steps out into a post-apocalyptic world. So much had changed since she had last 'popped to the shops.' Step-by-step, she told herself. First, start the car, get through the electric gates and past the reporters.

Start the car. Amelia nervously jangled the keys in her hand as she shut the front door behind her and stepped out into the glaring sunshine, relieved that she was wearing her Jackie O' sunglasses and her enormously wide-brimmed hat. Protection both from the sun and from the paparazzi. The car, a mud-brown, 1970's Ford Capri that used to belong to Dennis, Nell's father, was parked haphazardly at the edge of the drive, its bonnet partially concealed in a rose bush. Amelia had been in the passenger seat when Nell had parked it there, if you could call it parking, after their one trip into town together. Unable to open the passenger door due to the vehicle's proximity to the shrubbery, Amelia had had to exit the vehicle by clambering across the driver's seat. Nell had let out a loud peal of laughter watching Amelia grapple with the gearstick and swing her legs across the seat, her skirt riding up and her limbs tangled as if she were playing a children's party game.

The memory floored her.

When she made Nell smile, Amelia felt triumphant.

But when she made Nell laugh, Amelia felt complete.

Amelia wasn't laughing now. She turned the key in the ignition and set about reversing from the undergrowth, fairly certain that the *Vintage Car Owner's Manual* would not advocate parking your esteemed, collectable classic in a thorny hedge, and leaving it exposed to the elements for weeks.

But then to Nell it wasn't an esteemed classic, was it? It was just four wheels and an engine.

Amelia sighed. Some people had it all and didn't even realise.

Surprisingly, the car didn't seem all that worse for wear, considering its neglect. Amelia swung it round in a wide arc to face the gates. Courtesy of the enormous drive, she was still too far away to be newspaper fodder. She readjusted her hat and her sunglasses in the mirror, checked her make-up (a little shiny but not dripping off her face) and took a deep breath.

Putting her foot down on the accelerator, the car cruised forward. So far so good. The gates opened automatically ahead of her, and the gathered journalists sprang from their camping chairs, cameras lifted, microphones angled.

'Ms Early,' (they knew her name!) 'Ms Early, can you tell us more about the day Nell Davenport went missing?'

A rap on the car window, reporters standing so close she was scared of moving forward in case she ran them over. More raps. More questions.

'Ms Early, have there been any updates? What are the police doing to find her? What do you think has happened?'

As a child, Amelia had loved attention, fought to be in the spotlight. In her teens, she'd even contemplated an acting career. Now, it seemed that desire had laid dormant but not disappeared. As she slowly wound down the window, the vintage lever mechanism lending her the melodrama she craved, and took stock of her audience, a shiver of excitement ran through her.

'I'm afraid...' she paused, purposefully, enjoying the moment and her hold over the throng, without letting her façade slip. 'I'm afraid there's no news.' Her voice trembled but she wasn't acting now. 'I have no idea what's happened to Nell. None of us do.'

Her hands were shaking on the wheel, sweat beginning to dampen the armpits of her dress, after all. She would have been a bloody awful actress, unable to conceal her real emotions.

'What are the police doing to find her? Have they got any leads?'

'I'm sorry. I wish I had more to tell you. Now if you'll excuse me...' The words came out in a babble. Amelia wound the window back up, the handle jerking and resisting each rotation, making the glass judder its way back into position. Not so Jackie O' now, Amelia considered.

Thankfully, the old car pulled away without stuttering and stalling (one of its bad habits, she'd learnt the day she'd gone out in it with Nell) leaving the reporters unsatisfied in its wake.

The route into town was straightforward enough, which was lucky, as Amelia was feeling very strange indeed, her hands still shaking, and her thoughts muddled. It must be adrenaline, she thought, opening the window a little and taking deep breaths in an attempt to calm herself down. The wild expanse of moor visible from every angle did nothing to relax her; formidable granite tors, treacherous rushing rivers, sinister ancient woodland. Amelia was glad when finally the car left the moor behind and passed through farmland – vast, stunning yellow rape fields. But it wasn't long before they too added to her sense of unease, the height and mass of the flowers only leading her to think of their capability to confuse and conceal, giving them a portentous quality she sincerely hoped they didn't deserve. Aware that she was now sweating profusely, Amelia wafted her dress loose from under her armpits where it had stuck. As the road twisted and turned, snaking its way down from the moor, the harshness of the landscape hit home. Did Nell enjoy the isolation? Amelia had never asked her, hadn't even considered the question pertinent before to be honest. It's what you want in a writer's retreat, isolation, after all.

She was relieved when houses began to pepper the road, and the town of Stonebrook spread out in the dip of the valley below her. Following signs for the town centre, Amelia parked the car at the bottom of the main street.

She was barely out of the vehicle when she noticed two women staring in her direction, both in their late thirties, wearing running shoes, but with not a hair out of place. Too perfect to have actually done any exercise, she caught herself thinking, before mentally chastising herself for the judgement. Maybe they knew Nell? As she considered approaching them, the women turned and jogged away.

Runners after all.

Milk, alcohol, bread and cheese, painkillers: Amelia ran through the shopping list as she walked up the street.

Was she imagining it, or did conversations stop as she passed? And what on earth was happening with this weather? The day continued to get hotter, the sweat patches on her dress were no longer a distasteful possibility but an awful reality. She'd never had an issue like this before; huge, dark wet circles spreading like gunshot wounds from each armpit. This was mortifying. Keeping her arms close to her body, she walked faster, mentally reordering the priority of items on the list, striking off nail varnish remover and cotton buds. What had she been thinking – so frivolous? And she could order it all online anyway. Anything would be preferable to this heat and this feeling of…. She paused to catch her breath and consider it for a moment. What was it? Anxiety? Worry? Fear? Being watched?

When she later picked apart the events of the next few minutes, Amelia found herself questioning her mental state. It was bloody hot, she didn't feel well, her nerves were shot, and the cumulative effect of many sleepless nights must have been getting to her. The old lady couldn't really have reached out and grabbed Amelia's arm, making her shriek in surprise and shock. She must have misheard the old woman as she leaned in close to Amelia's ear and whispered thickly into her hair:

'She thought she was better than us, in that big house looking down on us all, writing about us all.'

Although she was certain that she didn't imagine the sour smell, lingering in the hot air or the white imprints left on her wrist. The old lady, layered in scarves despite the weather, hobbled past her down the street.

'Excuse me. What did you just say?' Amelia called to the hunched, retreating form.

'What's that luvvy?' Like an owl, the old woman turned her head without moving her body. A startling degree of rotation for any human being, let alone a person of that age. 'I said, I thought the weather was supposed to be getting cooler, Luvvy. That's all.'

Forget the shopping. Forget all of it. They would survive without it. Amelia's heart hammered in her chest and her breathing grew rapid, her respiratory system out of control. She found herself gulping in vast quantities of air as her lungs screamed that they were drowning on dry land. Get back to the car. Get back to the car.

Somehow she made it, a mixture of running and stumbling back down the hill, avoiding the looks of concern from the people she passed. Upon locating the key in her handbag and jerkily, clumsily turning it in the car door, the terror began to subside. But it wasn't until she was safely inside and had popped down the lock on the driver's door that relief washed over her and her breathing began to return to normal. What the hell had just happened? Was that a panic attack? Whatever it was, she was in no hurry to see if it happened again. Breathe, she told herself. Calm. Down. It's okay. She wished she had a brown paper bag. That's what people always used in situations like this. The thought appealed; a dark, cool place to stick her head inside sounded pretty perfect right now.

It was then that she noticed a small blue piece of paper tucked beneath the right-hand windscreen wiper. Too small to be the usual adverts for car washing services or touring circuses. Intrigued, despite the recent drama, Amelia slowly wound down the window and reached under the windscreen wiper to grab it.

Hi,
I wonder if you could call me. I wanted to talk to you about Nell Davenport.
Annie Barnes

Annie Barnes had printed a telephone number below her name. The note was brief, and to the point, Amelia supposed, but surely if this Annie Barnes knew anything about anything, then she would have already told it to the police.

Leaving the note strewn next to her bag on the passenger seat, Amelia started the car and glanced in the mirror before pulling away. Her fringe clung limply to her forehead, the hair under her hat, hot and damp. Under the sunglasses her eyes were puffy and bloodshot. Sighing, Amelia began the drive back to Moordown. A long, winding residential street, sleepy in the hot sunshine, led her out of town. Children's voices carried through her open car window; sounds of splashing and laughter came from paddling pools in backyards, and she began to feel normal again. She followed the road up onto the moor, leaving the houses behind, crossing the cattle grid that marked the start of open moorland and rough grazing. Her eyes itched, whether from the plant pollen or the lack of sleep, she wasn't sure. She checked her mirrors like a good girl – no one around (she was in the middle of nowhere after all; what was she expecting?). Keeping her right hand on the steering wheel and her eye on the road, she reached into her handbag and pulled out the small bottle of vodka she'd taken to keeping with her. Thank heavens she hadn't run out. Her hand shook as she unscrewed the lid and let it fall into the footwell. She took a greedy swig. It tasted so good, like lemonade on a hot day as a child. Another swig. The constricted feeling in her chest was loosening at last, her shoulders dropped an inch.

A small pony, with coarse, wild hair, meandered out into the road, the epitome of the day itself, slow, sleepy and lacking any direction. Amelia brought the vehicle to a standstill on a grassy verge to admire it. It was a beautiful beast, with wide-set eyes beneath a floppy auburn fringe. It looked a bit like Nell. Nell the horse, Amelia thought, and giggled.

Dear Lord, was she drunk already after only a couple of sips? She glanced at the bottle on the passenger seat. Alright, maybe more like a quarter of a bottle than a couple of sips, but who could blame her. It was such a hot day, she was dehydrated, and she'd had that horrible encounter with the old lady. Not her fault at all.

Amelia's phone vibrated within her handbag and it took a moment or two for her to identify then locate the source of the noise. She held the phone up to her face, squinting at the dark screen, cupping the device in her hands to prevent the glare of the sun hitting it. A text from her sister, asking if she was okay and if there was any news.

Phone in hand, Amelia's eyes lit upon the piece of paper that woman, Annie Barnes, had left on her car windscreen. Annie Barnes: the name wasn't the slightest bit familiar. In all the time that she'd been staying with Nell, she hadn't heard her mention the names of any friends of hers in Stonebrook. Maybe Annie was Huck's teacher, or Nell's Doctor, or the dentist, or, the pharmacist (pharmacists know everyone and everything), Amelia thought. Or maybe Annie worked with Nell at the paper. Or, the thought came quickly, slithering into her mind, maybe Annie wasn't a friend at all.

Only one way to find out.

Emboldened by the vodka, which she had tucked carefully away into her bag, having retrieved the lid from the depths of the footwell, she dialled the number. It took two attempts; her fingers were clumsy. Before she'd had a chance to prepare what she was going to say, the ringing tone sounded in her ear.

'Hello?' A questioning voice, caller unknown.

'Hi. My name's Amelia Early. I think you might have left your number on my car...Nell Davenport's car... in town today.'

Amelia could hear footsteps, muffled noises, then a door closing.

'Hi, yes, I did. I hope you don't mind. My name's Annie. Annie Barnes. I just wanted to talk to you, about Nell. I haven't spoken to the police, because I don't think it's my place, but I wanted to tell someone, in case it means anything.' Annie was talking in barely more than a whisper and straining to hear her was making Amelia feel queasy.

Amelia tugged gently on the zipper of her handbag whilst she tried to gauge the age of the woman on the end of the line. Mid-thirties maybe? It was hard to tell. She'd never been good at guessing a person's age from their appearance, let alone from just their voice.

'It's just that...' Amelia heard a deep intake of breath. 'It's just that, I had my concerns. About Nell Davenport and her husband. I cleaned for them, you see. I came twice a week. Some people think that's a lot, but Nell, well, she wasn't exactly house-proud if you know what I mean. She probably had more important things on her mind. The place could get in a bit of a state. Mr Dalton and I agreed twice a week would work well, to try and keep on top of things.'

Amelia stopped fiddling, straining to catch every word that Annie was saying.

'Anyway, what I wanted to tell you – it's a bit personal. That's why I didn't go to the police, because it could be something or it could be nothing, and I didn't want to get Mr Dalton into any trouble. I always thought he was a good man. But the thing is, the last few times I went over, they were arguing. Properly arguing. They'd given me the code to the gates so maybe I took them by surprise, but I could hear them before I'd even got out my car in the driveway. They'd stop as soon as I'd ring the doorbell, and that'd be the end of it. But the thing was, it wasn't just arguing as such. It sounded more like Mr Dalton was angry at Mrs Davenport for something. He was the one letting rip at her. I could hear her saying sorry over and over. I can't imagine what she might have done. I'd always thought he was a good man, but you just never know, do you?'

A long pause followed. Too long, Amelia realised. Her turn. She should have said something. The vodka had slowed down her reactions.

'When did you last go there? To clean? I've been there for over six weeks now and I've never seen you.' Amelia knew she sounded accusatory but buoyed by the vodka, didn't care. She didn't know this woman, didn't owe her anything.

A pause followed by a sigh.

'They don't need me over the summer. Mr Dalton, Edward, said that seeing as it was the school holidays, their son, Huck, would be around a bit more and he'd be able to take on the chores for a bit. He thought it would be good for him. I never got a chance to speak to Nell about it. He said they'd want me back after the summer though, when Huck went back to school.'

'I see.' Amelia could see the sense in that. Huck had been helping out around the place. Well, as helpful as teenagers tend to be.

'Anyway,' Annie had the tone of someone who'd reported a car crash and was about to continue their journey. 'I just wanted you to know that. Do what you think you need to with the information. I'll come and talk to the police if you want me to, whatever you think.'

'Thanks. Thanks, Annie, I appreciate you getting in touch,' Amelia said, forcing herself to find the right words. 'I'll try to get to the bottom of it and see if I can find out what they were arguing about. Just in case it has anything to do with Nell's disappearance.'

'Just don't say it was me, if you can help it.' Annie clearly wanted her job back in September, and Amelia didn't blame her. They might need her back sooner; the place was a tip.

'I won't. Don't worry. And thanks again.'

Amelia hung up. The pony had gone. Her head felt strange, foggy and slow. She needed to get back and lie down.

It was mid-afternoon when she pulled into Moordown, praying that the reporters couldn't smell the booze on her breath as she wound down the window to enter the code for the gates. Once safely inside, she went straight to her room, shut the door, collapsed on the bed and fell into a restless sleep, her dreams full of ginger haired ponies galloping through never-ending fields of maize, whilst an old lady who looked like an owl hooted from the branches of a tree.

Saturday 24th August

The Butterfly and the Moth

From: Nell Davenport
To: Frank Hannock
Subject: The Butterfly and the Moth

A small, blue butterfly was resting on a garden wall, soaking up the sun's rays, when it spied a leaf, high up in a tree, covered in delicious, sugary, sticky honeydew.

'What a feast,' thought Butterfly, fluttering her beautiful blue wings, to reach the tasty treat.

At the same moment, a large, brown moth, its wings faded and ravaged with age, lit upon the same leaf.

'Go away, Moth,' Butterfly said. 'I got here first. This honeydew is mine. It is daytime. You feed at night. Go away and hide in the dark and shady wood. You don't belong here.'

Moth looked at the beautiful, blue butterfly and felt ashamed. She opened her dull, brown wings, and flew away into the gloom of the wood.

Later that day, gathered on the long, spiked trusses of the purple buddleia bush, Butterfly told the other butterflies about Moth. The more her butterfly friends laughed, the more she embellished her story.

'How absurd!' laughed Butterfly. 'That Moth thought she was welcome in our garden, when she is so different to us. Moth is dull when we are beautiful. Moth gathers food at night whilst we gather food in the day. Moth rests with her wings open, whilst we rest with ours closed. Moth is not like us. Moth is a strange creature. We must not trust her.'

'Moth is a strange creature. We must not trust her.' The flutter agreed.

The next day, Butterfly was exploring the woodland when she spotted some more delicious honeydew, high, high up in the branches of a willow tree. Excited, she flew higher and higher towards her prize. Poor Butterfly, she hadn't spotted the bird camouflaged in the branches. But it had seen her. It swooped, its sharp beak trying to catch her, to rip and to shred her. The attack was over in a second. By some miracle, Butterfly evaded death, but not the damage wrought by the hunter's beak.

Butterfly struggled home to her buddleia bush where the other butterflies looked at her in horror.

'Your wings are torn, and your colour is gone. You are not like us. You look like Moth. Go away from here. You do not belong in our garden.'

Broken, Butterfly spread her colourless wings and flew into the anonymity of the shady, dark woods, where Moth happened to be feeding.

'Why are you not resting?' Butterfly asked, despite her shame. 'It is daytime. Moths rest in the day and come out at night.'

'But I am not a moth,' replied Moth. 'Why can't you see? I am a butterfly as you are a butterfly. We are both a type of butterfly. I may not look like you; I may not act like you, but we are not all that dissimilar, you and me. You are afraid of me, and so you tease me, you banish me. But now, perhaps, you understand me.'

We only see what we want to see.

Frank

'N ell, Nell, Nell,' Frank Hannock muttered under his breath, the blue light of his computer screen illuminating his face. The rest of the office was blanketed in darkness, as you'd expect for 2:17 a.m. on a Saturday.

He re-read the last line of the email.

We only see what we want to see.

'Nell, Nell, Nell,' he said again. Habit, more than anything, stemming from way back when she'd hand over a story, and refuse to sit whilst he read it, instead pacing his office, noting every smile, eyebrow raise and chuckle that escaped his control. Every bloody time he read her work as a critic, not as a friend. It's how he'd come as far as he had in the industry. And every bloody time he was awed by her talent.

'Well, well, well. What have we here, my dear?' he asked the screen, reading the email again before pressing reply.

Nell? Where are you? What's all this about?
You know the police are searching for you? You need to get in touch.
Dalt's a mess.

(He deleted the last sentence. Emotional not practical. Unhelpful).

Frank

Nell would have known, all too well, that Frank would be editing
the newspaper right now, as he did every Friday night, which would
bleed into Saturday morning without Frank noticing, whilst the
residents of Stonebrook slept. And here he was, as always, making last minute changes, correcting errors and proofreading before
the paper went to print. Here he was, when 'ping', the email alert
sounded, and her name flashed across the screen.

Thirty-five years as a reporter and in that time, more missing
people than he cared to recall. Missing people cases were always
troublesome. He'd seen his share of them over the years. Some mis-
pers, as they were called in the business, turned out to be abductions
– custody battles that had reached breaking point, forced marriages,
or worse, victims of serious crime. Then there were the accidents,
the misper found injured or worse, dead. Then there were those who
chose to disappear.

Heart-breaking, he'd always thought, never to know what had
become of a loved one. Were they dead or alive? Were they eating an
apple in a town far away, or were they floating face down in a canal?
The not-knowing has to be the worst.

It turned out it was. The not-knowing was destroying him.

There was no Mrs Hannock. Frank had dedicated the first half
of his adult life to war reporting and the second half to the *Stonebrook Gazette*. Mrs Hannock just hadn't appeared, and frankly, war
reporting had taken its toll on him. Post-traumatic-stress-disorder, a
doctor had later diagnosed (too much later to be of any help). He'd
got over the worst of it by then, the worst that came in the form of
panic attacks in the middle of the night and cold sweats in the queue

at the newsagents. He'd gotten over the worst of it thanks to Nell and Dalt. They'd fixed him up better than any drug ever could have.

Nell, Nell, Nell.

'We should run a piece on the famous author that lives on the edge of town,' one of the Bright Young Things had suggested years ago, at the brainstorming breakfast meetings they used to hold every Monday morning. 'Nell Davenport. She's just released a new book, part of her Daniel Hargreaves detective series. She's doing the PR rounds for it. We should try and get an interview.'

Famous author on the edge of town? It was the first Frank had heard of it.

'Good idea,' he'd said. 'I'll get on it, see if I can arrange a meeting.'

Nell Davenport had been hard to get hold of, impossible in fact. On numerous occasions her phone line rang out until his hand grew tired of holding the receiver, and he never received a reply to any of the emails he sent to an address he had found for her online.

Meanwhile, in the office her mystery deepened. Highly educated journalists could be found gathered around the water-cooler, discussing the myth that was Nell Davenport in the same way that the local kids gossiped about the neighbourhood's haunted house at Halloween (although in this case it seemed they were one and the same, Nell Davenport's reputation spanning generations).

'I've heard she's a total bitch, looking down from that house like Lady Muck. People in town don't like her.'

'She put that house on the market when her father died, then snatched it up herself when there was a whiff of interest in it, that's what I heard.'

Reporters could be damn harsh.

See for yourself, had always been Frank's motto. Don't take anyone else's word for it. Form your own opinions. He needed to run a staff training day on this apparently.

Hard to see for yourself though, when you're not given a chance.

'She's always out running. She's got a tiny baby, but she still goes out for hours each morning.' (How did they know these things? He supposed it was a reporter's job to get the inside information, but still, it was a little creepy).

And so it was that Frank began to run.

The road out of town up to Moordown was unforgiving, steep and exposed. Luckily for Frank, there were also trails out of town that headed up to the moors taking more meandering loops, avoiding the worst of the climbs and offering shade and scenery with them.

He'd go out early, before work, walking mostly at first, then running a little, building up his speed and stamina. At first, he felt ridiculous, an imposter in lurid green running shorts, a man who had never owned sportswear suddenly fixated on shoe tread and foot strike. The miles between his house and Moordown took months to conquer. But the act of running, rather than finding the author herself, became Frank's focus, the movement of his limbs melting away the memories that haunted him. Running therapy, he started to call it.

He almost forgot that he was looking for her when he found her. Or rather she found him. He'd bent to tie his shoelace, little realising that the long grasses of the moor had camouflaged him. Lace tied, he'd stood up at the exact moment that Nell Davenport happened to run past.

When Nell retells the story, which she does from time to time, she doesn't mention how loud she screamed that day. Or how loud he screamed too for that matter. Instead, she teasingly calls him, 'My Little Green Man,' an ode to his top-to-toe camouflage-green running attire, and jokes about how long he must have been hiding in the grass, waiting for someone to run past.

That day, when they had both got over the initial shock, they had run together. Frank had been surprised to find that conversation came easily. Another reason to never believe what you hear. Nell Davenport was intelligent, funny and charming – the perfect running companion. Rumour would have had it that she was rude, bordering on offensive, anti-social, but he had long known what he thought of rumour.

The meeting that day and the subsequent run that followed turned into another, and another and another. Nell was a creature of habit, running at the same time each morning. She wasn't hard to find, in fact, Frank didn't have to even look. Nell took to waiting each day by a marker stone not far from where they had first met. If he timed it right, they would run a few miles together, before she headed homeward and he back towards town. With their common bond of a love of words, Nell Davenport and Frank quickly become firm friends. In time, Nell introduced him to Dalt and to Huck. Frank, in turn, introduced Nell to the paper. Before long, Nell was writing a weekly common for the *Stonebrook Gazette*. Frank could hardly believe this best-selling author would deign to grace the local rag with her work.

But that's friendship for you.

That was fifteen years ago, and Frank hadn't made many other friends in that time. Neither had Nell.

Her disappearance had shaken his world.

'Nell, Nell, Nell.' Frank sighed to himself, scanning the email again. 'What's going on?'

Dalt

The noise penetrated the depths of Dalt's heavy, dreamless sleep. Part of his brain was aware of the sound, incessant and unrelenting, and fought against his reluctant body, dredging him up through cloudy layers of silt to consciousness against his will. Damn noise and damn sleeping pills. His mind felt slow and encumbered, his thoughts a dense fog. Make it stop. Pulled nearly to the surface of consciousness, he realised at last that the source was the ringing of his phone. Blearily, his fingers groped for it, swiping air at first, then the hard surface of his bedside table before they connected with the cold, hard screen.

'Hello.' Dalt knew he sounded awful, hoarse and groggy. Funnily enough, just like a man woken from a drug induced sleep.

'Dalt, it's Frank. I'm sorry to disturb you, but there's something you should know. I've just received an email from Nell's email address.'

The words tumbled through the air into Dalt's head, where they whirled before arranging themselves into order: an email from Nell, sent just now – what the...?

He was suddenly awake, his heart pounding. 'Forward it to me, now. And come over.' Dalt reeled at his unlikely shift into Man-of-Action mode.

The bright screen of the laptop blitzed away any residual effects of the sleeping pill. His fingers working on autopilot, Dalt had Frank's email open within a minute and read within one more.

Twenty minutes later, Dalt pressed the release switch for the electric gates, at the same time noticing the silent, shadowy forms of the reporters' vans, stationed on the road outside. Frank's black hybrid pulled soundlessly into the drive. Dalt gestured for Frank to stop short of the house itself. For the first time in weeks, Dalt noticed a chill in the air.

In one fluid motion, Frank undid his seatbelt, opened the door and stepped lightly out of the vehicle, his feet crunching softly on the gravel as he drew Dalt into a short, bolstering embrace. Wiry yet powerful, Frank did not fit the stereotype of a newspaper editor. He was more likely to be found at a vegan restaurant than a fast food stand, drinking kelp shakes instead of takeaway coffees, but he had the energy of a man fuelled by caffeine none-the-less. Dalt had known Frank for fifteen years and considered him the closest thing to a friend in Stonebrook that he had.

Frank was also good in an emergency, a skill he had honed during his years as a war reporter, and his calm presence stilled Dalt, who, minutes before, had been frenziedly pacing the driveway, tense, agitated and loaded with questions. Dalt knew better than to ask what Frank was doing, checking his email in the early hours of a Saturday morning. Friday nights to Frank were like Christmas Eve to Santa, hallowed vigils, honed to perfection, of reading, correcting, organising and ultimately, sanctioning the weekly publication of the *Stonebrook Gazette* in order for it to be printed and on the shelves by Sunday morning as coffee pots were warming.

No time to go inside, better to speak out here, far enough away from the gates that the reporters wouldn't hear.

'Is it Nell's writing? You know her style better than anyone, Frank. Do you think she wrote that?'

Frank looked deep into Dalt's eyes before replying, as if in doing so he might find the answer.

'I'm sorry, Dalt, I just don't know. It's not her usual style – not her style at all. It's just so random, so obscure – cryptic even. But it is from her email account.' Frank looked confused.

'Have you replied to it?' Dalt asked.

'First thing I did.' Frank wasn't a journo for nothing.

'If it wasn't sent by Nell then who else could have sent it? Does anyone else at the office know Nell's password? Could her email account have been hacked?' As Dalt posed the questions, he realised that he didn't know what the ideal answers would be. A niggle of a thought was forcing its way into his mind. Nell – safe, alive, typing and emailing but choosing to be gone – was this possible? Was this better than the other possibilities? What even were the other possibilities?

'Nell used her own laptop for work. As far as I know, she never logged into any of the office computers; she rarely came to the office anymore. As you know, she'd taken to writing at home and emailing her pieces to me on a Friday. I suppose it's possible that someone at work knew her password, or hacked her account, but who would do that, or why?'

'Anyone, anywhere, could have hacked her account if they knew how. Maybe it's some sick person's idea of a joke.' Maybe, maybe, maybe – Dalt's head was buzzing with maybes. It was taking all his mental strength and focus to swat the ideas away, before they settled like flies.

It had been two weeks since Nell had disappeared. The police focus so far seemed to have been concentrated entirely on the moor.

The environment, as he knew from fourteen days of his own relentless searching, was unforgiving: steep cliffs, rocky tors and vast expanses of water. A news reporter on television the previous evening had described the landscape as, *'awe-inspiring but formidable.' 'The precarious ridgeways,'* he had said, *'and the exposed moor, with its potentially lethal mine-shafts, combined with the extraordinary, unprecedented temperatures we have been experiencing over the last few weeks, make the search for missing woman, Nell Davenport, most difficult and challenging and the chances of a positive outcome....'* Dalt had muted the television before he could hear the rest of the sentence and felt a sudden rush of contempt towards this man, cosseted away in an air-conditioned studio, knowing nothing of the true meaning of *'difficult and challenging.'* Dalt had watched with blurry eyes as images of helicopters and teams of police officers with search and rescue dogs flashed across the screen, freezing at last on the photo of Nell on that bloody rowing boat, a phone number flashing below the picture. *Call if you have any information.*

But the crazy thing was that nobody knew anything. Rather, everyone knew nothing, the police least of all. There were no leads, no sightings, no suspects. And yet, Dalt suspected, they were all suspects. Such a cliché, but Nell seemed to have disappeared off the face of the earth. Gone without a trace. Whilst an accident was the preoccupying line of enquiry, abduction, or something as of yet unspoken but more sinister was undeniably lurking in the shadows.

But Dalt knew something. Something he wasn't sharing: he knew that Nell had disappeared on the anniversary of Toby's death.

He'd intended to call the police straight away with news of his discovery. Instead, he'd sat in the drawing room, staring at the photo on the wall. Nell and Toby. What would the police think?

He knew what they'd think. They'd think she'd had a reason to disappear. They might even think she meant to harm herself. They'd divert the search to look at the areas where a suicidal person might go. They could even scale down the search altogether.

He didn't believe it. Nell wouldn't have harmed herself. He couldn't let this happen.

So, he'd kept quiet.

He realised Frank was staring at him.

'Sorry, my mind's all over the place,' Dalt said, grateful for shadows that hid the red flush he knew was spreading across his cheeks.

Frank nodded sympathetically.

'What does it mean, though?' Frank had produced a paper copy of the email and offered it to Dalt. Dalt moved closer and they each took a corner to examine it. The porch light provided just enough light to read by, Dalt's large frame throwing a dark shadow across the printed words.

When Dalt first read the story on his laptop, his instinct had been to feedback to Nell, as he always did when he read a piece of her work. Nell hated surprises and perhaps she assumed Dalt did too, or maybe she just wanted to save Dalt the time and effort of going out for a paper each Sunday morning. Either way, when it came to Nell's weekly column, Nell would email him a copy of her feature like clockwork on a Friday evening. He would read it slowly and carefully, savouring it, noticing the twists and turns in the plot, the well-chosen vocabulary, the skill and ease with which she wrote. He noticed lately too, the way that reading what she had written made him ache inside, evoking a feeling comparable to loss, the same feeling he got looking through old photos, a yearning for what had gone before.

'You're missing an apostrophe, second line,' he'd shout.

'Idiot,' would be the reply.

But this story was just plain odd. Nell wrote about people, not animals. She wrote complex thrillers for adults, not fables for children. He tugged his corner of the printout to see it more clearly.

Frank, absorbed in rereading, held the opposite corner tight and the paper tore a little under the strain.

'Butterflies and moths? I can't make any sense of it. What's it supposed to mean?' Dalt couldn't contain the anger in his voice, the feeling of frustration, like someone was teasing him but he wasn't in on the joke. 'Is it based on people we know? People Nell knew? Is Nell Moth?' Wow, that was a sentence Dalt never thought he'd say. The total absurdity of the situation almost made him want to laugh.

Dalt caught the measure of concern in Frank's glance.

Frank was a facts man, to the point. If Dalt expected them to hypothesise and procrastinate together he was barking up the wrong tree.

'I can't make any sense of it either. We need to show it to the police. They might be able to pinpoint the location of the sender using the IP address. At any rate, the police need to know about it.' Frank, true to form, was practical and blunt.

They'd talked for a few minutes longer. Frank would phone the police station and forward the email. As the lights of Frank's car disappeared down the drive, Dalt looked up at the house and let in the thought that up until now he'd refused to acknowledge. They all knew her password – he, Huck and Amelia – all three of them knew it. The damn thing was taped to the wall behind Nell's desk. In fact, Nell was probably the only one of them who could never remember it. Stupid, to keep it on display, but typical Nell.

The email could have been sent by any one of them.

Huck

'How are you doing?' Dalt had asked Huck this morning.

'How are you doing?' An innocuous question when asked once, even twice maybe, but not when asked by every person he encountered, their faces different but their tone and expression the same mixture of pity and sympathy with a dash of, 'thank god it's not happening to me,' thrown in for good measure. 'How are you doing?' from his dad, Amelia, police officers, support workers, bloody everyone who turned up at the gates, and that was bloody everyone. If living with Mudder had verged on hermetic, living without her was proving to be one long open-house social. And how did they expect him to be doing, anyway? Angry, exhausted, illogical, emotional, anxious – had he mentioned angry? He was all of the above and more. His mother had disappeared. How the hell did they think he was doing?

'Frank received this in the early hours of this morning,' Dalt said, ignoring Huck's sullen look and silence, thrusting a sheet of paper into Huck's hand.

Huck could feel Dalt's eyes on him, as he lifted the document and read.

'What the hell is this? Where...' Huck, absorbed in the story, didn't finish his sentence.

'It was sent from Mudder's email address.'

'I don't get it,' Huck said, straightening up, passing it back. 'Do you think it's from Mudder? What do you think it means?'

'I don't know, I really don't. And Frank has no idea either. It's from her email account, but we don't know if she wrote it. Or what it's about. Frank forwarded it to the police. Maybe they'll be able to tell us something more.'

And now it was 10 a.m. Officers Pearson and Henley were back. Back, and armed with a renewed vigour. He could almost smell the excitement dripping off them like sweat as they crowded around Dalt's laptop on the kitchen counter. Maybe it was sweat actually. The temperature in the room must have been close to twenty-five degrees already. He pitied the officers in their heavy uniforms. He felt uncomfortable just looking at them.

'We'll get the tech department on it. They're good with this kind of stuff. They'll use the IP address to try and locate where the email was sent from. It doesn't always work, but hopefully they'll get lucky. We also need to check all the electronic devices in the house – laptops, phones – anything you could send an email from.' (What was Officer Pearson implying? Was he hoping to find Mudder, typing away on her laptop, if they had another peek in the study?)

'Now, as to the content of the email...' Huck's vision was obscured by Amelia's face, which was inches away from the screen. 'Well, it's a bit cryptic isn't it? Any ideas what it's about?'

Blank looks. Confusion.

'It isn't Nell's style. Frank and I agree on it. It's too simple. Child-like. And confusing – the fable makes no sense,' Dalt said.

'Hmmmm,' Officer Pearson looked disappointed, as if he'd expected the whole mystery to be unravelled Scooby-Doo style in front of him. 'I'd like you all to think carefully. If Nell did write this, then we need to make sense of it. We need to know who the characters could be, if we related them to Nell's life.'

Officer Pearson looked at Officer Henley, as if to ask, 'Was that okay? Did I cover everything?' With a (patronising?) nod of her head, Officer Henley took over.

'Obviously, this email is opening up new avenues of investigation.' New avenues? Were they serious? An avenue, singular! So far this was all they had.

'Avenue A: this email could be from Nell. She could be safe and well and choosing to disappear.'

In his head, Huck imagined Avenue A: tree lined and regal, it led to an impressive fountain, beside which Mudder casually stood, wearing the smile she wore the time she'd fooled them all on April 1st, by telling them there was a leak in the bathroom. When Huck and Dalt went to see, armed with towels and a tool bag, there was indeed a large leek in the bathroom, only it was fresh and green with soil still on its roots.

'Leek. Leak! Don't you get it?' Mudder had exclaimed, not realising that Huck and Dalt's confusion wasn't caused by their grasp of the wordplay on the homophone but by the fact that she had played a joke at all. Avenue A dissolved before his eyes.

'Or – Avenue B: Nell has nothing to do with these emails – in which case, who does? It could either be someone who is involved with her disappearance, or somebody entirely unconnected, a fan, or just an IT geek with an agenda, sensing an opportunity.'

Officer Henley's voice had grown in volume and spirit, and as she ended her hypothesising, Huck had the urge to stand and applaud. 'Oh Captain, my Captain!'

But before any of them could comment, a muffled, crackling voice shattered their thoughts. Both Officers reached simultaneously for their radios, holding them close to their ears whilst making a hasty exit into the garden, before reappearing moments later.

'That was a call for all officers in the area to attend an incident immediately. Sorry – it's an emergency. We'll be in touch.'

Amelia rushed to the front door to see them out and Huck felt a flash of annoyance. Why did Amelia have to be so damn helpful? They didn't need her here. When was she going to realise that?

His father's sighs brought Huck's attention back to the fable.

'It's okay. We'll work it out,' he told his father. 'And they'll be back.'

Amelia

It had started with the email to Frank. A development, she'd thought – progress even. The only lead they'd got since Nell had disappeared. She could feel it, the atmosphere charged with a new energy. They had something to go on. It was almost exciting.

The police officers had thought so too. Frank had called them first thing. They'd wasted no time getting to Moordown. The reporters at the gate sensed a breakthrough. She'd heard their questions and sensed their anticipation.

There was no sitting today. They'd all gathered around Dalt's laptop that sat open on the kitchen table, Dalt pacing, questioning, Huck more animated than she'd seen him for weeks. The officers hadn't disappointed, had sprung up to catch the bone and were tearing off small fragments of meat.

There had been talk of IP addresses and tech departments. Talk of tracking, tracing, locating and identifying. A lot of it had gone straight over her head, but the general feeling was positive. At last, something could be done.

Then, they'd been interrupted. An urgent call on the police radio, the police car had sped away, as quickly as it had come, across the moor. Amelia turned quiet and pale, standing in the hallway in the officers' wake, her thoughts spilling like vomit onto the granite floor.

Maybe they've found a body.

Maybe they've found *her* body.

From the kitchen she could hear Dalt and Huck's voices.

'This is worse than not knowing anything.'

'Where have the police gone?'

'Did Nell even write that?'

Her head was beginning to throb. A tension headache for sure. Returning to the intense atmosphere in the kitchen wasn't going to help. Guiltily, Amelia slipped up the stairs to her room, where she lay down on her cool, soft bed and closed her eyes.

'Ommmmmm,' she began. Always so self-conscious at first. Would she ever get over this, the ego, the sense of self? Did monks look around the room and check each other out when they meditated? Did they eye up one another's robes or giggle at each other's vibrations? Of course they didn't. She needed to pull herself together. Grow up.

'Ommmmmm.'

Yet the sense of calm and peace that was supposed to suffuse her was proving evasive.

It was hardly surprising that she couldn't focus. She needed to cut herself some slack. The two police officers had just sped off across the moor to find god knows what... a body? It was going to take a lot more than a bit of humming to take her mind off that. Distraction, that's what Doctor Yung would recommend. Think about something else. The fable then: the quandary of *The Butterfly and the Moth*.

A fable: a simple story, replete with animal characters, with the ultimate purpose of teaching the reader a moral message or lesson. Amelia could reel off the definition as well as any dictionary because

Amelia had always loved fables. In primary school, she would sit transfixed in assemblies, oblivious to the cold, hard floor and her fidgeting classmates, soaking up the words of the fables which flowed like poetry from the mouth of her petite and wise headmistress. *The Hare and the Tortoise*, (slow and steady wins the race), *The Ant and the Grasshopper*, (there's a time for work and a time for play) and her favourite of all, *The Fox and the Crow*, (you shouldn't always trust those who flatter you, as they may not have honourable intentions). Oh, the sweet anticipation of what was coming, the glorious knowledge as she listened, that she knew the right thing to do, that she knew which animal was clever and which was the fool. Then, a pantomime urge to shout out a warning, 'Keep your beak shut, Crow, the Fox is trying to flatter you – to get your cheese.' With the trick successful, the prize lost and the inevitable suffering of the foolish creature, the fable's message became clear to all. Yes, Amelia loved fables; the way they made her feel so safe and so sure, how they gifted her with foresight and wisdom and certainty of the ways of the world.

Usually.

Amelia had read the fable over and over since Dalt had shown it to her that morning, and instead of feeling enlightened, she felt the exact opposite; ignorant, foolish and unsettled. There was only one thing that Amelia did feel certain about. The animals had to represent people, and the story had to be important; it had to be linked to Nell's disappearance.

Was Nell Moth? A butterfly too, but different from the others, misunderstood and shunned (by whom?).

From what Amelia had seen since her arrival, Nell wasn't exactly surrounded by company. Nell and Dalt had lived here for over sixteen years, and, apart from Frank, Nell had never mentioned any friends at all. Amelia had suggested drinks in town one evening, 'a chance for me to meet your friends.' Nell had been dismissive, although Amelia hadn't thought much of it at the time. The pubs were claustrophobic, Nell had said, packed with tourists this time of year. Much nicer to have drinks in the garden, no need to go anywhere.

It had made sense then, but it made a different kind of sense now.

Nell had always been a loner. They'd met in the second year of university, when most friendships had already been formed and bonds cemented through drunken nights out and hashed retellings the morning after. Amelia's own set of friends from the first year had found a house to rent for the second year with the catch of only having four bedrooms. There being five of them in total, and apparently, Amelia being the fifth, she'd found herself cast out to find her own place to live.

So had Nell, although Nell had no such backstory. It was just Nell.

They'd both responded to an advert in the paper. House share for students, close to campus. Four rooms available. They'd taken the same bus, ridden a seat apart, disembarked at the same stop and walked within metres of each other to the house. Amelia had sat behind Nell, curious about the girl totally immersed in her book and completely unaware of the carnage her backpack was causing, blocking the central aisle, the girl who was oblivious to the tuts and looks thrown at her by the other passengers. Later, Nell admitted she hadn't even noticed Amelia, who was pretty hard to miss by anyone else's standards, with her multi-coloured hair and her khaki army jacket covered in badges.

Two of the rooms in the house share had already been taken. The two that were left were cramped and dingy and on the ground floor, the lounge, it appeared, having been sliced in half and rather shoddily partitioned to create them both, and more importantly for the landlord, the extra income.

'I'll take it,' Nell had said of the worse of the two rooms, plonking her bag down. Matter settled. Job done. Amelia couldn't believe this girl. Hadn't she noticed the black mould spores creeping out from behind the hideous monstrosity of a wardrobe. Did she not see the sprawling, damp patch extending directly over their heads? Even the landlord had looked taken aback.

'I guess I'll take the other one then,' Amelia had said, as if she was under some sort of spell. There was no way she'd have considered the room were it not for the bewitching action of the strange creature who was going to be her housemate.

'I need a desk. Do you know if there are any second-hand furniture shops around here?' Nell had said to Amelia the moment the landlord left.

'There's one just around the corner.' Amelia had seen it from the bus. Eagle-eyes, her mum used to call her.

Sitting here now, at the kitchen table at Moordown, with Nell missing and the fable in front of her, Amelia wondered if she deserved the nickname of eagle-eyes after all?

They had become friends. Housing had brought them together and time had sealed the contract. They'd ended up living together for two years, until graduation, before real life had seen them scattered in different directions. Amelia had other friends, girls she knew from her course, the girls she'd known the year before. Nell didn't, but her coolness and the air of superiority she carried told Amelia all she needed to know. Nell had chosen her, when she hadn't chosen anyone else.

But Nell hadn't just chosen her. Nell had needed her. Amelia had quickly learnt that much as a chameleon changes its colour to blend into its environment, Nell's icy cool exterior, quick wit and sharp tongue were a well-crafted defence system to protect her from the world. And these defences could only take her so far. Like a tourist in a foreign land, Nell needed not only a friend, but a guide

– an interpreter. Someone to lead her through the practicalities of everyday life. Someone to make sure she remembered to eat, to sleep and to turn up for lectures. Someone to help her interact with the people around her, from her professors to her peers to the kid on the checkout in the supermarket, who, to Nell, all seemed to speak in foreign languages. Left to her own devices, Amelia wondered whether Nell would ever have left the house.

Gladly, Amelia took on that role, became that person. Being with Nell was like being the bodyguard of a major celebrity. Nell exuded writing talent like film stars flashed smiles on the red carpet but lacked the ability to deal single-handedly with the world around her. Amelia steered her, guided her, advised her, mothered her, and in turn felt warmed by her glow, certain that the creativity that poured out of Nell would flow in her own direction.

Nell had written the first Daniel Hargreaves novel in that cramped, mouldy bedroom, at a small and battered wooden desk they'd found together in the second-hand shop that first day they met. Amelia had helped her edit the book, had proofread it over and over and over until they were both happy it was perfect. She'd helped Nell draft a letter to literary agents and had loaned her an outfit to wear for her first face to face meeting when one actually replied. She'd stood outside the goddamn door whilst Nell signed her first publishing deal.

Nell had thanked her in her own way.

On the very last page of acknowledgements in that very first book.

To my tour guide A.E. Thank you. I owe you – whatever you need. N.D

She'd always thought that Nell didn't need anyone else. That she let in the ones she wanted and didn't think twice about the rest.

But having read the fable, maybe she was wrong.

Maybe Nell was Moth, misunderstood and mistreated. But then, who were Butterfly and her friends?

Amelia sighed and massaged the area between her eyes with her fingers. Nell's disappearance was taking a serious toll on her health. Throw in the heatwave, and no wonder she felt so rough. Two weeks, and they were still no closer to finding her. It seemed unbelievable really, that outside these walls life was just carrying on, when here in this house it had frozen. Waiting.

People have no idea of the effect a missing person has on those left behind. They were living in Limbo, and it was not a town you would ever visit if you had the choice. A transient settlement situated smack bang in-between Hope and Hopelessness, Limbo offered no certainty, only uncertainty, no closure or resolution, no answers, only questions. In Limbo, a disease called despair was spreading, and the people were suffering. They were tired and stressed and their health was deteriorating. The police in Limbo had done all they could, but their enquiries drew blanks and they found only dead ends. The people of Limbo waited, not knowing.

She'd worked on this passage for a while. A little more polish and it might be book-worthy.

Worthy of *The Book*.

Just a little idea she'd had. An idea that was changing. Evolving. An idea to write a book about living through the disappearance of a loved one (and a famous loved one at that!).

But just an idea. Nothing more.

Whatever you need.

Honestly though, the not-knowing was awful. Officer Henley had given Dalt a telephone number for a missing person counselling service. Dalt left it on the chest by the front door, where it remained. Amelia contemplated calling it, but the question of entitlement hung over her head like a dark rain cloud. Not a day passed since Nell had gone that Amelia hadn't questioned her right to be at

Moordown, her right to cry, to worry and to fear for Nell's safety when she had only recently re-entered her friend's life after so many years of absence. It was an unusual situation that was for sure. She'd googled, *friend gone missing should I still stay at her house*, but (unsurprisingly) the search results were unhelpful. Was today the day she should get back on that train and go and stay with her sister? Get out of their hair and leave them in peace (oh, the irony)?

And why was she hanging around? It was pretty clear from Huck's body language that she wasn't wanted. Had probably never been wanted. What was her worth now? She had tried to offer domestic help, make sure they had enough food and clean plates, but she wasn't being hugely successful. She'd made the aborted trip to town and scheduled a couple of on-line deliveries, but she was hardly proving indispensable. With no dependants of her own she wasn't cut out for the role of housekeeper. They'd probably cope just as well without her. She'd tried to offer emotional support where she could but wasn't exactly excelling in this area either, not being very stable herself, often prone to loud, hiccupping tears and depressing thoughts. When she tried to reach out to comfort him, Dalt seemed suspicious, and Huck downright avoided her. Yet something was keeping her here. She couldn't just walk out and leave them. They were in this together. We've started so we'll finish.

There was one thing she was going to do for them, though. Find out some answers.

Starting with unravelling this fable.

Lucy Loxton

I t had been one hell of a Saturday morning.

It started with a lie-in, the alarm going off at 6 a.m. One whole hour later than usual. Dan had already left for the lake. He was even crazier than she was. The fish start biting early in the heat apparently.

Without Dan there to criticise her for keeping her phone in the bedroom, Lucy couldn't resist checking her blog page, the most recent post a photo of Lucy taken and uploaded the day before. She was modelling a multi-functional, UV+, 95% recycled, light-weight, seamless, comfortable, quick-drying, patterned headband. Even Lucy had rolled her eyes inwardly at the spin on that. It may have been her job to promote the products, take them out for a jaunt in the real world, photograph them, rave about them, show off their credentials, but even to Lucy that product description sounded like a lot of nonsense. A lot of nonsense she was getting paid for. And Lucy had really earned her money with this one. It had taken a whole twenty minutes and two hundred selfies to take a photo that didn't make her look like the love child of Axl Rose and Rambo. Lucy cringed a little at her gushing hashtag *#summerdays #hikinginthe-*

heat #wearitlikeiownit – she wasn't even sure what she meant by the last bit – but this stuff sold, and the comments were rolling in.

She was about to log off when the feed suddenly jumped down the page and a photo appeared in its place. Two people, sitting at one of those little round tables in a cafe, heads bent in towards each other

#blessed.

'What?' Lucy mumbled to herself.

One of those heads was clearly hers. Had she uploaded this somehow? But it wasn't her photo. She was in it, she couldn't have taken it, wouldn't have wanted to. But only she had the permissions to upload to her blog. How the hell had this photo got here, and why?

Shit, shit, shit.

Get a room, lovebirds. Ps Has Dan dyed his hair? Love it!

Such faithful followers. Too faithful, commenting on a blog post seconds after it appeared, at 6.10 a.m. on a Saturday.

They were spot on though – his hair did look different. Probably because it wasn't Dan.

Lucy's fingers felt slow and clumsy as she selected the dropdown menu to 'delete photo' and clicked. Instant relief.

She was still staring at the screen in confusion, when her phone pinged, and the new email icon appeared.

From: Nell Davenport

Confused, Lucy clicked on it.

Lucy Loxton, you have been personally invited by Nell Davenport to visit her blog. Please click on the link below to access the site.

This morning was weird. First the photo and now this. Nell Davenport, blogging? Lucy didn't know she could even send emails let alone blog! She wasn't the most social media savvy woman alive. That is, if she even was alive. The woman had been missing for two weeks, the whole country knew about it, the whole town had been involved in searching the moors. But it turned out she had just nipped off to set up a blog. Ah, that explains it. Call the search off everyone! Panic over, Nell was just doing a spot of web design.

Actually, Lucy considered, she wouldn't put it past Nell Davenport to pull off a little stunt like that. The woman had no concept of how the world worked. She probably thought it was okay to disappear for a few weeks or a month to set up a web page – she probably had no idea that people were spending valuable time and money looking for her, that her family were worried sick. That was Nell Davenport. Superior to everyone else, able to make her own rules.

One click on the hyperlink, and Nell's homepage appeared in front of her. There was no way Nell could have done this herself. A bottle green background, a border of vintage roses, and all the usual headings: *Home*, *About Me*, *Books*, *Blog*, *Contact*. It looked so slick, so professional, so expensive.

Lucy clicked on '*Blog*'.

The fable of *The Moth and the Butterfly* appeared on the page.

Was this for real, Lucy wondered. Wasn't Nell supposed to be an incredible writer? This story could have been written by an eight-year-old. It was all so bloody obvious. Surely the detective novels she wrote had to be better than this, otherwise you'd be able to guess who did it by the end of the first paragraph.

It was clear immediately to Lucy that Nell Davenport was Moth.

And she, Lucy Loxton, was Butterfly.

And Nell was being a bitch again.

At least she knew who had posted that photo on her blog now. It all made sense. Nell was getting her own back.

Getting her own back for the fact that it was her own husband in the photo. It must be why Nell had gone missing. Anger perhaps, then revenge.

The fool. But then, Nell had never been good at reading situations.

It must be her lucky day. An attempt to break up her marriage and shame her online, followed by a thinly veiled character assassination, all before breakfast.

Sinking back into her pillows, finger automatically hitting the refresh button on her own blog every few seconds, (would Nell repost the photo?) Lucy considered the situation – changed her password just in case.

Nell Davenport. Lucy had known of Nell's house before she had known Nell. Moordown House, high on the moor, an impressive stone structure, old and imposing, with magnificent views of the valley below. She knew it because she wanted it. Dan had just gone freelance with his consultancy business. They were free to move out of the city at last, to start a family. All they needed was to find the right place to begin the next phase of their lives together.

The town was easy. It had to be Stonebrook. Picture perfect, it was where they came on days off, to walk on the moor, then stop for a drink at the Greedy Goat. They would browse through the property listings in the local paper together, sating a hunger for property porn as well as their thirst. That's when she saw it. Moordown House, for sale. They'd left their drinks on the table unfinished, taken a drive there and then, up onto the moor to see it. As Dan drove, Lucy had read the specifics: six bedrooms, two reception rooms, acres of land, outbuildings. It was only ten minutes away, but Lucy had filled those ten minutes with the dreams and plans of a lifetime whilst Dan sat, bemused, in the driver's seat beside her.

'Take a left,' Lucy had said excitedly. 'It's along here on the right I think.'

Dan drove slowly, carefully, down the single-track road.

'There's grass in the middle!' Lucy had exclaimed, delighted by the three-part design of the road: concrete, grass, concrete, so rural!

'Yep, there sure is,' Dan had confirmed, not matching his wife's enthusiasm and trying to avoid the larger stones and rocks that threatened to damage the car's chassis.

'There, turn right there!' She had seen the for-sale sign just before she saw the majestic iron gates. She saw the winding drive moments before she saw the house itself. She saw the house right before she fell in love.

And that's where the story ends.

The gates were locked with a rusty old padlock. Lucy had phoned the estate agent, right there and then, from the road outside, her dream house still locked in her line of sight.

'I'm enquiring about Moordown House,' she had begun.

'Off the market already. Sorry. Original owner deceased, property handed down to his daughter... she's not selling after all.' A flurry of information delivered at speed.

Lucy remembered how she had ended the call without speaking. Dan had looked confused. He had looked even more bewildered when tears began to roll down her cheeks.

Ridiculous, to get so invested in such a short space of time, to feel so emotional about a pile of bricks.

In the end they had bought a house on Arcadia Drive. They were happy there. Their children were born there, first Harry and then Jake.

Fast forward three years. Lucy was in the doctors' surgery. Harry had a high temperature. Lucy was worried. That's when they rushed in. The man came first, the child wailing and flailing in his arms, the woman followed behind at his heels. Lucy admitted it, she'd stared, openly horrified. The boy's hand was dangling down, bandaged roughly with his father's t-shirt (she knew for certain it was his as he was somewhat distractingly bare-chested). Quite a sight that was for sure. Blood had seeped through the thin white fabric of the impromptu dressing, turning it a bright red, and a trail of red breadcrumbs had dripped across the surgery floor. Terribly dramatic for Stonebrook Surgery on a Thursday afternoon.

'He's lost the top of his finger!' The man ignored the queue, ignored everything, and rushed the boy straight to the stricken faced receptionist. 'It happened in the garden when my wife was digging. His name is Huck Davenport-Dalton. Huckleberry Davenport-Dalton.'

'Assistance,' hollered the receptionist, whilst simultaneously pressing a button under the counter. Two doctors came running at once.

The boy was whisked into a consultation room.

The waiting room collectively exhaled.

That was the first time she'd seen them. Lucy Loxton sat in her plastic chair, Harry's temperature forgotten, ruminating on the name. Davenport. Davenport. The bloody house.

She didn't see them again though, until Harry's first day of school – strange, in a small town, two mothers, their sons the same age – they must have met? What about the drop-in clinics, held weekly in the community centre, where they weighed their babies and chatted with the health visitors, fretted and compared notes about feeding and sleeping and minutiae they'd previously never dreamt of with other sleep deprived, conversationally starved mothers? What about the seemingly never-ending trips to the park, come rain or shine, loitering for hours by the climbing frame and jerkily pushing the swing back and forth, the hypnotic motion making their eyes glaze? Didn't they meet there? Or when they were pounding the streets with the pushchair, covering mile after mile, wishing buggies came with an in-built step counter. They must have met then?

No, no and no they never did. Although Lucy did learn their names. She made it her business to. She already knew the boy's name, from that day at the surgery. Huckleberry, how pretentious, she'd thought. She'd heard the rest from Mrs Baker, her dear neighbour and local expert on Stonebrook's social history (read: enormous gossip). Dear Mrs Baker, living alone must be so terribly dull – she did love to talk – but then so did Lucy. They chatted over the fence whilst hanging out the washing, the conversation mutually beneficial, Mrs Baker getting the interaction she craved, Lucy getting the information she stored away like bullets.

Mrs Baker knew everyone and everything; it seemed she'd been around since the beginning of time.

Mr Davenport (Dennis, Nell's father) had been a school chum of hers, married an 'out-of-towner', (she'd told Lucy this before realising her mistake and the offence she may have caused). They'd had one daughter (Nell) who, as it turns out was a similar age to Mrs Baker's youngest daughter Mary. 'Went all the way through school together, they did, but they were never friends,' Mrs Baker had said. When Lucy asked her why not, she had frowned and chosen her words more carefully than usual.

'She wasn't like the other girls, Nell Davenport. She was always on the edge of things. A sweet little dot, I always thought, but I could see why the other children weren't sure about her. She didn't care to join in their games, and when she did, it always seemed to end badly. She preferred her own company, it seemed. Then there was the tragedy. Dear Toby, he must have only been seven or eight, drowned in the river just down from the house. Awful, it was. Heart-breaking. Can't have been easy for them, up there. Her mother died shortly after, and Nell went away to an all-girls school on the coast.'

According to Mrs Baker, Nell Davenport had left Stonebrook for good at the age of seventeen and headed straight for Cambridge

University where she had studied literature. She'd graduated three years later with a double-first.

'Dennis was so proud of her. I bumped into him in the butcher's one day and he told me how she was doing. She was going to stay on in Cambridge, he said. She'd met someone – a man. Well – that surprised me. Nell Davenport meeting a man! She'd never seemed interested in other people. And then came the books. Dennis was proud as punch when they went on display in the window of Stoge's bookshop in town. They did look good – nice, shiny covers – Nell's face on the flysheet. I even went in and bought one for myself.'

Lucy had long ago run out of washing to peg and listened transfixed whilst Mrs Baker talked.

'But then, Dennis died. He was a good age. Just passed in his sleep's what I heard. I went to the funeral. There was a good turn-out. He was well-liked was Dennis – a good man, like I said. The house was left to her – to Nell – but she didn't want it at first. She put it on the market. Changed her mind though, when she came down to clear it out. She couldn't part with it, and her husband fell in love with it too. And that's where we are now, my love,' she'd turned to Lucy, back in the present again. 'We're up to date.'

When Lucy saw Nell Davenport on Harry's first day of school it had taken her by surprise. Nell had waltzed right on past the rest of the mothers, reassuring their young and each other in alternating conversations. Nell and Huck positioned themselves near the classroom door, on their own. 'Snooty', was what her mother would have called them. Snooty and standoffish.

Lucy remembered turning to Elliot's mum, Annie, whom she knew vaguely from toddler groups and incidental meetings at the park. She remembered telling her about the scene she'd witnessed in the doctor's surgery over the summer. The other mums had leaned in to listen and before she knew it, they were a huddle of shocked faces and over the shoulder glances. Not that Nell Davenport had even noticed.

Harry's class was small: thirteen girls and only eight boys. When you're going to be together for seven years of primary school, it's best to get on with everyone, Lucy thought, so she diligently invited the other boys and a few of the girls over to her house after school from time to time – 'playdates,' she called them. Most of the parents jumped at the chance: an opportunity to trash someone else's house for a change, with the kids' supper thrown in too – who wouldn't be up for a playdate? Nell Davenport – that's who.

Not quite true. She came along once, the second week of term, the first playdate Lucy threw. But even the invitation had been oddly received. Lucy had greeted Nell at the school gates, as they were dropping off the boys.

'Good morning! What a beautiful day for September,' Lucy had said chirpily. She was very much a morning person.

'Is it? The milk had gone off and Huck wouldn't put his uniform on. He very nearly came to school naked,' Nell had replied straight-faced.

'Ooookay,' Lucy smiled and ploughed on. 'I'm having a bit of a get-together after school on Friday for some of the children in Harry's class. A sort of 'get-to-know each other', for the parents as much as for the kids. Would you and Huck like to come?'

'Where do you live?'

Seriously! Imagine having the audacity to ask which part of town someone lived in before agreeing to a visit. Lucy had wondered which parts of town Nell would deem unacceptable and which would lead to a nod of the head and acceptance of the invitation.

'Arcadia Drive. 26, Arcadia drive, the end furthest away from town.' Lucy relayed the information, and found herself holding her breath, acutely aware of a desire to 'pass the test', even if she wasn't sure that she wanted the prize at the end anymore, simultaneously wanting to retract the invitation and impress Nell Davenport.

'What time?'

'Urm, straight from school? We can all walk there together.'
Heavens, thought Lucy, this woman was rude.

'Fine,' Nell had said.

Fine! Fine? Lucy was fuming. Who did the woman think she was, talking to her like that? It was too late to uninvite her, but she'd know better than to ask her again.

Friday came, and with it the children, flooding out of school at the end of the day, all excited about 'going to Harry's house', and looking forward to 'playing with Harry's toys.'

All except one child.

Huckleberry walked quietly alongside his mother, whilst the rest of the children ran ahead.

'Don't you want to join them, Huckleberry?' Lucy had asked.

'No thank you, Mrs Loxton,' he'd said politely. Too polite, that boy, oddly so. Nell had said nothing.

Nell said nothing whilst the other parents introduced themselves and chatted. Nell said nothing when they were seated in the garden, exchanging information about PE days, and homework, and what they all thought of Mrs Jamison, the Reception teacher. As Lucy leant down to place Nell's coffee on the table in front of her, Nell flinched – she actually flinched.

Nell Davenport was something else, with her house on the hill, her successful writing career and her perfect life. She thought she was above them all. Lucy was glad when the playdate was over. Nell's relief was evident too, in the speed with which she scooped up her bag and her child and was out of the front door. Behaviour which, quite frankly, was the last straw. That was the last time Lucy was going to invite Nell Davenport over. A shame really, as despite a few quirks, her son Huck was a sweet boy, quiet and unassuming, old for his years.

Coincidentally, or fortunately perhaps, Harry and Huck never bonded either, so Lucy didn't ever have occasion to invite Huck over again. She was civil with Nell Davenport at the school gates, but she went no further than that. Lucy wished she could say Nell was civil in return, but her replies to Lucy's daily platitudes were often rude and unfriendly.

That was all a long time ago now though – the days of standing together at the school gates were long gone. Lucy rarely saw Nell these days, perhaps an occasional sighting in the library or at the bank, but so infrequently it was hardly worth mentioning. When Lucy read about Nell's disappearance in the *Stonebrook Gazette*, her first thoughts were of her husband and son, alone in that big empty house. Would they stay there, if she didn't return? Stay at Moordown, without her?

She shouldn't have wasted her concern, she thought, as she scanned the fable again. What kind of game was Nell playing? Wasn't it all a bit over the top, for Nell to stage her own disappearance just to exact revenge upon Lucy Loxton and the husband Nell believed was cheating on her. Well, Lucy would have the last laugh; Nell Davenport hadn't even got her facts right.

The end of the fable was a little unnerving though. Butterfly meets her comeuppance. Is that what this was – the photo and the blog post – a public shaming? Lucy's comeuppance?

This morning had been intense, and it was only 6.30 a.m.

She needed to clear her head.

That was the moment Lucy's phone beeped again.

Meet me on the moor? Guller's Leap 7.30 a.m.?

This might help clear things up a little.

On my way, she dashed off in reply. She dressed quickly, grabbing the sunglasses she'd promised to promote for the eyewear shop in town, slipped the lead on the dog, and headed out the door.

MOOR DEATH: LOCAL WOMAN FALLS FROM ICONIC BEAUTY SPOT, GULLER'S LEAP

A local woman has died after falling from the popular beauty spot, Guller's Leap. Officers were called to the scene yesterday at 10.15 a.m., where Stonebrook resident, Lucy Loxton, was confirmed dead on arrival. Moor Rescue Volunteer, Lindsay Bell, raised the alarm after she made the shocking discovery of the body whilst carrying out routine fencing checks. Officers and rangers are currently working together to investigate the incident, but it is believed at this time to be a tragic accident. The woman, who was out walking her dog, is thought to have crossed the safety barrier to take a photo, before falling 200 feet to her death.

It is not uncommon for accidents to occur on Stonebrook Moor. Last year, a visitor died while hiking in wet conditions along the treacherous ridge close to the top of Guller's Leap.

'*Unfortunately, there is a history of fatalities in the area,*' said Ranger Robin Widder. '*People need to take care when walking out here. There are precipitous drops and the safety barriers are in place for good reason.*'

Guller's Leap is a popular look out spot offering scenic views of the moors, and the town of Stonebrook below. Guller's Leap itself is rooted in misfortune, gaining its name from an incident that is believed to have occurred in the late nineteenth century, in which a local boy, Tom Guller, jumped to his death whilst being chased by two village boys.

In more recent years, the popular overlook has seen its continued share of misfortune, becoming an unfortunate beacon for suicides and accidental deaths.

In his book, Mysteries of the Moor, local author Peter Squirely describes Guller's Leap as 'a magnet for the world weary.'

More on page seven.

Annie Barnes

She knew something was wrong yesterday morning, when two police cars and an ambulance sped silently past her kitchen window as she stood at the sink, washing up the breakfast things. She scrubbed at a stain as she tracked the journey of the vehicles, high up onto the moor. There was a riding school nearby, and the occasional accident. Maybe a rider had been thrown. The moor was uneven and hazardous, the horses often unreliable and unpredictable. It wouldn't be the first time.

But it hadn't been horses. God, she felt sick to her stomach. What was she doing the moment it had happened – the moment her friend had died? Drinking coffee, listening to the radio? Died. Dead. How was it possible, that she'd carried on her day as usual when her best friend lay crumpled at the base of a cliff?

It had been another of those blue-sky mornings, sunshine glaring through the window. Everyone kept saying how lucky they all were to have this heatwave, but Annie wasn't sure how lucky she felt, unable to sleep because of the heat, sticky and uncomfortable only minutes after she'd showered and dressed.

Often, Annie would join Lucy for her daily hike (since when had it become hiking, not walking, and what was the difference anyway? Was it the terrain, the speed, your mental attitude or what you were wearing that determined the correct verb choice?) Whilst Annie walked, Lucy most definitely hiked. But then, Lucy was being paid to wear and photograph 'hiking' clothes for a living. Annie could never quite believe it. Clothing companies paid, actually paid Lucy to wear a scarf, or gloves, or a new season coat. As an influencer, all Lucy had to do was take it for a walk (hike) and take a few (staged) photos then post the photo online with a gushing hashtag (*#autumndays #catchingleaves #autumnalcolours #snugasabug #livingmybestlife*) where her thousands of followers (thousands.... how was that even possible?) made comments that made Annie marvel, like, '*OMG I NEED that hat in my life*,' and '*You're rocking that scarf, where can I get my hands on one, NOW*?'

Annie secretly thought that the whole thing was sickeningly fake. But it could be fun too, better than cleaning houses for a living, like she did. Sometimes, when Lucy needed an accomplice, Annie would play along. They'd take it in turns to take photos of each other or squash together and take selfies. Lucy would do anything for a good shot; there'd been a couple of times when Annie had actually worried for her friend's safety, balanced precariously on a rock, stretching her arm out, moving the phone to the right then to the left and adjusting her clothing before resting her other hand on Annie's shoulder or making a peace sign above Annie's head, and grinning.

'Careful,' Annie would say, as Lucy angled to get them both in the frame, 'Careful.'

Maybe if she had gone with her yesterday it wouldn't have happened, and Lucy wouldn't have fallen to her death from Guller's Leap taking a bloody selfie. But Lucy hadn't sent her a message, hadn't invited her along like she normally did.

A tragedy, awful beyond comprehension. Lucy's family and friends left suddenly bereft. A woman dead, the triviality of the act that killed her the antithesis of the magnitude of death itself. Annie couldn't even begin to make sense of it.

Annie's son, Elliot, had been the one to break the news to her. He'd been at Lucy's house yesterday morning, hanging out with his best friend Harry, Lucy's son, when the police officers had knocked at the door, faces sombre. A glimpse of Baby, Lucy's dog, alone in the back seat of the police car parked on the street, had told the boys this wasn't good news.

The boys had brought Lucy and Annie together fifteen years earlier, although the women hadn't known then that they were the boys, just the bumps. Sometimes, as they grew up, the boys had nearly driven them apart too – they'd had their ups and downs over the years; it hadn't always been easy, but they'd been there for each other, and Elliot and Harry were older now – teenagers, nearly grown, and the women were having their own time again, their own fun. Or at least they had been.

Elliot had come into her room this morning with a cup of coffee and a slice of toast and had laid down on the bed beside her.

'I don't know what to say to him, Mum,' He confessed. 'I just don't know what to say.'

His eyes were red, and he looked like he'd slept in his clothes. Annie wanted to scream at this mess of a world, which took away mothers and wives and friends of mothers and husbands and sons.

She stroked his back as she gave him the only advice she had. 'You don't need to say anything. Just be there. He knows.'

She turned her attention back to the *Stonebrook Gazette*, spread open on the bed beside her. The article continued with a bunch of statistics. A recent study showed that at least 259 people in the world had died taking selfies. Incomprehensible. To lose someone at any time was heart-breaking: at war, at sea, in a car accident, but to die taking a photo! The boys had only been on their school holidays for four weeks. Exams over and done with; time to have fun and recover. But that wasn't going to happen. What was happening in Stonebrook this summer? Hadn't it been enough that Nell Davenport had gone missing? Weren't people distressed and on edge enough already?

She knew she was.

She couldn't stop thinking about Nell Davenport's disappearance. It's not like they were great friends, her and Nell – nothing like that – but Annie had been cleaning at Moordown House for years now. When you clean someone's house, you know people better than you probably ought to. Feel closer than you are.

She hadn't been over there for a while. Her last visit was a month or so before school broke up for the summer. She'd heard Nell and Dalt arguing. She'd heard Nell apologising. It sent shivers down her spine and made her fear for Nell and the secrets that lay behind closed doors. Her ex-husband used to like closed doors. They were good for banging her head against, or 'teaching her a lesson' as he used to call it.

Thank god he was gone and that was over.

She was always on the lookout for others in need. A hangover from her ex.

Perhaps Nell Davenport?

When she left the note on Amelia's car earlier in the week, Annie hadn't really known what she wanted to say – how to explain her anxiety for a woman she barely knew. When Amelia called her back, she'd been surprised. But it felt good to talk. To share the burden. She wondered what Amelia would do with the information.

And now Lucy. Dead.

Annie squeezed her eyes shut in an effort to stop her thoughts. Practicalities were the name of the game. She needed to keep busy – to help – then she might get through this day.

'Let's go over to Dan and Harry's and see if there's anything we can do.'

Elliot nodded and heaved himself up from the bed. Outside, the sun shone hard on the road, the tarmac black and sticky, the air shimmering and wavy, reminding her of childhood summers – ice-cream van melodies and games of tag in the street. The soles of her feet felt like they were burning in her worn-out flip-flops as they walked the short distance to Lucy's house.

Ten minutes later and Annie was standing in Lucy's kitchen (was it still Lucy's kitchen?) Harry and Elliot had gone straight into the garden. Now was not the time to tell Dan about the tobacco and rolling papers she'd found in her son's pocket earlier in the week. Dan was perched on a kitchen bar stool, his hands wrapped around a mug of instant coffee that Annie had just made. He had the look of someone who had just got back from a long run, flushed and full of adrenaline – but imminently about to crash.

'We were supposed to go out for dinner,' Dan spoke quickly, words and eyes darting about the kitchen. 'The new Mexican place next door to that coffee shop you girls always go to. It was the last thing we talked about. She asked me what time I'd booked the table. Seven, I told her. That's the last thing I said to her. Seven.'

Annie had the feeling that she got in the cinema during a really sad film, when her throat constricted and then throbbed from the effort of trying not to cry.

'Oh Dan,' was all she managed, but Dan was locked away in his grief, unaware she'd even spoken.

'Lucy's mum is on her way down from Manchester,' Dan said, 'and her sister is flying back from Australia, although she's got a family of her own over there, so I don't know how long she'll be able to stay. My parents are on their way. They'll be here soon. I had to identify the body yesterday. It was...' Dan's eyes were fixed on Annie's face, but he was seeing something else. Annie felt a wave of nausea.

Dan took a sudden swig of coffee that seemed to jolt him back to life.

'I don't understand how she could have been so stupid.' He stood up abruptly, two fingers rubbing his forehead, right between his eyes, rubbing so hard Annie wondered whether the action was providing pain or relief.

'Lucy knew that area of the moor as well as any ranger. She knew the dangers of Guller's Leap. Risking her life, crossing that barrier, just for a photo of some goddamn sunglasses,' he was pacing now, his voice loud and angry.

'They found her phone at the bottom, pretty smashed up, but somehow they've managed to access her photo gallery, and there's a series of photos...' Dan faltered again, his voice sounded strangled. He breathed in deeply and continued, 'Selfies, of Lucy, at the end. In the last one....'

Dan began to cry then, racking sobs, his elbows down on the counter and his fingertips pushing into his eye sockets, as if he could push the tears back in or stop them at their source.

'In the last one, she was screaming.'

Annie moved forward and instinctively placed her hand on his damp back. Her son was right. There were no words.

A photo on the fridge caught her eye: Harry, aged four, in a crisp, oversized school-uniform, low September sunshine making him squint. A rigid, nervous grin stretched across his small face. The school gates were visible in the background. The obligatory first day at school photo. Annie closed her eyes and replaced Harry's features with those of her own son, Elliot's, on the same day. She remembered it so clearly, those sweet, sweet boys. In fact, wasn't that Elliot in the background? She leaned in closer to see. No, it was Nell Davenport's boy, Huckleberry. And wasn't that Nell's hand he was holding in the photo? Annie had forgotten how similar Elliot and Huckleberry used to look. Huckleberry, the same age as Elliot and Harry, all starting school at the same time. Annie, Lucy and Nell, sending their firstborns off into the world together.

The vibration of Dan's phone on the counter startled them both. Dan shifted beneath the weight of her palm on his back and reached to answer it. Annie stepped back, her hand suddenly heavy, and listened for a moment to Dan's voice, catching in his throat, saying words that no one should have to say.

His family would be here any moment. Meeting Dan's eye and exchanging a small nod, Annie picked up her bag, and left the house by the back door, noticing as she passed, the plates and mugs accruing beside the sink. She'd come back later, wash it all up and maybe bring over some dinner. Dan needed space right now. She'd just say a quick hello to Harry and check he was okay. She followed the perfectly placed limestone paving down the left-hand side of the garden until she came to Harry's old treehouse, still going strong after all these years. The overly sweet smell of cannabis reached her nostrils the moment her hands touched the bottom rung of the ladder. Dan had built the treehouse when the boys were seven. Annie could bet that his design brief back then didn't contain, 'needs to be made of flame-retardant material for when my son and his friends smoke pot and get high.' At least there were gaps in the wood for the smoke to escape through. Annie watched now, as it curled over the curved wooden logs that made up the walls and then drifted lazily away into the hot summer air.

Give them this, at least, she thought, as she removed her hand from the ladder and quietly traced her steps back through the garden, this time following the path around the side of the house, until she stood once more on the street. Another car was parked in the drive now, and one in front of the house on the road. Dan must have received more well-wishers whilst she was out the back. At least he had company. Elliot would come home later, maybe even bringing Harry with him.

Lucy's house was at the newer, recently resurfaced end of the street, further away from the town centre. The houses this end were bigger, thoughtfully designed to blend in with the environment using natural materials – many incorporating solar panels and filled with natural light. Organic milk sat on doorsteps, delivered in re-cyclable glass bottles. Electric cars were parked in driveways, whilst expensive scooters lay abandoned on lush, green lawns.

Annie walked slowly towards her own end of the street, back towards town, where the houses became smaller and where playdates meant that children knocked on each other's doors with a packet of crisps and a football. It was a good street though, full of good people, whichever end you happened to live at.

Annie had grown up here on this street, just a few doors down from where she lived now. She remembered her dad, working class through and through, pouring scorn on the new builds up the road. 'What do they want all that glass for?' he'd say. 'The whole bloody place looks like an enormous greenhouse. More money than sense,' he'd grumbled.

Had he been envious or had his scorn been genuine? It was hard to tell.

Annie felt her generation was different, that they could see beyond the narrow mindset of their parents, beyond big houses and fancy cars and material possessions, beyond ends of a street, beyond walls of a house, to the person inside. They didn't judge.

Did they?

Uninvited, an image of Nell Davenport and Huck on that first day of school tore through her mind. The huddle of mothers, the rumours, the sideways glances, Lucy Loxton holding court. The memory made her cringe and her mother's voice nagged in her head.

'Bad deeds will come back to haunt you.'

Stupid. It had all been years ago, why think of it now? Lucy's death was a total accident. Wasn't it?

Dalt

'**N**ewspaper's arrived, mate. You might want to come and see this.'

7 a.m., Sunday morning. How life had changed in a couple of weeks. Instead of ambling to the mail box at the end of the drive, just the other side of the gates, as was his normal, pre-Nell-missing routine, one of the reporters stationed at the gate had buzzed the intercom to let him know of the weekly delivery of the *Stonebrook Gazette*.

They were alright though, the reporters. Gave him the dignity of not snapping his photo at least, as he trudged down the drive, all week-old stubble, unwashed shirt and bleary eyes. And there weren't as many of them as there had been at the beginning. Just three left now. Maybe some bigger news story had pulled them away.

'Here, have a read.' A guy with a heavy camera slung round his neck poked the paper through the metal bars. 'It's awful, but I'm just glad it's not your wife.'

Dalt read it right there, his face betraying the equal measures of disbelief and horror he felt inside.

Lucy Loxton, fallen to her death the day before from Guller's Leap.

Seeing that he had finished reading, the reporter was straight back to business. 'I'm surprised you haven't heard about it already.' Dalt was immediately on guard. Was the guy being genuine, or digging for a story?

'The cops were swarming all over the area yesterday. Special Teams sent out, even more dogs brought in, I heard them say.'

Dalt found himself dredging through the sludge of thoughts inside his head. Yesterday... the police had come, they'd left suddenly. And the rest of the day? It was the first day in two weeks that he hadn't spent trawling the moor.

'We were out in the garden.' Tending to Nell's vegetable patch, but he wasn't going to overshare. Who knew what slant might be put on the information he relayed?

Nell Davenport's family take gardening leave from their worries.

And that wasn't it at all. Nell had worked so hard on the vegetable patch, poured whatever was left after her busy days of writing into the earth. It was the least he (they actually... Huck, and then later, Amelia too) could do. Nell had planted cucumber, lettuce, spring onions, tomatoes, as well as potatoes and carrots and all manner of other vegetables. The unrelenting heat combined with weeks of neglect meant the earth needed watering and tending. Slugs and snails were rife. By tending Nell's garden, Dalt felt like at least he was doing something useful. In a crazy way it made him feel closer to her.

'We're all rooting for her, you know. My wife's a massive fan. So's Dave.' He gestured to a guy who raised his hand at the mention of his name, sitting on a fold-out chair in the shade of a sound van.

'Thanks. I appreciate that. Shocking news, though.' Dalt waved the paper both to clarify his statement and say goodbye.

Strange, he thought, as he walked back to the house, how quickly one's world could be turned upside down. How accepting one could be of a bunch of reporters hanging out in the drive, handing over the paper. How calmly one could receive the news of the horrific death of an acquaintance. Was he going mad? He felt like the heat had melted his pain receptors, leaving him robotic, unable to experience true emotions. Numb.

8 a.m. and Officer Henley and Officer Pearson arrived at the house, tired and distracted. Who could blame them? Stonebrook hadn't seen headlines like this since... well, since never. They stood in the kitchen bearing the same news that the reporter and the *Stonebrook Gazette* had notified the household of only an hour before. If Dalt hadn't been feeling so wrecked, he might have felt sorry for them.

'Terrible thing to have happened,' Officer Henley was saying. 'Shocking. And I'm sorry for the way we just dashed off yesterday. Must have left you all fearing the worst – thinking it was Nell.'

Dalt hadn't realised how tense he had been, until he felt his shoulders drop and his breathing regulate. It really was true. Lucy Loxton. Not Nell. Lucy.

'Coffee?' Amelia asked. Nods all round. Dalt noticed the shake in her hand as she depressed the plunger and poured the hot liquid into five mugs.

He felt a rare flash of gratitude towards her.

The Officers pulled out the bench nearest to them and sat down, Officer Pearson struggling to get his knees under the table. The kitchen at Moordown was enormous. Sixteen years ago, Dalt had envisaged it as the hub of family life. When he and Nell had first moved in after her father's death, the place had been in desperate need of refurbishment and Dalt had found himself in a whole new world of kitchen design. Correction – he'd found himself *alone* in a whole new world of kitchen design. He'd made all the right choices

(French style farmhouse, vintage green, rustic fittings, wide glass doors leading to the decking outside) and Nell had made all the right noises. The kitchen had looked incredible. Unfortunately, it still did.

He'd wanted the table to be the centre piece, running the entire length of the room, with long benches either side. It would be a table that people crowded around, squashed onto and passed steaming plates of food back and forth along, whilst chatting nosily together. It would be a place where his children (there would be two or three of them at least) worked in the evening, the low hanging spotlights illuminating the colourful art projects they were creating. He and Nell would potter around the kitchen preparing food or washing the dishes. It didn't matter if the table got scratched or stained. The marks would only serve as a reminder of the myriad of experiences they had shared together.

The table was in immaculate condition sixteen years later.

Amelia placed the coffee cups in front of the officers (using coasters, heaven forbid she damage the wood). They were all seated now, gathered around the end of the table nearest to the French doors which had been pinned back to let the air in. Another hot day.

The questions started immediately.

Did Dalt know Mrs Lucy Loxton? (Did he detect a slight emphasis on the Mrs?) He'd known her a little, he had replied. In town, everyone probably knew her a little. He was on safe ground. Lucy Loxton was (had been, he'd corrected himself, reddening) the kind of woman that people all seemed to know a little, community spirited and friendly, a well-known face about town and frequently in the local paper. He knew she ran a fashion blog that was so popular with a lot of women around here. She was a bit of a local celebrity he supposed. Amelia was a fan, it turned out and had followed *Lucy Loxton's Fashion Secrets* whilst living in London. 'She gives great tips on what to wear for weekends away in the country.'

Dalt stopped himself from rolling his eyes. Nell, unsurprisingly, had not been a follower.

'Huck goes to school with Lucy's son, Harry, is that right?' Officer Pearson had asked Dalt, notebook open, pencil poised.

'Yes, I think he does,' Dalt said, looking at Huck for confirmation as he spoke. Why were they asking him? Wasn't his fifteen-year-old son sat right there?

'Yes. Harry's in my year at school,' Huck said.

'Are you friends?' asked Officer Pearson.

'Urm. No.' Huck looked thoughtful. 'I've known him forever. We went to primary school together too. But no, we're not friends.'

'What's that got to do with anything, anyway?' Dalt sounded testy. He wasn't sure what the point of the question was? What were they doing here – playing six degrees of separation or trying to find his missing wife?

Officer Pearson looked searchingly at Officer Henley. The thin line of Officer Henley's mouth wavered with indecision, then she nodded her head.

'Mrs Loxton's mobile phone was retrieved from the incident site yesterday, at the base of Guller's Leap. The phone was pretty smashed up, but the tech team were able to examine it. There were a number of pictures taken that morning on Guller's Leap – selfies, we believe, that were taken by Mrs Loxton herself.' Officer Pearson paused, and Dalt had the impression the bomb shell was about to drop.

'Mrs Loxton had taken a number of shots before she stepped over the barrier to take what was ultimately her final photo. These shots were taken facing the other way, with the moor behind her. We believe she was trying to find the best angle to display the sunglasses she was wearing.'

Another pause. Officer Henley fidgeted on the bench.

'There was someone in the background of one of the photos,' Officer Henley interrupted.

Despite stealing his thunder, Officer Pearson looked nothing but relieved.

'We can't make out the figure clearly. Can't even tell if it's male or female. The photo has gone for further analysis.'

Officer Henley paused, making eye contact with each of them in turn. Dalt saw his own confusion reflected on the faces of Huck and Amelia.

'But there's more,' Officer Henley continued. 'Just after 6 a.m. yesterday morning, we can see that Lucy Loxton visited Nell Davenport's blog.'

'I'm sorry, her what?' Dalt was the first to speak.

'Lucy Loxton was emailed a link to Nell's blog just after 6 a.m. yesterday morning. The link came in an email sent from Nell's email address. Mrs Loxton clicked on the link. The most recent, and in fact, the only post on the blog, was a copy of the fable that was sent from Nell Davenport's email account to Frank Hannock in the early hours of Saturday morning. We are assuming that Mrs Loxton read this fable yesterday morning.'

'Nell doesn't have a blog!' Dalt pulled his phone from his pocket before Officer Henley had even finished talking. His fingers worked quickly to type '*Nell Davenport blog*' into the search engine.

He clicked on the top result.

Amelia and Huck were immediately behind him, heads straining to see the screen. The home page appeared, a photo and a brief biography of Nell Davenport, author of the Daniel Hargreaves detective series, then a list of the books in order of release date, with a brief synopsis of the plots.

Dalt skimmed the page, selected '*blog*.'

There it was, the fable of *The Butterfly and the Moth*.

'No way!' Amelia this time. 'Is it identical?' she asked Officer Henley.

'Yes, word-for-word.'

'How...?' Amelia's question trailed off.

'How, who, when, why? They're all questions we're asking, and we're looking for answers. For Lucy Loxton and for Nell.'

Huck and Amelia sat back down on the bench.

'We don't know yet whether the link that was sent to Nell Davenport's blog was sent to anyone else. Our guys are looking into it,' Officer Henley explained. 'We can only presume, as no one else has come forward at this time to say they have received a link to the blog, that Lucy was the only intended recipient.'

'Which means that the fable was aimed at Lucy?' Amelia surmised.

'Perhaps. This is the line of enquiry that we are currently following, in lieu of any other,' Officer Pearson explained. Was his tone gentler now? Was this his 'breaking bad news' voice?

'To clarify the timeline,' Officer Henley interjected. 'At 2 a.m. on Saturday morning, Frank Hannock received an email from Nell Davenport's email account, containing a short story: a fable. At 6 a.m. an author's webpage for Nell Davenport went live. At 6.15 a.m. Lucy Loxton received an email, again from Nell Davenport's email address, inviting her to view a blog on the aforementioned webpage, where the same short story that had been sent to Frank Hannock had been uploaded. We believe that sometime between 6.30 a.m. and 7.15 a.m. Lucy Loxton left her house with her dog. And at 10.00 a.m. a park ranger discovered the body of Mrs Loxton at the base of Guller's Leap.'

The timeline and its formal delivery were met with stunned silence. It had been just over two weeks since Nell's disappearance. Two weeks with no sightings, no clues, nothing.

And now this.

'We're looking for connections,' Officer Henley added.

Connections. Find your perfect match.

'We have to consider a number of different lines of enquiry at this stage,' Officer Pearson began. 'We need to consider the possibility that Nell herself is behind all this, the email to Frank, the website, the link sent to Lucy.' He ignored the incredulous faces of his audience and carried on. 'We also need to consider the possibility that Nell Davenport is *not* behind this. That someone else wrote the story, sent the email, sent the link.'

Stunned silence.

'Nell couldn't set up a website. She was one of those technophobes, or whatever you call them. She hated technology – that's why Huck hasn't got a phone or a laptop. There's no way she could have designed this.' Dalt waved the phone in his hand, the webpage still open on the screen, aware of his raised tone but unable to control it.

'There are many things we need to consider. We need to keep all lines of enquiry open. It's possible that Mrs Davenport had assistance. That someone is helping her.'

Huck's eyes narrowed; his voice trembled with emotion.

'You're saying that Mudder did this. That she chose to disappear, to leave us. That she wrote the fable, set up a webpage, killed Lucy Loxton?' His fist hit the table as he shouted the last three words.

'That's not what we're saying.' Officer Pearson was definitely using his 'breaking bad news' voice now. 'What we're saying is, we need to consider all the possibilities. We are also giving equal weight to the possibility that something has happened to your mother and someone else is involved.'

Huck rubbed his eyes hard with the palms of his hands, leaving them red and puffy.

'We want you all to read the fable again. We need you each to think carefully, to ask yourselves how this might relate to anything that has ever happened between Nell Davenport and Lucy Loxton. We're interested in how well your families knew each other. If there are any areas of overlap, we need to know. Were Nell and Lucy friends?' Officer Henley's pencil was poised to jot down information.

Dalt turned to Huck. Once upon a time Dalt would have known all the answers. Now Huck did.

'No. They weren't friends,' Huck said.

Officer Henley scribbled away in her notebook. 'Was there any connection between Lucy and Nell? Anything they had in common? Shared interests? Mutual friends?'

'Nell's not your average woman, officers. She is very focused on writing her novels. It doesn't leave much time for anything else: interests, or friends.' Or husbands, Dalt thought. 'As far as I know, her path and Lucy Loxton's rarely crossed. Maybe years ago, when the boys were young and Nell took Huck to school every day, but not for years. Nell kept herself to herself up here. In fact, I think she has a bit of a reputation in town for being a bit of a loner.'

The officers were nodding now.

'We did get that impression,' Officer Pearson said.

Dalt sensed the officer was being polite. Nell may have been well-known locally for her books, but Dalt had a strong feeling she was equally well-known for what the townspeople considered to be her aloof and superior attitude.

'What about the email to Frank?' said Dalt, straightening. 'Have you managed to find out where it was sent from?' He felt like he was harassing a customer service assistant about an undelivered package.

'No. It looks like the sender has used a VPN. A virtual private network...' Officer Henley clarified, seeing Dalt's confused expression. 'The email was sent from Nell's email address, but it's impossible to pinpoint the location of the device that sent it. The tech team are at a dead end.'

'So, her account has been hacked?' asked Dalt.

'No, not necessarily,' Officer Henley sighed. 'All we know is that a VPN has been used. Nell could have set that up herself.'

Dalt was aware his burst of laughter was inappropriate, but seriously, Nell, setting up a website, creating a VPN... sending untraceable emails. Next, they'd find out she'd been live-streaming her disappearance on social media.

'At the moment, that's all we've got. Mr Dalton, we're working on it. We're doing all we can,' said Officer Pearson. 'Did you phone the missing person support line number we gave you?'

Dalt wearily shook his head.

'You should give them a call.' He caught Huck and Amelia's eyes too. 'All of you should. They can help. Give you some good advice on how to get through this.'

Silence.

Amelia ended it. 'Thanks. We appreciate it,' she said, speaking for all of them now. Dalt wasn't sure how he felt about that.

Amelia gathered the coffee cups and carried them over to the sink. The police officers, taking this as a cue, rose from their seats as one entity, pushing the bench out behind them as they did so.

'Let us know if you have any more thoughts about any of this. Call anytime, you've got our number. In the meantime, we'll be deploying more officers to comb the area. We've already called in extra dogs and a specialised search team to see if we can find any evidence up there – any clues as to who the person in the background of the photo was, or where they went.'

Only Amelia went to show the officers out. Huck scrubbed the mugs, china clashing against china so hard it was a wonder they didn't smash. Dalt stayed where he was, lost in thought. What did any of this mean? How were Nell and Lucy Loxton connected? He kept picturing her, Lucy Loxton, sprawled and broken at the bottom of Guller's Leap. Couldn't get the image out of his mind.

Lucy Loxton. Would she leave a hole? He winced at his lack of tact, and the thought that she'd probably left a very real hole in the mud and earth at the bottom of the cliff, of the Roadrunner and Wile E. Coyote variety. But what of the holes she'd left in people's hearts?

The hole left by Nell was a concept Dalt had found himself returning to again and again since his wife had disappeared.

'Goodness Edward,' his mother had said, calling from New Zealand the day before. 'It must be so hard, living with a Nell-shaped hole,' and everyone from police officers, professional support agencies and even his friends kept referring to Nell's absence with the same turn of phrase. He had phoned the number on the card the officers had left – anything to try and make this sick, awful feeling at the pit of his stomach go away. The woman he'd spoken to had done her best. She'd known her stuff, had tried to reassure him with missing person statistics and helpful advice about how to get through each day, each hour, each minute at a time.

'It is incredibly difficult,' she had sympathised, 'living with the hole a missing person leaves behind.'

The hole Nell left behind. Sixteen years they'd lived together in this house, and they'd been together for five years before that. A hell of a lot of time. An enormous hole, a crater, surely big enough to swallow up this house and all of them in it.

He felt like a dead man walking, that was for sure. He was hanging in there on the surface, skirting around the edge of the abyss, trying to keep it together, trying to be there for Huck, trying to talk to his son, to keep him from falling in too. This, combined with liaising with the police officers, talking to concerned friends and family and just dealing with day to day affairs was sapping all of his energy.

But the nature of the hole was bothering him, and he was beginning to feel like a fraud. Was it a Nell-shaped hole he was avoiding, or just a hole created by the absence of routine and familiarity, dug deeper with stress and fear? Was it time to admit that he and Nell had drifted apart in the same way that they drifted around Moordown, focused on their own projects, their own goals, not noticing each other as they passed?

Twenty years ago, he would have noticed a Nell-shaped hole straight away and disappeared inside of it. He'd have felt her absence like a gap in his own chest, found it impossible to go on living if she wasn't there. In fact, he sometimes did. Back then, Nell would occasionally go away for a few weeks at a time. She needed quiet time, 'to concentrate', she said, 'to write it all down.' Alone in the poky flat they shared in Cambridge, Nell's absence was acute. Dalt missed her smell, a combination of orange peel and cinnamon. He missed her laugh, not always easy to trigger but well worth the effort for the voracity of the result. He missed the conversations they had together, Nell's wit and sharp tongue and her unorthodox way of looking at the world, so different to the other women he had known. What he missed too, although he never would have told her, was the way she made him feel needed. Nell was a lot of things, but there were a lot of things that she was not, and it was in the recognition of these flaws, these holes, that Dalt found himself falling the furthest.

Nell wasn't good in social situations; she avoided them where possible. Somehow, without meaning to, she managed to offend people. First impressions are formed so quickly – too quickly – for Nell. He'd heard some of the names that people at university called her behind her back: blunt, rude and arrogant. He presumed Nell didn't have many friends for this reason. She needed him, to walk her through a world that she didn't seem to understand, and that didn't understand her in return.

He remembered fondly the day he'd confessed the strength of his feelings to her. He'd cooked for her, in the tiny kitchen of that tiny flat, some pretentious dinner of 'pork three ways' (two ways too many in retrospect) and they'd sat at the tiny table in the cramped dining area, heads leaning together, hair touching as they ate. The intimacy of the moment, the candles, the wine spurring him on, he'd gone for it, proposed. And she'd said yes.

If she'd have disappeared then, there would have been so many holes to fall in, he would have been buried alive.

Huck

Yesterday, they'd had to wait. What else could they do, but wait, as the police car headed off across the moor, its blue lights flashing.

Wait, as they heard the sirens down in the town. Wait, when their thoughts could wait no more and sped them away, to the tors, to the gullies and quarries and water holes, to the dense woodlands and the ridgeways, to the rivers and the mines deep underground.

They'd fretted, they'd dozed, they'd paced. They'd ended up, all three of them, in the vegetable patch of all places. Tomatoes, potatoes, cucumber, radishes, all bursting with life, surviving, despite the temperature and the neglect. Ready to harvest. The labour had distracted him, temporarily.

There had been no calls, no news, no updates. That evening, they had eaten a cold supper and bid their goodnights, Huck thought, to lay on their separate beds in their separate rooms, with their shared pain.

And now they knew. His father had told him first, having heard the news himself from a reporter at the gate. Lucy Loxton, dead. The police officers had confirmed it.

She'd died at Guller's Leap.

Taking a selfie.

This topped going missing in a stupid t-shirt.

Lucy Loxton. Harry's mum. He could picture her so clearly. Not unusual, he supposed, when he had seen her every day, twice a day for all of his primary school years. And these days, she was something of a 'key player' in Stonebrook. One of those women who is always on every committee, hosting fund-raising evenings and appearing in the local paper for introducing a new 'Plastic-free Stonebrook' initiative. Super Mum.

He could still recall her voice at the school gates. Not the words themselves – no, those were kept for the select few – but the hushed, authoritative tone. He could picture her expression, sincere and beguiling and her body language. The frequent, confident tosses of her long blond hair, flashes of white teeth, conspiratorial glances. He could picture the huddle of heads in the playground like nodding dogs, lapping up every word, exclusivity exuding from Lucy Loxton like a limited-edition perfume, the scent a message communicating rank and status. Other heads turning to look, to catch snippets of conversation, not privileged enough to gain access, straining, edgy, lest they heard their own names on the wind.

He'd heard Mudder's name on the wind.

Patrick, the only friend he'd ever had, couldn't remember being four. In fact, Patrick couldn't seem to remember existing before the age of seven, and even his memories of then were hazy. Huck didn't know whether to tease him or be jealous.

Huck remembered everything clearly.

His earliest memory dated from when he was two. In it, he and Mudder were in the garden at Moordown. Mudder was digging out the old vegetable plot, unplanted for years, but suddenly an obsession. He could see her now, spade rising, falling, plunging, turning, rising, falling, plunging, turning, tendrils of her hair escaping the cloth wrapped around her head and falling in her eyes, the back of her t-shirt soaked through with sweat, her strength, determination and focus palpable. Hypnotised by the rhythmic rise and fall of the tool, she hadn't seen the glint of treasure overturned in the dark soil, didn't see the small hand of her son dart in to retrieve it.

Maybe, Huck considered, he remembered his memories because they were a lot harder to forget.

Shaken from a trance, Mudder had looked disorientated and confused. It had taken a moment for her eyes to locate the source of the noise, to fasten upon Huck, sprawled bawling in the earth, a small, balled hand clutched to his chest.

He remembered her lifting him, holding him out in front of her, as she ran to the house, screaming 'Edward, Edward,' He remembered her laying him out on the kitchen table, a boy made of mud and blood and tears. He remembered her stepping backwards, looking desperately over her shoulder towards the corridor for Dalt.

He remembered that Dalt had been angry, terribly, terribly angry, and that the bottle lid hadn't been worth losing the top of his finger for.

He didn't need to remember the feeling of guilt, he still felt it now. His own stupid action had got Mudder into trouble. All his fault.

After that, the visits from the lady started. Whilst he knew she wasn't Mudder's friend or a relative, at first Huck couldn't work out what or who she was. She came with her games and her books and her puppets, came with her smile and her charm and her clipboard. She'd sit on the floor beside him, chat, chat, chat, bubbles and bells – passing him toys, asking him questions. Mudder would sit straight backed on the sofa, indecipherable, impenetrable, sealed.

His fault.

Maybe, Huck thinks, he is jealous of Patrick's lack of memories after all.

Memories.

Lucy Loxton's voice carrying across the playground on the wind, to the ears of a four-year-old boy and his mother, on his first day of school.

'...lost the top of his finger... his mother did it... chopped it clean off.'

He had put his arm around Mudder's legs and held on tight. He had seen Mudder look over towards the woman with the low voice and the swingy ponytail and the pretty face, the people gathered all around her, and he had seen the flicker of fear in Mudder's eyes.

Amelia

Standing in the doorway, watching the police car drive away, Amelia felt overwhelmingly tired – probably all the adrenaline leaving her body, first the excitement, now the fear. The heat surrounded her like a swaddling blanket. She imagined giving into it, just closing her eyes and letting go. How glorious it would be to lie in the garden letting the gentle breeze lap over her, to hear the sounds of the water flowing nearby. How glorious it would be, to not think for a while, to not feel for a while.

Back in the kitchen, Dalt hadn't moved from the table. Slumped over, he looked exhausted. He'd lost weight; his face was thin and drawn. His shirt hung loosely on his large frame. Amelia feared he was in danger of disappearing too. Huck, propped up against the kitchen counter didn't look much better.

'This is worse than not knowing anything. Is she alive? Has she been abducted? Where the hell is she? And how does Lucy Loxton fit into all this?' Dalt shattered the silence.

'The figure in the background,' Huck said, as if he hadn't heard his father's question. 'There was a figure in the background in the photo.'

'Yes, but what has Lucy's death got to do with Nell?'

'Lucy Loxton hated Mudder.'

Amelia froze in the doorway.

'What?' Dalt said.

'She hated her. I don't know why, but she did,' Huck continued.

'What makes you think that?' Amelia asked gently.

'I don't think it, I know it,' Huck's voice rose shrilly. 'Lucy Loxton has to be the butterfly, otherwise why was the link sent to her? Mudder was the moth-butterfly. The butterfly gossiped about the moth, like Lucy Loxton gossiped about Mudder – it turned the others against the moth, just like Lucy Loxton did at the school gates years ago.' Huck looked red-faced and angry, but certain.

'What about the rest of the story?' Amelia asked. 'Butterfly gets banished. If Lucy Loxton is the butterfly, why does she get banished? That part doesn't make sense.'

'Enough hypothesising. This whole thing is ludicrous, reading things into a story, guessing at hidden meanings. We need real answers, physical answers. We need to stop messing around and get back out there and look for her.' Dalt was shouting by the end of his sentence. It wasn't often, Amelia thought, that Dalt allowed his true emotions to reveal themselves so publicly. She thought of her phone conversation with Annie Barnes, who'd hinted at a dark side to Dalt. Should she be taking Annie's words more seriously? Had the anger bubbling beneath the surface spilled over onto Nell?

When Amelia spoke, Dalt wouldn't meet her eyes.

'People are looking, Dalt. You've been looking! The police are still looking, searching the moor. They've got more officers up there now than ever before.' Amelia found herself in the role of peacemaker, chief negotiation officer.

'Not hard enough they're not. I'm going out.' Dalt knocked the table as he stood, sending newspapers spilling over the edge.

'I'll come.' Huck stood, eyes fixed on his father, ignoring the mess around him.

The men loaded up backpacks. Amelia, suddenly awkward in the space, filled a glass of water at the sink and looked out the window, across the lawns, to where the top of the willow tree was just visible, its long, green fronds swaying gently in the breeze. It seemed to be calling to her.

After Dalt and Huck left, Amelia walked barefoot through the long grass, carrying a blanket she'd found in the drawing room. The willow tree was as welcoming as she'd envisaged, enticing her in through the curtain to a cool, green wonderland. She tossed out the blanket to form a makeshift bed. The pleasure as she sank onto it was undeniable, the weight of the last few weeks and the heaviness of this morning's conversation lifted momentarily by the scent of the earth and the softness of the dewy green carpet. She let her fingers relax and stretch out over the edges of the blanket, stroking the feathery, thick grass, moving her arms up and down like a green grass angel. So therapeutic. She focused on her breathing, in, out, in, out, long, deep, slow breaths until her mind began to empty. In, out, in, out. She was just drifting off to sleep, when her fingers caught on something, closed around it, felt the shape of it and drew it in.

A round, hard something.

A ring.

Huck

Huck jogged over the uneven, rocky ground. Was he being slow or was his father trying to lose him? He'd spent the whole hike so far playing catch-up, striding forward to close the gap that had grown between them, only to find it had lengthened again moments later. Turnip lagged further behind still. They shouldn't have brought him; the sun beat down, relentless, unforgiving. Huck's backpack felt heavier than it should have on his back, his t-shirt soaked beneath it.

Dalt was in no mood for talking, which suited Huck just fine. They'd exchanged words briefly in the garden at Moordown: where they would go and how they would get there. They'd agreed on their destination immediately – Guller's Leap. It was decided they would take the direct route there, walking the road for half a mile until the T-Junction, where the right turn led into town and the left led to the open heart of the moor, but where, if you continued straight ahead on a lesser trodden path surrounded by purple heather, you'd find yourself at Guller's Leap.

Now side-by-side, Huck stole a glance at his father's face. Dalt's cap was pulled low over his forehead, his mouth fixed in a deter-

mined line, his breathing fast and audible, his chin covered in a thick
stubble, clamouring to be redefined as a beard. It had snuck up on
Dalt, like a game of *What's the time Mr Wolf?*, the wiry black hairs,
growing longer and longer each time Huck's back was turned. Huck
rubbed his own jaw line, comforted by its softness, its smoothness
and familiarity.

Dalt walked purposefully, his long stride only occasionally hin-
dered by the stones that littered the path. Not even 10 a.m. in the
morning, and yet so uncomfortably hot. Any other summer, and
they'd have been swimming in one of the many pools the moor had
to offer. Not the popular spots, not the ones all the kids from school
knew about, tourists following them there like unpaid teenage tour
guides. No, the hidden away places. The secret ones.

Stillpool, with its little sandy beach and its flat, well positioned
rocks, perfect for dreaming and sunbathing the day away; Marble
Falls, where the crystal-clear cascading water hammered his shoulders, stripping him of his breath and his worries, pounding his body,
clearing his mind. He ached just thinking of it, the shock of the icy
water, the honesty and simplicity of the pain, his world narrowed
for an instant to breath and to body.

Judd's pool was nearby. The thought of a quick dip crossed his
mind, icy cold-water numbing, cleansing, obliterating. Small and
deep, its inky black waters were shaded by the trees that protected it
and hid it from sight. The ponded section sat upstream of a natural
weir, a collection of gravel and stone built up over time, beyond
which the river flowed quickly, beginning its descent into the valley
towards Stonebrook.

Dalt had taught Huck to swim. Not here, in these pools. No,
these were the prize. He'd learnt in the community pool, with its
stark, unisex changing rooms and its bright lights and harsh smell of
chlorine. Every weekend they would go, from as far back as Huck
could remember, from before that even, from babe in arms. Why

Dalt thought it was so important for Huck to learn to swim, he had never said. Huck later realised, it had something to do with Mudder's dead brother – a shadow boy he'd only ever heard about in whispers and in warnings – a reaction to a tragedy. Whatever the reason, Huck saw it now as a gift, bestowed upon him by Dalt; a gift of freedom.

Huck had never heard Mudder voice any complaint to their swimming jaunts, despite her own terror of the water. She would usually go to her study to write when they went to swim, emerging only when his small fists pounded on her door upon his return, demanding to be let in, his hair still wet and the smell of chlorine clinging to his skin.

'My little water baby,' Mudder would call him, as he settled on the floor by her feet. He always sat there when she wrote, his fingers wrapped around a chunky crayon, or pencil, scribbling on the scraps of paper she handed to him like sweets.

As he'd grown bigger, the trips to the pool became more frequent. Instead of holding him, guiding him, coaching him, Dalt began to swim beside him. Over just a few short years, their strokes gradually became in sync, breathing on every two, at first, then every three: breathe to the left, one, two, three, breathe to the right.

In every other area of his life, Huck felt ungainly, clumsy and blundering. In the pool he felt different. Coordinated, agile and graceful. Complete and content. Free.

Then the day came that Huck ceased to swim beside his father and swam ahead of him instead.

They had both seen it coming, Huck had been getting fitter, stronger, faster, but he felt saddened, none-the-less. His mind conjured an imaginary banner, strung across the pool.

Congratulations boy, you are younger, quicker and more powerful than your father, it declared.

It was the flip side of the banner that bothered him, the side that proclaimed his father's diminishment: older, weaker and slower.

Hardly though, Huck told himself. Dalt was strong, athletic and capable. Maybe he was overthinking it. Dalt had probably dropped behind on purpose.

Dalt had begun taking him to the water holes on the moor the summer before Huck started primary school, at just four years old. They'd go when the sun shined and where the water was shallow. At first, Huck was unsure – it was so different to the community swimming pool – the water on the moor was cold. His feet slipped on weed and sank in mud. Ripples on the surface of the water would panic him, and he'd imagine the monster beneath that might have created such an effect. But with each summer that passed, Huck grew more confident. Grew to love the underwater secrets the pools held.

It was their 'thing.'

Some dads played football with their kids; some dads cycled. Dalt and Huck swam. Dalt wasn't much of a talker, and neither was Huck. Spending an afternoon with their heads underwater suited them both perfectly.

They'd passed the turning to Judd's pool and the moment to suggest a cooling dip had passed. What was he thinking, anyway? Frivolous behaviour, when one's mother was missing, and someone else's mother had just died.

'Remember the time we came across that bloke, stark naked at Judd's pool?' Dalt said suddenly, the first words spoken between them since they'd left the house.

'How could I ever forget?' said Huck, the memory making him smile before he could stop himself. 'I'm not sure who was more embarrassed, him or us?'

When Huck had first asked Dalt if he could swim in the pools on the river alone, Dalt's fear had not been that Huck might drown, but rather what he might live to see, wild swimming being the prerogative of aging skinny-dippers who left not only their clothes but also their inhibitions draped across the rocks whilst they embraced the magical properties of the water in their full-frontal glory.

It was the first time in a long time that Huck had heard his father chuckle.

'Remember the day you got me those new trunks: the orange ones? Remember how they billowed out in the water, and I thought it was the best thing ever, until the force of the falls pulled them right off me and they floated past the weir and disappeared?' Huck remembered how he'd had to walk home, tugging at the hem of his t-shirt, naked from the waist down.

Dalt was properly laughing now, rubbing at his eyes with the back of his hand. Perhaps Huck should have suggested a swim, after all. Maybe on the way home.

But Dalt's laughter stopped as quickly as it had started at the sight of the yellow and black police tape blocking the fork in the path towards Guller's Leap.

As a young boy, Huck had been fascinated, to the point of obsession, with Guller's Leap. In year seven, Mr Busby, the history teacher, had ordered Huck's class to conduct independent research projects on any area of local history of their choosing. Some kids researched the jobs people did back then, some kids researched education in days gone by. Patrick researched women's rights (but that was the kind of thing Patrick would do). For Huck, the choice wasn't hard.

Tom Guller was fifteen years old on the day he died. His portrait hung in the museum at the top of the stairs on the right, just above the eye level of an average twelve-year-old boy. Huck felt a kinship with the boy in the photograph, finding a shared dreaminess in their expressions and a vulnerability in their smiles. When the project was declared, Huck knew Tom was his man.

Besides, Tom Guller's untimely demise was a story that had transfixed children in Stonebrook for over a hundred years. What child wouldn't be interested in the ghoulish details that led to the immortalisation of a boy and place forever? A story told on cold, dark nights when the wind was blowing through the trees and the knocking of branches on glass could sound like the racing footsteps of a boy being chased to his death.

Huck had found a surprising amount of information about Tom Guller, thanks to a man called Albert Gresham.

In the late nineteenth century, Stonebrook was home to the Gresham Family, made rich by their booming textile factory operating at the height of the industrial revolution. Albert was the oldest son and heir to the family fortune, who found himself both very rich and very bored and therefore, most in need of a hobby. As a result, Albert had equipped himself with a box camera, a simple device, with a fixed-focus lens and single shutter speed. The rest was history – literally.

The town museum was plastered with black and white photos of Gresham's: the main street, the moors, the school, the factories – you name it, he shot it. As well as being a keen (and indiscriminate) amateur photographer, Albert was also something of a philanthropist, ahead of his time perhaps – maybe the photography made him so, allowing him to see first-hand how the poor lived, how the farm labourers toiled, how the women cooked and washed and brought up their young and he had a better understanding than many of his peers of the division between rich and poor. Gresham strived to address inequalities in his own unique way – through his photography and his writings. Albert photographed the people of the town and gave them the prints free of charge, as he knew they would not be able to afford them. This gesture made him well-liked by the townspeople, who would let him into their homes and their lives, making his pictures richer for their honesty.

Huck had learnt this from Gresham himself, who, being an educated man, had kindly kept a diary of his exploits from the age of eighteen until his death in 1948. The diary itself was displayed in a locked glass cabinet, on a plinth in the town museum, which had been the old schoolhouse many years before, and was opened to a rather innocuous page about film development. Huck was sure far juicer accounts of nineteenth-century life lay within those pages. He was later to discover, on a rainy weekend in mid-November, that the manuscript had been scanned, and was available to view in its entirety on an old computer in a quiet corner of the museum. He was right – it was juicy, and it provided perhaps the only written account of the story of Tom Guller.

He had spent days trawling through Gresham's manuscript for a sniff of the boy, but to no avail. It wasn't until his fourth day of searching that the aging custodian asked him what he was looking for, and directed him straight to page sixty-seven. There, at last, he found Tom's name. He wasn't the first to ask and the custodian told him with authority that she was sure he wouldn't be the last.

Good old Gresham, he didn't disappoint. A diary entry from August 1892 told the story of Tom Guller's life, as recounted by a random assortment of witnesses in the magistrate's court in Stonebrook at a hearing held to ascertain the nature of his death.

Gresham's account (as is the way of most stories, he imagined) was not the same as the tales Huck had been told as a boy growing up. Tales of how, hounded and terrified, Guller had launched himself off the cliff edge in an act of desperation, trying to get away from his tormentors, two local bullies, Peter Smythe and Billy Cluff.

No, Gresham's version was different. Very different.

Gresham described Tom Guller as a boy on the cusp of manhood, seemingly older than his fifteen years. Not the vulnerable dreamer that Huck had rather romantically attributed him to be, more of a wife-stealing, dirty, cheating liar as it turned out.

Molly Smythe was the wife in question, Peter Smythe's, obviously. According to Gresham, on the evening of Tom's death, Tom had been discovered in a somewhat compromising position in Peter's hay barn with Molly. Oops. Tom had scarpered, Peter and Billy (farmhand and friend) gave chase, up onto the moors.

In Gresham's account, Peter and Billy told the magistrate that they had never caught up with Tom Guller, that they'd lost him in the dark, presumed him hidden – that they'd gone back to town, to drown anger with beer. Tom Guller was found, soon enough though, at the base of a cliff. His cliff, from then on.

Huck had wondered why the spoken story that had been passed down through the ages, a story of a victim chased to his death by two school-yard bullies, differed so dramatically to Gresham's account. And he wondered which version was the truth.

On a school trip to the museum, the curator had pointed out the graffiti etched into the old schoolroom walls, left behind by the children from long ago. Huck had wanted to duck under the rope and dig his fingertips deep into the grooves; to see if Tom Guller had carved his name and to see if he could find any truth in the marks he might have left behind.

And now they stood, he and Dalt, the police tape ahead of them, facing another story that hadn't yet been told. As Huck stared at his father frozen before it, Officer Pearson's words echoed in his head,

'There was a figure in the background of the photograph.'

Friday 30th August

Annie Barnes

*T*he *Stonebrook Gazette* had run the fable of *The Butterfly and the Moth* on the page that used to be Nell Davenport's. Why the hell not, Annie supposed. The woman was probably still on payroll, they might as well get their money's worth. Nell Davenport was certainly doing her best to provide the town with interesting reading material in her absence. She always was one for a mystery.

The town was half crazed with it all. Everywhere you went, people discussing it.

Who wrote the fable?

What's happened to Nell Davenport?

I think the husband's behind it all.

Is Nell's disappearance linked to the death of that woman at Guller's Leap?

Everyone had something to say.

And Annie's personal opinion?

Following the trend for moral lessons, she'd have to say, 'You don't get something clean without getting something else dirty.'

Lucy Loxton had been a social butterfly, but she'd also been a social bully. Deep down, Annie knew it – had always known it, but she'd been too weak to admit it. Annie had witnessed first-hand the power Lucy had over the women of Stonebrook. Don't mess, she'd told herself. Go with the flow.

Nell Davenport hadn't gone with the flow. She'd flowed in a totally different direction. Annie had got to know her a little over the last few years as their cleaner. Yes, she was unusual, but she was also funny, articulate and interesting. Not all traits that Lucy Loxton could boast.

Ever since she'd seen that photo of the boys' first day at school on Lucy's fridge, Annie hadn't stopped thinking about Nell and Lucy. The rumours Lucy spread about Nell chopping Huck's finger off and the way Lucy turned the other mothers against Nell. The look on Nell's face as she stood alone at the gates, day after day. The look on her son's face as he stood by her side.

Was Nell Davenport cleaning up? And was she getting herself dirty in the process?

Amelia

A melia had kept the discovery of the ring a secret. She didn't know why. Nearly a week had passed since her fingers had clasped it and eased it from the mud. She'd taken it inside, blasted it under the hot tap, revealing the gold beneath the dirt. She'd felt like Gollum. She'd probably looked like Gollum, too – stringy unwashed hair, sallow face – the thought made her giggle out loud. Mad – like Gollum – driven mad by her precious.

The ring itself was pretty unremarkable. A five-millimetre-thick band of gold, average size, no stone, no distinguishing markings, no distinguishing features. She'd slipped it on her own average-sized ring finger and found it to be a little loose, leading her to think it could belong to either a woman or a man. Wow. She was really managing to narrow it down. She'd made a mental list of whose it could be, with Dalt appearing at the top, alongside Nell, Huck below them, then 'other' below that – 'other' to include Mr and Mrs Davenport Senior, and generations gone before, as well as accidental loss by friends or visitors.

But it most likely belonged to Nell or Dalt and could be the clue she'd been searching for.

The conversation with Annie Barnes kept playing out in her head. 'They were arguing. Properly arguing.' She pictured Dalt's anger in the kitchen days before, his body slamming into the table, the papers cascading over the edge. She owed it to Nell to get to the bottom of this. She'd made a promise that day on the moor to find answers. Yes, the police officers were out there, day and night, searching, looking for clues, but that didn't help shift the terrible thoughts she kept having: Nell, lying injured at the bottom of a cliff. Nell, kidnapped, bound and helpless. Nell, dead.

Dalt and Huck had been out searching the moor the day Amelia had discovered the ring, so she'd seized the opportunity and started her lines of enquiry immediately, in Nell and Dalt's bedroom. Her mission: to either locate Nell's wedding ring (if it wasn't out there somewhere on Nell's finger) or failing that, to compare the size of the willow tree ring against another of Nell's.

Amelia had been in Nell and Dalt's room only once before during her stay, and to be truthful, she hadn't actually been invited. She'd knocked, but Nell had been showering and hadn't heard, so she'd entered anyway, not thinking it to be a big deal.

It was a big deal.

Nell emerged from the shower room, turban and towel locked in place, and let out an almighty scream at the sight of Amelia standing just inside the door.

It turned out Nell valued her space and privacy rather a lot more than Amelia had estimated.

Amelia couldn't even remember what she had gone in there for.

But now Dalt was out and Nell was gone. Nobody was going to scream at her this time.

She turned the brass handle and stepped inside.

The room itself was grand – decadent even. Rich, velvet wallpaper covered the walls and an oriental rug of burgundy and navy hues was flung haphazardly onto polished wooden floorboards. But for all its size, the room had little furniture. The main feature, an enormous, eye-catching bed, took centre stage. It appeared to be a bedroom of two halves and Amelia was reminded of the room she used to share with her sister, Olivia, before she left for university. Olivia's side was neat and orderly (boring, she'd always thought). Books lined up in alphabetical order, ornaments arranged neatly on a display cabinet. Amelia's side had been a total pit, clothes on the floor, papers strewn all over the desk, photos, poems and pictures all over the walls. An imaginary line separated the two halves, as it did here to separate Nell and Dalt. Next to what had to be Dalt's side of the bed sat a bedside table, swarming with coffee cups, books, papers and magazines. Clothes were scattered all over the floor and pungent towels were draped over the back of a chair.

In contrast, Nell's bedside table was barren, save for a metal lamp. The floor beside the bed totally bare. No pictures adorned the walls, no cushions decorated the duvet. A chest of drawers sat primly at its foot, the surface of it uncluttered by photos or trinkets. Uncluttered, in fact, by anything at all. Next to the window, Nell's dressing table looked ironic with its plain and simple design. Weren't dressing tables traditionally frivolous, light-hearted affairs?

Quite functional. Quite Nell, thought Amelia.

Again, the surface of the dressing table was completely devoid of clutter. Amelia's dressing table at home (Henry Cooper's apartment was hardly 'home' now though, was it?) was covered in 'stuff', overflowing with 'stuff'. Necklaces and feather boas dangled from the mirror, perfume bottles, nail varnishes and make up bags peppered the tabletop whilst jewellery boxes spewed out tangles of bracelets and rings.

Amelia slid open the top drawer. Bingo! A small, wooden jewellery box, with Nell's initials engraved into the lid.

A ring box sat neatly inside, along with two necklaces and an emerald bracelet. Amelia plucked the ring box out and opened it.

Empty. A plump blue, satin pillow lined the base, with an indent where a ring had once sat. Amelia replaced the box with a sigh. The missing ring could either be on Nell's finger, or in Amelia's own hand, there was no way to know. She poked the necklaces disparagingly. Wait, was that a ring? Yes, buried beneath the coiled silver chain, a ring.

Holding it up to the light it was clear that the ring from the jewellery box wasn't Nell's wedding band. It was instantly familiar: a gaudy ruby, clumsily set onto a cheap, thin gold band. It had been Nell's mother's, Amelia recalled. Nell had worn it back in their university days.

Feeling in her pocket, Amelia pulled out the willow tree ring and compared the two. A pretty close size match; the willow tree ring could be Nell's.

Leaving the room as she'd found it, Amelia closed the door behind her and followed the ribbon of royal blue carpet that lay on top of the dark polished wood of the corridor, to the other side of the landing where the guest room (she still didn't think of it as her room) was situated. Not for the first time, she considered what a truly remarkable house it was. Two sets of staircases led to this, the first floor. A house with two staircases felt so terribly sophisticated. The apartment she'd shared with Henry Cooper had a mezzanine floor – terribly trendy, she'd thought at first, but she'd quickly realised this was essentially a small room higher up in a bigger room, visible to anybody below and accessed by what was termed a '*spiraling, steel stairway*' in estate agents particulars, but was essentially a perilous, twisting ladder, which quickly turned even more hazardous after a couple of G&T's. Not as covetable as it had initially sounded. No – this house was where it was at, with its shabby charm, an eclectic mix of flea market chic and antique furniture, ornate wall hangings and peeling paint. Nell didn't know how lucky she was.

Originally accessed by a narrow, wooden stairwell stemming from the kitchen, which stood in stark contrast to the wide, carpeted staircase that led to the main part of the house, the guest room was in what used to be the servants' quarters. The room itself was small and neat, a single bed in one corner, a bedside table with a solitary lamp next to it. A bright and colourful rug covered the worn wooden floorboards. A desk and chest of drawers completed the furnishings, the desk facing the window, with views to the gardens at the side of the house. Many nights since Nell had disappeared, Amelia had lain in bed, haunted by thoughts of the inhabitants of the room in years gone by, as if their toil and hardship had been absorbed by the stone walls, only to be reflected back on her.

She slipped her notebook out from under her pillow and jotted that last thought down. It might come in handy at a later stage. The writing was going well. She'd had to crack open a second notebook and was considering getting out her laptop to type up what she'd already written. She felt like a modern-day equivalent of those court artists, the ones who painted the accused as they sat in the stand, only she used pen instead of pencils and words instead of pictures. She would write that down too – that was good – poetic.

Netflix would thank her for it. She'd been thinking about Netflix a lot lately. Possibly too much (she wouldn't write this bit down, it would diminish the authenticity of the project if her writing looked premeditated, *Made for Netflix*). That did sound incredible though, didn't it? No – she needed to continue jotting down all the events as they happened, and then hope that at the end of it all (whatever and whenever that might be) someone (Netflix) might be interested in the fact that someone (she) had, by complete co-incidence, kept a day by day account of the 'missing' from a first hand, person on the ground, point of view. Then, when they made their ten-episode, crime thriller documentary, the diary would prove invaluable (as would her pieces to camera, the writing at the bottom of the screen introducing '*Amelia Early, author and family friend*').

Nell would have wanted her to express her feelings of loss, worry and sadness through writing. Nell would be proud of her, creating something at last.

Every page was dated and Amelia had recounted the events of the last few weeks, from the moment they realised Nell was missing, to the initial visit with the police officers to the news of Lucy Loxton's fall from Guller's Leap, and most recently finding the ring underneath the willow tree.

A gripping read.

I was hooked from the first page to the last sentence.

A masterpiece.

She could see it now.

When Amelia heard the front door open, and the voices of Huck and Dalt filled the hallway, she flew down the stairs to greet them.

'Any news?' she asked, her eyes loitering on Dalt's hands. 'Did you find anything?'

'Nothing. The place is crawling with search teams and reporters. It's pretty grim out there,' Dalt said, bending down to unclip Turnip's lead.

No wedding ring. No rings at all.

And now a week had passed, and Amelia had kept her discovery of the ring a secret.

Was it Dalt's? Quite possibly! Annie Barnes had heard arguing. Maybe Nell and Dalt were a couple on the edge. Had Dalt discarded his ring, declaring the marriage over? Had Nell left because of it?

Was the ring the key to finding Nell?

Saturday 31st August

The Magpie and the Sparrow

From: Nell Davenport
To: Frank Hannock
Subject: The Magpie and the Sparrow

One day, the birds of the trees decided it was time that their young were taught the ways of the world.

'But who will teach them?' asked Robin.

'I will,' said Magpie, certain that he was the most wise and knowledgeable of all the birds in the wood.

The next morning, the fledglings went off to school.

'First, we are going to learn how to sing,' announced Magpie.

All of the chicks nodded obediently, apart from Sparrow.

'I can already sing,' she told Magpie truthfully, 'I have a strong voice,' and she opened her beak to begin her twittering, warbling, strange song.

'That is not how we sing,' Magpie interrupted crossly. 'I am the teacher, and I will show you how we sing,' and he began his plain and simple song.

The birds nodded obediently.

Apart from Sparrow. Sparrow sang her own song under her breath and stepped from side to side on the branch.

'Today, we are going to learn how to catch food,' Magpie announced the following morning. 'I will teach you how to catch mice and pick the tastiest wild fruits and berries.'

'I can already find food,' declared Sparrow honestly. 'I am very good at catching insects and I know where to find the sweetest new buds.'

'That is not what we eat,' Magpie said angrily. 'I am the teacher, and I will tell you what we eat, and how we will catch it.'

The chicks nodded obediently. Sparrow fluttered her wings and stepped from foot to foot on the branch, but she kept her beak shut.

The following day, Magpie called his pupils to him and told them, 'Today we will learn how to fly.'

'But I know how to fly. I am excellent at it,' declared Sparrow excitedly, speaking nothing but the truth.

'Enough! Enough!' cawed Magpie. 'I am the teacher and you will learn from me.'

Magpie haughtily stretched out his wide, white-tipped wings, extravagantly fanned his sleek black tail feathers out behind him and stepped off the branch.

Whoosh. Goshawk, who had been watching the performance from the top of the tallest tree, swooped down, caught the noisy magpie in his beak, and carried him away.

Pride comes before a fall.

Ms Jamison

There were some children whose names I could never remember, even when they were in my class – Lilys and Lukes, Matthews and Katies. I'd look at their small, eager faces, indistinguishable from each other, staring up at me from the carpet where they sat, legs crossed, arms in laps, a sea of tiny yogis, and my mind would just go blank. Then there were the names I'd hold on to for longer, through seasons and siblings, until one day, wearing a secondary school uniform and a knowing smile, they'd pass me in the street and smile and say, 'Hi, Miss Jamison,' and I would smile back and say, 'Hello dear,' wracking my brain for the name that had been on the tip of my tongue moments and decades before, but had now seemingly deserted me.

Then, there were the names that I would never forget, the names that were engraved in my memory as deep and as raw as the initials that were scratched into the old wooden desks of my classroom with the sharp end of a compass.

Her name was one of these.

It's rare, but not impossible for a teacher's career to span two generations. I'm one of those rarities. I began teaching at Stonebrook Primary School, or Infant School, as it was known then, in the September of 1984. I was twenty-one years old, and newly qualified.

'Out of the frying pan, and into the fire,' the head teacher at the time, Mr Perkins, had joked.

It being my first day on the job, I hadn't wanted to appear contentious – he wasn't to know that I'd raised my five siblings practically single-handedly. I gave him a cool smile and the benefit of the doubt and stepped into the first classroom I could truly call my own.

Mine was the Reception class, at four and five years old, the youngest children in the school. On my application form I'd written of the satisfaction to be gained from imparting knowledge, the moral rewards of teaching right from wrong and the privilege and joy that came from creating relationships based on trust and respect with my pupils. To think that I once truly believed those words.

There were twenty-one children in that first class of 1984. Twenty-one names to remember, twenty-one faces to recognise, twenty-one characters to meet. But one stood out. She stood out right from the start.

Nell Davenport.

I'm not proud of what I'm about to tell you, not proud at all. I've taught for thirty-six years, and I made more mistakes in that first year than all the other years combined. You live and learn, I used to say, but little Nell Davenport, she had it the other way around. She had to learn to live.

Her chestnut red hair and her frown reminded me of a little Shirley Temple, but without any of the charm. I remember it as if it were yesterday, lined up in the playground on that very first day, Nell Davenport right at the head of the line.

'I'm first,' she told me, over and over. 'I'm first, I'm first, I'm first.'

Endearing, once maybe, possibly amusing twice, but by the end of the morning the child's voice was ringing in my ears.

Seated on the carpet, she rocked back and forth, humming, as if this was normal behaviour, acceptable even. 'It's the first day of school,' I told myself, 'the child doesn't know any better. My job is to teach her, to show her the correct way to do things.' But the first day passed, and the second, and the third, then the first week, and soon enough we found ourselves at the end of the first half term and, if anything, the girl's behaviour had grown worse. The rocking and humming had increased, Lord, the child could hardly stay still, and this was only the tip of the iceberg. The child was downright rude. She insulted the other children left, right and centre, making at least one-person cry on a daily basis.

There was the day Nell Davenport told little Francis Atkins that his grandmother looked so old she would most probably die soon. There was the day she asked the lunch time assistant why she was so fat, and the day that she told little Tommy Griffiths that he spoke in a funny way and that she couldn't understand a word he said (the poor child had a stutter worse than King George VI). Then there was the day she asked Mary Baker, whose beloved dog had just died, what the creature had looked like in his grave?

Those weren't the only difficult days. The most challenging days, the times that she made my blood really boil, were the days when she made me look foolish in front of the other children; the days she'd call out to tell me I'd made a mistake adding up, or that I'd misspelt a word on the blackboard or even that my use of punctuation was incorrect. Too big for her boots, I used to think. Little Know-it-all. Too smart for her own good.

But the day that will stay seared on my memory forever was Prospective Parents' Day. A day of great import, the teachers were all expected to put on a show.

'Impress and possess,' our Headmaster had delivered his punchy catchphrase in what he must have hoped was a rousing speech conducted in the staff room on the morning of the visit, when in reality his words were secondary to the sound of the kettle coming to boil.

'With new parents come new children, and with them, the funding to keep you all in a job. So do your bloody best,' Mr Perkins had commanded.

When Mr Perkins led his throng of prospective parents around the school, it just so happened that it was PE time, and the children and I were assembled in the hall ready to begin the session.

I was a stickler for following the rules, and the rules stated that girls must tie their hair up for PE. Nell Davenport's unruly mass of wild, red hair was down. Down and out and every which way but up.

'Nell Davenport, we need to tie your hair up,' I'd told her firmly.

Nell had taken a step backwards and said nothing. She had a habit of saying nothing if she didn't like what she was hearing.

'Here – I've got an elastic band,' I said, pulling one off my wrist that I kept exactly for moments like this, as I advanced towards her.

My fingers had hardly touched that mass of wild hair when she screamed. She screamed a scream so piercing and shrill that some of the children seated on the floor began to cry, whilst others clutched their ears for respite. As she screamed, she lashed out with her fists and her feet, a kicking, punching, screaming whirling dervish of a child. For my own protection, I stepped back from the girl and began to admonish her for her intolerable behaviour.

Then, as quickly as it had started, the screaming stopped. The child had a new idea. I watched her eyes dart manically around the room. Target locked in, she bolted at quite an unbelievable speed to the corner of the room where the gymnastic apparatus was stored. Like a mouse being chased she glanced over her shoulder at me, before ensconcing herself in the tiny space inside the vaulting box.

Twenty pairs of children's eyes looked from the vaulting box, to me, back to the vaulting box, to me again. Twenty pairs of children's eyes together with the bewildered eyes of at least fifteen visiting parents and one distinctly unimpressed headmaster.

I froze.

Mr Perkins ushered the prospective parents from the hall, uttering words like 'one-off' and 'unprecedented,' throwing a fraught, angry look over his shoulder in my general direction as the swinging double-doors closed behind him.

Coming to my senses, I gathered my class around me and eventually we continued our PE lesson, me, totally humiliated, bubbling inside with fury at the little red-haired imp of a girl who had made me lose face in front of all those people.

And Nell Davenport? Well, that nuisance of a girl stayed there, in that vaulting box all day long, rocking and humming, humming and rocking, until she rocked and hummed herself to sleep.

I am ashamed to admit that after that day I made her suffer for it. I'm not proud of what I've told you, not proud at all, but I was proud then. Too proud. I took what I thought to be the bad behaviour of a five-year-old girl to heart; I treated it as a personal vendetta. I realise how absolutely absurd, how totally pathetic that sounds.

The relief I felt at the end of that first school year was unimaginable. On that sunny day in late July, as I stood at my classroom door, and waved goodbye to my first class for the last time you'd have thought I'd have learnt a lesson.

I hadn't.

In every class after that, there was always a 'Nell'. That one child who couldn't sit still, who wouldn't listen, who thought they knew better. I made them pay. All of them. All of those children who didn't show me the respect I deserved.

And then, same door, same classroom, twenty-five years later – yes, you heard me right, twenty-five years later – who should I see in the yard on the first day of school: Nell Davenport, that's who.

I'd know that wild, red hair anywhere, that frown. A small boy leant against her. In contrast to the other mothers and children scattered around the playground, it looked more like he was supporting her than she was supporting him.

I am ashamed to admit that all those old feelings came pulsing back through my veins. Just looking at her made my heart beat faster.

This was going to be a long year.

The boy turned out to be quite a sweet thing: quiet, polite and eager to please. He found it difficult to make friends, but I don't believe it was his own fault as much as his mother's, who dressed him in over-sized, second-hand clothing, let his hair grow far too long and filled his lunchbox with fish and eggs and other foods designed to set the noses then the hearts of other children against him. His father was a dear, though, and most of the dealings I had with them were with him – parents' evenings and the like.

That was ten years ago. I am fifty-seven now and due to retire in just one more year. 'You're retiring early,' people say, and I want to laugh in their faces. Early? I taught for thirty-five years. Thirty-five years! In the same classroom, in the same school, in the same town. A lot happens in thirty-five years – a lot changes.

I check my work email daily; even at the weekend. There's usually some directive from above to respond to, but today was different.

Nell Davenport has invited you to view her blog.

I followed the link. I read the fable of *The Magpie and the Sparrow*, and I agreed wholeheartedly with the ending. Magpie had it coming; he deserved everything he got. My only question was how he had got away with it for so long.

When the phone rang this afternoon, and Rakim from the Department of Education informed me of my suspension pending an investigation, I was ready. And when Frank Hannock from the *Stonebrook Gazette* emailed over a courtesy 'heads-up' on an article they were running tomorrow, the headline didn't surprise me. I swear, I could hear Nell Davenport's sing-song voice reading it out, taunting me.

It had only been a matter of time before she formed a choir and their collective voices sounded, calling me out. Making me pay.

Dalt

Frank had waited until morning this time to tell Dalt. He'd turned up at the gates at 8 a.m. printout in hand. Dalt had buzzed him straight in, away from the ever-fluctuating throng of desperate reporters. They'd sat together over strong, black coffee (decaf for Frank), whilst Dalt tried to make sense of it. The first fable was only the warmup act. Dalt was getting the hang of this now, joining the dots of what little Nell had told him about her childhood, about her life, and matching the characters in the stories to the people and events she had mentioned.

Nell was easy to spot in the fable of *The Magpie and the Sparrow*. The self-assured sparrow, certain in her abilities, lacking charm, social skills and tact but truthful and honest nonetheless – Sparrow had Nell written all over it. And Magpie? Well, Dalt hadn't been given the chance to ascertain who Magpie really was. Frank had told him outright.

'The strangest thing, Dalt,' Frank had said, after Dalt had finished reading the fable. 'Our court reporter got word of a story last week. A local teacher is being investigated following allegations of gross misconduct, spanning thirty-five years of a teaching career. The story is scheduled to go out in the Gazette tomorrow. It's too late to pull it. Our reporter received an anonymous email, giving her a heads up on the case, advising her of the number of complainants and their campaign for a professional conduct hearing. The teacher in question is a woman named Ms Jamison.'

'Huck's first teacher,' Dalt said, picturing the formidable Ms Jamison, her joyless expression and her austere choice of clothing. She'd always struck him as the exact opposite of what a primary school teacher should be like. Was it awful, that the news didn't surprise him – that he felt no shock at the accusations, yet had left his son at school in this woman's care for a year, sensing something yet not acting upon it? It reminded him of when stories broke in the news, outing a celebrity for some morally deviant or socially unacceptable behaviour and his response (often the response of the nation) was one of *'well, we always thought that they were the type.'*

'But here's the rub. I found out this morning that she was Nell's teacher, too,' Frank said.

'What? How do you know that?'

'I did a little digging, after the email arrived this morning. The fable was too much of a coincidence. It was clearly about a teacher. I thought there was a strong chance there was a link between the fable and the allegations of misconduct. So, I went through the archives. Every September for the last thirty years, give or take, the Gazette photographer has visited the school to take a photo of the children who have just started school with their first teacher. Ms Jamison has taught the Reception class for thirty-five years now. That's a lot of photos,' Frank paused. 'And I found Nell.'

'You're not telling me you recognised my wife, at four years of age, in an old photo?'

'No,' Frank chuckled. 'I'm not that good! The children's names were listed underneath the pictures. In the very first photo, the one from thirty-five years ago, I saw her name. Finding her in the photo was a lot harder.'

At this, Frank produced a photo from a file Dalt hadn't even realised he'd been holding and presented it to him.

'Take a look.'

Dalt scanned the photo, curious as to what his wife had looked like as a child, certain he'd be able to pick her out. His eyes traversed the back row, middle row then bottom, taking in all the children, their small, anxious faces, their oversized uniforms, their cautious smiles.

But where was Nell?

'Found her?' Frank sounded almost gleeful.

'Nope. Maybe that one? No.' Dalt continued to pour over the photo, convinced he'd find that crazy red hair and intense stare.

'Give-up?' Frank asked, and before Dalt had time to reply he pointed to the edge of the photo, a blur Dalt had overlooked, but now saw to be the retreating back of a little girl, face turned away.

'Here's your wife. Running away from her first school photo.'

Forgetting himself, Dalt laughed appreciatively. Of course, she wasn't standing nicely, hands clasped neatly in front of her, hair tidily braided, smiling. This was Nell, after all.

'I've checked, it's her.'

Dalt didn't ask how, trusted him.

'Another connection,' Dalt said. 'The police are all about the connections. First Nell to Lucy, now Nell to Ms Jamison. Do they know any of this yet? That you received another email. That you've linked it to the teacher?'

'I've forwarded the email to the police. I've also given them a heads-up about the article we're running tomorrow: Ms Jamison and the allegations of misconduct. At least they won't have to waste time trying to work this one out,' Frank said.

'They'll have a field day with this. It'll add weight to their thinking that Nell is behind it all – the emails and the stories – like Nell's on some kind of personal vendetta to set people to rights.'

'And is she? Do you think they're right?' Frank asked.

Dalt hesitated – the million-dollar question – did he or didn't he, had she or hadn't she?

'I just don't know.'

He couldn't stand to admit that there was so much about Nell he didn't know. So much that she hadn't told him. Was there so much more too that she was capable of?

She'd been gone for three weeks today. Each Saturday that had passed since Nell's disappearance, marking another week of her absence, felt like a bad anniversary. An anti-versary. Another seven notches on the prison cell wall. Another seven days of missing, wondering, questioning, searching.

'And where are the police up to, with their investigation?' the reporters on the gate and the people that called asked daily.

Where indeed?

'No news. The police are doing all they can but with the death of the woman at Guller's Leap they've got a lot on their plate,' he tells them. A stock line – Dalt has realised lately that most of what he says are stock lines, responses that don't require any thinking, words spoken on autopilot, lacking meaning, feeling and even, occasionally, lacking the truth.

This is true though – the police are looking into Lucy Loxton's death. The figure in the photo at Guller's Leap is still to be identified. They are also continuing to investigate Nell's disappearance.

Dalt knows the *Police Missing Person Policy* practically inside out now. He knows that the police have pretty much ruled out that Nell is in the '*lost person*' category. She knew the moors better than any of them. Too well, perhaps? Anyway, search and rescue teams and volunteers have covered every inch of the moor for miles and found nothing. '*Missing under the influence of a third party*', was considered, but there has been no sign of a struggle, no sightings or reports from members of the public and no ransom notes posted through the door – if that ever really happens. No – Nell seemed to have been put into the '*missing person who goes missing voluntarily,*' category, simply for lack of other evidence. The report stated (and Dalt knew this part by heart) that '*this is someone who has control over their actions and who has decided upon a course of action, e.g. wishes to leave home or take their own life.*'

He's not sure where he stands on this. Nell was having a hard time. They were both having a hard time. But taking her own life? No. Not Nell.

Wishes to leave home then. He's had this discussion with Amelia and Huck over and over and over. It feels like all they have done this week is talk. There's suddenly a lot to say. Huck won't hear of it – that Nell's disappearance was her own decision. He's certain she's been abducted, or worse. They were so close. Too close, Dalt wonders? Huck sees it as a personal desertion. Dalt gets why that would hurt, he just can't make sense of it. Has she run away? Was it his fault?

Where did she go? Why did she go?

What did she know?

Huck

From his position on the servants' stairs, it was tricky to hear the conversation between his father and Frank clearly, but he managed to catch the gist of it: another fable, allegations of misconduct, the schoolteacher, Ms Jamison.

Ms Jamison.

Huck hadn't known that he and Mudder had shared their first teacher until earlier this year. How could he have known? Neither woman had ever told him. To the best of his knowledge, Mudder and Ms Jamison had never shown the slightest flicker of recognition or interest in each other during any of their interactions when Huck had been in Ms Jamison's class. Mudder had never allied herself with Huck in that first year of his at school, sharing stories of survival: kindred spirits in the face of a spiteful old bag in elasticated nylon trousers. Nothing. But then that was Mudder. Not one to share.

What was the old crone still doing teaching at her age? She must be in her late fifties now, approaching retirement age surely? Time to stop scaring the bejesus out of small children, time to find a different hobby.

Maybe this was just the little helping hand she needed.

What a coincidence, that someone had spoken up, that all the others had heard and come out of the woodwork. If he had access to social media he'd bet that there were many sites where one could post a comment about something – anything. How they had been abused by a teacher, a person in a position of authority and trust. He imagined how the comment would gain traction and snowball, picking up speed and voices, until that enormous, compacted, raging-for-justice orb crash-landed at the bottom of a mountain in the form of a series of allegations of gross misconduct. Allegations which could not fail to come to the attention of the current school head teacher, the governors and the local board of education.

If he was the betting type, that's what he'd wager might have happened.

And Ms Jamison? She deserved all she got. Cold, intolerant, ignorant. Call herself a teacher? Teachers were supposed to be kind, sympathetic and understanding. She'd never got that memo.

There used to be a shape sorter in Ms Jamison's classroom. A rectangular, wooden toy, with holes in the top. He remembered clearly the colourful, three-dimensional shapes that he would try to push into the holes, the pyramids, cubes and cuboids, how he'd turn them and twist them, until they sat flush. Then he'd knock them through to the other side of the hole with a small hammer and a grunt of satisfaction.

Ms Jamison was like a child with a shape sorter, the children in her class the shapes. She'd twist them and turn them, this way and that. Some shapes fitted easily into the holes and slipped through with no pressure. Some shapes needed a small push in this direction or that, some got wedged a little, needing a firm tap with the hammer to get them through the hole.

And some shapes didn't fit at all.

Like a frustrated child herself, Ms Jamison discarded those shapes, slung them into the far corner of the room, useless, unwanted, unloved. She didn't take time to examine them, to understand them, to question why they didn't fit or find different holes that they would fit into. Outcasts, undesirable, deviant.

Mudder must have been one of those shapes. She wouldn't have fit.

Had Ms Jamison picked up the hammer?

The therapist was Dalt's idea. Huck had overheard the conversation late one night, just after Easter, as he made his way back to his bedroom with a glass of water. He'd paused on the main stairs that met the first-floor landing and his parents' room then continued their way up to the second floor where his own room was. This house afforded many opportunities for listening, unnoticed. Huck knew them all, had honed the act into a craft.

He didn't need to utilise any extraordinary listening skills on a night like this though, when Dalt and Mudder's heated voices could be heard clearly from anywhere on the first floor and possibly further afield than that. He just needed to stay in the shadows in case one or the other of them burst from the room, as was often the case, and stormed down the stairs into the darkness (never upstairs, he need have no fear of that).

'It can't go on!' Did his father even realise he was shouting, Huck wondered?

'I'm sorry.' He heard his mother's voice, quieter but vehement in its sincerity. 'I'm sorry, I'm sorry, I'm sorry.'

Not a good move, Huck thought, not good at all. One apology is fine but apologising over and over sounds insincere. This was the way his parents' arguments played out time after time.

Dalt clearly thought the same.

'You always say that. Every time you say that, but nothing ever changes, does it?' Accusatory, fired-up anger spilling out and over and into.

His mother's voice again, desperate, pleading. 'I'm sorry, I'm sorry, I'm sorry.'

'Stop it. Stop saying it. You need to speak to someone, someone who can help. This is getting out of hand. I've got a number.' This last bit, hushed. Huck had to step closer, strain his ears to hear.

The crash when it came made him jump and high tail it up the stairs to the safety of the shadows. This was new. This was definitely new. This hadn't happened before.

His mother's voice now, whimpering, desperate, pleading. 'I'm sorry, I'm sorry, I'm sorry.'

'Goddamnit, Nell.'

Footsteps, the opening of a door, then a figure appeared in the hall. Mudder. Was he mistaken, or did she glance up at where he was hiding on the stairwell, into the shadows, into the crevices and the dark?

Then she was gone. Huck listened to the soft pad of her feet down the stairs, through the hall, through the kitchen. Far away, he heard the opening and closing of the back door.

He trod lightly on the stairs back to his room and crossed straight to the window, looking out across the moonlit lawn just in time to see Mudder break into a gentle run, feet bare on the spring grass. Luckily for Mudder, the night wasn't cold as she wore nothing but an old t-shirt and a pair of faded shorts.

This too wasn't new. It had happened before, but Mudder's Midnight Dash, as he had begun to call it, was becoming more and more frequent following the rows. He'd followed her once, crept down the stairs and out into the garden, right to the end of the lawn where the grass had turned to seed and sloped down to the river. He'd heard her before he saw her, talking to someone. He couldn't hear the words, only the murmur of her voice, which he followed until he caught a glimpse of her through the veil of the willow tree's branches. She'd paced the perimeter of the inner sanctum of the willow, paced and mumbled, paced and mumbled, but the only word he could catch was 'Toby.'

The therapist had appeared after that. Tall, thin and blonde with a severe ponytail, a fan of white blazers, white fitted trousers and shiny black shoes – medical professional chic slash life-sized cigarette. She wore the smell of antiseptic like a lotion and kept her hands tidily (obsessively, compulsively) on her knees throughout her visits, which were always conducted in the drawing room.

Mudder made no secret of it, rather the opposite. 'The therapist's here!' She would announce jovially, to no one and yet to everyone, as she led the woman ('Katrina, please call me Katrina,') into the drawing room, and closed the door behind them.

Huck asked her, after the first visit, why the woman had come, what they had talked about and whether she would be visiting again?

Mudder dismissed his questions with a wave of her hand.

'She smelt of disinfectant, it was quite distracting,' was all she had said, and Huck had laughed.

Dalt hadn't been laughing when Huck had passed their bedroom door that night, unseen in the shadows.

'I've paid for five sessions. You need to take it seriously, Nell. You need to talk to her.'

The following week The Cigarette was back. Same time, same ponytail, same colour scheme, same smell. Maybe, thought Huck, Katrina was the one who needed therapy.

The women sat in the drawing room, as they did before, in the lounge-style, white cane chairs, a small table between them on which rested two peppermint teas. The floor to ceiling glass window lending them generous views of the gardens. The Cigarette looked like she could be taking part in a shoot for a magazine, all clean, straight lines and crisp folds. His mother didn't.

From his somewhat reclined position (totally horizontal in fact) behind the sofa on the opposite side of the room, Huck could hear their conversation perfectly.

Conversation: a talk, especially an informal one, between two or more people, in which news and ideas are exchanged.

Correction: this wasn't a conversation. It was totally one-sided. From his somewhat reclined position (totally horizontal in fact) behind the sofa on the opposite side of the room, Huck could hear Katrina's calm (patronising), slow (condescending), gentle (really irritating) voice clearly. She'd been blathering on using psychoanalytical jargon ever since she'd arrived. Crap about 'early memories being key', and 'breaking down subconscious barriers.' Huck had to stifle a laugh when Katrina squeezed the words 'repression, disassociation and resistance' all into the same sentence. He couldn't see Mudder from where he lay but was certain that would have generated a cynical smile.

'That said, I want you to think about the adults in your life, the people who you interacted with on a day to day basis at a very early age. Last week we touched on your mother and father. I'd like you to tell me about your school years. What were they like for you? Do you remember your first teacher?'

A pause, so long that Huck had to fight his instinct to protect, to defend. How dare this woman probe his mother like this, this was none of her business. Mudder was fine. Just fine.

'I remember her clearly. Her name was Ms Jamison. She was a bitch.'

Ouch. Mudder would have done that on purpose. She liked to shock. She'd got a two-for-one with that bombshell though. Ms Jamison had been Huck's first teacher too! Why had Mudder never told him that?

'Okay.' A long pause, playing for time, covering surprise. 'Why was that?'

Another pause, Huck braced himself for his mother's sharp, quick tongue and callous sense of humour.

It didn't come.

A deep intake of breath, a slow, measured release.

'She disliked me. I don't know why, but she did, right from the start.' Mudder sounded different, deflated, honest, raw.

'What makes you say that?' Katrina continued to probe.

'I annoyed her. Everything I did annoyed her. She'd get angry, very angry. She said I was rude and unkind, that I couldn't behave. She said I was a mean child who would never have any friends.'

As the words fell, Huck could hear Katrina rummaging in her bag, for tissues he imagined. Was she internally high fiving herself for the breakthrough; would she annotate '*made cry*' in the margin of her notes?

The rummaging stopped when the laughing started. He could imagine Mudder shaking her head and chuckling as she spoke.

'It didn't bother me. She didn't like that about me either. Even when she locked me in the cupboard for a whole morning I didn't mind. It was quiet in there – better than being in the classroom. I quite liked it. I never minded when she shut me in there after that.'

A lengthy silence followed. Huck could only think that The Cigarette was either approaching the realisation that she was way out of her depth, or that she'd given up and left.

'Right. There's a lot to unpick here.' (You're damn right there is, Katrina. I hope you've got steady hands and a free weekend). 'First of all, you do know that what that teacher did to you was wrong – very wrong? That she could stand to get into a lot of trouble for her actions?'

'Could she?' Mudder sounded detached, disinterested, bored. Huck imagined she'd had her fun, spilled the beans and shocked the therapist. She was probably hoping The Cigarette would count her winnings and go home.

'Yes, she could. But it would have to be you that reported her. As part of our confidentiality agreement, I'm unable to disclose anything we discuss to any other party. But seriously, consider making a statement. I know a lot of time has gone by, but this teacher shouldn't be allowed to get away with this.'

Katrina had dropped the therapist voice. Now passionate, determined and fiery, Huck liked her a lot more.

The conversation circled, elements were pulled apart, expanded upon: how often, where, when and why? Mudder, child-like, obedient, gave the answers, but her tone was robotic.

'Tell Dalt. Dalt would want to know,' Katrina had said firmly, when the hour was up, and she stood to leave. Mudder made a throaty noise that Huck interpreted as a, 'Hell no,' and Katrina seemed to accept as an 'Okay, I'll consider it.'

'Same time next week?' and The Cigarette was gone.

Well, Katrina would be pleased now, Huck thought, as Frank and his father said their goodbyes and he slid back up the stairs, pleased that Mudder had spoken up, that Ms Jamison would get her comeuppance.

It wasn't right for people to treat others like that, not right at all. People who go around hurting others deserve to be punished themselves.

Amelia

*W*hose ring was lost, beneath the willow, and what other twisted secrets lay beneath its ancient boughs?

Amelia paused at the end of the sentence and chewed the end
of the pencil contemplatively; a bad habit she knew, but it could
be worse – she could be drinking. She wasn't though, had hardly
touched a drop all week. Writing was focusing her, giving her a
purpose that she'd been lacking for too long. It came at a heavy
price. The loss of her friend. The only hint of redemption lay in
the thought that this journal, Amelia's observations and discoveries
and attention to detail might be the thing that brought Nell back
somehow (Amelia wasn't quite clear on the actual how yet).

Annie Barnes.

Amelia wrote the name and underlined it, more decisively than
she felt, then added,

– *on /off cleaner.*

– *Made claims of heated arguments*

She'd done nothing with this information, hadn't told the police
and hadn't spoken to Dalt or Huck. There was investigating and
then there was prying. This would definitely be crossing that line.

Had Dalt and Nell argued more than any other couple? It was hard to define normal. Especially when one's own relationships involve a good deal of heated discussion (flaming rows). Yes, she'd heard Nell and Dalt arguing a few times, sure, but it was nothing major in her opinion. Never in front of her or Huck, always behind closed doors. But who was she to judge?

Who was she kidding? Of course, she'd judged.

She'd judged Nell's preoccupation with her projects, for one, whether it was running, writing or gardening. She'd noticed Nell pursued the task single-mindedly, obsessively actually, losing all track of time and neglecting everything else: her husband, her son, her appointments. Did they mind? Did Dalt and Huck feel second best? Had Nell always been like this? Amelia thought perhaps she had, but she, Amelia, had been so caught up in her own world that she hadn't noticed it (and as a student, wasn't it okay to eat, sleep and breathe your passion? It just wasn't quite so socially acceptable as a mother and wife with other obligations). Amelia thought, perhaps, Dalt did mind, although he did a jolly good job of keeping quiet about it (in public, at least). She'd seen Dalt's face, when Nell missed another dinner, forgot another appointment, when there was no food at all in the house, and Dalt had to take a trip into town to stock up. A distant expression, as if he was working hard not to care.

But they'd seemed okay. They weren't exactly holding hands and dancing around the kitchen, but they seemed content in each other's company. Amelia would settle for content.

But content didn't make someone disappear. And Dalt wasn't wearing a wedding ring.

She shuddered.

Fragments of ideas that she hadn't allowed in threatened to break free of their half forms and expand into fully fledged thoughts. Or nightmares.

A crazy stalker fan (who'd read Stephen King's *Misery*, obviously) had kidnapped Nell and was holding her hostage, forcing her to write... fables.

She shook her head. This was just ridiculous.

It was all so odd – the death of the woman, Lucy Loxton, at Guller's Leap. The email and the blog post sent from Nell's accounts. If she could only get some answers, to this part of the mystery at least, it might lead to a breakthrough in the investigation, the discovery of Nell, and then, when the smoke had cleared, the publication of her book.

Maybe she was letting herself get carried away, but she knew one thing for certain: she couldn't let the information from Annie Barnes just sit there. It was time to act. Time to find out what Nell and Dalt had been arguing about. Maybe it might shed some light on the ring and Nell's disappearance.

4.30 p.m. She'd spent too much time up here, in her room alone. Most of the day, in fact. It wasn't healthy.

And it wasn't going to help her find any answers.

Amelia made her way downstairs to the kitchen. Huck and Dalt were just coming in through the French doors, their arms laden with lettuce, squash, beans and tomatoes from Nell's vegetable patch. So much to eat. The thought had crossed her mind on more than one occasion: it was almost like Nell had planned this, readied this feast for them, to keep them fed whilst she was gone.

Together the three of them fell to the task of prepping the vegetables.

'There was another email today. To Frank, from Nell's email address,' Dalt said, without even looking up from the squash he was peeling.

'What?' Amelia's own knife clattered noisily out of her hand and onto the work surface. 'Why didn't you tell me earlier?'

She regretted the words as soon as they had left her mouth. Both Dalt and Huck turned to look at her. What right had she got to 'know' anything first, their eyes seemed to say. She felt their contempt washing over her. What was she even doing there, standing in their kitchen, peeling vegetables like she belonged?

Silently reproached, Amelia picked up her knife, aware of the two pairs of eyes upon her, as she self-consciously resumed her work with the beans.

'You've been up in your room all day. Sorry.' Dalt didn't look apologetic. 'There was another fable. Something about a school of birds and a teacher. Frank is on to it already. He said that the paper is running a story tomorrow about a woman named Ms Jamison, a teacher from Stonebrook Primary School, who's been charged with professional misconduct dating back thirty-five years.'

'She was my teacher,' Huck added. 'And she was Mudder's teacher, too.'

'Is that even possible? How old is she?' Amelia asked.

'It's possible. It's true. She's approaching retirement age,' Dalt sighed. 'Frank made the connection. He read the fable, then looked through archived photos of the reception class from thirty-five years ago. He found Nell's name. It can't just be coincidence.'

'What exactly are the allegations? What did she do?' Amelia asked.

'Frank says the paper doesn't go into detail,' Dalt sounded as vague as the article he was describing. 'But it can't be good.'

'And do you think Nell was... abused?' The word was difficult to form, hard to get out of her mouth, ugly and misshapen, a concept well outside her boundaries of comfort.

Dalt looked tired. 'I don't know. Frank's been in touch with the police. He's forwarded them the fable and told them about the allegations of misconduct and the article he's running in the Gazette, but I haven't spoken to them yet. Nell's connected somehow – the fable fits too well with the allegations of misconduct; it seems too much of a coincidence for her not to be involved.'

'Was an email sent to the teacher from Nell's account, inviting her to view the blog?' Amelia knew she sounded interrogatory, but she couldn't help herself.

'I don't know. I've been wondering this myself. I'm just waiting to hear from Officer Henley.'

'This is nuts.' Amelia couldn't hold herself back. What was it she was supposed to do? Count to ten, and ask herself *is what I am about to say valuable or adding value*? Too late for that now. She might as well carry on. 'Do you think it's Nell writing the fables?' She didn't pause for an answer. 'Because it doesn't feel like something Nell would do.' The fables, the revenge, it all sounded crazy – like a plot line from one of Nell's thrillers, not real life.

'I agree. It's crazy. I can't get my head around it either.'

For the first time in weeks, Amelia felt as if she and Dalt were on the same side.

'Nell wouldn't know where to start with all of this,' Dalt said. 'The tech stuff – the blog. She can send an email but that's about her limit. And she's not the kind of person to go missing – to choose to disappear without telling us, to carry out some vengeful attack on people who hurt her years ago. It's not in her nature to do that.'

'None of it makes sense,' Amelia agreed.

'I just want this to be over, however it needs to end. For the search team to find her. Or for her to come home,' Dalt looked the epitome of a man defeated, his strength sapped, his fingers slackened on the squash he was chopping.

'Don't we all?' Huck, washing lettuce at the sink, joined in the conversation at last. His voice was low and he looked on the verge of tears.

Half an hour later, they sat around the kitchen table. The atmosphere in the room was subdued. The salad they'd prepared sat barely touched on their plates. Dalt reached for a glass of water.

'Do you take your ring off when you cook?' Amelia asked, forgetting herself.

Dalt turned sharply, narrowed his eyes.

'I've lost it actually.'

Now was when she should have dug in her pocket, pulled out the ring.

Now was when she should have told him about her conversation with Annie Barnes.

But she didn't.

It was becoming clear that they didn't trust her.

Why should she trust them?

Dalt

When he said his wedding vows, Dalt was saying 'I do' to so much more than the 'seen-it-all' registrar and the two witnesses they'd enticed off the street with the lure of a free, celebratory pint had realised. 'I do' accept your social awkwardness and your hatred of small talk, 'I do' accept your sensitivity to touch and smell and taste. 'I do' accept your aloof behaviour and your need for silence. 'I do.' Quirks and all. He knew what he was signing on the dotted line for. He'd read the small print.

They'd stood facing each other, in front of the registrar in the tiny, bland room, Dalt grinning openly, Nell's expression reflecting their audacity, their spontaneity and recklessness, incredulous that they'd actually done it, gone through with it, and were now husband and wife. He'd squeezed her hand and she'd squeezed his back. We do.

That day was a bubble and they'd floated inside it. After the service, they'd walked and walked, through parks, past museums and coffee houses and book shops and streets they'd never seen before. They covered miles, walking, talking, laughing, observing, both the people they passed and each other, stopping to sit and to watch or to rest.

Back at their tiny flat that evening they'd shared a bottle of wine and some cheese and crackers, 'the wedding breakfast of kings', he had joked. Still in their bubble, still floating light and free but now with a rewarding ache in their legs and a different kind of hunger to appease.

They'd been studying for their degrees when he first noticed her; his, a BA in illustration, hers, creative writing. He'd seen her around campus – she looked detached and reserved. Not his type.

But then they'd been matched by the heads of departments – each creative writing student assigned an illustrator. The challenge: to write and illustrate a short story together.

His gut reaction? Honestly? Disappointment. He'd been hoping for the curly-haired girl who was always laughing, and he'd got the one he'd never even seen smile.

They'd met in the library that first time at 2 p.m. in the study room in the basement.

The meeting had been highly uncomfortable – painful in fact – with long, dense silences, a distinct lack of eye contact and audible sighs (her, all her).

Yet he'd found it oddly compelling.

He'd gone back to his shared house and told his friend about the meeting, exaggerating the interaction to make him laugh, making himself laugh too. But later, at his desk, he found himself reflecting on her, considering her factualness, her certainty and her composure, her individuality and apparent disregard for social conventions such as introductions and handshakes, idle chat and fake smiles.

So totally self-contained, so self-assured. So unique.

He smiled at the memory of the first words she had said to him as he approached the table where she sat.

'Are you Edward Dalton?'

'Yes,' he'd stepped forward, hand outstretched.

She'd ignored it completely, remained seated and looked into the air behind him with contempt.

'I have submitted a formal complaint to my head of department about this module. I do not wish to collaborate on this project. I work best alone and am a competent illustrator as well as a talented writer. I don't need your illustrative skills.'

Dalt froze in the process of pulling out a chair. Was this girl for real? She didn't look like she was kidding, but this was absurd – so rude, so blunt!

He'd unwittingly offered her a bewildered smile and an apology. 'Sorry. I prefer working solo, too. See it as a tick box – something to get over and done with.'

She'd screwed her face up. 'Tick box?' (She clearly thought he was an imbecile). She shook her head.

'As I haven't yet heard back from the head of department regarding my formal complaint, at this time I am still currently obligated to complete the task,' she'd sighed, loudly.

Dalt smiled, couldn't help it. Never before had he felt such a burden on someone. Never before had someone made it so blatantly, obviously clear that he was surplus to requirements – her honesty was refreshing (as well as offensive).

In the end, he'd pulled out the chair (she'd edged hers further away). There'd been no discussion like his tutor had recommended, where they got to know each other and worked out each other's strengths and weaknesses. No Siree.

'I write crime fiction,' she'd said. 'We'll create a crime comic, with a moralistic editorial tone and multi-panel sequence, complete with bold depictions of violence and criminal activity.'

He'd nodded, stunned.

'Meet same time, same place next Thursday? I'll bring the bones of the story, broken down into speech captions for each panel.'

She knew her stuff. He was silently impressed, a huge fan of vintage American graphic crime fiction, this was right up his street, even if she wasn't even in his neighbourhood (city, country or even planet).

'Sounds good,' he'd managed, feeling totally ambushed and he'd pushed his chair out and left, one hundred percent dismissed.

One hundred percent dismissed, and one hundred percent intrigued.

Thursday came around slowly and when it did, their meeting was as painfully awkward as before. If anything, Nell was even ruder and bossier, describing exactly what she wanted him to do, in such detail that he was tempted to tell her to do it herself. He had a feeling that this was exactly what she wanted.

Yet, sitting at his desk that night, reading the story she'd written, envisaging the characters and the layout, he felt invigorated and passionate, keen to do her writing justice with his illustrations, eager to prove that he wasn't as useless as she had him pinned down to be. Something sparked inside him.

He'd been pleased with the end product. He'd worked hard, kept his illustrations clean and tight, colourful and compelling.

Nell seemed pleased too, in her own way.

'I have asked for my formal complaint to be withdrawn,' she'd told him before she'd even viewed his graphics. He'd smiled.

The comic strip was ridiculously well received by both heads of department, who even suggested it should be submitted to a well-respected magazine. Never before had Dalt felt this level of achievement or pride in his work.

Dalt was on a high and he wanted more – of it, of her – of what they could do together.

They'd exchanged phone numbers early on, in the event that one or the other may have to cancel a scheduled meeting. He'd never called though, they'd never cancelled.

He didn't want to phone her now, either.

He found her, instead, in the library, same time, same table. He plonked his bag down on an empty chair and sat across from her. He thought she smiled.

That was the start.

Was this the end?

Or had the end come earlier, and he just hadn't recognised it?

Dalt was not a blogger or a vlogger or a tweeter or a Facebooker, not a social media user of any kind, so when Lucy Loxton approached him in the forecourt of the petrol station one Saturday morning earlier in the year, he had no idea at first what she was talking about.

'Hi, you're Edward Dalton aren't you? Huckleberry's dad?'

He'd spun around, pulling the nozzle from the fuel filler as he did, splattering the toes of his shoes. 'Yes, yes, I am. Sorry – I nearly covered you in diesel.'

The woman smiled. He recognised her, it was a small town after all, but he didn't know her name.

'I'm Lucy. Lucy Loxton. I should be apologising, not you – I'm the one that made you jump,' she smiled as she spoke, showing straight, even, white teeth. Nice teeth.

He was aware that the diesel nozzle was still dripping onto the floor near his shoe. He tilted it upwards. Lucy noticed and hurried to the point.

'You're an artist, aren't you? An illustrator?'

A horn beeped. He nodded, 'Yes.'

'I wonder if you might be able to help me. I write a fashion blog. Sometimes a vlog but mostly a blog,' she laughed, whether at her overuse of the word blog or at his expression, he was unsure.

'I've got an idea to use illustrations to accompany product photos. I don't suppose you'd be interested in a quick chat, over coffee maybe?'

The car honked its horn again, and Dalt turned to jam the nozzle back into the tank.

Little gambles. If he could fill the tank to fifty pounds exactly, then yes, he'd meet her and discuss her ideas – a penny more or a penny less – no. Little gambles were a wimp's way out, he knew, but a problem solving technique he employed on a daily basis all the same.

His index finger continued to pull back the trigger, watching the numbers tick by, waiting and calculating. Now! He'd always had good reflexes, nozzle released, fifty pounds on the nose.

Little gambles.

'Okay, sure. I'm pretty busy at the moment, but I can let you know the next time I'll be in town, see if you're free for a quick chat?'

She smiled again. Those teeth.

'Great. Great – thanks!'

She gave him her number. He saved it under '*Dentist*' to help him remember.

He was a sucker for good teeth.

Sunday 1st September

The Stonebrook Gazette

LOCAL TEACHER INVESTIGATED FOR GROSS MIS-CONDUCT

An investigation is underway after allegations of gross misconduct were made against local teacher and Stonebrook resident, Clare Jamison, who taught at Stonebrook Primary School, previously known as Stonebrook Infant School, for over thirty-five years.

Ms Jamison, who was teaching at Stonebrook Primary when the allegations of misconduct were made this week, has since been suspended whilst the investigation is carried out.

It is thought that the allegations were first made by an ex-pupil on a popular social media site. Other pupils from as far back as 1984 have since come forward to add their experiences of mistreatment.

Clare Jamison has been unavailable for comment. The Teaching Regulation Agency is investigating the claims.

Saturday 7th September

Dalt 2 a.m.

He had stayed awake this time, expecting it. Waiting for it. Frank had received the last two emails at 2 a.m. on a Saturday morning. Dalt felt sure this morning would herald the third. He looked at the glowing green light of the digital clock. Half an hour to go. He was tired, and the words from a call with his mother the previous evening played on a loop in his head. 'Life goes on, Edward,' she'd said, in that no-nonsense voice he recognised from his childhood. 'Life *has* to go on.'

Life does go on. And whilst living in the midst of a missing person investigation wasn't getting any easier, it was becoming more normal. Dalt's feelings towards his wife's absence still fluctuated wildly throughout the course of a day, from absolute, sheer terror at what may have become of her, to anger at her for disappearing and leading a merry dance of them all in her wake. Reflecting the expertise of the Stonebrook police department, whose manpower into the investigation had begun to decrease as the likelihood of Nell being alive and well and typing away on her keyboard had risen, Dalt had downgraded his personal level of worry and anxiety from high (immediate and current danger to Nell's life) to orange (risk of harm possible but not likely). There were even moments where he loitered on green – she's on a beach somewhere with a mojito.

Conversely, whilst the risk of harm to Nell herself had fallen, concerns had risen around the risk of harm to members of the public of Stonebrook. Dalt was no fool and neither was Frank. It looked like people were being picked off, one by one. People who had caused his wife suffering or hardship. According to the Stonebrook police, anyone who had reason to believe they may have done wrong by Nell had reason to fear.

First Lucy Loxton, then Ms Jamison. Who would be next? Dalt was painfully aware that if he was asked that question he wouldn't be able to give an answer.

He knew this for a fact as he had been asked that question.

Officer Henley had worded it as tactfully as possible, but it wasn't easy to tell a man his wife was a suspect in a murder case and a potential witness to another case currently under investigation.

'I'm going to be straight with you, Mr Dalton. We are narrowing our enquiry to focus on the emails that have been sent in your wife's name, and the uploaded blog posts. At this time, our concern lies not only with the whereabouts of your wife, but also with the safety and wellbeing of our community at large.'

Fair enough.

He could see how it may appear to outsiders that this was Nell's retribution, a one-woman crusade to right personal wrongs.

But seriously, Nell, doing this? The thought was so totally and utterly ludicrous that he was finding it difficult to suppress the bubble of manic laughter that threatened to spill out all over Officer Henley's crazy theories. He wanted to burst into Nell's office and tell her all about the ridiculous goings on in Stonebrook, share with her the absurd notion that she stood accused of masterminding her own disappearance, writing childish fables, creating a blog, pushing a woman off a cliff and getting another arrested for gross misconduct.

Nell! As if! He wanted to say, to the police officers, to the reporters, to anyone who would listen. As if Nell, my wife, would be capable of any of that! But he kept quiet. Didn't say it. Out of respect for Lucy Loxton and for Ms Jamison. Out of respect for the lack of evidence.

And there was something else that was holding him back. When the urge to laugh died away, Dalt felt something else in its place. A new hurt, a pain, that kept him wondering, reliving conversations, situations from the last twenty years with his wife. There was a new not-knowing. Not only was Dalt clueless as to where his wife had gone, it appeared he was also clueless about her life – important parts of her life – facts he couldn't dispute. What kind of a husband was he? What kind of husband doesn't realise that his wife has been ostracised by her peers? Bullied, by all accounts. What kind of useless husband doesn't know that his partner of over twenty years was abused as a child by her schoolteacher? A pretty inadequate husband, that's who.

Why didn't she talk to him about any of this stuff? Had she let it build up inside, let it fester and eat at her? Could there be any truth in any of the accusations being made of her? He was willing to admit there was a lot he didn't know. Maybe he didn't know what she was capable of either.

He'd known something was wrong. It had been building the way it always did, with increasing episodes of Nell's absence. Preoccupied with writing to the point of obsession, she'd spend days holed up in her study. She wasn't eating unless reminded, and even then only picked at her food absentmindedly, physically present but mentally far away. There had been arguments, too.

He'd persuaded her to see a therapist.

'She's beginning to open up', were the words Katrina had used on the last occasion she had visited. With hindsight, maybe opening up hadn't been a good thing. There'd been a story in the news just this week – a volcano in New Zealand had erupted, killing handfuls of tourists who had paid to climb up to its crater and peer into the depths. Was Nell like that volcano, persuaded to reveal her true self, only to explode and harm the people around her? Maybe the therapist had been a bad idea and Nell's feelings would have been better off staying buried deep inside her, if this was the effect opening up had on the world. Maybe, like the volcano, it was dangerous to get too close to his wife.

If it was Nell writing the stories, sending the emails, updating the blog, then where the hell was she? That was the biggest problem with this line of thinking. There was no trace of her – no sightings and no cash withdrawals from her bank account. How could someone just disappear like that? Or more to the point, how could Nell just disappear like that?

The police were no closer to tracking down the location of the sender of the emails, or the creator of the blog. Who were these computer nerds anyway? Hadn't Microsoft got a nine-year old kid on their team? Stonebrook police seriously needed to up their game.

2 a.m. Dalt pressed *F5* and refreshed his screen. Frank had promised he would immediately forward to Dalt and the police any messages he received.

A new envelope appeared in his mailbox.

From: Frank Hannock
Subject: Fwd: The Cat and the Piglets.

The Cat and the Piglets

Once upon a time there was a farm, high on top of the moor, exposed to the sun and the wind and the rain. The farm was home to many animals, including Mother Cat and Mother Pig.

Mother Pig slept in a pig sty with her six piglets. The pig sty had a tin roof to keep it warm and dry. Mother Pig and her piglets had a whole field to roam in, full of lush green grass with trees and mud holes for shade from the hot sun.

Mother Cat lived in the farmhouse with her three kittens and the farmer and his wife. She liked to be cosy and warm and spent a good deal of her time preening herself on the rug in front of the fire.

One hot summer's day, Mother Cat and her kittens took a walk through the fields searching for tasty mice to eat. They passed Mother Pig and her piglets, wallowing in a pool of mud in Pig's field.

'Mother Pig is a disgusting creature,' Mother Cat told her kittens. 'Mother Pig is smelly and unhygienic. Mother Pig enjoys rolling in mud and digging in the dirt.'

Mother Cat and her kittens stalked past Mother Pig and her piglets, their tails held high in the air, keeping to the short grass and avoiding the mud.

One of the piglets, the smallest of the litter, had stopped at the edge of the mud hole to listen to Mother Cat as she passed. The little piglet looked at her mother, rolling in the mud, and thought of what cat had said. 'Mother Pig is smelly and unhygienic. Mother Pig is a bad example to her piglets.'

Piglet took a step away from the mud hole. She didn't want to be dirty and smelly like her mother. She would listen to cat.

Mother Pig and her piglets spent the day in the mudhole. As the sun went down, they made their way back to their sty.

The littlest piglet tried to trot along with her mother, but soon had to stop. Her back was itchy and sore. Her skin was dry and cracked. She did not feel very well at all.

Mother Pig turned to wait for her and noticed the little piglet's burnt red skin and her dry snout.

'You're sunburnt,' she told her littlest piglet. 'Why didn't you come and lie in the mud with us to keep the sun from burning your skin?'

Piglet felt ashamed. 'I heard Mother Cat say that you were dirty and smelly. I didn't want to be dirty and smelly too. I wanted to be clean like Mother Cat.'

Mother Pig shook her head sadly. 'We are not dirty and smelly. We are just as clean as Mother Cat. We lie in the mud to stop our skin burning. Mother Cat doesn't understand pigs. Mother Cat doesn't know of what she talks.'

Later that day, Mother Cat and her kittens walked back past the pig sty. Mother Cat saw the littlest piglet, squealing with pain and red from the sun. Mother Cat shook her head in disgust, despairing at Mother Pig's poor mothering skills, smug that she was so much wiser.

There are two sides to every story.

Dalt

Dalt opened the attachment, speed read the story.

It hit him straight away. Goddamnit, the social worker, why hadn't he thought of her before? Angered by his own stupidity, he brought the palm of his hand crashing to his forehead, once, twice, three times. Joan Matthews, harbinger of months of anxiety, worry and doubt. The woman who had nearly stolen their son. The woman who did not end up taking Huck but took something else instead – Nell's spirit.

Nell had been broken by the case after the incident with the finger. They'd lived for months in limbo (a little like now) unsure whether their son would be taken from them but powerless to stop the wheels of the system turning. Thank god for that doctor, the one who spoke up at the hearing and ultimately saved their family. They'd kept their boy, but Nell had taken months to recover. The repercussions were far-reaching. Life-changing. The ripples sent out by the event forming a tsunami on their shore.

It became clear that there would be no more children. The chaotic household he'd once envisaged was not going to become a reality.

'I nearly lost the one I had,' Nell said, whenever he brought the subject up. 'I'm sorry. I'm not capable. I don't think we should have any more.'

No amount of persuading could talk her into it.

Nell had become more isolated than ever yet at the same time, more self-sufficient. She reminded him of the land girls in the war, out in any weather, digging, planting, and sowing the vegetable garden like her life depended on it. She'd bought chickens, built a run for them with her own bare hands. Wrung their necks with them too, when the time came. She'd made her own bread, repaired all their clothes. He hadn't realised at first what the show of self-sufficiency was all about, had seen it as a hobby or a distraction. Now he could see it for what it was: a show of not needing anyone or anything, a declaration of Nell's lack of trust in the outside world.

She still trusted Dalt though. Dalt and Huck.

It had fallen to Dalt to run the truck into town for milk and supplies that couldn't be grown or made at home. He didn't mind. Truth be told, there were often times he felt isolated and lonely too, in that big house high upon the moor, his wife consumed by her projects, his son her little shadow.

Joan Matthews – Mother Cat – making poor judgements about other people's behaviour. She'd nearly ruined their life, but Nell had rebuilt them stronger.

Nell had tightened her arms around the three of them and pulled them in closer. Locked the door and kept out the world. She'd kept them safe.

And what of Joan Matthews? Where was she now, Dalt wondered? Should they be concerned for her welfare? Unless Officer Pearson and Officer Henley had really done their homework (which Dalt somewhat doubted) the officers were unlikely to be able to make sense of this most recent email. He needed to speak to them urgently and to fill in the gaps. Picking up the phone, he dialled Officer Henley's private number. She picked up on the first ring.

Huck

F unny, how things change. In term time, a Saturday morning for Huck would have meant a much longed for lie-in, a protest against the early starts that school demanded. And now it was September: term time again – the school holidays were over. But Huck hadn't gone back. The head teacher had phoned, had spoken to Dalt, was aware of the situation. Exemptions had been made. Exceptional circumstances. Blah-de-blah-de-blah.

Saturday mornings held a different routine now.

7 a.m. and the newest fable appeared on Mudder's blog, as if by magic.

Huck heard his father on the phone downstairs. Taking the servants' stairs, he entered the kitchen just as Dalt finished the call and laid his phone down on the kitchen counter with a sigh.

A movement at the kitchen table – Amelia held a mug out towards Huck, gesturing at the cafetiere. He took the cup, filled it and leaned against the sink.

'Here – there's been another fable.' Dalt handed a printed sheet to Huck. 'I've just been on the phone to Officer Henley. They're on their way over.'

Huck quickly read the fable of *The Cat and the Piglets*.

'I've worked it out,' Dalt said, as soon as Huck glanced up. 'I'm annoyed that I didn't think of it sooner. I don't know if you remember this, Huck, but when you were small, maybe two or three, you had an accident in the garden. Mudder was digging...'

'The tip of my finger,' Huck interrupted, holding up his hand to show the scar. 'Of course, I remember. Why's that matter now?'

'You know that bit of the story,' Dalt said, as gently as Huck could ever recall him speaking. 'It's what happened next that you might not. The Doctor who stitched you up alerted social services to the situation. He'd got the wrong end of the stick, thought Mudder had been negligent,' Dalt paused. Was he trying to gauge Huck's response?

'A social worker began to visit. You know how Mudder can be with strangers? How she can come across as rude? Well, the social worker misread the situation, she thought that you weren't safe here. She thought she was protecting you,' Dalt paused again, for longer this time. Who was *he* trying to protect here, wondered Huck?

'She recommended that you should be put into care.'

Amelia gasped.

'But I wasn't. Why not?'

'There was a hearing. A panel of experts were called to discuss the evidence against Mudder. A young doctor spoke in defence of Mudder's behaviour. The case was dropped.'

'I never knew this. Why did Nell never tell me?' Amelia sounded indignant. Why she should have known this, when it was clearly private family business was quite beyond Huck.

'We tried to put it behind us,' Dalt said quietly. 'Nell didn't want to be reminded of it. And also, Amelia, to be quite honest, there were a lot of years when you and Nell weren't in touch. A lot happened in that time. A lot that you don't know about.'

Good answer, thought Huck, very good answer.

Amelia looked suitably chastised.

'But, seriously, that's shocking. How could anyone think that Nell was a bad mother?'

'You know how she is as well as anyone. Nell's different. We all know that. She can be blunt, sometimes to the point of rudeness. She struggles to engage with people. The way she acts, the things she does... people thinks she's odd. People are scared of what they don't understand, and a lot of people don't understand Nell, so they're afraid. Their fear manifests itself in different ways. The social worker was just another person who didn't understand.'

'I'm sorry, I don't understand.' Amelia looked totally confused. 'What has this got to do with the fable that Frank received this morning?'

'The story is about parenting,' Dalt plucked the printed sheet out of Huck's hands and offered it to Amelia. The moral was that there are two sides to every story. It has to be about Joan Matthews – the social worker. She saw what she wanted to see, an incompetent parent. There was another side to the story, only she couldn't see it,' Dalt added.

But they were all seeing it now, weren't they? All these things they'd missed, brought to life, examined under a flood-lit, human-life-sized microscope. Huck watched his father sag against the counter he was leaning on. He looked terrible. Worn and old.

And lost.

But not as lost as Mudder, he found himself thinking, resentfully.

It was Dalt who had gone astray first. Only he had been lucky. He had managed to find his way back.

Joan Matthews

Keeping children safe was my number one priority. Every morning before going to work I would look in the mirror, look myself straight in the eye, and repeat the words of Rosa Parks, '*You must never be fearful about what you are doing when it is right.*' Such was my conviction; such was my determination to serve and protect.

Did I look myself in the eye the morning I signed the written notice to start care proceedings in the case of Huckleberry Dalton? Have I looked myself in the eye ever since?

Huckleberry Dalton. Not a name one could forget in a hurry. I've re-read the file so many times I have the details and the dates committed to memory. Huckleberry Dalton, referred to me by Dr Warner, of the Stonebrook General Medical Practice, on the twenty-seventh of June, 2006, aged two and three months, following an incident in the family garden in which his mother chopped off the tip of his index finger on his right hand with a spade.

Dr Warner's notes, in the manner of many Doctors, were hard to decipher. Amongst the scribbles were the words, '*guarded,*' '*withdrawn*' and '*unapologetic,*' used to describe the child's mother, Mrs

Nell Davenport, when her son was being examined and treated for the injuries sustained to his finger.

Doctor Warner (General Practitioner for many years and a man I highly respected for his strong, traditional family values) had continued on to describe Mrs Davenport's behaviour as '*inattentive / negligent?*'

To quote directly from that first correspondence, Dr Warner had written: '*I have serious doubts regarding Mrs Davenport's ability to parent, and therefore serious concerns for the welfare of the child. It is our duty to intervene and prevent the child suffering further harm.*'

A call to arms if ever there was one.

I was assigned the role of Lead Social Worker, a position that came with a crushing weight of responsibility. God forbid anything should happen to a child under my care. It was my duty to formulate a detailed child protection plan and ensure its implementation.

But first, I needed to meet Huckleberry Dalton. I needed to visit the family home and assess the boy. Observe the mother. I needed to obtain a full understanding of the family history and secure information from any other agencies involved. I needed to see the family interact with my own eyes and plan any interventions that needed to be made.

Rosa Parks had been with me when I'd stood in front of the mirror that morning, fearless, bold and ready for battle, my brown checked jacket and matching skirt pressed and stiff, my heels tapping intimidatingly on the wooden floorboards. The way one looks says a lot about a person. I poked one last pin into my bun, ensuring not a hair was out of place, then picked up my black leather briefcase before addressing my reflection sternly, '*You must never be fearful about what you are doing when it is right.*'

Rosa was still with me when I pushed the heavy gates aside and stood on the doorstep of Moordown House for the first time and rang that tarnished old bell, the force of her passion inside me.

They'd been advised I was coming, as was protocol. I didn't agree with it. In my opinion, it would be better to conduct spontaneous spot checks, to catch people unawares and unprepared, no time to pretend. But I was resigned to saving that battle for another day.

Edward Dalton opened the door. He had featured surprisingly little in Doctor Warner's report. I dredged up the words I recalled the good doctor using: '*amiable, compliant and protective.*'

Mr Dalton had greeted me in a polite if somewhat cool manner. I was used to this in my line of work. He led me through to the drawing room.

Nell Davenport stood to greet me. I offered my hand, but she didn't take it.

'Good afternoon, Mrs Davenport,' I began. 'I believe you know why I am here. You have received a copy of the report from Doctor Warner. It is my duty to complete an assessment of your child and your family.'

She wouldn't even look at me. Her eyes flew around the room, above me, to the side of me, but never for a second did they rest on me. I identified it immediately as skittish, guilty behaviour.

'We got the letter,' she began. 'I believe there has been a misunderstanding. It was an accident, Huck's finger. Just an accident.'

The defence of a person who is guilty, I thought to myself, as I laid my briefcase flat on a table, pulled out my clipboard and pen and immediately began taking notes. Intimidating her. I was not about to stand by and let this remorseless woman mistreat this powerless infant, whilst her naïve husband turned a blind eye.

And still she stood, hands on hips, all pointed angles and garish, mismatched clothes. Had the woman no pride? Pretty enough but doing herself no favours swamping herself in that enormous cardigan and floor length skirt, trailing along the floor after her, picking up dirt no doubt.

'Mudder?'

The boy appeared from behind a piano, using the furniture to balance himself, a shock of red curls about a china delicate face, improperly dressed in an oversized t-shirt and nappy, with his legs and feet bare, an urchin Michelangelo.

'Mudder.' His arms reached out to her but he wasn't crying, or even pleading. His voice lacked emotion of any kind.

She didn't answer him or respond to him in any way. *Cold. Uncaring. Neglectful.* I jotted a note on my pad.

I walked towards him and noted the way he flinched. Was he afraid of me? Afraid of women because of his mother? I dropped to one knee in front of him on the blue and cream Oriental rug and as I did so a cloud of dust rose up and entered my nose and throat making me cough. The child stared. Mental note: *house unclean, an unsuitable environment for a child to crawl around in, hands in dust and dirt, then into his mouth, the way of all toddlers. A recipe for disaster.*

'Hello Huckleberry. My name is Miss Matthews. I've come to visit you and your mummy and to have a little chat.'

Nothing. No response.

'Where are your toys? What do you like to play with?'

Still nothing.

The child continued to stare, as did his mother – ogling me, the pair of them. I turned my attention to her.

'Do sit down, Mrs Davenport.'

Thankfully she did, although she certainly didn't look comfortable, perched on the edge of a straight-backed chair like she was poised to leap off and scarper at any moment. There was something most odd about this woman, with her lack of effort to make small talk, her shifty looks and her clear disdain for my presence. Haughty and arrogant, she clearly thought I had no business in that grand house of hers. A house like that hides many secrets I can tell you. Most mothers I visited would be spewing out their stories by now, desperately trying to demonstrate their excellent parenting skills in an attempt to rewrite the script, to get me off their case. Nell Davenport was quite the opposite. So composed, so steely, so indifferent. So guilty.

I opened my briefcase and pulled out a small cotton bag.

'Would you like to see my bag of tricks?' I asked the child.

He nodded uncertainly. He was most likely unused to being played with, communicated with even. I needed to take it slowly.

The bag contained four puppets, supposed to represent a family: the father, a mother and two children. I could work magic with these four toys, moving them this way and that, making them speak and show emotion. I'd seen the eyes of the most stubborn, uncommunicative children light up and witnessed barriers break down. I'd watched children who were mute play with the toys in a way that provided me with a thousand words.

What I'm trying to say is, they were my secret weapon. They had never failed me so far.

I held the bag of puppets out towards Huckleberry. With his one free hand, the other holding the sofa's edge to keep himself upright, he grasped the head of the one of the puppets poking out of the bag and tugged. No good. The puppet was stuck. Removing the hand that held onto the sofa, he added it to the top of the puppet's head and pulled again. Determined, I noted, with the ability to problem solve; a child already used to fending for himself.

A popping, ripping, tearing noise and the child was falling backwards, crashing to the floor, a wooden stick and an exuberance of coarse brown wool in his hand. Dear Lord, the child had decapitated one of the puppets. I looked down at the bag in my hand where its torso remained, grotesque and ruined.

These dolls had served me for five years. Handmade, by a puppeteer in Oxford, I'd bought them shortly after qualifying, an entire month's pay they'd cost me. An investment, I'd thought at the time.

The child had begun to cry.

'Now, now.' I used what I thought of as my Mary Poppins' voice, my calm-yet-assertive, matter-of-fact voice that disguised the annoyance I felt at the violent beheading of my prop. Ever the professional. 'There's no use crying over spilt milk is there?'

That was when she rose out of her chair, and towered over us both, scrutinising the scene of the incident – the puppet's severed head and her weeping son.

'He's crying about the puppet,' she told me. Told me – *me* of all people – the one person standing in this room with a masters in child psychology and five years on the job experience.

'I know he is crying about the puppet,' I spoke through clenched teeth; the woman was an imbecile. Perhaps that was the root of the problem – processing issues, or something similar.

'You told him not to cry over the spilt milk, but he's not crying over milk. He's crying because the puppet is broken.'

In all my years in this job, I'd never been belittled like this. Oh, she thought she was smart, this one, ridiculing me, making me look stupid.

That was the moment I vowed to get that little boy out of there.

I visited weekly. My notes grew into a file, with subdivisions: *Interactions with Son*, *Interactions with Husband*, *Evidence of Neglect*. And so on and so forth.

With each visit, a snippet more evidence for the file. The child was naked, running in the garden on a hot day – he would get burnt or get stung or worse. The child wasn't potty trained; she was waiting for him to 'be ready to do it himself.' Whoever heard of such a thing? Lazy. Neglectful. The child barely spoke. Hardly surprising, I wrote, when his mother didn't communicate with him. Evidence building up, up, up. Words repeated over and over: *unsuitable, neglectful, unconventional, and harmful.*

Did I really believe it? Was I really channelling the spirit of Rosa Parks, demanding change and justice for the wronged and abused, or was I ploughing ruthlessly onwards down the only path I had chosen to see, so certain that what I was doing was right, a blinkered horse hauling a dead weight, unable to turn around, to go back?

Or did my actions stem from anger? And did that anger stem from my own insecurities? From the moment I entered that house, I felt lesser, insignificant. Did she make me feel small, with her superior, cool demeanour and her blunt manner, with her big house and her obvious success?

Status anxiety – that's what a psychologist on one of those morning television chat shows called it. The fear of being perceived as unsuccessful – a destructive behaviour, I realise now, that came close to ruining the lives of a family I was put in a position to help.

The television is on all day in this place, I have to hear it, whether I want to or not. I'm powerless now – like she was then. Karma. I heard about that on the television, too.

I submitted my report. I recommended that the boy be removed from the family home.

It was vetoed. A *Section 47* enquiry was carried out. A specialist police officer interviewed both mother and child, and an independent doctor carried out a medical examination. My findings were presented, alongside theirs, at a child protection hearing called to assess the case. My report was dismissed. No cause for concern noted. The child was not thought to be at risk of significant harm, or indeed, any harm at all; he was not neglected or abused or mistreated in any way, according to the experts brought in to assess the case alongside me.

I remember the independent doctor well – a young woman – articulate and passionate. Holding my report in her hand, she addressed the attendees of the hearing, as if she were giving evidence in court at a murder trial. *'A naïve and incorrect interpretation of reality,'* she called my report. *'A blatant misunderstanding and wrongful analysis of actions and intent.'* A fancy way of saying my report was a load of old rubbish – that I'd got it all wrong. She turned on her computer to present her own report, this knowledgeable young doctor, a PowerPoint, would you believe it?

Autism.

The title on the first page shook my foundations, tore at my blinkers. I began to see.

She'd recognised it straight away, she'd said, but then, she was fresh out of training, filled to the brim with all those new-fangled ideas and studies. With her computer presentation and her words, this doctor ripped my observations apart. Nell Davenport was a *'classic case'* apparently, exhibiting a lack of understanding of social rules and conventions, having difficulty expressing herself to professionals and often appearing rude or uncaring. Apparently, I had *'totally misunderstood Nell Davenport's behaviour'*. I had judged her to be an inadequate parent, when in fact she wasn't. She was a good mother – I just hadn't seen it.

Blind, or blinded?

A happy ending. No harm done, right?

Wrong.

Stonebrook was a small community. Word got out. Word got around.

Life wasn't easy for either of us after that. In fairness, it wasn't easy for Nell Davenport before, but it certainly got worse when whispers passed like smoke between lips as ignorant as my own. The townsfolk didn't understand. They didn't care. To them she was just 'odd.'

And as for me, my career was over, my credibility gone. I'd recommended a child be removed from his family home and be committed to care and I had got the entire thing wrong. Colleagues offered platitudes: '*It could have happened to any of us.*' '*Put it behind you and move on.*' '*See it as a learning experience.*' But I couldn't. The terrible thing, the worst thing of all wasn't the fact that I'd nearly taken a child away from his innocent mother, it was my own pride, my dismay at losing face and my fall from grace.

How selfish I was.

Karma. There was a whole television programme on it last year. Good karma: a doctor who saved the life of a dangerously ill baby was saved in return when he crashed his car, some twenty years later. The paramedic, his rescuer, was the man he had saved all those years ago. Bad karma: a guy waving around a gun, threatening to hurt people, misfires and shoots himself in the foot.

Karma: a woman trying to take away another woman's child loses something of considerable value to herself: her health.

The stroke happened later that year. They say stress may have caused it. Personally, I think karma caused it, but apparently that's not a medically acclaimed attributing factor. It should be. I've learned my lesson. They thought my speech might return, with physiotherapy, with therapists, with time. It hasn't. Neither has my strength. My notes describe me as '*gross motor function classification system IV. Walking ability severely limited even with assistive devices.*'

Karma.

Years ago, I saw her on television too. Like I said, it's always on. Most of us 'facility users' can't tell them to turn it off. We're parked up in front of it, blankets thrown over our knees, heads held straight by foam supports and the padding on the backs of our wheelchairs. We can't look away; we are forced to see what's in front of us, to look it in the eye.

Karma.

She looked well, Nell Davenport. She was at a book signing, sitting at a table piled high with books. She'd done well for herself. The queue stretched out the door. She was quick – efficient. She didn't waste time with chit chat. Didn't even look up from her table. Some might call that rude. I wouldn't.

Then a few weeks ago, she appeared on the screen again, on the news this time. They say she's gone missing. My first thought was for the boy. I hope he finds her.

The strangest thing, though. On a Thursday morning the readers come. Volunteers – teenagers mostly – armed with smiles and books and enthusiasm. They sit with us, chat to us and read us a story.

Today is Thursday and they were here. A boy sat with me. I'd not seen him before, but that's nothing new. He wore a black cap and blue shorts. He told me it was hot outside.

He pulled a book from his backpack. *Aesop's Fables*, it was, but the story he read to me wasn't one I had heard before. It was a story about a pig and her piglets and a cat and her kittens; a story of parenting and judgements. A story of me and of her, a cat and a pig. A story all too familiar.

He read well, the boy, his voice strong and clear. He didn't stop when my tears began to fall. He didn't stop when my nose and throat filled with mucus which my useless body couldn't clear away. He must have read that same story three, four times over, as I writhed silently beside him.

He left abruptly. They gave me an injection to relax me. Agitated, they said I was – upset. They suggested I type my thoughts down. I can do that, you see. It's the only thing I can do now.

And so here they are, and I feel a little better for getting that off my chest. I hope he finds his mother, that boy. She was nearly taken from him once. It shouldn't happen again.

Amelia

O nly 7.30 a.m. and the surprises were coming thick and fast (albeit surprises more akin to treading on an unexploded landmine than a *surprise it's your birthday* party). This latest revelation about the social worker recommending that Huck be removed from Nell and Dalt's care was mind-blowing. It bothered Amelia immensely that Nell had never spoken to her of these events – the incident with Huck in the garden, the social worker, and the death of her brother, too. Nell had been opening up to her in the last few weeks before she disappeared, but Dalt was right. There were too many years that Amelia hadn't been in touch, years when Amelia had kept her distance – jealous – of Nell's family, of Nell's success. Amelia had failed her. She should have been a better friend. A better person.

You had to admire Nell though, if this was her doing. An eye for an eye, and all that. Soon the whole town would be blind.

There had been a shift in Amelia's thinking at some point this morning, a movement towards the idea that Nell was alive and well, hiding away, a cat on her lap which she stroked absentmindedly, a twisted smile on her face, in an evil supervillain sort of way.

Such a masterful plan, a stroke of genius really, to just vanish, leaving everyone questioning, wondering, worrying. Then, to strike – to get even, to make reparations for those years of torment and anguish at the hands of these fools (was she getting a little dramatic? Perhaps, but still, what a masterful plan indeed. What a clever woman Nell was).

Finding this social worker, Joan Matthews, seemed more important right now than locating Nell.

They needed to find her and make sure that she was alright.

Huck

J oan Matthews was not alright. She had died of a massive stroke on the evening of Friday 6th September. Arriving at Moordown shortly after 8 a.m., Officer Pearson and Officer Henley divulged the shocking news.

They hadn't been able to connect the dots without help. His father had phoned Officer Henley's personal number, as she'd requested, just after 2 a.m. upon reading the latest fable himself. Dalt's confidence in identifying Joan Matthews (Mother Cat) had been all the assistance the officers had needed. They'd quickly traced her to a care home just outside of Stonebrook and the officers had used their authority to obtain the necessary information.

Hats off to the officers; they'd upped their game. They'd swapped shifts apparently, so that they would be on duty at 2 a.m. when a new fable might be emailed to Frank. Were they enjoying this, Dalt wondered? Was it like a crime thriller come true? Did they feel like Morgan Freeman and Brad Pitt in *Seven*, following the clues, solving the case?

'Such a strange coincidence,' Amelia was saying. 'Dying now, of all times. Just when we want to speak to her.'

Amelia's words amused him. How terribly rude of Joan Matthews, dying like that – so thoughtless.

But Officer Henley had nodded her agreement and helped herself to a biscuit. Seated around the kitchen table, Huck, Dalt, and Amelia watched as Officer Pearson counted out mugs, and poured them all more coffee. These two were certainly starting to make themselves feel at home.

'We're going to the nursing home next,' Officer Pearson said. 'There are a few more questions we'd like to ask, although it doesn't look like anything of a suspicious nature has occurred. Apparently, Mrs Matthews was seated in the communal television area yesterday evening when she had the stroke. Death by natural causes. The timing must just be one of those strange coincidences.'

'I listened to a radio phone-in about strange coincidences once,' said Amelia. 'It was unbelievable. A mother had tried to call her son's phone number, but misdialled, and called the number of a phone box instead and who should be walking past, who should answer, but her son!'

Amelia may have misjudged her audience. Perplexed faces stared back at her, but Huck agreed she was right about one thing. This was one of those unbelievable coincidences.

'We know there's a rough pattern; first the fable emailed to Frank in the early hours of a Saturday morning. Then the fable appears on Nell's blog. Then the individual named in the letter is brought to justice in some way. Although this time, the events didn't happen in quite that order. Ms Matthews had passed away before the fable was sent to Frank.'

When Officer Henley paused for breath, Officer Pearson immediately picked up the baton.

'There's a difference with the emails too. Lucy Loxton and Ms Jamison were both emailed a link to the blog from Nell's email account. But there was no link emailed to Joan Matthews. We'll ask the nursing home if Ms Matthews had an email account. I'm guessing it is unlikely.'

'But if the purpose of the fables is to bring someone to justice – to make them understand the impact of their actions – then what was the purpose of this fable? It doesn't sound like Ms Matthews would have seen it.' Dalt looked confused. 'Lucy Loxton obviously saw her fable. And Ms Jamison read the fable meant for her. They knew they were being held accountable for their actions. What was the point, if the social worker never saw the fable? Do you really think it's a coincidence that she's dead?'

Heads nodded around the table.

'A very good point,' Officer Henley agreed. 'It seems very odd that Ms Matthews died yesterday. But when we spoke to the woman in charge of the care home this morning, she said that Ms Matthews had been unwell since Thursday.' She must have noted the unconvinced expression on Dalt's face. 'An autopsy will be performed, to determine the exact cause of death, of course.'

'Maybe she did see the fable! Maybe Nell sent the fable in a letter?' Amelia interjected excitedly.

'Oh, so you're accusing her now are you?' Huck felt a sudden burst of anger towards Amelia. Was this a game to her? It was Nell Davenport, in the care home, with the letter opener.

Amelia reddened. 'No, I... I was just thinking out loud. Sorry. I'm not blaming Nell. I just got carried away,' Amelia shook her head. 'Sorry.'

The apology hung in the warm air of the kitchen like a bad smell.

'Look, let's focus on what we know,' said Officer Henley. 'Whilst the acts of writing the fable and publishing the post online seem relatively innocuous, there have obviously been significant repercussions to the individuals involved: two deaths and a pending court case. Whilst the likelihood of risk to Nell has been downgraded, our duty of care lies with protecting the people that are being targeted.'

'What are you saying?' Dalt brought his mug down so suddenly that coffee sloshed violently onto the wooden tabletop.

'Look – we're not saying Nell is responsible for these acts. In fact, there is no direct evidence to link Nell to the death of Lucy Loxton, or that of Joan Matthews,' said Officer Pearson, 'and we're still investigating who filed the complaints about the schoolteacher. But what we *are* saying, is that the timing of these events is all most unusual.'

Huck watched his father, his face contorted into a tight ball of anger, shake his head from side to side, but the gesture seemed to go unnoticed by the officers.

'We need to take pre-emptive action. Think about who might be next. Is there anyone else, that any of you can recall, that might have upset Nell in any way?' asked Officer Henley.

Huck looked at his father who looked deep in thought. Dalt shook his head again and shrugged his shoulders. Eyes turned to Amelia. Another shake of the head. Then the focus was on him.

'Sorry, no.' To his ears, his own voice sounded fake, insincere, hollow.

'This is important. People are getting hurt. Let us know immediately if you think of anything. Anyone.' Officer Pearson glanced at his watch and nodded to Officer Henley who closed her notebook and put it into the briefcase at her feet.

'We're due at the care home. We'll be in touch if we have any new information.'

'Is that it then? A few questions about a social worker who visited over a decade ago, and you're off?'

All heads turned to look at Dalt.

'What are you doing to find her? Are you even looking?'

Huck jumped at the volume of his father's voice. It was rare for Dalt to get angry, let alone shout so hard that spittle flew out of the corners of his mouth.

'Or are you just blaming her? Accusing her? What if she's being held by someone, some freak who thinks this is a game? What if she's injured? Tell me you're doing something apart from ringing care homes and analysing fairy tales!'

'Mr Dalton, we are doing all that we can,' Officer Pearson kept his voice level. 'The search teams are still being deployed – the helicopter went up again today, and the search and rescue crew have been out again with the dogs since first light. Yes, we've had to scale down the search, but believe me, it's still happening.'

'Mr Dalton, we are lucky it's still happening. The situation is being reviewed daily and let me tell you, as new information has been received, we've had to fight tooth and nail for the continued deployment of those specialist agencies,' Officer Henley's eyes narrowed and her expression hardened as the volume of her voice rose. 'We are doing all we can to keep the search for Nell a priority. In light of the continuing developments, it has not been easy. So please trust us to do our jobs.'

Huck could see his father was shaking as he brushed past the officers, pushed the screen door aside, and stormed into the garden. Huck watched his back as he strode towards the river, the same path forged by his mother all those weeks ago.

Officer Henley placed a hand on his arm.

'Look, I'm sorry. I shouldn't have spoken like that. I know how hard it is for you all. I promise you, we will keep doing everything we can to help find your mum.'

'You might have to find my dad too, the way things are going,' Huck joked wryly.

Both officers smiled.

'He'll be back when he's cooled off. And we'll be back tomorrow. Let us know if there's any news before then and we'll do the same.'

Huck walked the officers to the front door. His palms were so sweaty he struggled to turn the doorknob.

'Thanks.'

As the officers crunched across the gravel to their car, Huck's thoughts turned to the moor, to his missing-in-action, techno-in-competent mother, to his angry father.

And to the laptop secreted away beneath his wardrobe.

Time might be running out to find Mudder. He couldn't let them withdraw the search teams. So what was he going to do about it?

May (before)

Dalt

Two weeks had gone by since Lucy Loxton had given him her phone number at the petrol pump. Truth be told, he'd not given the encounter a second thought since, but the lack of milk at breakfast and the imminent need to pop into town to stock up on provisions had jerked his memory.

He pulled his phone out of his pocket. It was early. 7:30 a.m. Nell was out running. He would go into town this afternoon. He fired off a quick message: *I'll be in town later, if you would still like to meet.*

As he scrolled down for her number, the memory of her white teeth came back to him and selecting *Dentist* he watched the envelope on the screen grow wings and disappear.

Her response pinged back promptly.

Glad you got in touch, would love to meet. 2 p.m. at the Frothing Frapp?

He sent a simple, *Sounds good*, and slipped his phone back into his pocket.

Dalt always looked forward to the weekend. Whilst Saturdays were much the same as any other day of the week at Moordown for Nell, who was a creature of habit and ran and wrote on Saturdays and Sundays just as she did on every other day, Dalt and Huck would find themselves restless and in need of adventure.

For them, weekends were about walking on the moor and swimming in the streams and rivers. They'd begun when Huck was three, his swimming things packed into a tiny backpack he took great pride in carrying himself, sandwiches, water and blankets loaded into Dalt's. They'd only be gone an hour at first, then two, then three, until whole days disappeared under ever-changing skies, and nights beneath blankets of stars. On a Sunday evening they'd return tired and aching but replenished in spirit.

Huck was Nell's boy though, through and through. Just as some parents have a favourite child (as much as they may laugh and protest it), some children have a favourite parent. Huck's favourite was Nell. When Huck was tiny, this had given Dalt cause for concern. Huck had been breastfed for the first year of his life. Dalt had patiently waited this out, accepting that he couldn't compete in this arena, knowing his own time would come. But weaning came and went, and Huck was as firmly attached to Nell as ever, paradoxical really, as Nell did nothing to invite this intense bond, to further it, or encourage it, only be the way she always was. Dalt loved Huck even more for that – for choosing Nell as he had chosen her, accepting her and loving her absolutely.

As a toddler, Huck would spend his days nestled at Nell's feet whilst she typed, playing with his toys or humming to himself. He'd pull at her clothes until she lifted him, then fall asleep, content, in the dip of her lap, his small fingers entwined in her long hair, as if to keep her close whilst he slept.

Dalt owned one baby book. An old child rearing manual he'd picked up at a village fete and presented to Nell shortly before their son was born. Nell had examined the cover, read the blurb, thanked him, and never looked at the book again. But Dalt had. In a chapter entitled U*nderstanding Your Baby*, the 'expert' author wrote of how babies communicate with the parent mainly through body language, through 'cues' that we have to learn to understand. Not just the obvious one like crying or smiling, but stiffening of the fingers, clenching of the hands, yawning and fussing or gazing, with wide open eyes.

The fascinating thing was that at Moordown, this process appeared to be happening the other way around.

Huck's bond with his mother grew stronger with each month that passed. Nell would sigh when the doorbell rang, and carrying Huck on her arm, go to open it. More often than not, she would scowl at the person on the step. Huck would smile and gurgle and charm, assisting his mother by diffusing the situation the only way he knew how. The pressure was lifted from Nell to perform these dreaded social interactions. Huck had made it his duty to help. When Nell sighed, the child cooed and gurgled and stroked her face. When she sat for hours at the computer, locked in her own world, he would start to cry and pull at her hair until she released her focus and returned her attentions back to her small family.

By the time Huck went to school, he and Nell were so well attuned, it was like they had a language all of their own. This bond had never been broken. Now fifteen and practically a man, Dalt knew Huck still cared intensely for his mother, although he'd never admit it.

The moor had been their saving grace, he and his son's. For all the things that Nell could give Huck, long days of adventure and abandon didn't feature on the list.

But Dalt could offer that. Weekends were their time, his and Huck's.

But not this weekend.

Huck wasn't well. He'd told Dalt at breakfast. He was feeling feverish, he said. Hot then cold. Wobbly. He did look pale.

'Take it easy today,' Dalt told him, tossing him the remote control and leaving him in peace on the sofa.

Dalt had spent the morning with Turnip, an ever-ready companion, albeit one who couldn't offer too much in the way of conversation (not always a bad thing) on a circular walk he favoured up to the local beauty spot, Guller's Leap, then back down through Pike's Pass. Fascinating, all the people who had unwittingly lent their names to these places: rocks and cliffs and valleys that displayed the infamy of those who had gone before.

He'd checked on Huck as soon he got back home. Laid out on the sofa watching an old film, his son had gratefully accepted a cup of tea and some toast, before Dalt left him alone again.

Next, he'd knocked on Nell's study door, more tea and toast in hand, again both gratefully received. They'd exchanged a few words whilst he lingered in the doorway. She looked preoccupied, he thought, like she wasn't really listening. She probably wasn't.

'I'm popping to town,' he told her. 'If there's anything you need?'

A shake of her head signalled his dismissal, and now, here he was, walking across the market square towards the Frothing Frapp to meet Lucy Loxton. Her name reminded him of the story book character Foxy Loxy.

'What are you smiling about?'

Dalt looked up to see Mrs Foxy Loxy herself standing right in front of him.

'Perfect timing,' she said, smiling and holding out a hand. He shook it obligingly. 'Follow me. There's a little table at the back where we won't be disturbed.'

This woman was fresh out of the British School of Social Etiquette, graduating with a first no doubt. A bit different to his wife.

He followed in Lucy Loxton's footsteps as she glided across the busy café, smiling and greeting people casually yet politely as she went.

Once seated (she was right, the table was a good one, set back from the general noise of the café and offering the perfect opportunity to talk uninterrupted) with coffees in front of them, Lucy launched into her idea.

Dalt knew he was something of a Luddite, they all were in his family, but Lucy's nonchalant use of technical vocabulary still blew him away; if it hadn't been for Lucy's excitement and her energy for the project, Dalt would have allowed himself to zone out completely. But her enthusiasm – a passionate, articulate woman focused single-mindedly on achieving her goal – kept him engaged. A spark reignited.

He picked out and hung onto the words he was familiar with and asked her to explain those he did not: graphical interface, metadata, indexing – the words and their explanations fell easily from her – gracefully and uncontrived. Ironic, really, when a quick look at her online persona revealed the opposite: Lucy, posturing and posing amidst a pseudo-reality of filters and effects – hard to believe this was the same woman as the one that sat opposite him. She was clever, that was clear. She knew her stuff – there were brains behind the brand.

'What I need,' she was saying, looking at him earnestly, 'is an illustrator. You. I need you.' Dalt felt himself begin to redden but forced himself to maintain eye contact. It had been a long time since anyone had said those words to him, even if they were only being said in a business context. Also, the eye contact was strangely disconcerting. He wasn't used to holding a woman's gaze like this, so intently, for so long.

'I've seen your work. You're good.' Flattery now too.

'Thanks.'

'I'm picturing some sketches that would accompany my social media posts – simple pencil outlines of a figure. My figure, I suppose I should say, illustrated with the clothes I'm describing in the posts themselves. I'm picturing bold sketches, showing colour and pattern and print, as well as obviously shape and design. I'm picturing sketchbook-style, whimsical even, with a French feel.'

Dalt wondered if he should feel worried that she had said 'I'm picturing...' three times in one breath. It felt ominous, reminding him of the time when, as a teenager, he'd described a particular hair cut to a bemused looking hairdresser, beginning his sentence with those fateful words, only to emerge from the salon half an hour later, clipped, feathered and quaffed within an inch of his life, weighted down with gel and hairspray but more memorably with an enormous burst of laughter as the salon door swung shut behind him. He'd stopped 'picturing' things after that.

She was waiting for a reply. He took a long swig of his coffee.

'You're asking for a fashion croquis.' Now it was his turn to bandy around technical terminology, but he was quick to explain, as she had been. 'It just means a quick sketch of a figure, with a loose drawing of the design of the clothes. It's been a long time since I've done one – college, probably.'

He paused and took another drink.

'We were paired up with the fashion students at one point: they'd give us their design briefs and we'd provide the sketches. It's easy enough.'

Lucy was nodding and looking at him expectantly.

'If I emailed you a photo or a description of an item and what it would be teamed with, do you think you might be able to whip up a croquis? You could just scan your work and email it back to me. I'd pay you for the time taken.'

Dalt paused again. This wasn't a big deal. A sketch like she was describing would take minutes to do. What was holding him back?

Her gaze hadn't shifted. He thought of that game Huck used to like to play, '*the one where the person who blinks first loses, Daddy!*' She'd be amazing at that game.

'Okay. I'm in.'

She smiled.

She smiled like a girl in a toothpaste advert.

He knew why he'd been holding back.

It was late afternoon when he arrived home. He'd picked up the groceries and ticked several chores off his list whilst in town. Moordown was quiet. He placed his keys on the chest in the hallway and knocked gently on the door of Nell's office. No reply. She must have gone out.

As he reached the kitchen, he heard Nell calling from the study.

'Yes? Come in. You don't need to knock.'

He retraced his footsteps and pushed open the door.

'I'm sorry. I was engrossed...' Her explanation trailed off as she abandoned her apology before even finishing it and returned her gaze to the typed papers in front of her.

She didn't notice him leave. How could she, when she hadn't noticed he was there in the first place?

In his study, Dalt slid open the top drawer of his desk and pulled out a fresh, white sheet of paper. There was nothing quite like a blank page, anticipation and uncertainty mixed with a quiet expectation of what it might become. He closed his eyes, pictured Lucy Loxton, and began to sketch.

Sunday 8th September

Huck

'Think about who might be next. Is there anyone else, that any of you can recall, that might have upset Nell in any way?' Officer Henley had asked.

Huck's English teacher at school had a penchant for character analysis. Draw your character, she would say, then annotate it. What are your character's physical characteristics? What's their personality like? What's their background, their relationship with others? You've got to truly understand them, to know what motivates them. You've got to get inside their skin before you can write them.

As a result, Huck had formed a habit of mentally pinning people onto an imaginary, life-sized pin board as if they were rare specimens and he an entomologist. He'd adjust his exhibits carefully, sometimes stretching the torso, straightening the limbs, centring the gaze, then he'd scatter words around them: *creative, strong-willed, articulate, determined, focused* (Mudder), or *precise, practical, polite, methodical, distant* (Dalt).

If he, Huck, were to be caught in a net, pinned tenderly onto a board, examined, scrutinised, deciphered, he wondered what words would decorate him?

Deceitful, for one.

He had a laptop. It had been borrowed from the English department at his school at the beginning of year eight for the purpose of completing his homework and carrying out research. Mrs Forbes had kept him behind one afternoon, pulled up a stool, and used that soft, gentle voice that he knew was meant to say, 'Talk to me; I'm on your side.'

Surprisingly, she was. Having noticed that Huck was struggling to complete homework tasks and was spending an inordinate amount of time before and after school in the library, Mrs Forbes had worked out that Huck did not have access to a computer at home. 'Money issues?' she'd enquired tentatively. He'd just nodded – it was easier than explaining Mudder's archaic ideas (that the internet was unsafe, dangerous, and unsavoury, that social media was a waste of time – mindless, pointless and filled with drivel, and that screen time could lead to blurred vision, eye strain and near-sightedness, and worst of all, a lack of imagination).

Denied access to a computer, bereft of a mobile phone, Huck was, and always had been, a social pariah. Perceptive Mrs Forbes, with her smock dresses and her chunky knit cardigans, was his saviour. The laptop she found for him wasn't new, it wasn't shiny, but it was his. It fit perfectly in the small gap beneath the oak wardrobe and the floorboards of his bedroom. Hardly the best hiding place in the world, but as neither of his parents ever entered his room it was perfectly safe. He probably could have left it out on his desk. No one would have noticed, until Dalt gave the police officers permission to search the house that is. Then Huck had been forced to hide it. The moor was perfect for keeping secrets. Rocky outcrops created perfect little hidey holes where he used to keep his treasures as a boy:

coins, pencils and special stones. He'd known the perfect place to stash his laptop. He hadn't left it there too long though; the police officers and their dogs were back on the moor in no time at all.

Okay, add *unscrupulous* and *underhand* to the words on his butterfly board. Confession time: Huck wasn't just using the laptop for homework and research. Nope – googling '*why Henry VIII dissolved the monasteries*' was only the tip of the iceberg. The rest of the iceberg, about ninety-six percent of it in fact, along with the rest of Huck's time, was spent submerged in the depths of the web, in the deep and the dark, where it was harder to see and easy to get lost, where more harmful enterprises haunted the gloom. '*But what's a nice boy like you doing in a place like this?*' The truth was too predictable to bear thinking about. *Bored, disillusioned teen seeks power trips and cheap thrills.* Hardly headline material. Embarrassing, really.

Or it might be, if he wasn't so damn good at programming, coding and basically messing around where he wasn't invited. Infiltrating, penetrating, hacking, whatever you want to call it. He called it a calling.

Huck/Hack, even the words shared an affinity.

At the start of the year, a careers fair had visited his school. Stands were set out and representatives from different vocations had done their best to polish, sell and glorify their chosen profession. He'd left feeling heavy, melancholy, pensive. Nothing jumped out at him, nothing said '*Hey, I'm for you and you're for me.*'

A few months later he found the dark web. Huck met Hack.

He'd started off small – bought a lifetime subscription to a hacked Netflix account for the price of a pint of milk. The hit that came with the illegal procurement felt so good. A jolt of adrenaline, like the feeling he got when diving into an ice-cold pool with Dalt, only Dalt was too busy to do that much these days. 'A new project,' was all he'd said when Huck had recently asked. Whatever it was, it seemed to be giving Dalt the same kind of thrill Huck was getting.

One thing led to the next, led to the next: the acquisition of a credit card, the purchase of a reprogrammed mobile phone, and the downloading of illegal hacking software.

Dark web videos and chat forums told him everything he needed to know, and a lot more that he didn't. It was all there, whatever he wanted, and he discovered that he wanted all of it.

It took time. Most of the posters on the forums he frequented seemed to have been born knowing how to program a computer. Huck had to start from scratch – everything from the position of the keys on the keyboard to the vocabulary of coding was new to him – but it didn't hold him back. Basic scripting, manipulating computer code, programming and modifying; his skills developed quickly.

Like any good student, Huck interspersed his theory lessons with more practical ones. First and foremost (he was nobody's fool) he learnt how to hide his IP address, masking his location and identity. Safe in the knowledge that he couldn't be found, he began to enjoy himself.

Next: how to find someone's physical address. He didn't do anything sinister with the information, he wasn't a creep, but the knowledge that he could find it, the power that came with knowing how to carry out this act was enough. Tutorials on how to penetrate the fortified walls of a private PC came next, and after that, how to hack a mobile phone. He had a lot of fun with that one. Who'd have thought that Dom Jackson, the most popular and sporty kid in his year, was into online chess, or that Juliette Treavy, the willowy, softly spoken brunette who sat across from him in religious studies was obsessed with the occult?

Or that his father was arranging to meet up with Lucy Loxton?

There were things he took for granted: the rough, wet slop of Turnip's tongue on his cheek when he greeted him in the morning, the sound of the back door shutting as Mudder returned from her daily run, and the invisible but unbreakable bond between his parents.

So, Harry Loxton's mum?

When he'd hacked into his father's phone early one Saturday morning (just to see if he could) and seen a message exchange between his father and Lucy Loxton, he'd squinted hard at the screen. Weird, for sure, that his father should be messaging Lucy Loxton. Stranger still that they should be arranging to meet later that same afternoon.

2 p.m. at the Frothing Frapp.

Sometimes you just want to keep on taking certain things for granted.

He'd feigned a fever. Had spent the morning slumped on the sofa watching some old western.

That afternoon, the moment Dalt left the house and was clear of the gates, Huck had jumped on his bike and followed him into town. He'd lurked outside the coffee shop, unnoticed. He didn't know why but he'd taken a photo of the two of them through the steamy window. He was home and back on the sofa before Dalt returned. Mudder wouldn't have even noticed he'd been gone.

He'd kept tabs on Dalt after that, hacked into his computer, checked his email.

Just a few days after their meeting in the Frothing Frapp, his father sent Lucy Loxton an email.

Huck had opened it, clicked on the attachment. A sketch of a woman's body appeared before him, clearly drawn by his father's talented hands, the quick and easy pencil lines that formed the well-proportioned figure of what had to be Lucy Loxton's torso.

And underneath, the writing simply said, *I hope you like it. Let me know when you want to get together next.*

Dalt? Seriously? It couldn't be true.

His father and Lucy Loxton had exchanged emails every week or so since then. Only ever sketches. Only ever the briefest of messages that gave nothing away. He couldn't believe his father was really doing this (whatever this was) behind Mudder's back.

Huck had shaken his head in the kitchen yesterday, when Officer Henley had asked her loaded question.

'Think about who might be next. Is there anyone else, that any of you can recall, that might have upset Nell in any way?'

Dalt. Oh Dalt. He made a mental note to add *'dark horse'* to his father's character assimilation. But whatever his father may have done, he wasn't about to dob him in to Officer Henley. He wasn't about to throw him to the wolves.

Dalt had taken him fishing a couple of times when he was younger, but Huck hadn't particularly enjoyed the experience. He didn't think Dalt had either. A show of manliness, perhaps, a fatherly performance – this is what fathers do with their sons.

'You've got one. It's yours,' Dalt had said, as Huck's line pulled taut sending vibrations quivering through his tensed hand. Reel it in. Had Dalt been expecting to see pride, joy, fulfilment in his son's face at the sorry creature hooked on the end of the line? And wasn't Dalt's face supposed to mirror these emotions? Huck recalls instead that his father's expression was confused, uncertain, lacking.

They'd stood on the riverbank, as the small, brown trout floundered on the ground in front of them. Its body jerked, its tail raised, and it was momentarily suspended in the air – a fortune fish on a hot hand (love or hate?) then slap – caudal fin followed by dorsal fin striking viscous mud, a sucking, pulling, glooping sound as the creature twisted again and again, its lower body sucking, pulling, farting from the mud, only to splat once more into the ground. Rasping, dragging, silent screaming. Was that him or the fish?

'Dad,' he'd said. 'Dad, do something.' Huck had looked to the rock clasped uselessly in his father's hand, to the fish, to the rock and back again.

Dalt had moved forward, stumbled, and loosened his grip on the rock which fell uselessly to his side. In a turn of events that seemed surreal then and downright weird when he later recalled it, Dalt had swung his leg and booted the fish high into the air. Time turned to slow motion as the creature completed a graceful arc, droplets of water scattered in the air, before normal speed resumed, and it slapped clumsily back into the cold waters of the river.

Too small, Dalt had said, turning to his son after a moment. Not worth it.

Later, when a second trout had lain flapping on the bank before him, Huck hadn't paused. He'd reached for his father's discarded rock and without hesitation brought it down hard upon the fish's head, right above its eyes. A second blow, and the creature lay still.

He learnt a valuable lesson that day. Two, actually. Firstly, his father was no fisherman, and secondly, putting an end to suffering was better than watching it.

Dalt

'Think about who might be next. Is there anyone else, that any of you can recall, that might have upset Nell in any way?' Officer Henley had asked.

Dalt kept quiet and focused on keeping his expression inscrutable, a passable imitation of a man deep in thought, taking a situation seriously.

He often felt like this – removed – as if he were acting moments instead of really living them. Maybe it was a subconscious method of self-protection.

Or maybe it was because he wasn't telling the truth.

Because he did have his doubts about someone. The only problem was that the person in question was currently sitting only a few inches away from him, sipping a cup of coffee.

When had he first suspected that Amelia was up to something? He'd felt uneasy since the day she'd arrived, the moment she'd thrown her arms around his wife and moved her bags into the spare room.

But he wasn't suspicious then. There had been no reason to be. He'd thought it strange, of course, Amelia turning up unannounced at the house of a friend that she hadn't seen in over fifteen years, carrying on as if time hadn't passed: strange, but not suspicious. He knew that his wife felt indebted to Amelia; Nell had never made a secret of the fact that it was Amelia who had helped her navigate university life – Amelia who had helped her get her first book deal. Dalt felt indebted to Amelia too, as if they were all part of the same relay team and Nell was the baton that Amelia had successfully passed into his outstretched hand. The baton with which, together, they'd won the race. So, when Amelia had knocked on the door, he hadn't been the least bit surprised that, despite her love of solitude, Nell had invited her old friend straight in.

Whatever you need.

But his suspicion had grown, fuelled by little things. Tells. Slips. The prawn risotto that Amelia made for supper one day, only to be politely reminded by Nell that she was allergic (to put it mildly) to shellfish. Just touching a prawn could send his wife into anaphylactic shock. Proximity to prawns and particle inhalation alone could make Nell's lips and tongue swell and her breathing become laboured. Dalt had grabbed all four plates, swept them off the table and hurled their contents into the outside bin. Nell had been fine, but he had been fuming. Amelia had appeared distraught. She'd quite forgotten, she said. Dalt was not sure how one could 'quite forget' something so important. Hadn't Nell told him a story once, of how she had ended up in hospital for a week after eating some chips with Amelia that had been cooked, unbeknownst to them, next to some scallops? Amelia had had to rush her to hospital. Wouldn't you remember that?

There were other things, too. The boating excursion. Amelia seemed completely unaware of Nell's fear of water. Why would Nell have stepped foot on the boat given the traumatic events of its past?

Even before Nell's disappearance, Dalt had begun to watch Amelia closely. A guest in the house always takes a little getting used to, but Amelia felt less like a guest and more like a downright stranger, and a stranger in the house, well, that's just dangerous.

But she was the perfect house guest in those first few weeks, early to rise, eager to please.

'Eggs? Porridge? Coffee? What can I get you?' she'd ask, when he or Huck wandered into the kitchen bleary eyed in the morning.

He hadn't had a problem with that. It had been a long time since someone had made him breakfast. Nell wasn't much for that sort of thing, particularly as she wasn't even there in the morning, always out running.

Amelia was cheery too and brought an energy with her that the house had been lacking. The radio was often on in the evening and Dalt would hear her singing along to songs as she helped prepare the evening meal. Sometimes, Nell would even join in, a rare occurrence that he could only be thankful for, as he enjoyed the sound of their laughter spilling out of the kitchen.

Amelia had her merits. If she made Nell happy, then surely he should be happy.

But it didn't feel right. *Trust your instincts*, Mr Moustache whispered in his ear. *Trust yourself.*

Amelia had her flaws, too.

Insecurity tainted every move she made. Like an uncertain Midas, Amelia infused all her creations with doubt: her writing, her relationships, her cooking, the woman was eternally questioning herself. *Was it any good? Did it sound okay? Did it taste okay? Did it read okay?* She could have written *War and Peace* only to talk herself out of a publishing deal. It drove Dalt mad, the constant self-examination and need for reassurance.

This insecurity underpinned the entire framework of her being, like the main sewer pipe, running fetid beneath the belly of a city, into which the tributary pipes of lack of confidence and low self-esteem shat their rancid waste. Insecurity, the mother of all flaws, which led Amelia from bad decision to bad decision, drama to failure to catastrophe.

He almost felt sorry for her.

'Do you remember Henry? Henry Cooper?' Amelia had said to Nell the day she turned up at Moordown. He'd overheard the conversation from the kitchen, where he'd been reading the paper. Amelia hadn't waited for an answer – had rushed on with the news of the breakdown of her relationship, trying to outrace the opening of the sewage gate, before it released the backlog of waste that threatened to engulf her.

Amelia's suitcase was barely upstairs before Dalt had typed Henry Cooper's name into a search engine.

Henry Cooper: fifty-five, senior commissioning editor at a very well-known London publishing house.

Good for you, Mr Henry Cooper, life sounded just peachy.

Fact-checking complete, Dalt hadn't probed any further. But when Nell disappeared, and Amelia began acting suspiciously, creeping around, always carrying that damn notebook, Dalt's curiosity about her sudden arrival was piqued once more, and he couldn't resist calling the office where Mr Cooper worked. What on earth he was going to say when he had the man on the phone, he didn't know.

Dalt needn't have worried.

Mr Henry Cooper is out of the office. If you need immediate assistance, please contact Janine Heatherington on the main switchboard.

It had taken two weeks of calling sporadically and listening to this pre-recorded message before Dalt decided to phone the main number.

'Good morning, Blackdown Press, Janine speaking. How can I be of assistance?'

Janine, hi, my name is Edward Dalton. Henry Cooper gave me his card at an event a few months back. I wondered if it would be possible to speak to him?' A small, white lie, fluid, easy and plausible.

A pause. The silence itself informing him of Henry Cooper's continued absence before Janine Heatherington did.

'I'm sorry, Mr Cooper is on extended leave, and I'm unable to say at this time when we are expecting him back. Is there anything I can help you with?'

'Thank you, no. It wasn't important. I'll try again in a few weeks.'

Dalt had ended the call before Janine could respond.

Was it odd, he'd wondered, that Henry Cooper had taken extended leave from work when his relationship ended – a little melodramatic even? Yes, Amelia had packed her bags and boarded the first train out of London, but Henry Cooper? Dalt didn't know the man, but it sounded like he had serious responsibilities: his job, for one, a house, dependants from a previous marriage, (thank you, again, Google). Was the man really so cut up about Amelia that he had disappeared (hadn't he been the one to end things with her?) or was something else going on here? It didn't make sense.

More delving was required.

Through a combination of hard work and rich, dead relatives, Henry Cooper was in the enviable position of being the owner of a two and a half million-pound house in South West London, where he had lived since the breakdown of his marriage nine years previously. As a highly regarded, senior member of staff at Blackdown Press, Cooper had the power to decide which books to publish and which to leave at the bottom of the slush pile. With a string of successes tucked under his belt, and a recent deal secured with an '*up and coming new author*' who had stared broodingly at Dalt throughout his breakfast earlier in the week from the *Review* section of the newspaper, Henry Cooper was clearly a man on the up.

Until he disappeared.

Okay, Dalt had no real evidence to substantiate the disappearance claim, but he felt it in his gut.

And there was something else, something closer to home.

The day that Nell disappeared, whilst Dalt had been looking for her in the garden, he'd found something, a scrap of paper, blown against the trunk of the willow tree. At first he'd thought it was a note from Nell. It wasn't. It appeared to be the bones of a conversation, recorded in a hasty hand, illegible in places and occasionally nonsensical, punctuated with the odd word underlined or starred. Two speakers were obvious, marked by an *N* and an *A*. *'Stand down Bletchley Park, I've got this,'* he'd thought wryly.

A was clearly asking *N* questions, although the answers in shorthand were hard to decipher, but why? Had Nell agreed to this, or was Amelia taking advantage of their friendship, interviewing the world-famous author unawares, recording her revelations? What was Amelia planning to do with this material, and did dear old Henry Cooper have something to do with it?

He'd stuffed it into his pocket, to look over properly later.

It had slipped his mind, understandably, as the events of the day had unfolded. It was as he hung his trousers on the line to dry a week later, the pocket flapping open, soggy and empty, that he remembered the paper he'd stuffed in there.

Had Nell found out that Amelia was writing about her? Had Nell felt betrayed by her old friend? Is that why she'd disappeared? Or was it a combination of factors: the anniversary of Toby's death, memories of the past coming back to haunt her, Amelia's actions proving the last straw?

Or had Amelia got something to do with Nell's disappearance? How desperate was she for a story? For glory of her own?

He needed to talk to her, get it all out in the open, but what if he was wrong? What if he was losing it? He was a wreck. No proper sleep for weeks and a constant sense of unease and worry. Distrust penetrated his rational thought. Maybe he was wrong about Amelia. He couldn't risk it yet. Didn't want to add upsetting Amelia to his list of worries if his delusional, sleep-deprived, anxious mind had made it all up.

Dalt needed to pull himself together. He had behaved appallingly the last time the police officers had visited. He shouldn't have shouted. Shouldn't have stormed off, but he was approaching overload. All the information to take onboard – the fable, the social worker, dead – an impossible coincidence. All those bad memories revisited. And the fingers of blame all pointed at Nell. But it seemed that no one was listening to what he was saying. The world was going mad.

Where the hell was Nell?

What the hell was going on?

And when would it end? His life on hold. Nell, out there somewhere, injured? Forcibly held? Insane? Which was it? And how did time just keep on turning? He wasn't sure he could keep on turning with it, all the twists were disorientating him, sending him spinning.

'Think about who might be next. Is there anyone else, that any of you can recall, that might have upset Nell in any way?' Officer Henley had asked.

Amelia Early, Dalt thought.

I'm watching you.

Amelia

'Think about who might be next. Is there anyone else, that any of you can recall, that might have upset Nell in any way?' Officer Henley had asked.

Amelia had watched as Dalt shook his head and shrugged his shoulders, a childish gesture of orchestrated nonchalance. Huck shrugged too, an imitation of his father, and she, Amelia could feel her cheeks reddening as Officer Henley turned her gaze in Amelia's direction. Would that later become a note in a file: '*incriminating body language*?'

Frauds, all three of them, secrets spilling from them like water off the edge of a fountain.

This house was stifling; she pulled at her collar to loosen it, let in some air. They were rotting here, in this house, all of them, squashed together like ripe fruits on the cusp, starting to split, to ooze their sticky liquid onto each other. Not long before the wasps amassed, before they were all ruined. Note-to-self: jot that down later.

Dalt was clearly losing it; they could all see it. Letting rip at the police officers like that and then storming out into the garden. She looked out, through the glass doors Dalt had pushed aside. No sign of him.

She'd overstayed her welcome. Every day she was in the house felt like a day on borrowed time. The police officers were the only people who seemed to accept her presence. Dalt and Huck were acting more distant each day. Who could blame them? Amelia was an interloper. She didn't belong here, and they were making it very clear.

Could she just leave? Were there police rules in a situation like this, with a missing person enquiry underway? Would fingers point in her direction if she, too, suddenly disappeared?

But what if she could get some answers? They'd thank her then, wouldn't they?

A lie down might help give her a chance to gather her thoughts. Meditate on it.

In her bedroom with the door shut behind her, a glance in the mirror confirmed what she already knew; flushed red cheeks, frizzy hair and damp armpits were not a good look. Lately, Amelia had visions of herself disappearing, melting into her own pool of sweat like the wicked witch in *The Wizard of Oz*.

She thought of Nell, cool and composed in her author photo at the back of her latest book. Hardly the time to compare, but old habits die hard. Amelia felt that familiar twang of envy, disappointment and failure. A fresh start, that's what she needed, a new image to see her through this time of transition.

In the shower, the cold water on her body felt incredible, reminding her of the river. Reminding her of Nell.

As she dried herself, she looked around the room. It wouldn't take long to pack up her things, the few clothes and books that she'd brought with her. Her notebooks were already squirrelled away in the zip compartment of her suitcase. Four notebooks in all, full of, well... full of everything, right from the start. She really had something here, she could feel it. A fly on the wall account of the mysterious disappearance of a woman. But not just any old woman, no – which is where the genius lay – the disappearance of a woman who wrote novels about disappearing.

It was perfect. Nell's fans (of whom there were millions) would be all over this like a rash. This was Amelia's moment to shine. At last. It had been long enough coming, but now it was here she was going to grasp it with both hands and kiss it full on the lips (with tongues).

If only this niggling feeling that she was doing something terribly wrong would go away. She'd tried to ignore it, but it was always there. Niggle, niggle, niggle, putting her off her food and infiltrating her dreams. Last night, for example, she'd been enjoying a magnificent dream. She'd been wearing a rather spectacular red blouse, no... there was more to it than that. She was at a book signing – her own book signing, wearing a rather spectacular red blouse. The table in front of her was piled high with shiny, hardback copies of her book. The queue of people wanting a signed copy stretched out the door and into the street. Dream Amelia (in that amazing red blouse) smiled and picked up her pen.

'What shall I write?' dream Amelia had asked the featureless woman at the front of the queue.

'Snake.'

'I'm sorry, who would you like me to dedicate this to?'

'Snake, snake, snake, snake, snake, snake, snake.'

It started quietly, then grew to a crescendo. The whole crowd hissing as one, a cacophony of reptiles, calling her out.

Amelia woke up, heart racing, bed sheets damp.

And wondered if there would be any way to track down a blouse like that.

Seriously though, the dream had unnerved her. She needed to talk to Dalt. She needed to be honest, so that there could be no chance of accusations of underhand behaviour later on. She could just imagine the conversation.

'*Oh, by the way, Dalt, I've been writing a biography of your wife. No, she didn't know about it. Yes, it was mostly factual and observational. No, Nell hadn't shared the innermost workings of her mind and soul with me – I suppose I was going to pad it out with anecdotal accounts and 'Nell trivia'. But I was going to ask her permission before I approached any publishers with the project. I'm sure she would have supported the book.*

Then Nell went missing, but I didn't let it stop me. Instead, I altered the premise of the book and turned it into an account of what it's like to live through a family member's disappearance. Yes, I suppose I have been privy to a lot of private moments and confidential conversations. Yes, it is an incredibly difficult and personal time for you and Huck, but I feel that I, (we? you?) owe it to Nell's fans to give this to them, to help them understand.'

Understand what though? Amelia realised she wasn't quite sure. She hadn't joined up all the dots yet. Nobody had. She hadn't got any answers.

Her book had no ending.

Here, again, like she had been so many times before, so near yet so far.

No ending. She hadn't voiced the thought until now, but it had been lurking, dormant in a dark cavern of her brain waiting for a moment like this to pounce.

It was why she hadn't yet left, she realised. She couldn't, with the story unfinished.

This was her time, maybe her last shot. If the story needed an ending, then she would jolly well have to come up with one, wouldn't she?

And to do that she'd have to get a grip of herself. Starting right now.

Hair pinned up off her face (the cool air on the nape of her neck felt transcendental) and wearing the most light-weight dress in her wardrobe (feeling quite the bohemian author) she was ready to brainstorm. Propped up on the bed with some blousy pillows, she opened a new document on her laptop.

SYNOPSIS

That sounded decisive. She felt strong.

Following the breakdown of her marriage (an exaggeration, but this needed to be punchy) and liberated from familial ties, Nell Davenport – woman on the run, takes the opportunity of anonymity to wreak revenge upon the citizens of Stonebrook who have wronged her.

Yes, yes, yes! This was good stuff!

This was coming together.

MIDDLE SECTION

Details of the fables and the women that they belonged to: Lucy Loxton, Clare Jamison, Joan Matthews.

It was like Nell was still giving her the information for the book despite her disappearance.

ENDING... ?

Well, either the fables would continue, or they wouldn't. Amelia was going to have to give it more time. Some things can't be rushed. This was one of them. She was just going to have to hold steady and see what happened next.

It was win-win, however you looked at it. If Nell stayed 'lost', then Amelia's theories couldn't be disproved. If Nell returned, then she could abandon the project. The whole thing would doubtless be forgotten about, the wonder of her reappearance cancelling out any little 'exposés' that may have been bandied about.

If only all of Amelia's writing sessions were so productive.

Amelia saved her document under _Ending_. The feeling of urgency to leave Moordown that had overwhelmed her this morning had dissipated, leaving a sense of renewed purpose in its place.

No, there was no rush now. She'd stay a while longer, see what happened next. Then, when it was all over she'd go back to London with everything she needed.

Monday 9th September

Huck

He'd found the fables the day Mudder went missing.

Dalt had gone out to retrace the route Mudder might have run that morning. Amelia was looking through the calendar.

He'd gone straight to Mudder's office.

Office had never seemed the right name for the room where Mudder spent most of her time writing, the word holding connotations of business-like efficiency, agendas and deadlines when in reality, Mudder came to this room to be free of all that; to be in her own, fictional world. *Fantasy Zone*, suited better, or *Isolation Suite*.

Huck knew where to look. The space between the bottom drawer of Mudder's desk and the floorboards used to be his own little hidey-hole, back when he was a toddler playing at Mudder's feet. He'd pull out the drawer, then post his crayons into the gap down the back.

'Hidey, hidey!' he'd declare happily, and Mudder would feign surprise.

'Where have your crayons gone, my little Huckleberry?' she would say, laughing whilst pretending to look confused.

'Here!' he would say, reaching in, grabbing a handful of colours. 'Hiding.'

Mudder would laugh and he would laugh, then she'd turn back to her writing and he to his colouring.

Kneeling on the floor, he'd pulled open the drawer and stuck his hand down behind it, his fingers connecting with a sheaf of paper. Hidey hidey! He pulled it around the bend of the back of the drawer and drew it free, taking the bundle over to Mudder's chair to examine. Had he ever sat here, in the chair itself, before? It was incredibly uncomfortable: ancient and lacking padding of any sort. It was a chair version of Mudder herself, Huck thought with a wry smile.

Huck knocked the bottom edges of the papers onto the desk to neatly align them, then took a moment to gently, reverently, thoughtfully thumb through them from back to front, not permitting his eyes to focus enough to read his mother's writing. The spidery, familiar scrawl made his heart quicken. There was something indefinably thrilling in discovering another's secret scribblings, each word a golden nugget of treasure to be savoured.

Unable to stave off the anticipation any longer, Huck allowed his eyes to focus and began to read. It took a few pages to understand what was in front of him: short stories, for children. He hadn't known Mudder was writing a children's book. A new avenue. Well, good for her, he was sure she'd be very successful. Everything Mudder wrote was received with acclaim.

But as he read on, Huck began to question the nature of the stories. Not stories, after all: fables, each with a moral – a lesson to be learnt. The flames of recognition began to spark: a description here or there, the actions of the characters, their very characteristics, the situations they found themselves in – it was all achingly familiar.

How often his English teacher had asked the class to find the hidden meaning. Eat this, Mrs Cunningham; how's this for analysing the hell out of a text. This was no collection of short stories for children. If he wasn't mistaken, this was Mudder's autobiography sitting in pieces before him. How very Mudder. He could see her now, disguising herself in the form of a moth, a baby sparrow, a mother pig, removing herself just enough to be able to revisit the tribulations of her past, able to remember and retell events through the voice and thoughts of somebody else. Wasn't there a technical term for this, transference, or something?

But that wasn't important. What was important was that these experiences had been significant enough for Mudder to commit them to paper. These events had shaped her, changed her; scarred her even.

Huck pulled open the top drawer of the desk, took a sheet of plain paper from the neat pile and a pencil from a plastic pot that held ten identically sharpened, yellow and black pencils. (How were they all the same length? Did Mudder have to sharpen them all whenever just one was blunt, to retain consistency in length, or did she rotate them, using a different one in turn each day, to ensure they stayed the same size?) A snapshot into the weird and wonderful world of Mudder, he thought. Dear Mudder.

Pencil in hand, he read through the fables again. There were four in total, each set in a different location, each containing a different set of creatures, yet all with one thing – one character – in common: Mudder. How did he know it was Mudder? Why was he so sure? Misunderstood but trying to understand, shunned by others, who else could it be?

A trickle of anger seeped into his veins as he read, moving slowly at first, then flowing through him quicker and stronger before turning into a torrent, leaving him prickling with rage. How dare these people treat his mother like this? After all he'd done, protecting her, guarding her. Ignorant, narrow minded morons. The room suddenly felt too small; the desire to walk, to run, to swim, to plunge into an ice-cold pool, to blow it all away consumed him.

Deep breaths. Slow, deep breaths. He needed to work out who the other people in the stories were. Deep breaths. Focus.

He could fix this. Make it right.

He heard the front door open. Heard Dalt call for Mudder, then for him.

He'd shoved the papers back where he'd found them.

When Mudder hadn't returned that evening and the police officers came, his thoughts were still on the fables. That night, when his father and Amelia had gone to bed, he'd returned to the office, gathered the stories and taken them up to his room.

For the first few days that she was gone, the fables and his thoughts of revenge had distracted him from the act of missing her. They'd given him structure and purpose, something to hold on to. Dear, dear Mudder – even in her absence she had planned for him. She must have hidden the fables there, knowing he'd find them. He was carrying out her will, an avenging angel.

It hadn't taken long to crack the first fable: Butterfly was 'beautiful', she gossiped and laughed with her butterfly friends, she spread rumours like she was spreading pollen. There was only one place where women acted like this that Huck had experienced. The school gates. It had to be one of the school mums – those side-glancing, hushed-voiced, judgemental women that stood in the playground like a ring of ancient standing stones, impregnable and worshipped. There were lots of these women, seven, maybe eight, but there was only one who stood out clearly in his mind.

Lucy Loxton.

Had Mudder known about Lucy Loxton and Dalt – their meeting at the coffee shop, the emails and the sketches? She must have known. This was too much of a coincidence otherwise.

Lucy Loxton. Even as a four-year-old he'd understood how manipulative she'd been, in that smiling-to-your-face, talking-disparagingly-about-you-behind-it kind of way. He remembered the playdate at her house, Mudder, quiet and subdued, out of her depths with these women who'd flitted around her examining her, comparing her, judging her.

Then they'd cut her out altogether, stopped the games and openly ignored her. Told their children to avoid him too.

It had hurt, at the time. No one to play with, no one to share a snack or a secret with. But he'd got over it, and he thought Mudder had too. But for her it must have been one more brick in the wall of hostility that the community was building around her.

First Lucy Loxton had messed with Mudder, then with Dalt too.

He'd see to it that she was punished.

At first, he didn't know how.

He'd trolled her online, dropped some catty comments here and there and fuelled himself with how pathetic she was, a woman of no substance, the type who might blow away in the wind like the scarves she modelled. Materialistic, shallow and vain, she took photos of herself in freebie clothes for a living, and yet had the audacity to criticise others. A fake, a fraud, a cheat, posting photos of her amazing life. Her and her husband holding hands, the picture taken from behind by their son; her and her husband walking their dog, both grinning, him looking at her, her at the camera.

Fake. Fraud. Cheat.

He needed to reveal her for what she really was.

If you can't beat 'em, join 'em.

Mudder had only been missing for four days when the plan had come to him. He would create a website for author, Nell Davenport, with its own blog page. He'd upload the fables to it. He'd let the world (or at least the citizens of Stonebrook) know the truth about the way she was treated.

Mudder's wasn't the first website he'd designed. He had created several different sites for paying clients on the dark web and had become quite adept at it. His practice had paid off. Mudder would have been proud. Actually, she would have hated it, with its twee border of entangled roses, and swirling script, but it wasn't like she was here to comment. And being able to program didn't naturally endow him with any design sense.

It was a Friday night – Mudder had been missing for nearly two weeks – when he finished designing the website. The blog post ready and waiting, Huck typed up the fable of *The Butterfly and the Moth* and prepared to upload it.

And then he realised the problem.

Lucy Loxton wouldn't see this. And wasn't that the entire point, for her to see what she'd done?

In fact, no one would see this. Nobody even knew Mudder had a blog (technically, she didn't yet). It wasn't as if she was out there doing her own PR for it. How would anyone know it existed?

He could email Lucy Loxton, with a direct link to the blog post. She'd get the message quick enough; she'd know it was about her.

And while he was at it, he'd post a few photos onto Lucy Loxton's blog (hacking this was easy enough), incriminating pictures that would shame her the way she'd shamed Mudder. He knew the very one he'd use. The one he'd taken that day at the Frothing Frapp.

It was when he was creating a message to Lucy Loxton from Mudder's email account that he happened to see Frank Hannock's name in her inbox and another idea came to him.

He could send the fable to Frank too. Frank would no doubt tell Dalt, and the police. It would keep the officers on their toes, give them another reason to keep trying to find Mudder and they'd have a field day trying to work out what it meant. Frank might even publish it in the Gazette. There was a blank column ready and waiting with Nell Davenport's name on it after all.

In the early hours of that fateful Saturday morning on the 24th of August, Huck sent the fable of *The Moth and the Butterfly* to Frank Hannock.

At 6 a.m. he uploaded the photo of his father and Lucy Loxton at the Frothing Frapp.

At 6.15 a.m. he emailed a link to Lucy Loxton.

He had sat back on his bed, mission complete.

Only he didn't feel complete. He felt hollow, unfulfilled, dissatisfied. Lucy Loxton's reaction was a complete unknown. She might be as blasé about the fable as she was about her fashion sense.

He needed to see her face. He wanted to hear her say sorry. He'd ask her about the fable, remind her of how she'd turned the other mothers against Mudder and made Mudder's life miserable.

He'd wait for an apology.

The place they should meet was obvious. Guller's Leap. He'd seen her up there before, walking her dog. It was quiet and secluded. He doubted there'd be anyone else there, especially that early in the morning.

And so, at 6.30 a.m. he had hacked into Dalt's phone and sent Lucy Loxton a text message, arranging to meet at Guller's Leap in an hour's time. He'd felt wired and energised but at the same time he'd felt at peace in a way that he hadn't been for weeks. Whilst everyone else sat around doing nothing, getting nowhere (Dalt, Amelia, the police officers, the whole town in fact), here he was, the good son, following leads, finding the truth, helping Mudder.

But then it all went wrong.

It wasn't his fault. Let's start with that. It wasn't his fault.

Would it have happened if he wasn't there? No. No, it probably wouldn't. But he didn't touch her. It was like dominoes falling, a series of events, unstoppable once set in motion.

At 7 a.m. Huck had snuck out the back way, the way Mudder went the day she went missing, down the lawn behind the house, not through the electric gates. He didn't want to alert anyone to his absence.

Lucy Loxton was already at Guller's Leap when he arrived. She had that dog with her, the one he'd seen online, an enormous creature (a Great Dane?) ironically named Baby. Huck ducked down behind a rock, suddenly terrified of what he was about to do. What *was* he about to do? He hadn't thought this through. It was okay though. She hadn't seen him.

She was halfway between his rock and the viewing point right on the edge of the cliff with her back to him and her arm stuck out in front of her angling her camera this way and that.

Was she taking selfies? For that blog of hers?

Shit. He ducked back behind the rock.

When he looked again a minute later she'd moved closer to the edge of Guller's Leap and was facing in his direction, although she didn't appear to have spotted him. She was wearing the most ridiculous sunglasses that made her look like a bug.

What was she up to now?

She was right next to the safety barrier. Not just next to it, straddling it! Huck watched in horror as she swung first one leg over and then the other. Was she crazy? The cliff dropped steeply away just inches from where she was standing. What the hell was she doing? His heart pounded in his chest as he watched her hold on to the barrier with only one hand and lean backwards.

Snap, snap, snap.

Jesus Christ this woman was insane!

Only inches from the cliff edge and certain death, who in their right mind would risk their life for a photo?

Suddenly a wet tongue rolled across his face and a moist nose nudged him. Baby may have been enormous, but with her sloppy, friendly greeting she was no guard dog. Surprised, Huck leapt to his feet.

'Huckleberry? Is that you?'

She'd seen him. He just hoped that now she'd get away from that cliff edge. It was making him feel sick.

'Yes, Mrs Loxton,' he gave a schoolboy response. Polite. Unnerving? Lucy Loxton's expression was impossible to read behind her bug-eyed glasses, but when she spoke her voice was uncertain, hesitant, shaky.

'What's going on, Huck? I thought your father was coming.'

'I came here to ask you the same question.' Huck felt a sudden rush. He was doing it. He was really doing it. He was going to get the answers. This one's for you, Mudder.

'What's going on with you and my dad?'

And then it happened.

A beautiful, small, blue butterfly alighted on Lucy Loxton's shoulder.

It flapped its wings once, twice, three times: spellbinding. Transfixed, they both stared.

Then – and this is the part he could not comprehend – the part that seemed absolute madness – she reached out her phone, angling it for the perfect photo.

Time froze, stood still, ceased to be. Beat, beat, beat. Hearts and wings, wings and hearts. The stillness of the air, the heat of the morning, the coincidence of the nature of the insect creating a moment of absolute clarity. Everything was revealed. Nothing was revealed.

The dog sprung forward, attracted by those flapping wings. Five bounds and it had reached her, its mammoth front paws reaching over the barrier and connecting forcibly with her chest.

And she was gone.

A beautiful, blue, butterfly flapped its wings at the cliff edge, unaware, whilst another tumbled to her death.

For a fraction of a moment, as he watched the dog whining at the top of the cliff, Huck felt his mother's presence. It couldn't be a coincidence, the butterfly killed by the butterfly. It was meant to be.

Then it swept over him. Absolute, sheer terror.

Get out of here, move, go, now.

Trying not to vomit, head spinning, body drenched in sweat, running back the way he came, racing over the bushes of gorse and heather. Home, home, home. At no point did he stop to glance behind, to glance down.

Through the back garden and the side door, straight to his room, straight to his laptop, to delete the incriminating digital trail: the photos he'd taken and uploaded, the emails he'd sent. He hacked into Lucy Loxton's email account and her phone one last time and deleted the entire back and forth conversations she'd had with his father. His fingers were shaking as he deleted the text from that morning, arranging to meet at Guller's Leap. He deleted it all, any trace of contact between his father and Lucy Loxton. Blood was blood after all. Actually, Huck didn't want to think about blood right now. He wanted Dalt to learn a lesson about fidelity, not get sent down for murder.

He knew that it was possible, with a bit of effort and the right forensic computer tools, for the police to recover some of the information he'd deleted, but it was going to take them time. He reckoned he had a few weeks before anyone would be onto him. That should be enough time to work out what to do about this almighty mess.

Lucy Loxton. An almighty mess at the bottom of a cliff.

He closed his eyes tightly. It wasn't just his hands shaking, his teeth were chattering violently now too. Get a grip, he told himself, you didn't do anything. The dog did it – it was an accident.

Deep breaths, a quick shower, a change of clothes and he'd be okay.

When Huck entered the kitchen minutes later he got the impression that his father had been waiting for him. Did Dalt know he'd been gone? If he did, he didn't say, just pressed the fable of the *The Butterfly and the Moth* into Huck's hand and watched intently whilst he read it.

Was he being tested?

Did he pass?

Thursday 12th September

Dalt

It had been a strange seven days, which was saying something, considering how totally bizarre the last five weeks had been.

Dalt had watched Amelia like a hawk stalking its prey. But like the hunted, she was wily, watching him in return, planning her escape routes in advance, leaving rooms as soon as he entered.

On Wednesday he'd decided to do a little undercover work. Amelia's bedroom door had been ajar, an opportune breeze blowing it open an extra foot as he passed. Slowing his pace, footsteps light (two can play at that game), he'd craned his neck to see in.

No sign of Amelia. No sign of much at all. The room didn't look lived in. Odd. The single bed was neatly made, the bedside table clear of the normal detritus of nocturnal needs. He didn't mean to judge, but she struck him as the kind of woman who lived amidst a clutter of ointments and potions and sprays. She carried scents on her like layers; he could always tell if she'd just been in a room by the heavy fragrance she left in her wake. Dalt stepped around the door, half in, half out of the room, on the edge of reasonable excuse territory. '*I thought I heard a tap running.*' No clothes draped over the wingback chair, no towels scattered across it, nothing, nothing, nothing anywhere. Very odd.

Just the edge of a red suitcase jutting out from under the bed.

Footsteps. Dalt was out the room, across the hallway and back in his own room before Amelia even emerged from the servants' stairs.

Was she planning on leaving? When? Soon?

Why hadn't she said?

He'd seen the way she watched him. When had they turned into adversaries? At what point had their shared worries and fears morphed into mutual suspicion?

It takes a thief to catch a thief.

And he knew she had been stealing. He'd read her notebook one day, when she'd left it by accident on the kitchen table. Private moments, confidential conversations, raw emotion, intimate thoughts. He knew she had jotted them down, taken them. And he knew what she had done with them – locked them up, password protected on her laptop, to peruse at her leisure, to form into sentences, paragraphs, pages, chapters until ultimately, there, sealed in a book, released to the world, was the ultimate theft – their story. Huck's story, Dalt's story. Nell's story.

Not Amelia's story.

Dalt could see that she had been left behind over the years, whilst Nell rode a wave of success that never seemed to come to shore. It couldn't have been easy for Amelia, watching from afar, trying so hard herself, but never quite making it.

When Amelia had first arrived, Dalt had offered to help illustrate her children's story, do what he could to get her work out into the world.

Two things had put an end to that. The first was that the book she had written was really, truly awful. Oddly familiar, in fact disconcertingly recognisable, its plot centred around a young girl who, having recently discovered she was a witch, had been invited to attend a school of witchcraft and wizardry. Upon her enrolment, together with her motley pals, all sorts of escapades and adventures ensued.

This book wasn't going anywhere, and he was pretty sure Amelia knew it.

The second turning point had occurred one evening at supper, a week or so before Nell disappeared.

They'd all been there, all four of them. The evening was warm, and they'd eaten outside. It was a Friday, and the wine was flowing. Nell was on top form. Amused and amusing, sharp tongued and witty, relaxed and off-guard, his wife at her best. Amelia was seated next to her at the long table, flushed and giggly. He recalled how she kept placing her hand on Nell's arm. Was he jealous? No, he didn't think so. It was when the conversation took a more serious path that warning lights began to flash.

'Do you remember when we lived together?' Amelia reminisced. 'In the flat with the mould behind the wardrobe and the woman upstairs who did exercise videos at 3 a.m.?'

Huck had spoken before Nell could reply.

'Is that when you wrote your first Daniel Hargreaves novel, Mudder? I remember you mentioning something about writing through the night when you couldn't sleep.'

Amelia placed her wine glass on the table with unnecessary force, spilling the dark red contents onto her hand.

'Yes, I think it was,' Nell had replied, seemingly oblivious to the change in her friend's demeanour, the charge in the air.

'What were you writing then, Amelia?'

Huck was baiting her. Was it the glass of wine Huck filled for himself, challenging Dalt with his eyes as he did so, or the charged atmosphere that loosened his son's tongue, dared him to dip his toe into foreign waters?

No hesitation on Amelia's part.

'I'd just submitted a series of short stories to a publisher.'

'Did they like them?' Quick fire. Dalt flinched. Huck was like a cattle prod, poking, poking.

'No.'

The word sounded sharp and bitter on Amelia's tongue.

Dalt watched as Huck leaned back in his chair, his work done.

'No, they didn't like them. '*Not what they were looking for,*' apparently, '*not right for the current market.*'

Huck lifted the bottle of red, refilled Amelia's glass. Taking her to the slaughterhouse.

Amelia drank deeply.

'Story of my life. Rejection, rejection, rejection. I'm sick of waiting for it to happen. I've worked bloody hard.'

And there it was, the ugly inside, laid out on the table.

Entitlement – success a prerogative, not a possibility.

She sounded like a petulant toddler, '*But it's my turn now, my turn,*' in denial that the toy she wanted wasn't hers to have.

Enough of this game of Huck's. Dalt lost any sympathy he had for Amelia then, pushed his chair back from the table and gathered his glass and plate to take his leave.

Just as Nell leaned over and awkwardly half rubbed, half patted Amelia on the back.

Nuts. His wife could never read a situation. Nell had no idea how jealous and how resentful Amelia was of her and that this wasn't exactly the top characteristic you look for in a friend.

And now Nell was gone, and he was sure Amelia was taking advantage of the situation. She didn't care about them. All she wanted was her fifteen minutes of fame.

And what publisher would be able to resist the true, fly-on-the-wall, blow-by-blow account of the seconds, minutes, hours and weeks surrounding the disappearance of one of the nation's favourite writers? It wouldn't matter that Amelia, the author, was a previously unpublished nobody.

But Dalt wasn't about to let that happen. There was no way Amelia would leave this house with that story.

It takes a thief to catch a thief. A funny old saying that.

Amelia had violated their trust, stolen a story

Dalt lay back on his bed, closing his eyes for a moment.

He, in turn, had violated their story, stolen trust. There were things he hadn't told Nell. Secrets he'd been keeping, even though he wasn't sure why. Whose crime was worse? And would stopping Amelia make reparations for his own wrongs?

Friday 13th September

Huck

A fter the incident at Guller's Leap, Huck had laid low.

Funnily enough, a dead body hadn't been part of his plan. He hadn't even had a plan.

Nobody was supposed to die.

It was an accident. It was an accident. The mantra played over and over in his head, but the knowledge didn't help alleviate the guilt. His thoughts kept returning to Harry Loxton, Lucy's son. He, Huck, knew the pain of losing a mother. Now, Harry was suffering the same. This wasn't what Huck had intended, not at all. He'd just wanted to talk to Lucy – shake her up a little.

He hadn't meant for her to die.

Huck had spent the next three days in a haze, hardly eating, barely sleeping, biting his nails until his cuticles bled. Unbelievably, scarily, (worryingly?), nobody seemed to have noticed. One of the perks of his mother being a missing person; he was allowed (expected even?) to be an emotional wreck.

But by Wednesday he was feeling marginally better. His right eye had stopped twitching uncontrollably and his hands had mostly stopped shaking.

He needed to finish what Mudder had started. It was the only thing that made any sense.

He'd hidden the fables under a loose floorboard beneath his bed. It was an effort to get out of bed, to get dressed and to retrieve them.

But once the stories were in his hand he felt focused. Purposeful again.

Next on the list was the tale of *The Magpie and the Sparrow*. Huck hadn't needed to work this one out, he knew it straight away. It helped that he'd eavesdropped on Mudder's conversation with The Cigarette, Katrina, and he'd heard first-hand how Mudder had been treated so cruelly by their shared teacher, Ms Jamison. He knew immediately that Ms Jamison was Magpie.

It wasn't hard to find others who'd suffered at the teacher's hands as Mudder had. It turned out that the town museum (good old museum, coming up trumps again) had copies of class photos from the last forty years at Stonebrook Primary School on microfiche. He'd spent a whole day trawling through the pictures, writing down the pupils' names listed beneath the black and white images. Back home, in the privacy of his room, using a false name, he'd set up a private Facebook group, *Former Pupils of Stonebrook Primary School*. Using the names from the school photos, he'd sent out invitations for others to join. This had been a bit hit and miss – many of the girls, now adults, must have got married, changed their names. He just hoped that the invitation would reach a few of the right people, and snowball from there. He was lucky. It did. Soon, the group had over five hundred members, many posting photos on the timeline, and reminiscing about days gone by.

It didn't take much to kick-start an online conversation about Ms Jamison. Huck created another false account (he could do this with his eyes shut). Using yet another false name (he'd gone for Amy Smith: easily forgettable) he'd commented underneath a photo posted by a Hamish Turner, showing all the teachers in their magnificent eighties glory (thanks Hamish).

Woah, blast from the past! Ms Jamison? I don't think I'll ever forget her after she shut me in her store cupboard for an entire morning. What a b**ch!

All he had to do now was sit back and watch the action unfold.

Mudder had been right, he mused, as over the course of the next few days the number of comments under Fake Amy's post entered triple digits. Social media was a waste of time – vacuous, shallow and filled with drivel, but it also had its positives. You could raise an angry army in no time.

Melanie Bateman, class of 1994: *No way! I thought I was the only person she'd done that to. Surely she wasn't allowed to do that?*

Catherine Pickering, class of 1989: *Oh. My. God. Ms J rapped my knuckles with a ruler more times than I can remember the year I was in her class. I never told anyone because I thought it was my own fault for being naughty.*

Peter Graham: *It wasn't just girls. She shut me in her stock cupboard too. I was a bit of a nightmare kid. I was diagnosed with ADHD in secondary school. I didn't deserve that though.*

Interspersed with these confessions were the voices of justice.

Sarah Anthony: *You need to speak up, now. It's not too late.*

Gordon Fraser: *Ms J can't get away with this.*

And so on and so forth.

Eventually, Melanie Bateman started a new thread:

If you were mistreated in some way by Ms Jamison, PM me. We need to make a list of all of us affected and get this out in the open. I'm prepared to speak up about this.

The post received over thirty 'likes', which Huck took to mean at least thirty people were sending her private messages.

Later that day, Huck resigned from his role as page administrator, ensuring he'd left no online trace, and withdrew back into the woodwork.

His work was done.

Nearly.

Just the fable itself to type up and send to Frank in the early hours of Saturday morning, as before.

And two more fables to go.

Amelia

S he couldn't hang around for an ending after all. She couldn't stay here any longer. Her skin prickled, both from the heat, and from the sensation that she had carried with her all week that someone was watching her. Yesterday, she could have sworn she'd seen a shadow across the hallway as she entered her room and she'd had the strangest feeling that someone had been in there before her. She'd outstayed her welcome that was for certain. This sense of trepidation, that something was coming for her, was playing havoc with her mental health.

Last night she'd dreamt of this house. It was some other time, sometime long ago. Gas lamps stood on low tables and sent out gentle arcs of soft, yellow light. Shadows danced on the walls and somewhere far off, someone played the piano.

In her dream, she'd walked the hallways, calling out Nell's name, calling it into every room she passed. Floorboards creaked beneath her bare feet as she pushed open door after door, walked up stair after stair.

It was only when she reached the very apex of the house, a room, high in the attic, and looked out of the window that she saw the townspeople, hundreds of them, gathered on the lawns below, brandishing flaming torches high above their heads, pickaxes, scythes and shovels trailing along the dewy grass.

Traitor, traitor, traitor!

The air around her vibrated with sound, her whole body pulsed with it.

Traitor, traitor, traitor!

And at their fore, a woman with a mass of fiery auburn hair, flaming torch raised highest of all, voice audible above the mass.

Traitor, traitor, traitor!

The floorboards of the attic floor creaked behind her, and in the dream, Amelia turned to see Dalt and Huck enter the attic room. They joined her at the window, and together the three of them watched the angry mob.

Traitor, traitor, traitor!

The house was burning now, flames licking the steps, the porch, the front windows.

'Up there!' one of the villagers shouted, pointing up at their three faces in the window.

The red-haired woman stepped forward.

And Amelia woke up, the acrid smell of smoke burning in her nostrils.

Were those cries of traitor for her, or for Dalt or for Huck?

Weeks ago, before Nell went missing, before any of this, Amelia had got embarrassingly drunk at supper. It had got unpleasant. She vaguely remembered bemoaning her lack of success. The details were blurry, but she remembered Dalt looking scornfully at her, and the feeling of shame burrowing under her skin. But Nell had made it better. Dear Nell had bent to Amelia's ear and whispered, 'You'll find your story. It's coming, I can feel it.' Or something like that. Amelia had definitely been rather tipsy.

Nell was offering her something incredible. A chance. Amelia had convinced herself that somehow Nell knew about the biography idea. Amelia had been asking a lot of questions, after all; Nell must have worked it out.

But the cries of *traitor* and *snake* in her dreams were unnerving her, making her question herself.

Making her question them all.

It was like that quiz show where you could hold on to your winnings or gamble it all for the ultimate prize and end up walking away with nothing. No thank you. She'd take what she'd got and run, thank you very much. It was time to leave.

Huck

The third fable, the one about *The Cat and the Piglets*, hadn't been so easy to decipher. A story about parenting and judgements, about different approaches and consequences. The perpetrator didn't immediately jump to mind.

He'd found himself absent-mindedly rubbing his thumb and his shortened forefinger together as he read, a habit he'd had as long as he could remember, the action soothing him like a baby sucking its thumb.

The accident. Was it linked to the accident? The time Mudder accidentally chopped off the tip of his finger? The buds of an idea developed in his brain; he tried to grasp it, tease it out. Funny, how the brain works, the subconscious mind storing it all away and informing the conscious mind when the time is right. What else was hiding in his head that he wasn't allowing himself to think about?

After the accident, that woman had come to visit. What if the fable was about her? He remembered her now, crouching on the carpet, a bag of puppets in her outstretched hand. He hadn't thought about her in years.

Was she Mother Cat? Was it her?

His memories of her were few. No name. No real idea of what she had even looked like. Her hair had been hard, he remembered. He'd touched it once, and had recoiled, his fingers sticky, his stomach queasy. Unnatural.

Not like Mudder's hair. Soft, long, comforting, he'd always loved playing with it, twisting it around his fingers.

He missed her so much it hurt.

Drawing a blank on any further details of the mystery visitor, Huck thought carefully about where to turn. He couldn't ask Dalt about the identity of the woman without raising suspicions.

There had to be some paperwork somewhere about the finger incident. He could try the Doctors' Surgery – his medical notes maybe. Was he old enough to access them without parental permission? He didn't want to alert anyone to his investigation.

There was an old metal filing cabinet in Dalt's study, the kind that topples over with the weight of itself when the top drawer is extended. Huck knew this from experience. As a child it had overbalanced, coming close to crushing him as he cowered in its shadow. That had been weird too, looking back. Mudder, who had been stood in the doorway talking to Dalt at his desk, had screamed in absolute terror. A scream Huck had only heard that one time before in the garden. Dalt had crossed the room like a shot, catching the cabinet before it crushed Huck, whilst Mudder looked on in horror.

Turns out Huck had been fine, but Mudder hadn't been fine. It had taken the rest of the evening for Dalt to calm her down, to stop her rambling. He'd run her a bath, and when that didn't work, taken her upstairs and helped her to bed. Huck had stood by, watching, scared, confused. It was all coming back to him. Funny old things, brains, he thought again, staring at the cabinet, slowly connecting the dots.

She'd been afraid, hadn't she? Terrified when the filing cabinet fell that he would get hurt, and that she would get in trouble – get in trouble for another accident. Get in trouble with that woman.

He opened the filing cabinet with care. It looked well organised. Folders titled *Car Documents*, *Birth Certificates*, *Tax*, and *Medical*.

Medical – that was the one he was after. He pulled out the entire folder and dumped its contents onto Dalt's desk. Letters. Lots and lots of letters, referrals, appointments, hospital names and addresses, department extension numbers, assessments, observations. His name, over and over. His name and Mudder's.

But there was another name that appeared time and time again: *Joan Matthews, Regional Social Worker*.

'Joan Matthews,' Huck tried it out. It echoed in the room, cold, steely, unforgiving.

Joan Matthews. Hairspray, bun, minty breath and a bag of toys, Mudder perched on a sofa, anxious, bewildered, uncertain.

It had been his fault Joan Matthews had ever visited them. His fault that his fingers got in the way of Mudder's spade. His fault that this woman had ruined Mudder's life, reduced her to a shell of the mother he'd had before the accident.

Only he could fix this.

And so, once more, he had.

Time flowed differently since Mudder's disappearance. There was more of it, for a start, day and night blurred together. There was way too much of it and nobody seemed to care what he did with it. Nobody noticed when he was in the house or when he left it, in the same way that he didn't pay much attention to the actions of his father or Amelia.

Every man for himself, seemed to be their coping mechanism.

This freedom had its benefits.

Back in his room, Huck slid the laptop out from beneath the wardrobe. He typed '*Joan Matthews social worker*' into a search engine. Nothing relevant at first. Scrolling far down the page, a link to a newspaper report.

September 2006, Joan Matthews, Stonebrook social worker, recommended a two-year-old boy be removed from his home following allegations of neglect. A hearing followed; scholarly evidence presented on the subject of *'autism in mothers.'* *'Case turned on its head'*, the article stated. *'Accusations revoked.'*

Autism? Mudder?

The diagnosis didn't surprise him. He'd known it all along, understood it right from the start, he'd just never said the words out loud.

And Joan Matthews, what of her now?

What of her indeed.

A lengthy call to the local county council social work team (most of it spent on hold listening to jarring, jangly music) gave him the beginnings of the breadcrumb trail he was searching for. Joan Matthews was no longer registered as a social worker. She'd left the profession in December 2006, the same year as the court case. The woman on the phone had been surprisingly chatty (or Huck had been surprisingly charming). Huck had tried to guess her age: late fifties, he'd decided, three cats and a husband who made all the right noises but never truly listened.

'I wanted to find her,' Huck had simpered down the line at her, 'to say thank you, after all these years, for everything she did for me when I was younger.'

Cat Lady was probably imagining a camera crew recording the telephone call, which would later be played on a big screen in a television studio to a live audience on Saturday night TV, whilst on the stage itself *Young Boy In Need Now An Adult* was reunited with *Joan Matthews, Social Worker Extraordinaire Who Changed His Life Forever.*

Or the woman had just been off sick the day they rolled out the data protection training. Either way: win, win. He had her right where he wanted her.

'Oh, my love, now isn't that wonderful. It's not often someone calls to say thanks.'

A few more gushing adulations and Cat Lady ('Barbara, my dear, call me Barbara,') was cracking open the case file on Joan Matthews (or typing her name into the personnel database) keeping up a stream of conversation as she did so. He hoped she worked in the office alone, both for his sake and for Barbara's.

'Do you know, I remember Joan Matthews. I'd only just started when she left. It was the saddest thing; she had a stroke. Shocked us all – she must have only been in her late forties. Terrible it was.'

'That's awful.' Huck's response was genuine.

'Here, I've found her details now. December 2006 it happened. As I recall, Joan was in hospital for a good bit, physiotherapy and all that, but I don't think it made much difference. There's an address for her here on the screen. It hasn't been updated for a while, but she might be there still. It's a nursing home.'

'You've been amazing, Barbara,' (genuinely, she had been. Loose tongued and unaware of any legal implications of handing out addresses to strangers over the phone, there weren't many Barbaras left in the world). 'I'll just get a pen and paper,' (as if he wasn't already poised and ready to go).

Effusive thank yous followed, in which he promised to let Barbara know how it all went by means of a follow up phone call (sorry Barb, never going to happen).

When the call ended, Huck sat in quiet contemplation, staring at the scrap of paper in front of him.

The Tudor's Nursing Home, Warren Farm Road, Stonebrook.

He could end it all right now and not take this any further. Call it divine retribution – the woman had already had a stroke.

A vision of Mudder pulling at weeds, digging, planting, hands raw, determined to be self-sufficient, to rely on no-one flashed through his mind. Mudder screaming as the filing cabinet toppled.

He couldn't end it here. He needed Joan Matthews to know what she'd done to Mudder.

The Tudor's Nursing Home seeks to provide the highest standard of care to our residents. Individual care plans are formed and residents are actively encouraged to exercise choice and to enjoy life to their full potential. The website promised.

Huck scanned the list of activities offered to the residents of the Tudor's: *quiz night, bingo night, volunteer-led reading sessions, board games, exercise classes.* This was more like a five-star hotel than a nursing home.

Volunteer-led reading sessions.

The idea came to him straight away. Joan Matthews had already had her punishment, but he, Huck, needed closure. He'd visit, read her the fable, make sure she realised it was her story. Remind her one last time. That was only fair, wasn't it? He, Dalt, Mudder – they were all still wearing the scars Joan Matthews had given them; Joan Matthews needed to see the damage she'd caused one last time.

And so, he'd arranged it, phoned the Tudor's, given a false name and a mawkish spiel about 'giving back to the community'. He'd snuck out the back way, had to push his bike over the uneven ground of the moor until he'd met the road, but he'd made it – no one had seen him leave. And boom, there he was: Thursday morning reading session. He'd pulled his cap down low, in case he was recognised and merged into the handful of other volunteers waiting in the lobby.

As the readers trooped into the residents' day lounge the smell of overcooked vegetables and old age hit him in the nostrils. He wanted to gag, wanted to be high, high upon the moors, with the warm wind and the fresh air buffeting his face. This was grim.

A large room filled with every shade of brown (who knew there were so many?) housed the elderly occupants of the Tudor's. A television played in a corner of the room but as far as he could tell, no one seemed to be paying it any attention. Heads hung low, rasping breath emanated from bunched up airways. Eyes followed the volunteers, whilst the bodies they belonged to remained inert. Coughing, wheezing, grunting, Huck didn't know how they'd have heard the television even if they wanted to.

Is this what it meant to be old? Did your need for fresh air and your enjoyment of colour diminish along with your eyesight and gross motor skills?

The residents were arranged in a semi-circle facing a glass window that ran the entire length of the room, and looked out onto a flat, green lawn. Outside, numerous sprinklers showered the grass, grass that was defying the summer, defying the environment it lived in, and thriving despite the heatwave.

'Derek, here's Quinn. You boys are flying through *Treasure Island*, you must be nearly finished?' Judy, a bustling (and busty, in a can't help but notice but don't want to look kind of way) care-worker was organising the volunteers, depositing them like drops of water onto withered plants, and didn't expect an answer.

'Quinn, squeeze in there next to Derek,' Judy was saying. 'Pull that chair up from over there, the one next to Joan.'

Joan.

Joan Matthews?

Yes, according to the name badge she had pinned to her chest. From his position towards the back of the line, Huck eyed his target. As an undercover operative, he couldn't be further from James Bond. And slumped in her wheelchair dozing, Joan Matthews couldn't be further from Blofeld. Huck felt like he was going to war with a machine gun whilst his enemy held up a blade of glass. Joan Matthews probably couldn't even hold a blade of glass. Her hands lay uselessly in her lap, placed there, he assumed, by a member of staff, her wrists scrawny, blue, fragile like porcelain. A blanket covered her, thick and warm, with thin blue lines dashed across it like waves. A splash of colour in this bird's nest of brown. Her face looked anxious, even in sleep, or one side of it did at least, the other side was slack, saliva clinging to her lip and chin.

Yes, Joan Matthews was being punished enough. But he was here now, he had to go through with it. No one had said this was going to be easy. This was atonement, and it turned out atonement could be downright ugly (as well as mute and infirm).

Huck slipped out of the line of waiting volunteers, and quietly pulled up a chair next to Joan. He opened the book of *Aesop's Fables* he had been carrying and, aware that Judy had finished despatching the volunteers and was scanning the room to make sure all was as it should be, Huck launched into the tale of *The Boy Who Cried Wolf*. When he next looked up, Judy had gone, probably making the most of her teenage babysitters and putting her feet up for five minutes.

Huck paused in his reading to assess the situation. He was sat to the right of Joan Matthews. Her good side, he supposed. He hated to be predictable, stereotypical even, but the old lady smelt overwhelmingly of urine. Did she remember his mother? Was this even worth it? What was going on inside her head?

The old lady's right hand jerked (involuntarily?). He jumped in his seat. How ridiculous, he chastised himself, feeling like he was watching a bad horror film, one where you think the villain is dead and then they take one last shot.

But her right hand flapped again, and her chin lifted from her chest. A string of garbled sounds tumbled from her mouth, rasping noises that made no sense but indicated a need, a desire.

She wanted him to keep reading.

He began to read again, quickly.

Her noises stopped. She wasn't as vacant as he'd thought. She definitely wanted to hear the story. Maybe she had that 'locked-in syndrome' thing. He'd watched a film about a guy with it. You can't talk or move or anything, but you know what's going on around you. It sounded horrific. It sounded a little like being Mudder.

That refocused him. He placed the book on his lap and looked into her eyes; pale blue and watery. He wondered if she saw him.

'It's hot outside.' Small, inconsequential, but he thought she nodded.

He smiled at her, couldn't help it, a reflex reaction forged from pity and fear and sorrow – for her, for Mudder and for himself, all encapsulated in the lift of the corners of his mouth.

From in-between the pages of the book, he pulled the loose sheets of paper, the fable of *The Cat and the Piglets* and settled it squarely in front of him.

He began to read.

When he was twelve his grandfather had died. At eighty-six, Charles Dalton had been an intimidating man, never the grandfatherly figure Huck had imagined (wanted, hoped for).

There had been a service, held at the local parish church. Local to Charles, not Huck. His grandfather had lived up north, a solid five hours' drive away. On the long car journey, Huck's stomach had clenched tighter with each mile that had passed, a bleak, harrowing gnawing feeling sweeping in like dark rain clouds over the sea. The anticipation of his role in the church service, a poem that he had been instructed to read, a poem he clutched in his hand, made him breathe too fast then panic that he couldn't breathe at all.

The following day in church, when the moment finally came, he'd stood petrified at the front looking at the faces of strangers, at the coffin of his grandfather, at his father in his grief.

And he'd read.

He'd read that damn poem like he meant it. Like he'd loved and lost and would remember and all the other sentiments it spouted.

People had reached for tissues, dabbed at their eyes. There'd been audible swallows and looks of admiration, and (would you believe it) a small ripple of applause at the end. He'd almost bowed. He should have, really, it was all just an act anyway, wasn't it?

He'd realised then that he had this ability, skill, call it what you will, to lock away his true feelings, bury them deep, and get on with the job in hand.

So that's what he did now.

He read.

Is there anything more powerful, in these lives of ours, than words? Words can appease or anger. Words can provoke tears and laughter and evoke memories and moments that we'd long considered lost in the sands of time. Words can sink and words can save. How powerful we all are, he thought, as he watched Joan Matthews' face. How powerful we are without lifting a finger.

He was three quarters of the way into reading the fable of *The Cat and the Piglets* when he saw the first tear fall. By the end of the story, Joan Matthews' face was wet, her breathing quick and shallow. He fought the urge to take a tissue and clean her up, her absence of dignity hard to bear, but instead he gripped the papers he held tighter, and began to read again, glancing around the room to see if anyone else was paying them any attention.

No, the other readers were all absorbed in their own stories, attentive to their own listeners. No sign of Judy either.

He started reading the fable again, slowly at first, then speeding up, reading with focus, with intent. An eye for an eye, he told himself, in an effort to calm his own racing heart. Tit for Tat. Deep down, he wasn't sure he believed it, but the thought of Mudder kept him going. He read the fable three, four more times, all the while Joan Matthews' agitation becoming more apparent. Gurgling, wheezing, drooling, by the end of the final read through, she really was in quite a state.

Mentally exhausted, he placed the papers on his lap. Enough. Perfect timing, he could see Judy in the hallway on her way to the day lounge.

'Judy,' he called, standing and pushing his chair back, 'Judy, I think something's wrong with Mrs Matthews. She doesn't look well at all.'

Judy pressed a button attached to a belt around her waist and an alarm sounded further back down the corridor. Behind Judy, footsteps came running and within moments, another two nurses were at Mrs Matthews' side, speaking in calming voices and wiping her face.

'Thank you, readers, we're going to have to finish early today. Thank you all for coming and we do hope to see you again, same time next week.'

The speedy evacuation reminded him of the time James Turner had smashed the fire alarm during a mock science exam. His peers looked then as they did now: sheepishly relieved that the session had come to an end sooner than expected. They filed out obediently, books tucked under arms, down the grand steps of the nursing home into the glaringly bright sunshine of the morning.

He thought Judy might want to question him, to ask him what had occurred to make Joan Matthews so distraught, but no. Judy shut the door behind the last volunteer and that was that. Perhaps residents choking on their own tears was an everyday occurrence here.

As he approached the clump of trees at the foot of the drive behind which he'd stashed his bike, Huck realised he still had the sheets of paper in his hand. He knelt at the side of his bike, pretending to fiddle with the lock long after he'd opened it, until the last of the other volunteers had dispersed. Taking his lighter from his pocket, he knelt amidst the tree roots and nettles and shredded the paper into tiny pieces. Taking his time, choosing thin, dry twigs, Huck built a small pyramid over the words that had done their job. It was time to release them. They'd done some research at school into ancient cultures and their beliefs. He'd been fascinated at the time by the practice of building sacrificial fires – that which is burnt turns to smoke and is thought to return through the air to the gods. Not his smoke though, not today.

'Back off, Gods,' he whispered as his thumb depressed the button on the crappy lighter and the flame shot out, the edges of the paper and twigs catching quickly. 'This one's for you, Mudder.'

Acrid words floating into the air. Would they reach Mudder, would she realise what he was doing for her? What he'd done?

But it wasn't over yet. There was still one last fable.

The Willow Tree and the Conifer

A t the bottom of a grassy bank, a willow tree grew. It was a thing of great beauty and people came from far and wide to admire it. Its branches, laden with bright green leaves and yellow flowers, reached down to caress the gently flowing water of the river running past. Its thick trunk offered itself as a home to squirrels and birds and insects of a hundred different species. Never had there been a more magnificent tree. The townspeople loved and cared for the tree. They would use its willow to make charcoal and to weave baskets. They used its wood to make beautiful sculptures and placed them at the tree's trunk as offerings of thanks.

On the other side of the river grew a conifer tree. Its branches were thin and spindly, no good for shading the grazing cattle that roamed this side of the river. Its timber was weak and prone to rot, no good for building boats or houses and its fruit was hard and woody, no good for the children to sit and gorge upon.

The conifer on the far bank would gaze at the willow tree, with the townspeople gathered around it. How it longed to be like its neighbour: idolised and adored. Didn't they share the same soil?

The same sun and wind and rain. How unfair life was, to bestow the willow with so much, and yet the conifer with so little.

The conifer tree's grumbles were carried on the wind to where the willow stood. Day after day, night after night, year after year the willow listened to the moans of the conifer, until one day it could take no more.

'Listen carefully to me,' the willow called across the water. 'Listen and heed my words.'

Surprised, the conifer tree ceased its grumbling and turned to hear what the willow had to say.

'Because my wood is so useful, my branches are cut from me. Because my bark is so special it is stripped from me and used to make medicine. Because my leaves hang so low, people gather under me all day long to find shade from the hot sun. I am never left alone. The people mean well, but in the end, they will kill me.

'And you? You sit in a beautiful, quiet field, full of long grass and butterflies. Nobody bothers you. Nobody wants anything from you. You are free to grow, to be exactly what you are, with no expectations, no demands. You are free to flourish simply as you. Do you know how lucky you are?'

The conifer tree looked at the willow tree then, like he was seeing it for the first time. It looked tired and old. There were scars in its bark from the villagers' knives and stumps on its trunk where its poor branches had been sawn off. The willow tree bowed its head deep and low and spoke for the final time.

'Take what you have, be who you are, without envy, without doubt, without sadness. Only when you release yourself of these afflictions will you be truly free, and only when you are truly free will you see what you are truly capable of.'

The more you can let go, the happier you can be.

Huck

One last fable. The fable of *The Willow Tree and the Conifer*, all typed up and ready to go.

The plan, to send it to Frank, as usual, in the early hours of Saturday morning – the last piece of the puzzle.

Dear Mudder, never good with spoken words but a dream with paper and pen, Huck's admiration for her pulsed as strongly as ever.

Years ago, his teacher had invited parents into school to talk about their careers. Huck hadn't asked Mudder. He knew she wouldn't (couldn't) sit in front of a class of thirty children and talk to them in a way that they would understand. He understood. But Patrick's mum had come in, much to Patrick's embarrassment. She was a scientist, an aquarium research assistant to be exact. Her role, carrying out research to tackle fundamental gaps in understanding of coastal ecosystem responses to artificial light at night. The way she talked, the way she described the moonlight shimmering on the ocean, made even a bookworm like Huck sit up and listen. Patrick's mum was truly fascinating. She managed to make the observation of larvae and the collection of data sound as incredible as a trip to the moon. He'd stared adoringly up at this magnificent woman, hanging onto every word that had fallen from her lips. At the end of the talk, he'd turned to Patrick, keen to catch his friend's eye, sure he'd be grinning and proud, but Patrick's face was buried deep within his hands, his hands resting on his knees; his whole body tightly curled into a ball. He reminded Huck of a hedgehog, a scruffy tuft of black hair poking through where his fingers met.

Huck didn't understand him at all. He was nothing but proud of his mother.

When Huck had read Mudder's fables that first day in her office, the fable of *The Willow Tree and the Conifer* had been at the bottom of the pile, written in a different pen to the others, the handwriting looked messier, as if it had been written in a hurry.

Amelia was, of course, the conifer.

Mudder had meant Amelia to be last, because this was the part where the cymbals clashed, and the symphony ended. Deal with Amelia, and afterwards, when the ripples of the vibrations had died down, everything would be resolved.

Mudder had known how desperate Amelia was to be published. The Amelia that had turned up unannounced two and a half months earlier had been beaten by the publishing industry. Against her nature and her solitary instincts, Mudder had taken Amelia in, fed her with stories, nursed her with words and healed her with hope. Hope of her own story.

He'd overheard them on occasion, sitting out on the decking of an evening. Amelia hadn't exactly been covert. Amelia had openly asked Mudder questions about her writing, her ideas, her routine. She'd openly jotted down Mudder's responses too. Mudder must have realised something odd was going on.

Despite this, or maybe because of this, Mudder never gave much away. Amelia was having to work for what she wanted and how much she wanted it was clear.

And it wasn't just Amelia who would want it. A biography of the elusive Nell Davenport would be something an awful lot of people would be desperate to get their hands on.

Amelia had seemed focused and purposeful. He could imagine that feeling, knowing that she was on her way to publishing her first book, a biography of one of the country's most beloved authors. Amelia's intentions were clear to Huck. But had Mudder known what she was up to?

Then it all went wrong for Amelia.

Mudder went missing.

But Amelia had flipped it around! Huck had seen her, skulking around with her notepad, recording the days, the events, the progression of Mudder's disappearance. He'd snuck into Amelia's room, read extracts of her diary. Amelia hadn't been knocked down by the absence of her friend. If anything, she had been built up by it.

Mudder's disappearance would, of course, add an incredible layer of intrigue to Amelia's biography. It would make it topical and relevant, even more desirable. Amelia would have struck literary gold, a fly-on-the-wall account of a vanishing author and the holes she'd left behind.

But there was a twist at the end waiting for Amelia. Mudder was no fool. She wasn't master of the thriller genre for nothing.

Amelia had a lesson to learn. So terribly clever. Hadn't the willow told the conifer to listen? '*Heed my words.*' Mudder had tried to warn Amelia of the dangers of fame. She'd tried to tell her that the way to be happy was not through success but through letting go of expectations. Through letting go of books that were half written.

Some lessons just had to be learnt the hard way.

Mudder would have known Huck would get there in the end – that he would execute this vitally important final part of the plan. There was no way Amelia was going to be allowed to leave with the notes she'd made. In order for her to be happy, Amelia needed to be able to let go. It was up to Huck to help her.

He had a feeling that parting (tearing, ripping?) Amelia from her story was going to be the most difficult task of all.

Amelia

The dream from the night before had played on a loop in her head all day. Flashes of flaming torches and shouted threats had left her feeling quite anxious. She'd barely left her room, and now it was 5 p.m.

From her vantage point on the edge of the neatly made bed, Amelia inspected the room. Clean and tidy, she'd made sure of that this afternoon. She felt bad enough leaving without saying thank you or goodbye, let alone leaving a mess behind in her wake. Her red suitcase lay packed and zipped up at her feet, a backpack next to it containing her laptop, wallet and notebooks. Best to keep those on her at all times.

Would Nell approve of the book? She'd been pondering the question for days. Today, she'd tried meditating in an effort to find an answer. She spent a large part of the morning lying on the floor, stilling her mind and body, opening her heart and lifting her consciousness in order to achieve a transcendental state. It hadn't been easy though. It was cramped down there between the bed and the chest of drawers, and her foot kept knocking into the door to the bathroom, making it swing open then closed again. She'd bet the Dalai Lama didn't have to contend with this sort of nonsense.

She'd waited patiently at the end of the meditation for divine guidance to come but all she got was another bloody mosquito bite.

'Have faith,' she imagined her Zen master reassuring her in his (slightly sinister) breathy tones, *'the answer will come when you least expect it. For now, use your common sense. And give thanks.'*

In the end, the decision was going to have to come down to her gut instinct. Her intuition.

Henry Cooper had agreed.

He hadn't been part of the plan. Of course, he hadn't been part of the plan. Amelia had come here seething mad at him for dumping her out of the blue. She'd also discovered since, from a friend in London, that the swine had taken the tickets she'd purchased for Rome and used them for his own holiday. So, Henry really couldn't have been further from her first choice of publisher.

But when she'd submitted a synopsis, and the rough draft of the first five chapters of her manuscript, to a number of highly regarded publishers last week, her first choice, then second, third, fourth and fifth had all turned her down. *'It's something of a sensitive area, don't you think?'* and *'Perhaps, when we know what has happened to Ms Davenport, we might consider it. When we're sure we won't be prosecuted for defamation of character should Ms Davenport reappear in the meantime.'*

Amelia had had to start looking elsewhere.

Luckily, Henry Cooper was a man of few principles and poor morals (it turned out he hadn't gone to Rome alone, but with some random stranger he'd met in a bar at the hotel airport the night before).

'You're lucky to have caught me,' he'd drawled down the phone line earlier that afternoon. 'I'm literally just back in the office. Took a bit of time off – been seeing the sights.'

Amelia could imagine what sights he'd been seeing, the creep. What had she ever seen in him?

She'd nearly hung up there and then, would have, had she not glanced down at the notepad on the desk in front of her, covered in the names and telephone numbers of all the publishers she'd already called. If this was going to happen, she was going to have to make some compromises.

Or one enormous, hideous, smug and balding compromise at least.

It was a price she'd have to pay.

He hadn't been able to contain his excitement when she talked him through her manuscript. Amelia could practically see the dollar signs ching ching above his head and hear his hands rub together with glee.

'And Nell Davenport isn't going to contest this, should she reappear anytime soon? Are we clear on that?' His chuckle was positively repulsive, but even Henry 'The Weasel' Cooper didn't want to get sued for libel.

'I've been staying with her. We're great friends. She'd be happy it was me that wrote it, not somebody she didn't know making money off the back of someone else's tragedy.'

Amelia tried to ignore the feeling that this was exactly what she was doing.

'I need you to come and get me.' Amelia hadn't realised she was going to issue the command until the words had left her mouth, but she liked the way she sounded. Powerful. In control.

Henry had begun to laugh in a sleazy, 'you're joking' kind of way, before realising the silence on her part meant she most definitely was not.

'Er, what, now?'

'Yes. Now.' Wow, she was good at this. Maybe she should have tried this years ago, instead of playing the simpering female-in-need role.

A pause and the shuffling of paper before he spoke again.

'Where are you? I'll write it down.'

Amelia could hear the scratch of a pencil in the background as he took down the details.

'Is it sat-nav-able?' The lazy drawl was back.

'Yes. But you won't be able to get in the gates without the code. Actually, forget the gates, I'll meet you on the road outside. Text me when you get here.'

'I won't be able to leave London until at least six. I shan't imagine I'll be there before eleven. Can I stay the night and we can drive back to London in the morning?'

Amelia glanced around at the packed suitcase, the backpack beside it, the tidy, empty room and the single bed for one.

'No, I need to leave tonight.'

Henry accepted this without further questioning. Amelia had a feeling he was rather enjoying this new, bossy side to her.

It had been 3 p.m. when she'd hung up the phone. A bad taste lingered in her mouth. Had she made a massive mistake, a deal with the devil, or was she just being dramatic? Whatever she'd just done, it didn't feel good.

Just the afternoon to kill, then she was out of here.

A little more meditating (which accidentally turned into a two-hour long nap) and the hands of the clock had turned to point to five, at which Amelia had gone downstairs to prepare dinner.

Or 'the last supper,' she'd thought wryly.

It was while she was grinding up pine nuts and basil for a home-made pesto and worrying about her midnight escape that the idea to drug Dalt came to her. The pack of sleeping tablets on the kitchen shelf caught her eye and the plan began to form. Placing the pestle down gently, Amelia examined the packet. Dalt's name was on the label. Only a couple had been taken. That was Dalt through and through, unable to accept help, sure he could power on, get through it on his own. If it was her, she'd have finished that packet by now and would be demanding a repeat prescription.

Drugging Dalt and leaving unannounced was the coward's way out, but Amelia was certain that Dalt knew of her intentions to publish the book. If he knew she was leaving, she was sure that he would try to stop her. Stop her and make her promise not to do anything with the story.

A promise she was not willing to make.

Anyway, if she were to put these tablets in his food it would be the best night's sleep Dalt would have had in weeks. Amelia would actually be doing him a favour.

And Huck? Should she give them to him too?

What was she thinking, drugging a child? Huck was less likely to hear her leave, anyway, tucked away on his own on the top floor. She was pretty sure he was nothing to worry about.

The spaghetti had been bloody good, even if she did say so herself. She'd ground five of Dalt's pills into his portion. Five seemed the right amount, she didn't want to kill him.

They'd eaten in the garden. Her idea. They'd sat outside on the decking. The air seemed different – charged – and for once the insects didn't bother them. The cushions had been left out on the chairs for weeks. When Nell was here, would she have brought them in each evening, Amelia wondered? She couldn't imagine it – Dalt's job perhaps, in that life before. What else had gone undone in the weeks since Nell disappeared? Would these small duties now abandoned, cushions left to the will of the weather, weeds left to grow rife amongst the herb garden, in time be gathered up again, given the import they once had, or had the small things gone forever? Would they pick up the pieces, or decide the pieces weren't important after all?

This question would have provided the perfect epilogue to her book. But that question would have to go unanswered since Amelia wasn't about to hang around any longer to discover the answer for herself. She sincerely hoped that Dalt and Huck discovered it though and found a way to make the small things matter again.

There was little chat throughout dinner, but the silence felt amicable. Amelia watched Dalt twist long strands of glistening spaghetti, flecked with vibrant, green pesto, around his fork. She had no idea how this was going to pan out. Would it be like in films, when the character who'd been drugged would suddenly collapse, head lolling, into their dinner? Dear god she hoped not. Huck would think his father had had a heart attack or something. The poor boy didn't need the worries of another parent exiting his life in a sudden manner. She'd only given Dalt five tablets in the hope that he would be able to recognise his own drowsiness and take himself off to bed like a sensible grown up to sleep it off.

Thankfully, with the meal just finished, Dalt did exactly that.

'That was delicious, Amelia. Really delicious. If you two don't mind, I'm going to have an early night.'

Huck looked surprised.

'Okay, night,' he said.

'Good night,' Amelia echoed. 'Sleep well.'

Sleep very, very well indeed.

And Dalt was gone.

Huck helped her clear the table and wash the dishes. It hadn't taken long. It was still only 8 p.m. and Amelia wasn't expecting Henry Cooper until closer to eleven.

Huck went to his room just after nine. Feeling wistful, Amelia took one last walk through the downstairs rooms of the house, reflecting on the events of the summer. So much had gone wrong,

starting with her break-up and ending with the mysterious disappearance of her old friend. It had been intense, living in the af-
termath of such turmoil. But whilst she was still at Moordown,
she felt connected to Nell. Amelia feared that the moment she left,
she would become a stranger to the house and its occupants, her
connection to Nell severed as if it had never existed.

She wished it hadn't ended this way. She'd trade the bloody book
any day, to have Nell here again.

Amelia peeked in on Dalt in his room on her way past – his door
had been ajar (she'd shut it firmly). He'd been curled up on the bed
in his clothes in a foetal position. Yes, she'd definitely done him a
favour with those sleeping pills.

Two hours and she would be gone.

Saturday 14th September

Dalt

His head hurt. His mouth felt dry. Disorientated, Dalt sat up in bed. Is this what it felt like to sleep through the night? If sleep felt this bad, he was better off staying awake. He rubbed his forehead with his fingers and looked at his watch. 9 a.m. on Saturday. How the hell had he managed to sleep for that long? This must be how rock stars felt, entire decades lost in drug induced blurs. '*Oh, the eighties, man, yeah, I dunno what happened to them, man.*' He could say the same about Friday night.

Unsettling, to say the least.

And the house felt unnaturally quiet.

Something wasn't right.

He cast his memory back. Amelia had been behaving oddly at dinner last night – she'd kept looking at him when she thought he wasn't watching and staring at him as he ate. She'd made spaghetti. Dalt had complimented it, he wasn't churlish, and it was delicious. Amelia had looked pleased and when they had finished eating, Dalt had taken himself to bed.

Now he remembered. He had been overcome by a wave, no a tsunami, of tiredness. He'd been too exhausted to question it, had just wanted to lay down, to sleep.

But thirteen hours later he was beginning to smell a rat.

Had Amelia drugged him? He couldn't believe he was asking himself this – the idea like something out of a bad murder mystery. Although, it wouldn't have been hard to do. He pictured the sleeping pills on the kitchen shelf, the pestle and mortar on the counter, the dinner he had devoured.

But why?

Today was Saturday. Saturday! The fables.

Where was his phone?

Not on the bedside table. He fumbled down the side of his bed and his hand found the smooth edge of his mobile.

Yes. There it was.

He paused before opening his email. For that split second, he was in control, reality suspended.

But he couldn't stave off the truth forever. He clicked on the email from Frank that was waiting for him, as he'd known it would be, unprepared but acceptant of the next twist in the road.

He read the fable of *The Willow Tree and the Conifer* slowly. Would it be wrong to say he enjoyed it? Of all the fables so far, this one resonated with him the most. Maybe, because he'd just been thinking about her – the Conifer. Amelia. The jigsaw was fitting together now, pieces sliding into place smoothly and easily, edges completed and only the gaps in the middle left. It was just a matter of twisting the pieces, turning them to make them fit.

He pictured Nell (he was certain that she had written this). His undemonstrative, composed, inscrutable Nell, choosing her words, arranging her sentences, ordering her thoughts, demonstrating the depth of her care and her compassion through the means of the fable. A cry from a woman who never cried out, to a friend who was about to walk in front of a truck. Don't do it, Amelia. Stay where you are.

Amelia!

Had she seen the fable yet? Had Huck? Had it been uploaded to Nell's blog?

There were definite advantages to sleeping in your clothes; Dalt was up and out of his room within seconds. Ignoring the main stairs, he crossed the hall to the servants' steps leading to the kitchen. Amelia's door was shut. Was she still asleep? He tapped politely but clearly on her door. Open it, Amelia, open it.

Nothing. Three more raps were met by further silence. He was about to knock again when he heard footsteps crossing the hallway from the direction of the main stairs. Huck.

'You've read it?' his son asked.

'Yes. Do you think Amelia has? Have you seen her?' Dalt said, realising they were both whispering.

'She's not downstairs,' Huck said.

Dalt's fingers grasped the door handle, twisting and turning it with a sudden urgency.

Amelia's room was empty of all her belongings. No suitcase poked out from beneath the bed. Had she left? Would she really have gone, without telling them, just like that? Like Nell?

And if she had gone, then how? Had she taken a car? Had she walked?

'Is the car here?' Huck must have had the same thought at the same time. They crossed to the window and checked the drive. Two cars. All accounted for.

Huck swung the wardrobe drawers wide. Nothing. Nothing in the chest of drawers either, and the en-suite was the same. No bottles littered the edges of the shower, no toothbrush sat next to the sink.

'Did you know she was planning on leaving today?' Huck asked Dalt.

'I had an idea she was thinking about going soon, but not like this – not without telling us.'

'Strange,' Huck said.

Dalt pulled his phone out of his pocket and called Amelia. It went straight to voicemail.

'Let's drive into town, see if we pass her on the road. Or maybe she's waiting at the station. We can't let her just leave – she's been writing about us. We can't let her go without talking to her about what she's planning to do.' Dalt felt panicky. Breathless.

Huck nodded his agreement and within minutes they were through the gates, no reporters in place to question them, and on the road, cutting through the moor, eyes peeled for movement.

Moor turned to town but with no sign of Amelia.

'She must have left late last night or really early this morning,' Huck suggested as they pulled into an empty short stay parking bay at the train station.

'But surely we would have heard something?' Dalt wasn't ready to share his theory that he had been drugged the night before. In the car, in the daylight, it seemed far-fetched, like something out of one of Nell's thrillers.

Huck shrugged, 'I didn't hear anything.'

The station was busy. They stood, scanning the queues at the ticket machines, the row of people at the information desk. No Amelia.

'Let's check the platforms,' Dalt said. 'I'll go across to the other side, you check this one.'

Without waiting for an answer, he was off, through the crowded entranceway, up the stairs and over the bridge down to platform two. No Amelia.

Huck stood facing him on the opposite platform. It was Dalt's turn to shrug. He retraced his steps and they returned to the car, half formed thoughts falling like rain between them.

Had something upset her?
She seemed quiet at supper. Did you notice?
But to leave without telling us?
Especially after Mudder...
What was she writing about?
Did she walk? Get a taxi?
Where do you think she went?
Had she read the fable?

By the time they were back home, the burst of adrenaline that had sent them in pursuit of their quarry had worn off. Dalt's head was pounding. The air in the room, thick and heavy. Maybe a coffee would help. Dalt turned on the machine whilst Huck sat at the kitchen table.

'We need to tell the police. About the email, and about Amelia leaving,' Huck said.

'I'll call them after coffee.' What was the point though, Dalt wondered? What good would it do?

They sat opposite each other, neither speaking now, Dalt mirroring the posture of his son, elbows on the table, chin cupped in his hands.

When Huck was small, Dalt used to read him stories about a family of elephants. The elephant children were loud and chaotic and often badly behaved, their parents were often tired and weary. Huck had demanded the stories over and over. What transfixed him so, Dalt never understood. He found even reading the stories quite exhausting, glad of their own home and its sense of calm and purpose.

Dalt felt that calm now, washing over him in waves, as he looked at his son, propped up across from him. Amelia had been like one of those elephant children, he realised, and as the story used to say, now, there was peace at last.

Huck looked like he felt the same. His breathing was slow and steady, his expression soft, as if something had left him, left them both, in peace.

Where was the anger? The bubbling fury Dalt had felt only days earlier at Amelia for intruding on their darkest moments, for recording it all to reveal to the world, was gone.

Let her do what she wanted with it, Dalt decided. Life was too short. There were more important things to worry about.

'Do you think they will ever find Mudder?' Huck spoke so quietly it took Dalt a moment for the words to collate and form as a question he was expected to answer.

'I don't know,' Dalt looked straight across the table, directly into his son's eyes. 'I really don't. But we'll be alright.'

An admission that life would go on. His first. A proclamation that they would survive, pick up the pieces, keep going. He exhaled deeply. The surprising thing was, he meant it.

He looked at his son. Huck looked exhausted. Dalt was overcome by an urge to throw his arms around him. Pull him close. Had he done that, since Nell had gone missing? He couldn't recall.

'We'll be alright,' he repeated.

He called the police, still felt that obligation to report and to update, but the need to demand answers was gone, his role now of messenger rather than protagonist. His breathing felt lighter, easier, than it had in weeks, his mind clearer. Yes, there had been a fable intended for Amelia. Yes, she was missing, but she wasn't in any danger – this disappearance was no mystery; her bags had been packed. She'd left. Her choice. This is what the women round here seemed to do.

And the day was young – young and extraordinarily muggy. The late morning air was dense and devoid of any breezes that would cool the skin. The perfect day for a swim. Dalt could practically feel it already, the ice-cold water taking his breath away, forcing his chest to contract, the rapid, desperate gulps for air and the sudden surge of adrenaline, the uncontrollable urge to scream, to shout, to laugh. The release.

Huck was sitting reading in an old sun lounger under the shade of an oak tree – one of Nell's favourite thinking spots – when Dalt found him.

'Fancy a swim? We could go to Dalberry pool.' Dalt needed give no further persuasion, Huck understood what was on offer.

'Sure. I was just thinking the same. Let me just grab my stuff.' Huck swung his legs over the side of the lounger and jogged to the house. How tall his son had grown. Fifteen, almost a man. How had he not noticed? It was time to stop focusing on what was gone and start seeing what remained.

'Tur-nip? Tur-nip?' Dalt split the two syllables of the dog's name up so distinctly it sounded like the creature had a forename and a surname.

Where was he, anyway?

The poor creature had been neglected in his wife's absence. Dalt had just about managed to feed him each day, and lock him in at night, but he certainly wouldn't be winning any *Pet Owner of the Year Awards*. But Turnip loved to walk on the moors and would surely join them for this morning's outing. If only Dalt could find him.

'Turnip! Turnip! Turnip!' he called as he crossed the lawn, away from the house now, down towards the river. 'Turnip! Turnip!'

Movement in the grass ahead, rustling and scraping and the dog's oh-so-familiar whine. It was coming from inside the curtains of the willow tree.

'Turnip?' he tried again, but whatever had caught the dog's attention was keeping it. Intrigued, Dalt quickened his step, bending forward into the fronds of the willow, leaves touching his face as he stretched his arms out in front to sweep the trailing branches out of the way.

'Turnip, what have you got, boy?'

The dog turned its attention to Dalt for a fraction of a second, before returning to furiously paw at the earth, at an exposed, raw, peaty-black mound that was totally at odds with the lush green blanket of grass that surrounded it.

What on earth?

Fear flooded through him, cold and raw. His heart hammered in his chest, a floodgate of thoughts opened and threatened to overwhelm him. Tangled for a moment, caught in the fronds of the tree, then running, running, running, flight instinct well and truly activated, down to the river, legs pounding through long grass, brambles whipping at his bare legs.

Far enough away, bent over and gasping for breath, Dalt tried to calm down, to breathe and gather his thoughts.

He'd checked underneath the willow tree when Nell disappeared, he was certain of it. But doubt was seeping in. He'd been in a daze then and in the weeks that followed. Had he checked? A mound like that wasn't something you would fail to notice. A body-shaped mound like that wasn't something you could just ignore. Shit, he'd let the thought in – body-shaped. Shit. The fear that came with the recognition winded him again, kept him doubled over, struggling to breathe.

Calm. Down. Calm. Down. Deep breaths, repeat the mantra, calm down.

Minutes passed before his breathing began to regulate. Minutes in which shame crept in – shame that in this one, testing moment he had crumbled. Shame, that he had run rather than faced whatever lay beneath that pile of earth. He shook his head violently to banish the thought. Shame, shame, shame, that in a moment like this, a life-defining moment, he'd chosen to flee rather than face.

But face what, exactly?
What or who?

Huck

The night before, his father had gone to bed suddenly, straight after supper. Huck had been lurking on the stairs, he'd seen Amelia grind those sleeping pills into his father's food. Huck would have stopped his father eating them if he hadn't thought it was such a good idea. Wished he had thought of it himself.

It had got him thinking, though. Why would Amelia want to be so sure that Dalt was in a deep sleep? She had to be planning on leaving. Her bag had been packed for days, her room clean and tidy (yes, he was keeping a very close eye on her).

She wasn't about to get away with it that easily.

He'd gone up to his room at 9 p.m. He'd heard Amelia on the stairs not long after, heard her bedroom door shut. What was her plan? Would she wait until she was sure he was asleep and take Mudder's car? Would she drive it all the way to London, or leave it at the train station? Did trains even run to London at night? A quick online search told him that they didn't. She must be taking the car then.

And what was he going to do about it?

Lucy Loxton, Ms Jamison and Joan Matthews, all problems he'd solved effectively – from a distance. He'd not laid a hand on a soul. He didn't want to. After all, he hadn't asked for this job, this mission, this crusade. He was just Mudder's agent, carrying out her will. He was no 'baddie.'

But Amelia, she was a different matter. He couldn't allow her to leave with her laptop and her notebooks and her intent, ambition and her scheme – yes scheme – to publish a story about them. No, Mudder had shown him through her fables that he needed to help Amelia to be free of this aspiration. He needed to stop her.

A lightbulb moment. He didn't need to use force. He'd use the fable itself, tell Amelia about the fables, all of them. How he'd found them hidden in Mudder's office. She'd understand, wouldn't she? How could she fail to, when she read her own story of envy and resentment and learnt for herself that the answer was to let go of all desires? Amelia was into all that flowery, hippy Buddhist stuff. This should be a piece of cake.

At 10 p.m. he'd trodden lightly down the stairs, checked briefly on Dalt (dead to the world) and crossed the landing to stand right outside Amelia's room.

He had paused for a moment, listening, noting the creak of a bed and the quiet turning of pages.

He knocked, two short, quiet raps, and waited.

'Urm, yes?' Amelia's voice was unsure, wavering.

'It's Huck. Can I come in?'

'Hold on.'

Without waiting for consent, Huck had turned the handle and stepped into the room. An ambient light from a bedside lamp cast a soft glow over Amelia. She stood to greet him.

'Sorry to disturb you,' he began, noticing that Amelia was still very much in her day clothes, right down to the boots that she was wearing. Boots on the bed? The relaxed, easy manner with which he'd entered the room slipped fractionally. He wasn't priggish, but there was something distinctively wrong about boots on the bed – an implication of ownership, territory and rights that came from placing ones heavy, dark, leather onto clean white linen. An irrational wave of frustration swept through him.

'I wanted to show you something.' His voice was gruffer than he'd intended.

Amelia looked bewildered as he passed her the piece of paper upon which was written, in Mudder's handwriting, the fable of *The Willow Tree and the Conifer*.

Did he detect a shake in her hand as she clasped the paper? Her expression was focused. He followed her eyes as she read twice, three times from start to finish, followed her eyes as tears began to appear.

Phew, this wasn't going to be so bad after all.

'How have you got this? It's only Friday night? The fables are always sent to Frank in the early hours of Saturday morning?'

Her eyes were focused on the paper as she spoke, but Huck was sure she wasn't reading. Was she aware that something was about to happen, holding onto this moment to delay the next? Perceptive of her. He was grateful, too, for a moment to recalibrate, grab hold of his intentions and steer them in the right direction.

'Mudder wrote all the fables. I found them in her office. I typed them up. I've been emailing them to Frank. I set up the blog and I posted them on there.' The words came out steadily, articulately, defiantly. He wasn't ashamed. Why should he be?

Now he had her attention. Her mouth had dropped and her hand holding the fable had fallen to her side.

She looked at him for a long, hard moment.

'Why?'

Why? Wasn't it obvious? Hadn't she clicked, like he had, that this was what Mudder had intended, that this was Mudder's grand plan, that he was a pawn carrying it out?

'Because that's what Mudder wanted me to do.' He almost added a *'duh.'*

He hadn't bargained for what happened next. Like watching a ragdoll come to life, Amelia's face passed from confusion to pity, then settled upon fury.

'How do you know that? Did she ask you to do this for her? Or did you decide that this was what she wanted? Wait, do you know where she is? Have you got something to do with this?'

It was highly disconcerting, the way Amelia was looking at him as if he was nuts, as if he was dangerous – the way she arched her body away from him. Highly disconcerting. He'd thought he could be honest with her. That she would understand.

She must have recognised the change in his face.

'Wait,' (why was she telling him to wait? What did she think he was going to do?) 'You've been going through a tough time. You must miss her so much. God, it must be so hard.'

What was she doing now? Going gentle on the mentally unhinged kid? Did she think he'd lost the plot?

It clicked. She must think he'd somehow been responsible for Lucy Loxton's death, and for Joan Matthews' untimely demise.

'I don't know where Mudder is. I haven't hurt anyone. I promise. All I've done is share the fables and made sure the right people saw them. I didn't lay a finger on anyone.'

That didn't sound right. That still sounded very, very wrong. This was harder to explain than he'd thought it would be. Maybe it was best to just get to the point.

'I know you've been writing about us – about this whole thing. You can't publish it. You have to destroy all your notes, everything on your computer – everything.'

Amelia looked back at him, horrified, her face shiny with sweat and tears.

'Nell wouldn't have minded.' Amelia wasn't even sure she believed this herself anymore, but now wasn't the moment to back down. 'This is madness – what you're doing – hurting people because of a bunch of fables. Nell wouldn't have wanted that. Nell would never want to hurt anyone.'

Amelia was talking madness. Dreams of success were clouding her rational thought. Saying the fables were not part of Mudder's plan, that Huck had misinterpreted Mudder's intentions, implying that Huck's actions since were misguided and unhinged? How dare she? The idea that Amelia knew what Mudder would have wanted better than he did was unbelievable. Huck had always been there for Mudder, understood her when no one else did. What claim did Amelia have to her?

Anger. Wave upon wave of anger surged through him. Anger like he'd never felt before. She had it all wrong.

Suddenly, his hand was on her wrist, pulling, twisting. Amelia dropped the paper she held, fear and panic in her eyes and jerked her arm away. He reached to grab her again, as she kicked him hard in the stomach. Winded, he dropped to the floor.

There was a moment then, when things could have gone in one direction or another. A sliding doors sort of moment of different choices, different roads, with vastly differing endings and consequences.

When his fingers reached out and found the stone door stop, when he stood with it, lifted it, raised it high and it met with the thin, delicate skin of Amelia's hairline, the only road he saw was the one leading back to Mudder.

Dalt

Now.

You panic now. Now, when there's a fresh burial mound under a tree in your garden, and a second woman has gone suddenly and mysteriously missing. You definitely, definitely panic now.

Gather thoughts. Get it together.

What if it's Nell under there? What if it's Nell?

What if it's Amelia?

Get it together.

Someone did this. Whatever this is – someone did it. Where are they now? What the hell is going on? Are they still here? Are they going to come for him next?

Or Huck?

Huck.

Where was Huck? It wouldn't have taken him long to go back to the house and get his swim shorts; why hadn't he reappeared and called for Dalt to let him know he was ready to go?

Was Huck okay?

Shit. Huck.

Dalt moved from bent over to standing so suddenly that the lack of blood to his brain caused his eyes to blur. The long grass swayed around him and he felt dizzy and sick.

Huck. Find Huck.

The searing pain in the back of his head came out of nowhere. He felt his legs buckle, felt himself fall, the long, soft grass rising up to meet him, and then he felt nothing at all.

It was still light when he opened his eyes. Or tried to open them. They felt crusty and sore. Instinctively, he reached his fingers up to rub them, but his hand wouldn't move. Was he lying on it? Was he in his bed? This had happened in bed before; he'd fallen asleep on his arm and his hand had gone numb. Pins and needles were sure to follow shortly, then he'd be able to feel his fingers again. Although Dalt couldn't remember going to bed, couldn't even remember what day it was, come to think of it.

This didn't feel right. This wasn't his bed. He was sitting upright for starters. Grimacing with pain, Dalt managed to open his eyes enough to squint at his surroundings. Where was he? Outside, that much was clear. He could feel a breeze, and an earthy smell reached his nostrils. His thoughts were coming slowly, wading through deep, thick mud, wearing oversized wellingtons, getting lost on the way, not making it to the surface. His head throbbed; his mouth felt parched. What was going on?

Black dots danced in his eyes. He lost consciousness.

The sky was darker when he opened his eyes for a second time. His awareness focused immediately on the pain in the back of his head and neck. He noticed the chill of his skin for the first time in weeks. What had happened to his hands? Forcing his brain to cooperate, Dalt tried to move them from side to side. They seemed to be tied behind him. His fingers brushed against something rough and ridged, sensed grooves and indentations. Bark – a tree. He was sitting against a tree, hands tied behind his back.

What tree? Why?

Still his thoughts refused to obey him, swirled and sunk in the bog water of his mind.

His neck, so stiff. No wonder. His chin was on his chest. Hard work just to lift it even an inch, to squint into the half-light.

When he did, what he saw made him retch, made his stomach heave uncontrollably. No, he couldn't be, this couldn't be...

Was he tied to the willow? And that, that mound of earth in front of him...?

Despite the cold he began to sweat. His heart raced and a deep, primeval fear stirred his senses, jolted them back into being. The discovery of the pile of earth earlier in the day (assuming it was the same day) came back to him. He'd run away. Then, nothing – this was where his memories ended.

And now he was back here. Tied to the tree.

Alone? It seemed that way, although his vision was severely limited by the throbbing pain in his skull and the fact that he couldn't move his head. Alone, but for the mound.

Stay calm, breathe deep.

The mound.

Amelia? He retched again, forced himself to look at the pile of earth. None of this made sense. What was he doing here? Who did this? Why?

He pulled at his hands again, but they were bound tight. It was then that he noticed the clipboard on his lap, a typed sheet of paper gripped between its shiny metal teeth.

There was just enough light left in the day to make sense of the words written upon it.

The Dog and the Baker

A poor baker lived with an old, lame dog on the outskirts of a village. The baker worked hard all day long, until his fingers ached and his back groaned. He got up at five in the morning, every day of the week, to make the dough for his bread, and went to bed long after all the other villagers, when his floor was swept and his body tired.

The baker had no family to help him. His wife had died two years before, and his son had moved away. All he had was the dog, who had turned up on his doorstep the day he had buried his wife.

He welcomed it into his simple cottage, let it warm itself by the fire. When it flinched at his touch, he made it a promise.

'I will look after you, dog. I promise I will never hurt you and you shall never go hungry again.'

Now this was a very bold promise to make. The baker had very little to eat himself; all he baked, he sold, and with the money he made, he bought more flour to make more bread. He ate the stale crusts and burnt ends that people wouldn't buy, and often went to bed with his stomach growling hungrily.

But he kept his promise to the dog.

At the end of each day, the baker would turn the sign on the door of the shop to 'closed' and gather the few morsels that hadn't sold. He would sit at the small table by the window and divide the food into two piles.

Slowly, savouring each mouthful, the baker would eat, feeding first the dog, then himself in turn, until the piles were gone.

The villagers thought he was mad, sharing what little food he had with a mangy old dog, but the baker had made a promise and he always kept his promises.

May Day arrived, as it did every year, bringing with it a flurry of customers, keen to buy bread for their picnics. The baker baked and baked all day long, using up all his flour and all of his butter, eggs and milk, until he had no ingredients left at all. At the end of the day, when every loaf had been sold and the baker had turned the sign to closed, there came a sharp rapping on the door.

A beautiful woman stood there, covered from head to toe in expensive scarves and elaborately patterned cloths. The baker noticed her red lips and her perfect, shiny white teeth.

'Have you any bread to spare?' she asked.

'Only these few scraps my dog and I were about to eat,' said the baker.

'I will take those scraps, with thanks,' said the woman, taking them from his hand and setting off down the street.

Sighing, the old man locked the door once more, and turned to his dog.

'I am sorry, dog. I cannot keep the promise I made you.'

The dog looked up at the old man, his eyes full of sadness and betrayal.

Then he gobbled him up.

Always keep your promises.

Dalt

D alt may have sustained a serious head injury, but even with possibly impaired judgement, he knew that this fable was ridiculous. There was an imaginary line, and this story had definitely just crossed it, moved into a surreal new territory. He'd have been tempted to laugh out loud and call it comedy if it hadn't been for the fact that absolutely nothing else about the situation was funny. Maybe this is what happened when you were knocked out and tied to a tree next to a dead body – you gain a little perspective.

Time to put his Freudian glasses on over his seeping, painful eyes and analyse the hell out of this thing, though. That's what he was supposed to do, right?

'Right?' he called, into the half-light. 'You want me to read this? To work it all out? Who's who, and who hurt who and who's going to pay and all that?'

He paused. Was he losing his grip? Who was he even talking to?

There were three options.

His wife. His son. Or Amelia.

So why was he so scared?

'You want me to find the deeper meaning in this thing, then what?' No response, the swish of willow in the wind.

'Then I get my comeuppance? I get punished for what I've done?' Nothing, nada, zero.

He wasn't about to let that put him off.

'And what have I done, exactly?'

Did he hear an intake of breath, a crunch of a footstep, or was it the wind which had suddenly picked up, hearing rumour of a change in the weather, violently swishing the fronds of the willow tree?

'Okay, I'll play along, but only because I haven't got anything better to do.' Despite his dry mouth and throbbing head Dalt was beginning to warm up, adrenaline and fear pulsing through his veins, pushing his limits.

'I'm the baker and Nell is the dog. I promised Nell everything, and then according to the fable, I cheated on her with another woman. So she ate me.'

Dalt's voice emptied into the air.

It didn't bode well, being eaten by an imaginary dog. It wasn't the ending he'd hoped for.

'I didn't though. Cheat, I mean. I didn't cheat. So, whoever wrote the fable has got it wrong. I never cheated. I kept my promises.'

All this talking was making him feel woozy. The back of his head felt wet and sticky. What was he doing, tied to a tree jabbering on like an idiot? At least do something constructive, he told himself, pulling at the rope around his wrists, trying to loosen it. At least try to escape.

He must have passed out again. He was woken by a rumble of thunder. A flash of lightning, followed seconds later by more thunder. The moon was partially visible through the curtain of swaying green branches, reminding him of a spontaneous camping adventure years before. He and Huck had loaded their bags and set out on the moor. They'd taken a different path to the one they normally chose and had only been walking for about an hour when they came across a deep blue pool, hidden by a copse of trees. It wasn't a water hole Dalt had seen listed in any of his walking books. Was it possible, they'd wondered, to find a pool so close to home that no one else had discovered yet? Huck had thought so. Let's name it after us, he'd cried exuberantly. They'd tried various combinations of their names: Duck's pool made them giggle, Hulk's pool had seen them describing the mythical beast who lived in the pool's depths (green, obviously, and muscly, as well as very slimy). Eventually, they'd settled on Dalberry's Pool. It's made up of the best bits of both of us, Huck had said. It belongs to us.

They'd swum and splashed and messed around, the day passing before they realised how late it was. Huck had been more than happy to stay the night, to let the adventure continue, and so they'd slept under the stars wrapped in their towels, the cool night air kept at bay by the warmth of their bodies mashed together, the moon bright above them, as it was tonight. They'd had one last dip in the chilly waters as the sun rose the following morning, then packed up their things and headed towards home.

What would it have been like if Dalt had been the one to go missing? The question struck him, not for the first time. What would the hole he'd leave behind be like? Vast and cavernous, or quickly filled in with fresh soil? He'd like to think it might be somewhere in the middle. Large enough to be noticed, obstructive even for a short while, with Nell and Huck struggling to walk past it, around it, over it. Tripping, and falling in from time to time. But he knew he'd want them to fill it in, gradually, slowly, shovel by shovel, until they could start again.

What had gone wrong in his small family?

So much had gone right: the love he had for Nell, the love he had for his son. But sitting here, tied to a tree, aching hands working ceaselessly to loosen the rope at his wrists, Dalt had to admit that there had been failings. Normal families don't knock each other out and tie them to trees next to sinister mounds of earth. Or do they? You never know what happens behind closed doors. But he suspected they didn't.

And he suspected that Huck was responsible.

'Huck?' he called into the night. 'Huck?' It was worth a try, but no answer came. 'Huck, whatever you think I did, I promise you I didn't. If you think I had an affair with Lucy Loxton, then you're wrong. I sketched her. It was work. That was all.'

Perhaps his son was there, silently lurking in the shadows. He might as well set the record straight.

'Your mother and I had been arguing. But it wasn't because I was cheating. It's complicated. She's complicated. But that's why I love her. I accept her, Huck. I have done right from the start. I miss her.'

It was only whilst saying the words that he realised how true they were. There really was a Nell-shaped hole, he could see it now. Ironic really, the last time he'd been beneath the bows of the willow, he'd been with Nell. They'd been arguing, she'd stormed out of the house and come here. Dalt had followed her. Nell had been upset. She'd even thrown her wedding ring at him, saying something about how he'd be better off without her. They'd both fallen to the floor to look for it, but it was gone from sight. How quickly it disappeared into the long grass.

God, this was like therapy. Concussed Tree Therapy they should call it. A little extreme perhaps, but one could really look inside oneself, right into the true nature of one's being when tied to a tree next to a dead body.

No point shouting for help. The reporters had gone, when police interest in Nell Davenport as a missing person at risk had diminished. '*We're more at risk than she is,*' he'd heard one of the reporters joking, shortly before the vans drove away.

The hoot of an owl, the brushing of willow against willow, the sway of the grass. In the gaps between gusts of wind, these small night-time sounds became magnified, almost imperceptible until you really opened your ears and started to listen. Perhaps acknowledging these sounds are there in the first place is half the secret to hearing them. Creaking trees, flowing water. Layer upon layer of sounds that he hadn't noticed before.

And it wasn't just the sounds he was hearing for the first time; he was seeing things for the first time, too.

Like how strong his son had become, knocking him out, moving him and digging a gra... Dalt stopped himself, wouldn't allow the thought – digging an extremely large hole.

How good at knots his son was.

And how messed up.

How had he missed this?

The five weeks that Nell had been gone had been tough on all of them.

They'd been particularly tough on Dalt.

Had Dalt looked outside of himself enough? Had he paid enough attention to his son? No. He'd been so consumed with his own feelings and then more recently, fixated with Amelia's behaviour, that he hadn't noticed where his attentions really should have been.

Another lightning burst.

'I'm sorry, Huck.' The night swallowed his apology, spat it out as a roar of thunder. 'I'm sorry if I haven't been there for you these last few months. And before that. I'm sorry.'

What was his son playing at? Anger surged through him now, anger at his own helplessness, at his renegade son.

What was he trying to do? Punish anybody who'd ever upset Nell? What did he think this would achieve? Did he think it would bring her back? And what did he plan to do with Dalt? Would he kill his own father?

More lightning. More thunder. The gap between the two getting noticeably shorter. The moon now obscured beneath a foreboding sky.

His entire body felt cold. After a whole summer of heat, day after day of unrelenting sun, his body permanently uncomfortably hot, he was now freezing. His head throbbed, his arms and back ached. Everything turned to black as he drifted into a restless sleep.

Sunday 15th September

Huck 5 a.m.

He couldn't sleep.

He'd knocked two people unconscious. One of them being his own father.

He supposed that the inability to fall asleep in a situation like this wasn't unusual.

Abduction for Beginners: Chapter One: Be prepared to stay awake for a very long time.

He'd whipped up the fable of *The Dog and the Baker* yesterday, to pass the time until Dalt regained consciousness. He hadn't hit him that hard; he wouldn't be out for long. Huck was a sucker for a pattern. Dalt needed a fable – needed to know what he'd done, just like the rest of them did. He hadn't posted it to the blog, though, or sent it to Frank.

He was feeling pretty tired of all the games. This was just between them, now. Just between him and Dalt. And Mudder.

But he needed to sleep. If he slept, then maybe his brain would clear itself of this fug, this fog, this haze. Maybe he could get his thoughts straight.

The rumbles of thunder didn't help. Neither did hearing his father calling out from where he'd left him, tied to the willow tree at the bottom of the garden. Maybe he should close the windows. It wasn't like shutting out the unwanted sound of a lawn mower when he was trying to read. One's own father, cold, injured, tethered to a tree and shouting in distress was a little harder to ignore.

If only he could get his head around the recent turn of events and the dilemma he was now faced with. It seemed he had made a mistake. His father had not cheated, not according to Dalt, anyway. According to Dalt, he hadn't done anything wrong. A bit annoying, thought Huck, that he'd only found this out after he'd knocked him unconscious with a spade. The same spade he'd lost the top of his finger with all those years ago, probably.

But, these things happen, he thought. We live and learn.

The problem was that now he was going to have to go and untie Dalt and explain the unfortunate mound of earth beneath the willow tree at the same time. It was clear that he hadn't thought this whole plan through. Knocking Amelia out had been rash, spontaneous, unplanned. An unforeseen act that had led to events spiralling out of control.

Abduction for Beginners: Chapter Two: Never lose control.

There were many facets in the role of redeemer. There was no way he could be adept at all of them.

He'd have to tell Dalt about Amelia.

No rush. Dalt seemed to have stopped shouting. It wouldn't be fair to wake his father up if he was sleeping. He'd use this time to get the facts straight. He was going to have quite a lot of explaining to do.

The facts. They'd begun to blur. They weren't straight at all; they were undulating, multiplying, slipping out of control, like a handful of lassos thrown at once onto the necks of wild stallions, who galloped further and further away, pulling Huck helplessly along behind.

The starting point.

The day Mudder left.

Fact one: Mudder had left a note.

Even admitting this fact to himself made Huck screw his eyes shut and cover them with a hand in denial. Yep, she'd left a note.

Fact two: he'd read it and gone after her.

Fact three:

He didn't want to think about fact three. He'd have to come back to fact three.

The note then, focus on the note.

That morning all those weeks ago, just after he'd seen Mudder running across the lawn, he'd gone downstairs to make coffee. He'd seen the note straight away, propped up next to the kettle, both his name and Dalt's on the envelope.

He'd pulled out a small yellow sheet of paper and recognised at once Mudder's distinctive writing, all capital letters.

DEAR D & H,
SORRY FOR SUDDEN EXIT. THOUGHT EASIER. AM
FINDING THINGS DIFFICULT. AM GOING AWAY.
MUCH LOVE
NELL

More like a telegram than a letter, and hurtful without meaning to be. Typical Mudder. But he couldn't very well let her disappear feeling like that, out on the moors.

Fact two: no time to wake his father, who would sleep for another hour yet, Huck had stuffed the note into his pocket, pulled on his trainers, shut Turnip in the drawing room and headed across the lawn after his mother, driven by instinct more than reason. He had runners' genes, Mudder always said, and he felt grateful for this now. Despite rarely moving faster than a quick walk, he was able to effortlessly up his pace to a decent jog.

He'd run alongside the river at first, then up onto the moor, his feet springing lightly over soft heather, tree branches and small streams. The early morning sun was warm on his neck and he felt good. After ten minutes, he saw her far ahead, leaping, as he was, over the natural obstacles the moor liked to present to its intrepid explorers.

'Mudder!' he shouted. She didn't stop. Too far away to hear him.

Increasing his pace, he followed a sheep trail winding between large rocks, the grass high around him.

'Mudder!'

She'd dropped down again, out of sight. Disorientated, he reached the top of a hill. He could see the sheep trail continuing along the top of the ridge ahead of him for what he guessed to be another half a mile, where it crossed a steep, rocky field, at the foot of which ran a stream. Further still to the right, surrounded by large, flat rocks, was a pool. It took a few seconds to work out where he was. His and Dalt's pool. Dalberry's Pool. The one they had discovered and camped out at. And there was Mudder, running alongside the stream towards it.

Legs pumping, he followed, racing along the ridge, high above her, keeping her in his sights.

And then he froze.

She'd come to a standstill in front of Dalberry's Pool.

'Mudder!' he screamed. 'Mudder!'

But he was still too far away for her to hear him.

Fact three: here, his memories began to blur.

She'd kept her backpack on when she waded in, he knew that much. The water grew deep quickly, too quickly: over her knees then thighs, waist then chest.

And like her younger brother Toby, all those years before, the water claimed her.

'Mudder!' His legs were useless, jelly; he'd never make it in time. He sank to the floor, screaming her name.

Choose your own adventure.

He'd loved those books as a kid. Yes, they were a bit naff, not exactly highbrow literature, but who doesn't want to dictate the story, to be in charge?

Totally submerged. Killed herself. Dead.

To be with Toby?

Choose your own adventure.

Life had overwhelmed her.

Choose.

In front of him was the truth. He could choose to carry on.

If you choose to go down to the water and find the body, turn to page 48.

But the truth was too awful. He could never choose that.

Choose again.

If you wish to make a call to the emergency services, turn to page 52.

No phone with him. Not an option.

Choose again.

If you wish to return home and tell your father what happened, turn to page 54.

Tell his father of his failure to save her. How he'd stood and watched?

Choose again:

If you wish to return home and pretend that you are unaware of the events of this morning, turn to page 63.

He chose.

Would he choose the same again? Hell, no.

His grief and his guilt had made the choices. He knew that now. He'd been out of his mind. In denial. Not thinking rational thoughts. He'd watched his mother drown. It was his fault. It must be. He had heard his parents arguing, sensed his mother's unhappiness, and done nothing.

If he had the choice again, he'd turn the pages back, in a flash. Back to the start of the book, where he could have talked to her. Where he could have helped.

But he'd turned to page 63, and from there the paths he picked had taken him further and further away from the truth.

And now, despite being in the bedroom he'd slept in all his life, he was lost.

So many turns.

If you wish to redeem yourself and atone for your mother's death turn to page 72.

Turn.

If you wish to infiltrate the dark web and reek revenge on those that have hurt your mother, turn to page 78.

Turn.

If you wish to sabotage attempts for a family friend to cash in on your mother's disappearance, turn to page 85.

Turn.

If you wish to punish your father for an affair you believe he has been involved in, turn to page 93.

Turn.

Your father is tied to a tree in the garden. If you wish to come clean and tell him the truth turn to page 96.

Stupid book. Stupid choose your own adventure. A fad, that was all. No one really wants that responsibility, even if they think they do at the time. All we want are happy endings, predictable storylines, the meet, lose and get back of a romantic comedy.

He'd taken so many bad turns he'd ended up in the middle of nowhere, the voice of sat nav the only reason left. He hadn't intended to get to this point. This wasn't his destination.

Turn around where possible.

Not possible.

He'd thought the search teams would find her body. They had divers, dogs, kayakers, helicopters. He hadn't thought it would take this long or get this far. They'd find her and it would all be over.

Only they hadn't. Dalt had always told him that some of those pools were deep; some were even rumoured to be bottomless. Old quarries filled with water. Things could get lost forever in a place like that, he'd said, and it seemed he had been right.

If you want to confess your actions to the police, turn to page 97.

If you wish to end your own life, turn to page 98.

Page 98 sounded like possibly the best option at this point. Although, he dreaded to think of the specific choices that particular page would have to offer.

If you wish to hang yourself, turn to page 99.

If you wish to take an overdose of alcohol and painkillers, turn to page 101.

This was becoming too depressing. The options were closing in on him. The book was running out of pages.

Amelia

She was still coming to terms with the events of the last day and a half. Her head throbbed just thinking about Friday evening. Reaching her hand to her scalp, Amelia caressed the egg-shaped lump, the action triggering a memory of her eventful escape from Moordown in the early hours of Saturday morning, the delightful Henry Cooper her unlikely saviour.

Thank god for Henry bloody Cooper. Six words Amelia had never imagined saying out loud, let alone meaning. But she had said them, right there on the road outside Moordown at 11.30 p .m. on Friday when she spotted the headlights of his silly little car approaching. For once his timing had been impeccable, unlike his timing the day she'd returned home early to find him seducing the cleaner, but she wouldn't dwell on that now.

Her excitement at seeing him had been short lived.

'Will you leave it alone? Poking it is hardly going to help, is it?'

Amelia had pulled her hand away from the sore area on the back of her head, as if she'd been slapped. He may have rescued her, but that hadn't made him any more charming. Henry Cooper had turned his attention back to the road, sighing irritably.

'You're telling me that he took everything? Your notes, your laptop, memory sticks, everything? And that you hadn't backed it up anywhere, not even emailed it to yourself, nothing?'

It was her turn to sigh. Seriously, they'd gone over this at least three times already, and his lack of concern for her physical state was verging on negligent homicide.

'Yes, yes, yes and no. For God's sake Henry, if I can let it go, why can't you?'

She'd known full well why he couldn't let it go. The promise of the story was the only thing that had brought him out here, driving through the night to the middle of nowhere to get her. And now they were in his tiny sports car, barely big enough for two people, heading back towards London empty handed.

But he owed her far more than a taxi ride home; she wasn't going to let him make her feel bad about this. Henry seethed beside her, eyes locked on the road.

'You should go to the police. He's committed a criminal offence; he knocked you out! Aren't you concerned that if he could do this to you, then he might have done something to his own mother?'

'No. I'm not worried. I think he was right, anyway,' she'd said into the frosty silence.

He'd turned to glare at her.

'You what? He hit you over the head, knocked you out, left you for dead as he stole an entire novel from you, and you think he was right? Perhaps we should get you to the hospital after all.'

Amelia had known that his concern wasn't for her. Any concern he had was rooted firmly in the loss of *The Book That Got Away*. She rather liked that title. But that was all over now.

'I do, actually. I got caught up in the moment. It was intrusive and morally wrong to take their private moments and record them.' Amelia knew she sounded robotic, but she'd been repeating this phrase in her head and it was definitely making her more certain that she had done the right thing.

'And you're realising this now?' Henry Cooper banged his hand down hard on the steering wheel. What an idiot she had been to mourn the loss of this man.

'Yes, I'm realising this now.'

Not strictly true. She'd begun to realise it as she regained consciousness on the bedroom floor at Moordown, woozy and confused at her predicament. She'd consolidated her feelings in the passenger seat of Henry Cooper's car, when a hunch had told her to use his phone and check Nell's blog. The fable of *The Willow Tree and the Conifer* that Huck had showed her on Friday evening, when he forced his way into her room shortly before he'd knocked her out, was there online for all to see.

Amelia read it again.

The more you can let go, the happier you can be.

Yesterday, when Huck had shown her the fable, she'd felt affronted. It stung, being compared to a stupid tree. But perhaps all the spiritual guidance was paying off. The more she considered it, the more the story of the two trees spoke to her. She knew this sounded corny, but she'd had a moment, an actual moment – an epiphany or whatever it's called, where she saw everything clearly. Huck was right. Maybe not right to hit her over the head and steal her possessions, but right to stop her publishing the story. It wasn't hers to give. She needed to be her own tree, in her own field, happy in her own roots. The fable was spot on.

Still, epiphany or no epiphany, she wasn't keen on hanging around to discover what Huck had planned for her next. She'd regained consciousness on the floor of her bedroom, her belongings gone. She wasn't about to find out if Huck was planning on disposing of her after he had disposed of her things. She'd been out of those gates and off down the road like a shot, eternally grateful of the sight of Henry Cooper's silly little sports car coming towards her.

So self-absorbed, he hadn't even noticed her lack of luggage, and she hadn't explained what had happened at Moordown until they were over an hour's drive away, for fear that Henry would swing the car around and demand they go back and retrieve the possessions. When she had told him, he'd still swerved the car dramatically across two lanes of the motorway to the hard shoulder, ignoring her shrieks of distress. Even Henry Cooper couldn't pull off a U-turn on a motorway though, and so in the end they had kept going, and he had kept sighing and grumbling.

She must have dozed off.

'Where are we?' she'd asked.

'About two hours away from London.' Was Henry sulking? The expression on his face was no brighter, despite an increasing proximity to their destination. He was like a boy-man, a petulant child trapped inside an adult's body.

Half an hour of gazing out the window and quiet contemplation (she hesitated to call it meditation: it was hardly focused and restorative listening to the constant sighing of the man beside her) had led her to the following conclusion; Huck had tried, in his own 'assault and battery' kind of way, to help her.

Now she needed to help him.

She wouldn't report this to the police.

Yet.

Yes, he'd knocked her out, caused grievous bodily harm, but her instinct told her he hadn't intended to really hurt her, just stop her from taking the story.

And the others? Lucy Loxton, Ms Jamison and Joan Matthews?

Well, he'd meddled, that much was clear, sending emails, uploading fables onto the blog he'd created.

But he claimed he hadn't hurt anyone.

She remembered his words clearly. 'I haven't laid a finger on any of them. I promise.'

And she believed him.

She needed to help Huck, but she'd interfered enough already.

Huck needed to be the one who told the police everything. Not Amelia. But she needed to give him time to reach this conclusion himself. He'd told her that there were only four fables. It was over now, there was no risk of harm to anyone else. They had time.

Time for Huck to process everything that had happened.

Then he'd surely speak to Dalt and the police about what he'd done. Amelia had done a hell of a lot of therapy. She knew how it worked. And she, Amelia, was going to help him with the process.

She would write another fable. But this time for Huck. It would guide him to do the right thing.

They had got home at 4 a.m. Or what used to be home. Henry Cooper had reluctantly taken her back to the house they used to share. It wasn't ideal, but he had no choice. With all her belongings, including her phone, still at Moordown, Amelia couldn't very well call a friend or stay anywhere else. Henry had disappeared immediately into the spare room, mumbling something about driving all night and being an unpaid taxi service.

Not that she'd cared.

She'd needed a shower and a change of clothes, then access to his computer whilst she sorted her life out.

Her scalp had stung like crazy when the water and shampoo touched it, but in an odd way, she had been thankful for the pain. This was all part of her journey. Her healing. She was The Conifer Tree! She would get in touch with her therapist later; talk through this revelation. It was good to be back in London! She'd missed The Sanctuary and her network of support!

It had felt wonderful to be surrounded by her things again too. Henry had kept everything exactly as it was when she'd left. Not because he'd missed her, but because he'd been away on an extended holiday.

The idiot.

It had its benefits though. She'd pulled on some pyjamas and brushed her hair. A little sleep, and then she'd be fresh and ready to get her life back on track.

The little sleep had turned out to be a big, long sleep. She had probably been pretty concussed.

There had been an awful lot of admin to do when she woke in the late afternoon. She'd contacted the bank, reported her phone as lost, and spent hours on hold to the insurance company in the attempt to wrangle a new one.

And she'd been starving. Henry had ordered her in a sushi delivery before disappearing out for the evening. Sushi was something else you didn't get in Stonebrook. London had its perks. Her conifer was learning where its roots belonged.

Finally, yesterday evening, she'd sat down at Henry's laptop to write the fable.

The Tale of the Fox and Her Cub had unfolded seamlessly, a story she knew but hadn't allowed herself to recognise: an unhealthy relationship between a son and his mother. The moral, albeit dark, designed to help Huck save himself, to stop his self-sacrificing vendetta before it was too late.

The moral: *revenge will hurt the avenger.* Stop this game, Huck, before you get hurt. Don't end up dead, like the fox cub nearly did in the fable.

It was late when she finished it. She'd send it in the morning.

And now it was Sunday. She'd woken early, the fable the first thing on her mind. It was only when she sat down at the laptop to send it that the dilemma of how to get Huck to see it occurred to her.

She would follow the pattern of all the other fables. She'd send the fable to Frank. Frank would forward it to Dalt like he had with all the others. Then (hopefully) Dalt would show Huck.

She found Frank's email address on the *Stonebrook Gazette*'s website, created an anonymous email account, attached the fable and pressed send.

That was easy.

Now, she needed the chain to work: Frank to Dalt to Huck to putting an end to this thing.

Huck

A phone vibrated, startling him back to life.

Dalt's phone. He'd taken it the night before. Blearily, he reached for it, tapped the screen.

An email from Frank – subject: *The Tale of the Fox and Her Cub.*

This was a new one to him. He felt sick. Faint.

His vision blurred, a blackness drawing in front of his eyes like curtains closing. Sinking to the floor, back against the wall, he closed his eyes, forced himself to slow down the shallow, quick breaths that threatened to spirit him away.

Fear.

He recognised it even if he couldn't look it in the eye.

Fear of reparation.

A fable has been sent that you did not write.

If you wish to read the fable, turn to page 105.

If you want to confess your actions to the police, turn to page 97.

If you wish to end your own life, turn to page 98.

Choice, choices, choices. Choices that were getting narrower and less appealing by the moment.

Minutes passed. His breathing evened, the urgent need to vomit or pass out diminished.

He opened the attachment. He began to read.

The Tale of the Fox and Her Cub

I n a den deep in the ground and deeper still in the woods, Mother Fox returned from her evening hunt, a juicy rabbit dangling from her jaws.

Together, Mother Fox and Cub tore at the rich flesh. Bellies full, they lay on the soft earth.

Cub nestled in as close as he dared to Mother Fox and breathed deeply. Warm and content, he drifted off to sleep.

The following evening, Mother Fox turned to Cub.

'Come with me, Cub,' she said. 'You're old enough now to learn to hunt.'

Cub was excited. His mother was an expert hunter. She always returned with her mouth full of delicious meat and their bellies were always full. How he had longed for this day when he would learn to hunt just like her.

They poked their heads out of the den into the bright, moonlit night. An owl hooted overhead. This night-time world was very exciting.

'This night-time world is very dangerous,' said Mother Fox. 'We must stick together and be very careful. We must look out for each other.'

Cub nodded his head obediently, but he was not afraid. Not with Mother Fox by his side.

Night after night, Cub followed Mother Fox as she hunted. He learnt how to smell the air, he learnt to notice the direction the wind was blowing, he learnt how to follow a scent.

When two months had passed, Mother Fox showed Cub the farm a mile away, where the farmer kept a barn full of fat, noisy chickens. She showed him the tunnel she had dug that popped out in the barn, where they could eat their fill.

Night after night they feasted upon chickens, their stomachs full to bursting and their hearts happy.

Until the night the farmer came.

He had been waiting in the chicken barn at the mouth of the tunnel. As Mother Fox emerged, the farmer had brought the shovel down hard upon her head with a bellow.

Cub grabbed at the fur on her hind legs from behind, pulled her back through the tunnel into the woods, pulled and dragged her until his mouth ached and his muscles burned and until they were home.

The other animals of the wood watched, saw the trail of blood she left behind, worried that they would be next.

For many months, Cub nursed Mother Fox. She was not the same creature that had taught him to hunt, that was bold and fearless, strong and brave. Instead, she was frightened of the world outside the den and the creatures that lived there.

'I will hunt for us,' Cub told her bravely. And each night he poked his nose out of the burrow, sniffing the air like Mother Fox had taught him.

Over time, Mother Fox grew strong again, and eventually the day came when she was ready to leave the den and hunt once more. Cub stayed firmly by her side.

The years passed. Cub was no longer a Cub and Mother Fox was no longer afraid, but still Cub stayed by her side, for Cub had never forgotten the hurt the farmer had caused Mother Fox.

One night, when the wind was wild and his anger even wilder, Cub could not hold back any longer.

Quietly, he left the den without waking Mother Fox, and ran quickly through the woods until he got to the farm. He scrambled through the old tunnel into the chicken barn, his mind full of all the chickens he would kill, and how the farmer would pay.

Just in time, he saw the snare, carefully positioned at the mouth of the tunnel.

Just in time, he avoided the wire coil around his neck, and just in time, he returned sheepishly to his mother in the den.

Revenge will hurt the avenger.

Huck

R evenge will hurt the avenger, well isn't that the truth?

The cub may have escaped, just in time – clunky ending but nice touch, anonymous author – he could see what they were trying to do. The 'not-so-thinly-veiled' offer of hope for him. It could all still work out okay.

But he didn't agree. He was beyond saving. It was too late for that.

From his position on the bedroom floor, Huck surveyed the room for a noose.

He wished that noise would stop.

His father (Huck never called him that, why did it feel right to do it now, after he'd tied him to a tree and left him for dead?) had started singing. Singing! At the precise moment when Huck needed silence whilst he contemplated the best way to depart this earth, Dalt had broken into song. Huck could picture him under the tree, hungry, tired, cold and bored, but rather satisfied with his song choices, nonetheless. First there'd been *I Want to Break Free*, by Queen, followed by *Live and Let Die*, (the Guns and Roses version he thought; something about the way Dalt spat out the '*d*' of die and dragged the word out until it hurt to listen). His father was halfway through the opening line of Celine Dion's *All by Myself* when Huck finally closed the window.

A new day.

The last day? No more choices. Nothing left. All out of road. All out of pages.

Water, he had decided, was the answer. If it worked for Virginia Woolf it could work for him. Besides, the air in the room felt stale – cloying – and he was dying for a dip. (It was becoming more apparent, having heard his father's singing, where his dark sense of humour originated from).

When you're up shit creek without a paddle, he figured, you might as well sink with a smile.

Although, he didn't really feel in the mood to die. What he really felt like was lying down in a field of grass so tall that he could become invisible and then falling asleep. Sleeping for days. Weeks. Months. Whatever it took for all this to be over. This massive mess he had got them all into. All his fault. Always his fault.

Water was the next best thing, he supposed. Being in water had always felt so right, the cold water annihilating any worries, leaving him at peace. And that's what he needed now: to feel oblivion, peace, nothingness.

He hauled himself up from the floor. Whoever wrote the fable (and he was almost certain that it was Amelia) was right. Revenge will hurt the avenger. Enough already. He just wanted the hurt to stop. He couldn't live without Mudder. Ironic really, when he'd always thought it was the other way around.

Time to go.

Should he leave a note?

It seemed as though he should. Look what had happened when Mudder had left without a note. Although, of course, technically she hadn't. He'd burnt her letter with his lighter on his way home that day. A reflex action, but one that would have reeked of guilt should he have confessed to it. So, he didn't.

There were enough notes circulating, in the form of the fables. Wouldn't the last fable, *The Tale of the Fox and Her Cub* explain everything? He really wouldn't need to say much. Credit goes to unknown author.

He knew all he needed to say.

Sorry

There, scribbled on one of Mudder's yellow sheets of notepaper.

Sorry Mudder

Sorry, sorry, sorry, sorry, sorry, sorry.

One apology from Lucy Loxton

One from Claire Jamison

One from Joan Matthews

One from Amelia

One from Dalt

And one from him.

He hoped he wouldn't be misunderstood. He wasn't apologising for what he had done to the others. He was apologising to Mudder for what they had all, collectively, done to her. All of them. They had all mistreated her, one way or the other. Now it was his turn to pay as the others all had.

He left the note on the kitchen table and opened the door, immediately noticing the fall in temperature. The sun would soon rise but dark, heavy clouds hung ominously above. He paused on the decking then walked slowly, pensively, ('mindfully,' Amelia would have said) towards the river, his pockets heavy with the rocks he collected along the way.

Dalt

He'd gone through pretty much his entire range of emotions over the last twenty-four hours, and it appeared that he was left with mild to middling hysteria which was presenting itself in the form of hilarity. Nothing about his situation was funny, and yet everything about it was hysterical. Tied to a bloody tree, probably by the hand of his own son, next to a shallow grave, whilst a storm continued to intensify around him. He couldn't contain the bubble of laughter.

Headlines flashed in front of his eyes:

House on Horror Hill

The enquiry into multiple bodies found at the home of missing author Nell Davenport continues. Police remain confounded by the series of events which led to the bizarre deaths at the property and can only hazard a guess that the whole family was totally nuts.

Yes, that would sum it up.

He wasn't dead yet though, was he? Another burst of laughter escaped as he contemplated his situation. He was merely tied to a tree. Tied to a tree remarkably well by some very strong rope and some even stronger knots. Oh, the irony that he himself had been the one to teach his son these survival skills. That had backfired!

Get a grip, he told himself firmly. Remember the man who fell down a ravine, dislodging a boulder on the way and found himself pinned to the side of a canyon wall in the middle of absolutely bloody nowhere? The man that spent days hacking his own arm off with a pocketknife in order to free himself then hiked seven miles to safety? Remember him? Another uncontrollable burst of laughter. He bet that man wished he'd been sat sheltered beneath a willow tree, bound only by a bit of thread. What was Dalt worrying about?

What, indeed, was Dalt worrying about?

Just the small matter of a son gone rogue, a missing wife and houseguest, and a disturbing patch of freshly dug earth.

Up, down, up down, he moved his arms like a bear rubbing against a tree on a nature documentary, rope against bark, bark against rope, imagining the rope thinning, strand by strand, until soon he would be free.

More thunder, then the heavy thud of footsteps approaching. His instinct was to call out, but something made him hold his tongue. He paused in his rubbing, frozen with anticipation.

The footsteps passed by.

Then he heard the splash.

Huck

U pon reflection (perhaps a little late) it occurred to Huck that Virginia Woolf had probably approached the matter of taking her own life with more foresight than he had and had probably sewn the rocks into her pockets in order for the event to go smoothly. (The event indeed! How presumptuous of him, to term it an event). How big must her pockets have been, he'd wondered, that she could stockpile enough rocks to keep her under the water? Maybe she'd been pretty tiny and hadn't needed too much to anchor her. It seemed, however, that he was going to need more than just a few rocks to stay submerged, possibly a large lump of cement or a shovel full of bricks. He was also going to need a better belt or some tighter shorts, the darn things kept slipping down with the weight of the damned stones. Virginia would have been wearing a dress, he realised... maybe he should... No! Imagine the gossip that would fuel. Think on your feet, he told himself sternly. You can do this.

A backpack full of bricks. That'd do it. Mudder had been carrying a backpack when she waded into the water. She must have had the same idea – filled it with something heavy. Hadn't Toby, too, had a heavy rucksack strapped to his back when he died? A macabre thread would join them all together: Huck, Toby and Mudder. This was meant to be.

Huck walked back up the lawn towards the house, droplets of water (and the occasional stone) splattering the grass as he went, his failed suicide attempt reminding him of the 'bloopers' outtakes at the end of films, canned laughter as his shorts slipped around his ankles and his body refused to sink.

'Idiot', he muttered under his breath.

It didn't much matter that he dripped water all over the kitchen. There was no one left to care. He found his school bag on the peg near the door and took it back outside, looking around for anything heavy to fill it with.

Ten minutes later he was back at the water's edge, the backpack, loaded with bricks he'd found near the barbecue, strapped firmly to his chest. Take two. Or should it be, final take?

He stood a moment in the shallows. A deep, guttural crash of thunder echoed in his ears and stuttering bursts of light filled the sky. Rain pattered the river around him. How beautiful they looked, the droplets, bouncing off the surface, dancing just for him.

What were you supposed to do in an electrical storm? Probably not stand in a river with only your head exposed. Oh well. It would put him out of his misery all the quicker.

The rain gathered ferocity, a violent, angry attack. A fitting end.

Now was the time to say something profound. Or at least to think it. Famous last words. But what was the point if there was no one there to listen?

He waded out into the water.

The Tale of the Goat Herd and the Wolves

Once upon a time, in a cave high in the mountains, there lived a goat herder, whose life's work was to guard the pure-white goats who lived in the field below the cave.

The goat herder lived a simple existence. He spent his days caring for his herd, protecting them from hungry predators and moving them on to new pastures when the grass ran low. He spent his nights sitting at the mouth of the cave, wrapped in heavy blankets, watching.

But he couldn't stay awake and keep watch all night long.

Every night without fail, just when the herder had fallen into his deepest sleep, the wolves would come.

And every night without fail, the youngest billy goat, a brave little fellow, would charge at the wolves, bleating noisily and angrily.

'Stay away from my herd. Stay away, or you will pay the price.'

'Out of our way, Little Billy Goat,' the wolves would laugh, as they tore through the herd to choose a delicious white goat for their dinner.

Night after night the wolves attacked, weakening the herd, reducing its numbers.

Day after day the goat herder would sigh and moan.

'Another goat gone, what am I to do? I am a useless goat herder. I am no good at looking after these goats of mine.'

Then came the day there were only a handful of goats left in the field beneath the cave.

The moon was high in the sky, the goat herder snoring deeply, when the wolves came as usual.

'Well, Little Billy Goat,' the largest of the wolves said. 'It looks like it is you that we are going to be eating today.'

The Little Billy Goat bleated as loudly as he could and stamped his hooves hard on the ground.

'You have done enough damage to our herd. Go away, before I make you pay the price.'

'What a lot of courage for a Little Billy Goat,' the biggest wolf said, hooting with laughter. Then he pounced, a creature made of teeth and jaws and saliva.

Bang, bang, bang, bang, bang.

Little Billy Goat looked up to see where the noise had come from. There, at the mouth of the cave above him, stood the goat herder holding an enormous AK-47.

Little Billy Goat looked down at his feet. There, dead on the grass, lay the wolves. All five of them.

He looked back again at the goat herder and gave a small nod of thanks.

The goat herder nodded back.

'I'm sorry I took so long.'

You sometimes have to wait for that which is worth waiting.

Huck

B lurred thoughts.

A voice.

'I'm sorry I took so long.'

Dragging, lifting, pulling.

Heavy. Helpless.

Landing, falling, rolling.

Sensations of touch: his mouth, his face, his chest.

Breath and air. Pressure and release.

Spluttering, jerking, spasming.

A hand, stroking, calming, soothing.

And a voice. A voice he'd have died to have heard again.

A voice that he almost did die to hear again.

'I'm sorry I took so long.'

Mudder

'Toby!'

Running down, down to the river. Water everywhere. From the sky. From the river. Wet. So wet.

A boy floating face down in the water. Lifeless.

Screaming.

'Toby, Toby, Toby!'

But no, it couldn't be. What was she thinking? Madness, Toby long gone. And yet history repeating itself.

That head of curly hair, not Toby. Not Toby at all.

'Huck. Huck!' Screaming like it would bring them both back. Screaming as she ran, then dived, then swam and waded until the curly hair was in her hands, the rain hammering down, making it hard to see.

Heavy. Why was he so heavy? Her hands felt the backpack on his chest, felt for the zip, tugged it. Bricks tumbling forth onto the riverbed, cascading like a waterfall. He was lighter now, ridiculously light for her almost man of a boy. She tugged at his clothes, pulled his face out the water, found the riverbed with her feet and dragged him, hauled him to the bank.

Get him flat on his back. Pinch the nose, breathe into the mouth, breathe, breathe, breathe. Rain mixed with river water running down both their faces. Heel of her hand on the centre of his chest now, fingers interlocked, arms straight and press, press, press, beating for the heart that isn't. Breathe, breathe, watch the chest rise. Press, press, press. Press and promise.

Promise that you won't go away again. That you'll be there, in mind as well as body. That you'll do better.

'I'm sorry I took so long.'

Choking, coughing, river water and bile.

Heaving him onto his side now, hands rubbing his back like she did when he was an infant, the action opening floodgates, memories surging through long dried up riverbeds.

Feelings of fear, inadequacy, self-doubt. Feelings of shame and uselessness.

He coughs again. Her son. He vomits. She carries on rubbing, her hand moving in soft circles, then he gulps, sucks in the air around him as if he has been starved of it. He has.

He flails, life returning. His hand slices air, then connects with her own.

He squeezes her fingers. She squeezes his.

He opens his eyes.

Dalt

S till here, still tied to the tree, still trying to piece together the events of the last ten minutes that he has heard but not seen.

Did Huck try to drown himself? And did Nell, his missing wife, save him?

Or has he, Dalt, totally lost the plot, been hallucinating? A result of concussion and sleep deprivation.

'Huck?' Dalt's voice is croaky and weak. Hard to be heard above the pounding rain. 'Huck! Nell! Huck!'

Footsteps approach at last. The fronds of his green prison are swept apart, and he sees her, his wife, who has been missing for five weeks.

She is soaking wet and looks almost as confused as he does.

'Dalt?'

And he laughs. He can't help it. The absurdity of it all. The fragility of each moment, the twists and turns a life can take in an instant. In the last hour he has pictured a life with neither wife nor son. Life without. Seeing Nell, he feels a neat joining, tectonic plates sliding perfectly back together after the earthquake.

Huck appears behind Nell. He looks pretty rough – pale, almost translucent skin, bloodshot eyes and soaked to the bone. But alive.

Dalt wishes he could freeze this moment, before anyone speaks, before life carries on. He wishes they could all lie down on the soft grass, stay inside this sanctuary, talking of neither the past nor the future. Just existing in the right now.

But life can't be paused for long.

'You're... you're alive! I... I don't understand. Where the hell have you been?' The ferocity of his own voice surprises him, the anger it contains.

Nell is painfully thin, malnourished even, dark circles under her eyes, stringy hair. And that same *Your pace or mine?* t-shirt.

'I had to go away. I'm so sorry.'

'Go away? Are you serious? Where? Why didn't you tell anyone? We thought you were dead! There's been police, helicopters, dogs, divers, all searching the moor for weeks. Where have you been?'

Nell looks horrified. Her whole body begins to shake.

'Can I sit down?' She doesn't wait for an answer and crosses the small space between them, sinking down in the grass beside Dalt, her fingers pulling at the knots in the rope that bind him. And he's free. His hands are shaking as he wipes his face, feels the mud and saliva beneath his fingertips. He feels her cold, shivering body sending vibrations through his.

'It was all too much. I wasn't coping. There was the pressure of the new book; you know how I hate all the PR nonsense... how stressed it makes me. On top of that, or maybe because of that, I started to think about the past. Obsess about it really. All the bad things that had happened to me. To us. Toby dying, then my mother. Horrible memories from my school days. People who seemed out to get me.' Nell stares at her knees as she speaks. Won't look at Dalt.

'Amelia had been talking about different therapy sessions she'd done. She'd said writing things down was a good way to release any worries. Write them down and let them go. I tried. But I couldn't even get the words onto the paper. Couldn't write about me and them. It was all too much.

'Then, the idea of the fables came to me. Writing the fables seemed to help at first: creating the characters, making them realise their mistakes, even making them pay made me feel better, like I was clearing it all out of my system. But rather than going away, the act of writing it all down, dredging up all the memories, reliving all the events began to make everything worse – fresher, if anything – more painful than ever and more real. I couldn't stop thinking about the past.

'It was all falling apart. It was the night before the anniversary of Toby's death. I was a mess. We argued. Again. I threw a plate at you! I was losing it, Dalt. I was worried, for the three of us. I thought you'd all be better off if I went away for a while. And Amelia was here at Moordown. I thought she'd be able to look after things for a while.'

'Amelia! You left us with Amelia! What kind of logic is that? You wrote a fable about her. She was part of the problem.'

Nell looks taken aback at Dalt's mention of the fable.

'Oh. Yes, of course, you've seen it. I wrote the fables as a release, for me. Amelia's fable was a little different to the others: it wasn't supposed to hurt her. It was supposed to help her: to set her free. She'd been asking me questions. It was part of the problem, really. She was bringing everything to the surface again. But it felt odd. It felt a little like she was using me. Probably just a neurotic thought... my mind was all over the place. But anyway – that's why I wrote her fable. I knew she didn't mean any harm. I knew I was leaving you in safe hands.' Nell seems pleased with her own logic.

'So you just left? But why didn't you leave a note at least? And where the hell did you go? A different planet? Somewhere they don't have news?' Dalt hadn't realised there was this much pent up rage inside him, until it comes raining down.

'She did leave a note,' Huck says.

Dalt turns his attention to his son.

'I saw it, the morning she left. I took it.' Huck looks at Nell, his expression unreadable.

'I saw you leave. I ran after you, got as far as the ridge that overlooks Dalberry's Pool.' His voice is shaking. 'You waded in with your backpack. I thought... I thought...'

Now it is Huck's turn to look to Nell for answers. None come.

'The note said you were finding things difficult. Then you wade into deep water wearing all your clothes, and your backpack. You can't swim for god's sake! I thought you had killed yourself. I thought you had drowned, like Toby. I thought I'd stood and watched you drown.' Huck is sobbing. Gulping, messy sobs.

'I didn't know you'd followed me. I was upset. I did wade into the water. It was the anniversary of Toby's death. I wanted to feel something. A connection.' Nell retells the facts without emotion. Pure Nell. 'But I wasn't trying to kill myself. I suppose it could have looked like that.'

'It looked exactly like that!' Dalt has never heard Huck so angry. His pallid skin is turning red with anger. 'You disappeared! You didn't come up!'

'I swam underwater. I got out. I was okay. I am okay.'

'You swam?'

'Amelia was teaching me. I wanted to learn. For you. For Toby.'

So many secrets.

Huck looks baffled. Dalt recognises the feeling. But there is still so much more to know.

'You didn't drown. You got out,' Dalt knows he sounds like the recap on a ten-part crime documentary, but he needs to set the facts straight in his own head. 'Then what happened?'

'I had to get away. I needed some time on my own.' Nell looks at Dalt and yet beyond him, as if she is picturing the day as she talks him through it.

'At first, I just ran. It was hot, I dried off quickly. It felt good to run. To not think. I knew where I was heading. I'd been running that way a lot. There's a cottage about fifteen miles north, on the outskirts of Rangdale. Annie Barnes told me about it once. She cleans there. The owners only visit once a year – every Christmas. I knew it would be empty.'

His wife, missing, feared dead, returns, right in front of him. A garbled story about drowning, or swimming, or running, or hiding. Too much information. Too much to take onboard. He can't even begin to process how he feels. Emotions coursing through him: anger, disbelief, horror, sadness, the whole range.

'And that's where you've been, ever since?' Huck picks up the interrogation. 'Hiding in some holiday rental whilst the entire town searched the moor for you, thinking you're dead?'

Nell's eyes narrow. 'I didn't know you thought I was dead. I left the note. I didn't know about the police and the search parties. I was feeling awful. Not thinking straight. It's not an excuse, but it's the truth. I can't even remember the first week in the cottage. It's just a blur. I broke in. I broke a window round the back. I went upstairs, lay down in the first bed I came to, and slept. I spent days sleeping, making it as far as the bathroom, then sleeping again.'

All those years ago, after Joan Matthews had tried to take Huck away, Nell had fallen into a deep depression. For weeks she'd lain upstairs in bed, refusing to re-enter the world. Dalt remembers endless trips up and down the stairs with tea and soup and kind words, coaxing her back into herself again. Then one day she'd got up as if nothing had happened, put on her wellingtons and gone out to dig the garden.

'Anyway,' Nell continues, 'That went on for a while. I don't know how long. I lost track of days. Eventually I went downstairs. I needed to eat. Wanted to eat again. The kitchen cupboards were well stocked with rice, dried pasta, tinned soup... I didn't eat much. I'm going to work it out with them... the food. The window.' She looks panicked, as if she's merely raided the minibar and left without paying the bill, rather than gone full Goldilocks on the holiday cottage.

'I thought of you, all the time. I just couldn't come home. I felt like I was dragging you down. Ruining everything. I thought you'd be better off without me.'

'This is crazy,' Huck interrupts. 'How could you not know everyone was looking for you? It was all over the news. Didn't you turn on the TV or the radio? Didn't anyone come to the door?'

'I had no idea. Do you think I'd have stayed away if I did? There's no TV. No radio. I just wanted to be alone. And no one came to the door.'

Fifteen miles away. Had the search extended that far, Dalt wonders? His personal search certainly hadn't.

'So why did you come back?' Huck asks.

'Annie came in the middle of the night. She said there was a storm coming. She was checking up on the house; making sure everything was okay before it hit. She let herself in and found me right there, sitting on a barstool in the kitchen. She seemed pretty shocked.'

'*Pretty shocked*,' must have been an understatement, thinks Dalt.

'She told me how I'd been headline news for weeks and that everyone had been searching for me.' Nell pauses and looks at Huck. 'She told me about the fables too, and Lucy Loxton, Ms Jamison and Joan Matthews.'

Dalt watches a deep red wash over his son's face.

'I couldn't understand what she was telling me; I'm still not sure I understand it now. She was talking about my fables being uploaded to my blog and being emailed all over the place. My blog?' Nell screws her face up and says the word *blog* like it is an insult. 'She said that people had got hurt. Annie thought it was me! She thought I was behind it all!'

Nell's face contorts into a picture of anguish, before upset turns to indignation. 'Sending the emails! Pushing people off cliffs! I told her I didn't know anything about it. We had a coffee...'

'You had a coffee?' Dalt can't help his tone, but it doesn't sound like his wife is taking things very seriously.

'Yes! Annie seemed to think I was in shock or something. Anyway, when I thought about it, I knew that the only person who would have looked under the drawer where I hid the fables was Huck. But then I realised that Huck couldn't have done all the techy things Annie had mentioned. Then Annie told me how she'd found a laptop under Huck's wardrobe when she was cleaning his room one day, and it all started to make sense.

'Annie tried phoning Dalt, but there was no answer. She tried Amelia's number, too. Odd – that she had it. No answer either, so we jumped in her car and she brought me straight over here. I left her in the driveway. She said she was going to call the police. I can't blame her. They're probably on their way.'

Nell turns to look at Huck. 'And was it you, Huck? What have you done? What's buried under that mound?' Dalt feels dizzy and weak, his mouth is dry, he needs a drink. But more than that, he needs his son to give him answers.

Huck approaches the mound and kicks at the soil with his toe. Five deep scuffs and his foot connects with something. He leans forward, brushes the soil away with the flat of his hand, closes his fingers around the object and pulls.

A laptop case.

Dirt scatters from it as Huck holds it aloft, before dumping it on the grass beside Dalt. He kneels and digs again. This time, the side of a red suitcase is revealed.

Huck hauls it from the earth and unzips it. Clothes, papers and random paraphernalia belonging to a forty-year-old woman spew from the bag, and Dalt mentally downgrades the potential criminal act committed from manslaughter to (merely) theft and possibly causing grievous bodily harm.

'It's Amelia's stuff,' Huck says, by way of an explanation. 'She was writing about Mudder and it wasn't right. I took her laptop, her notebooks, her phone and I buried it. It seemed like a good idea at the time.'

Dalt breathes out an enormous sigh of relief. Just stuff. No body under there, just a suitcase.

'Where is Amelia?' he asks his son.

'She must have left on Friday night. I didn't see her go. I've no idea where she is.'

'And the others? Ms Jamison? Joan Matthews? Lucy Loxton? Did you show them the fables? Did you hurt them?' Nell is looking at Huck as if she's never seen him before, doesn't recognise him.

'I didn't hurt anyone. I just wanted them to realise what they'd done to you. I made sure they saw the fables, but the rest was...' Huck falters, 'was fate, or karma, or coincidence.' His voice breaks. 'I didn't kill anyone. I didn't lay a hand on them.' No wonder Nell doesn't recognise him. He isn't the same boy she'd left behind.

'Why were you tied to the tree?' Nell turns her attention to Dalt.

'Because he had an affair with Lucy Loxton. I was teaching him a lesson,' Huck explains. Then, noticing Nell's alarm, he adds, 'Only he didn't have an affair. I got it wrong.'

What a mess. What a total, utter mess. Incomprehensible, the web of secrets they've woven, and now they are stuck like flies in the middle, unable to free themselves, thinks Dalt.

Nell turns to face him at last. Her eyes tear into his, searching for answers of her own. Dalt feels his heart quicken and is suddenly aware of his appearance.

'Sorry. I smell. I've been here a while,' he says.

'I really thought you boys would be fine without me. I thought Huck would tell you about the note. I thought you'd get it – that I needed time and space. I'm so sorry.'

Dalt looks closely at his wife. Her pale, tired face and sallow skin. 'You've only taken up all of the local police department's manpower and resources for the last five weeks. Huck and I have barely been able to eat, sleep, function really... your son has gone off the rails and decided to reap vengeance upon anyone that may ever have caused you any pain. But apart from that...' he pauses to study her face next to his and smiles, 'apart from that, it's been fine.'

A degree in husbandry – who had he been kidding? He'd spectacularly flunked the admissions test by managing to lose his own wife, and he'd followed that up by living with his son / cyber-criminal / deeply disturbed teenager, whilst being completely oblivious to what was going on right under his nose. Then, to make matters even worse, he'd sat tied to a tree, whilst his son tried (and very nearly succeeded) to drown himself. Heroic stuff, Dalt. Seriously, you've outdone yourself.

His wife, missing, presumed dead, seemingly disappeared off the face of the earth, then appears from nowhere in the nick of time. She throws herself into a deep river in the middle of a thunderstorm, despite the opposing factors of phobia of water due to past trauma and the fact that she can't swim. She rescues their son, drags him to safety, carries out spectacularly accomplished CPR. And then says sorry she's late.

Sorry she's late.

Annie Barnes had called the police. Officer Henley and Officer Pearson are probably moments away from finding them all here, under this tree. What are they going to make of all this? Of Huck, and what he's done?

Dalt reaches for his wife's hand and closes his eyes.

Afterwards

Huck

Not dead and not guilty: not a bad outcome, all things considered. The not dead bit was a two-for-one success. Mudder was alive and so was he. The moment in which he regained consciousness on the riverbank to the sound of his mother's voice was one that would stay with him forever. The not guilty verdict had taken a while longer to process.

The police had come, their purpose two-fold.

Firstly, they came for pilgrimage; to see with their own eyes the supernatural phenomenon of the woman returned. Mudder had greeted them warily, informed of, but still not truly comprehending the extent of the mystery and the man hours that had embodied her disappearance.

Secondly, they came for Huck.

He was no fool, he knew this was coming – it was why he'd waded into the river with a backpack full of bricks – but he had Mudder now, and Dalt. Together, Dalt told him, they'd get through this.

As it turned out, Huck hadn't actually done anything 'too' criminal. But, as Officer Pearson explained whilst Huck sat at the police station giving his statement (a process which took four and a half hours) it would all need to be investigated.

To summarise (because hell, somebody had to) the conversation went a little like this.

Lucy Loxton – knocked off a cliff by her own (enormous) dog whilst taking selfies.

Ms Jamison – tried and found guilty of gross misconduct.

Joan Matthews – died of a stroke. Definitely unsporting behaviour on Huck's part – stoking the fires of the past and upsetting a sick old lady. However, she'd ultimately died of natural causes.

As for all the internet stuff, the messages, the fables and the hacking, Huck had come away with a very stern warning. A warning and a job offer, should he wish to take it. During the inquiry into missing person, Nell Davenport, it had been brought to the attention of the local police that they had substandard knowledge and expertise in the area of modern technology. Turns out, Officer Henley knew 'just the man for the job.'

'In a few years, Huck,' she'd said (kindly, considering the circumstances). Go to university, get a degree, then get in touch.

'Get some therapy, too,' Officer Pearson had added jokily. They all knew he wasn't joking.

Huck thought he just might.

The media interest since Mudder's reappearance had been extraordinary. The reporters were back at the gate, far more of them than ever before, all desperate to get an exclusive interview with Nell Davenport.

Never going to happen.

But there was one person in the media she would talk to.

Frank.

Good old Frank, he spun his magic for all of them. They'd come out of it okay. And Frank had sold a hell of a lot of newspapers.

And Amelia.

Ah, Amelia. Now Amelia had decided not to press charges, despite having good reason to. Huck had confessed to causing grievous bodily harm and leaving her unconscious. But... good old Amelia – it turned out that this had been, 'just the awakening that I needed.' Who'd have thought? Many years of therapy sessions, counsellors, Zen masters and meditation groups, and all she'd needed was a good, solid, whack over the head with a door stop. She'd 'seen the light,' apparently – had some kind of an epiphany. *The Great Turning*, she was calling it. By 'it', Huck meant her best-selling book. Everywhere he went there were billboards for it, and life-sized cut-outs of Amelia Early herself, looking radiant and offering to bestow her newfound knowledge and serenity to the masses in *'ten quick and easy steps.'* He hadn't read it yet, but he wondered if one of the steps involved being knocked unconscious and losing everything. He wouldn't put it past her. Mudder was thrilled for Amelia, as was he. She really did deserve this. The conifer tree had come to fruit at last.

And Dalt? He hadn't pressed charges either. He would have been within his rights to, a fact he reminded Huck of daily. Whilst Dalt seemed to have missed out on The Great Turning for himself, he'd had a turning of sorts. Inward, towards his family. The summer had long gone, those endless, hot days and nights leaving as suddenly as Mudder had returned. In its wake came an autumn so rich it threatened to string itself up as a caricature. Leaves of gold, russet and yellow thick upon the mossy moor, the light imbued with a particular quality that only comes this time of year.

It was an autumn, Dalt had declared, for swimming.

A brave move, Huck considered, seeing as he had tried to drown himself. But if Dalt could overlook this so easily, then perhaps he should too.

Here Huck's therapy began. When he emailed Amelia (which he did frequently now) he might have referred to these swimming sessions as *The Great Turning*. Just the once.

It's no secret that water has incredible healing powers. When he dived into the cold, fresh water of the river (this time with both Dalt and Mudder), it was like a renewal of vows, a reconnecting and a coming home. A way to begin again.

Mudder was beginning again too. It had taken a while upon her return for her to understand and accept the events of the summer and Huck's role in it all. Huck in turn had been shocked and saddened to learn of his mother's depression. They were all starting again, getting to know each other and understand each other a little better.

Something had been bothering him, though.

Why had Mudder returned when she did, right then, at that precise moment? How had all the pieces of the puzzle fallen into place right then: Annie Barnes, the storm, the cottage, the discovery, the journey home? Extraordinary, inexplicable, miraculous. Her freakishly impeccable timing was the only reason he was alive. It was inconceivable, preposterous, and unimaginable that she should return at that exact moment, that exact yoctosecond (look it up) upon which his life hung in the balance. Sometimes (and he knew this sounded crazy) he found himself pinching his own arm, nerve receptors screaming at his brain, whilst he challenged his body to hold its hands up and say, '*The joke's on me – you're not really alive, kiddo. That would be friggin' impossible.*'

But it seemed it wasn't impossible, and Mudder had returned when she did, in the nick of Planck time: the briefest, physically meaningful span of time (getting an idea of how much time he was spending obsessing over this?)

Maybe, just maybe, she didn't need him to look after her, after all.

Mudder

All's well that ends well.

In parched, dry lands, fires spread quickly and burn hard. They decimate everything in their path.

After the fire has raged, and the old, dead trees are gone, the sunlight is let in. The soil is left fertile; new plants can grow, can thrive.

Nature is unusual in her methods. Sometimes it takes the destruction of everything that was, to make way for everything that is to come.

Acknowledgements

For a very long time I've wanted to write a book. But what good is a book, with no one to read it? So, firstly, thank you, dear reader, for choosing this book. I hope that you enjoyed it. That's what this whole thing was about.

Thank you to all the wonderful authors that I have read, who have inspired me, and made me want to create something even just half as good.

Thank you to my family and friends, far and wide, who have most definitely been on this journey with me. Sorry about that, and thank you all, immensely, for all of the support, encouragement and belief that each and every one of you have shown me. It won't be forgotten.

Thank you to my sister, Miriam, and to the wonderful Becky Beer, whom I have never met, for reading the first draft, which had to be practically pried from my fingers. You both gave me the confidence to keep going when I was about to throw in the towel. If it all goes wrong, I'll blame you two.

Thank you to my children for their unending support and optimism. Kitty, your motivational talks have been exceptional, particularly considering you're only eleven! Layla, your no-nonsense approach makes me get over myself and get on with it, and Leo – did you know I wrote a book?

And finally, and absolutely...

Thank you George. Without you, there would be no book. Or there would be, but it wouldn't have a cover, or a title, or a blurb, or formatting, or even possibly a plot that made sense. Thank you, for always believing in me, even when I didn't believe in myself. Thank you for scooping me up, time and time again, and persuading me to persevere. Thank you for your endless words of encouragement, wisdom and support that were always so very needed. Thank you for all the time and energy you have invested in this project of mine (and it has taken *quite* a long time!) But we got there in the end. I bet you're praying I never write another!

Author's Note

But I am writing another! It should be released into the world soon(ish).

If you sign up to my mailing list below I will let you know as soon as it is released.

www.tinyurl.com/rachelmahood

If you enjoyed reading *Seven Ways to Start a Fire*, I would be extremely grateful if you could leave a review wherever you bought your copy.

You can also keep in touch via social media.

www.facebook.com/RachelMahoodAuthor
www.instagram.com/rachelmahood
www.twitter.com/rachelmahood

Rachel Mahood lives on the south coast of England with her husband and three children. When she is not writing, Rachel can usually be found outdoors. Running, cycling or swimming, she's always up for an adventure.

Printed in Great Britain
by Amazon

27812820R00212